THE INCURSION

THE INCURSION

A NOVEL BY

Dirk Hanson

LITTLE, BROWN AND COMPANY
Boston — Toronto

FIRST EDITION

The characters and events portrayed in this book are fictitious.
Any similarities to real persons, living or dead, are purely
coincidental and not intended by the author.

The author is grateful to the following for permission to reprint ex-
cerpts from previously copyrighted material:

From *Ratner's Star* by Don DeLillo. Copyright © 1980 by Don
DeLillo. Reprinted by permission of Alfred A. Knopf, Inc.

From "My Generation," words and music by Peter Townshend. ©
Copyright 1965 Fabulous Music Ltd., London, England. TRO-Devon
Music, Inc., New York, controls all publication rights for the U.S.A.
and Canada. Used by permission.

From "Won't Get Fooled Again" by Pete Townshend. Copyright ©
1971 by Fabulous Music Limited. All rights in the United States, its
territories and possessions, Canada, Mexico, and the Philippines are
controlled by Towser Tunes, Inc. All rights reserved. International
copyright secured.

Library of Congress Cataloging-in-Publication Data

Hanson, Dirk.
  The incursion.

  I. Title.
PS3558.A5144I5   1987   813'.54   86-20977
ISBN 0-316-34374-9

RRD VA

*Published simultaneously in Canada
by Little, Brown & Company (Canada) Limited*

PRINTED IN THE UNITED STATES OF AMERICA

For Peter, the genuine article

When technology reaches a certain level, people begin to feel like criminals. . . . What enormous weight. . . .

— Don DeLillo, *Ratner's Star*

PART

ONE

ONE

IT WAS A beautiful fish, immaculately free of scars and welts, pale pink fading to silver along the flanks. It had run the gauntlet of seals and sea lions in the bay, rediscovering its natal river with mystical precision, working artfully past the rocks and shallow gravelly riffles, pounding steadily upstream for three miles. As far as this pool. As far as Peter's rod and lure. This far and no farther.

He had hooked it on his third cast into the first pool on the second Friday of December. It was Oregon steelhead season. For the record, he used a Bud's Little Steelie #2 Spinner.

He stood looking down at the fish as it thrashed and twisted in the wet grass at streamside. A sleek and muscular nine-pounder, fresh from the salt, homeward bound. This is perfect, he thought. This is as close to perfect as it gets. This is as close to perfect as I can probably stand.

He quickly gutted the fish and rinsed it in the stream, keeping a practiced eye on the darkening, unleavened sky. When he finished, he placed the carcass on the smooth inner surface of a strip of hemlock bark. Then, in the last light of the day, he sat down on a mossy rock and lit a joint — the better to examine his feelings about the moment. A gust of wind caught his thick blond hair as he smoked. It was about to rain again, hard. He could feel it coming.

He sat motionless on the rock, considering the attributes, the verifiable elements, of the frozen moment he was creating: his fish on the torn strip of bark; this uncontested stretch of creek; the many sounds of water moving. Vine maple turning crimson. Garlands of mist in the highest spires of fir. Fish Dog rooting and snuffling in the bushes. Everything simple and sane. Try paring away everything

3

that cannot be contained in a finite set of simple things. Yes, he thought, try that.

Peter sat musing in the gloom until he began to shiver from the sunset plunge in temperature. It was a simple thing he could neither freeze in place nor ignore. It's too cold for frozen moments, he decided. However useful they may be. He began scrambling up the steep stream bank, spinning rod in hand, two fingers crooked through the jaws of his steelhead, Fish Dog breaking trail for him through a nasty tangle of nettle and devil's club. When he reached the unpaved road, Peter continued uphill toward the dim outline of his car, listening to the sound of his boots as they dibbled and scraped through the puddles along the gravel shoulder.

Fish Dog was waiting for him at the back of the Jeep Scout. Peter unlocked the tailgate and the black Lab took up a guard position near his master's trophy. Peter told him not to worry. Trout bandits were scarce in these parts.

Peter leaned on the tailgate and replaced his boots with a pair of tennis shoes for the drive home. The boots were Fisherman's Specials from L. L. Bean, felt-lined and waterproof. They were absolutely perfect footgear for Oregon steelhead season and close to useless for anything else.

He broke down his fishing rod and stowed his gear and wrapped his fish in newspaper, just as it began to rain. Whistling Fish Dog inside, he closed the back of the Scout and climbed behind the wheel, contemplating with pleasure the solitary drive down the eastern slope of the coastal hills. Savoring the sheer uneventfulness of the evening ahead, he gunned the Scout to life and eased off the shoulder. Some popcorn, maybe a late-night movie. Nothing taxing.

He began sketching in tomorrow's clean slate as he drove, planning an early visit to a lovely and secluded tributary of the Alsea River. Tomorrow's prediction called for high winds and periodic spasms of heavy rain — the kind of weather you could count on to keep the tyros off the streams. On the weekends you had to get clever. You had to get high and go far away.

He relaxed himself behind the wheel, letting the lonely road work its magic. In these dark hills, plummeting toward the valley, he felt disassociated from his professional self, happily in suspension for the duration of the drive. He was ready to strike at first light, seeking just the right water, the proper bend and current. It was all chemistry, a particular concatenation of elements ignited by the flash and astonishing strength of the steelhead, the instant when it all dropped into

4

place, when a symmetry broke across your actions and you solved the problem. You balanced the thing. When there wasn't any way to improve upon what had happened. Like that.

Peter glanced over at the seat beside him, empty except for a manila envelope containing a paper he'd promised to review for a physics journal. He tried to remember whether he had promised to do it by this weekend. He thought not. There were things he could remember and things he couldn't. He could remember every steelhead and salmon he had ever caught. The river, the riffle, the time of day. The weather conditions. Whether it fought well or wisely. He could remember when rivers were high or low; when the tides swelled the lower reaches of the ones that debouched into the Pacific.

He knew when the fish ran, and where. He knew the particular geology of every peak he had climbed. And yet, he couldn't remember the first names of half his former co-workers. Where they lived. What they did for kicks. There were things that were important and things that weren't.

As he plunged downward, toward the outskirts of Portland, he remembered the best Chinook salmon run he had ever encountered. It was several Junes ago, just below the first dam in the southeast part of town. The salmon had come charging along the Columbia, branching into the Willamette right where it flowed through the city. Big ones. Trophies in downtown Portland. Who'd have guessed it.

It felt good to be unemployed. He was gone. Solid gone. Goodbye and good luck.

Driving with his left hand, he reached across with his right and rummaged in the glove box for his new Dire Straits tape. On impulse, he began to construct a mental list of the rivers that mattered to him; the ones that had begun for him as thin branching lines on the wall map in his childhood bedroom, only to become, in succession, problems to be solved, processes to be discovered, entities to be deciphered.

Running north to south, there were the Skagit and the Snoqualmie and the Toutle, this last now half-buried and diverted by the explosion of Mount St. Helens. There were the Columbia and the Willamette and the McKenzie. The Alsea, the Rogue. The Trinity. The rivers, all of them, were the successive rungs that defined in his mind the north-south mountain ranges of the Pacific Northwest. He had fished and camped in them all — the Kamloops of British Columbia, the saw-toothed North Cascades of his native Washington, the hooded Olympics of the Washington Peninsula, the gentler Central

5

Cascades of Oregon, and the parallel Coast Range, nearer the Pacific, through which he was now driving.

These mountains formed a long broken chain running from Alaska to California; two thousand miles of conifer and cone-top, the volcanoes shimmering on the horizons of his youth: Baker, Rainier, St. Helens, Hood, Jefferson, the Three Sisters, Diamond Peak. Mount Mazama, the long-vanished sire of Crater Lake. And below the peaks, the great lowland trough of Puget Sound, Oregon's Willamette Valley. Cedar and Douglas fir. The Indians of the region used to stand with their backs against the tallest trees of the forest, in order to draw power from them. Peter could see why.

The rain dwindled, becoming a fine mist. He drove through layers of wraithlike ground fog, alternating between high and low beam, notching up the heater for added comfort. As he rounded a tight curve, taking it slowly, with utmost respect, he caught sight of two black-tailed deer at the side of the road. Two does, plump rear ends facing him.

He once dated a girl from New York who informed him that there weren't any deer around anymore. Deer were an endangered species. The hunters killed them all. This came as something of a shock to Peter, who was used to driving the twisty wet roads of the Pacific Northwest, where the deer were fairly adept at killing people. Over the hood and through the windshield and into your lap at fifty-five miles per hour. Not a terrific way to go for either party.

The road continued to descend through the invisible hills, changing from Forest Service gravel to county blacktop to state pavement in the space of a few miles. He cruised automatically through the faceless bedroom communities south of Portland, absently fingering the beginnings of a bulge which lately, and for no apparent reason, had appeared around his middle. When he reached Interstate 5, he merged south and drove for twenty minutes along the broad run of the Willamette Valley. He took his exit and drove east, past the lumber mill that hadn't been running in eighteen months, the rusting wigwam burners that hadn't been fired in years. Twenty-five years ago, this was all timber country. People used to work in the woods with some regularity, back then. Times were tough.

* *

Peter was parked in his driveway beside the A-frame by seven-forty-five. He put his dog in the pen and his fish in the freezer, and the dog whined. Peter relented. Fish Dog loved popcorn. Everything else but his boots he left locked up in the Scout for the night.

6

Inside the house there was a thick pile of mail underneath the door slot. Peter stepped over it without a glance and went directly to the squat black wood stove in the living room. He stoked it with newspaper and kindling, and as he took a book of matches from the phone table, he saw that there were three calls logged on his answering machine. Three calls, meaning the usual dilemma — to answer or ignore.

The mail was easy. It could hold until tomorrow, possibly even longer. Back in the Stanford days he had once let his mail pile up, unopened and unexamined, for a full six weeks. Back in the university daze. As if you could produce the desired effect that easily.

The phone machine was a problem, though. He didn't have one ten years ago. He didn't even have a phone. He lit the fire and stood by the stove until he could feel the heat of it through his jeans. Then he went to the kitchen nook and took a can of beer out of the refrigerator. He felt obliged to remain optimistic. The calls *were* tapering down now, the machine becoming a little more forgiving every day.

Peter returned to the living room and sat down in his fireside chair, facing away from the telephone table. He took a sip of his beer and scooted his damp boots over closer to the fire. It felt good to know that none of the three calls on his machine was likely to have anything to do with work.

How many times had it happened? He pictured himself standing over by the phone, another perfect fishing weekend exploding into pieces before his eyes. Some engineer on the line, chasing a circuit glitch deep into the weekend. A systems analyst with a hard-on about testing data that wouldn't mesh. A research supervisor calling with a tale of woe about lost memory data, certain inelegantly delicate particle-to-particle energy transfers across the surface of a microchip. He would troop down to headquarters with the rest of them — blown Saturdays and Sundays all around — and he would become, for the day, just another overgrown Alice rattling down the rabbit hole, searching for subatomic culprits in the quantum dimension.

He was out of the loop now. They couldn't touch him. There had always been two good reasons for returning phone calls on the weekend — to keep his job or to get laid. Now there was only one. Peter put his money on a call from Sandy, and went to the phone machine to find out.

In the end, he hit the playback button like a good soldier. This much is on record.

It was Sandy. She was already a fair bit into her evening's wine, as he judged it. Taking things one step at a time, he stopped the machine and called her back. Sandy was lit; thrust and gentle parry. Not tonight. For the past several months Sandy had been dropping slowly, inexorably out of his life. Neither of them viewed this as any great tragedy.

"Peter," she told him, "there was this man on the phone today, at the hospital. He was doing a background check of some sort. I forget his name."

"Go on."

"I'm listed in the nurses' registry, I get lots of job offers. But this wasn't about *my* job. It was about yours."

"I don't have one," Peter said.

"That's what I told him. He said it was standard procedure at the DID Corporation. He called it an exit interview."

"What did he want?"

"He wanted to know if you and I ever talked about your job. The nature of your work, he called it."

"What did you tell him?"

"I told him no, of course."

"Thank you."

"What did you think?"

"Go on."

"He asked me, for example, whether you had discussed your work with me last night. Thursday night."

"He asked you that specific question?"

"He did, Pete."

"I was out fishing."

"That's what I told him."

Peter was silent for a moment. "You should have told him to fuck off. If it happens again, just hang up. It's your right."

"He hung up first."

"Hang up before that. Right after the point," he added, as gently as possible, "where you get the guy's name."

They made an extremely tentative date for the next night.

Peter dropped the receiver into the cradle, feeling a touch less optimistic than before. More exit interviews? They're thorough to a fault, he thought. His whereabouts on Thursday, December thirteenth? There didn't seem to be any point in that at all.

Peter returned to his chair by the fire, determined to finish his beer before returning any more phone calls. He would have to speak with somebody about the exit interviews. Enough was enough. It was proving

8

to be far more difficult to quit than anyone might have imagined. Much harder, in some ways, than getting hired in the first place. The DID Corporation had a thing about keeping its people — almost a mania. It had to do with the nature of the work performed there. DID was a very exclusive club.

*   *

Naturally, when he told them he was quitting, they wanted to know why. Almost exactly one month ago he was lying in his bedroom, pinned to his bed like some drugged insect, asking himself the same question. Searching the wreckage for clues. He could not rise. He just couldn't. It wasn't possible. He should have seen it coming. He *had* seen it coming.

At the time of his quitting, Peter Cassidy was a twenty-nine-year-old solid-state physicist, reasonably well known, very well paid — a five-year veteran of the DID Corporation. It occurred to him, as he watched his boots beginning to steam over by the fire, that it was possible to bracket his life between two identical mornings. Twin failures to rise, some ten years apart, like bookends. The second time it happened, he solved it by deciding to quit. The first time it happened, he never really solved it at all. Alison was not solvable. It lasted for three hours, that first time, or the rest of his life, he was never sure which. Alison was always with him.

The second time it happened, there was very little on the surface of his life to account for it. It wasn't like being lovesick in college at all. He remembered lying there, trying to figure it out. The work was prestigious as hell. His name was all over the journals — Supersensitivity, *see* Alpha sensitivity, *see* Cassidy, P. C., et al., "Threshold Energy States: The Special Case of Niobium Circuitry." He was a contributing member of the American Association for the Advancement of Science. He was also a lifetime subscriber to *Angler* magazine.

His most prized possessions were two in number: his mind, and his handmade nine-and-a-half-foot cane fly rod, with ferrules of marble, wrapped painstakingly with red and blue silk thread, stored proudly, permanently, in one sloping corner of his living room.

He had pressed on. He wasn't married, didn't gamble, had no yen to collect art, owned no scars with sinister stories to tell. He had never been in the army or in prison or to France. He wasn't a spy and he wasn't for sale. He had never been a member of a cult, unless the Presbyterians counted, and that was early on, under strict parental guidance. While it is true that he did not normally like to ski or drink heavily — peculiarities which tended to set him at a certain remove from great numbers of his professional colleagues — this was no major problem in his life. People at DID were allowed their privacy, of a sort. They just didn't have much of the real thing.

It wasn't the work itself. God, he thought, how I love the work. The research. Can't fake it or shake it. The work was unreal. That was the safest, the most accurate statement you could make about it. He worked with the newest ion-passivated microchips — spectral memory storage, response time in picoseconds, instantaneous and infallible. Power specs, energy requirements, so low as to be mathematically negligible. As to be slightly surreal. Alejandro's latest batch. So delicate and powerful. Unreal, the whole show.

But he was quitting, just the same. They wanted to know why. They were concerned. He could have tried to frame it as a simple case of burnout, something they could understand, but there wasn't much evidence for it — no staring dully out the windows, no lassitude at departmental meetings, that kind of behavior. He had done good work right up to the end. They were puzzled.

Would he consider a sabbatical? A consultancy? He would not. The quitting was the thing. There was nothing he could tell them, nothing they would understand. This whole business of electronics and computers — it was all supposed to be so faultlessly progressive, so evolutionarily ordained. So teleologically exact. But it wasn't any of those things. Not any longer. Not with the SEEK system. They were riding for a fall. He'd told them in his memos, but they were all too far gone to hear it. Even David, in his way. You had to believe in the infallibility of it all. You couldn't breathe the atmosphere around DID for six seconds if you didn't.

Thinking of David, Peter abruptly rose from his chair, grabbed a second beer from the kitchen, and went to take his second call on the answering machine. It was indeed David, no problem.

"Burgers at your place tomorrow night?" said David's taped voice, still holding a trace of Philadelphia in it after all these years. "Or what?"

Peter turned off the machine once again and dialed David's number, thinking about Alison.

It wasn't as if he had lost her. No. He never really had her. Never did.

David's phone began ringing. All those bright evenings and slow nights, Peter thought, all that sweet give and take. The whispered endearments. Alison's tanned thighs flexing and unflexing; sweat mingling and drying on the single sheet in the cool of the California midnight. Signifying what? It was supposed to signify something. There should have been signs. There *were* signs. He would have faked anything for her — highwayman, holy man, seller of insurance. Whatever she wanted. But not in time. Women are sometimes wrong about you, Peter thought.

"I have a question," Peter said, when David finally answered. "Of a technical nature. My question is this — "

"You know how I hate it when you ask me technical questions over the phone," David cut in tersely. Peter could hear some appliance or other humming in the background. "Especially over the phone. This is not, at present, a secure channel for person-to-person communication. If you understand what I'm saying here."

Peter paused.

"With respect to fielding questions of a technical nature," David continued, "I feel that burgers at your place tomorrow would be a better bet. This is my feeling."

Peter winced, taken rather completely by surprise, the implications inherent in David's weird, stilted preamble dawning on him only gradually.

David suspected a tap. How long had it been? No doubt it happened frequently, as a security check. Computerized, programmed to activate at the utterance of certain key words, word groupings. Sometimes there was even a specific reason for a tap. When that happened, it was almost always useful to know what it was. David probably did.

"I get it," Peter said. "You're saying you no longer feel that the state, corporate or otherwise, will wither away in our very own lifetime. Is that correct?"

"I feel very safe in saying that nothing of any magnitude is going to wither away by early tomorrow morning."

"I don't follow."

"A firm request for overtime."

"I see."

"A serious, highly pedigreed request."

Peter paused again, sorting it out. Pedigreed. Meaning classified. An emergency meeting of some sort. Clearances? The whole works? David doing the tap dance and background checks all the way to sweet Sandy. . . .

"David," he said, "I am disillusioned with certain facets of our free enterprise system."

11

"I share a measure of your disillusionment," David said. "It *is* disillusioning, in its way."

"I resent having to assume I'm being listened to."

"We know one thing for sure," David responded. "Burgers at your place tomorrow. Am I right?"

Peter agreed and hung up. There was an edge to these two calls that he did not like. Fish Dog began to whimper and pace, signaling extreme urinary distress. Peter threw on his fishing jacket and accompanied the Lab out the front door, in order to avoid taking the third call on his machine for a few moments.

* *

Outside, the night was trying to become beautiful, clearing again, letting the odd star through. Peter hunched himself against the chill and followed Fish Dog out onto the sidewalk, thankful as ever for the lack of streetlights on McKenzie Place. The street looked best at night when the seedy edges didn't show. When you couldn't tell the neighborhood from the neighboring woods.

He'd been reasonable about the quitting. He had tried to give them something. He even threw in a half-baked story about guiding in Canada for a season. His friend Buster owned a small fly-in fishing camp on the coast of British Columbia. He could still go up for the last of the season and help Buster out a little. Buster was a solid citizen now; he'd even sworn allegiance, or whatever you swear, to the Queen.

You drop out for two years and you're through. Washed out. You'll never catch up.

As Fish Dog did his business, Peter paused to drink in the awesome truth of the hulking Olmos RV, now docked on the far side of the street. Sig Olmos, Peter's neighbor down the block, had himself a rig and a half. You could play tennis in it.

There were only two or three dark cars parked along the street. On the far side, a few car lengths behind the RV, was a station wagon Peter didn't recognize. He could vaguely discern two figures, seated and motionless, in the front seat of it.

Two figures, motionless, on his nearly deserted street.

How abominably stupid. High drama in low places. You just don't *do* that on McKenzie Place.

I should have gone to Buster's, he thought. Right off the bat.

With a sudden, inward lurch, Peter remembered the unanswered call on his phone machine. There was no longer any question about that. The call would be a request for his attendance at tomorrow's

12

emergency meeting, the one to which David had alluded. Something had come up. Who knew what. Something having to do with the SEEK system. A security matter. An untoward event. Highly classified, whatever it was. Which explained the phone tap and the background checks. And the station wagon? The station wagon could best be viewed as an RSVP in advance.

Peter whistled for Fish Dog and walked slowly back home, remembering how concerned they had been at the abruptness of his resignation. They just wanted him to be happy. Would he consult for them at some future date?

It was possible. *Anything* was possible. The power of economic terror is undeniable. A man's gotta work for a living, his father used to say. Jesus, how he had hated that line. No deal, he thought. I'm unavailable. Currently pursuing personal research. Leave it at that. But you couldn't, of course. That was the hitch. The thing rippled out.

When Peter returned home, he opened another beer. For the first time in three years, courtesy of a crumpled pack that Sandy had left in his kitchen drawer, Peter had a cigarette. Well, shit, he told himself, what did you think? You should have gone straight to Buster's but you didn't. This security business — people get hurt when they take it seriously and they get hurt when they don't.

When he had finished the cigarette, he hit the playback button. The call was from the office of Colonel Robert Core, president and chief executive officer, the DID Corporation. The original good soldier. The woman who left the message had a clipped, irritatingly professional voice. She informed him of an emergency meeting on SEEK security procedures, eight o'clock tomorrow morning. His papers would be waiting in the lobby. Observe appropriate procedures with respect to Class 1 meetings. Call back soonest and confirm.

Peter turned off his answering machine for good and immediately returned the call. "There must be some mistake," he said to the woman, when he had been put through to the colonel's night secretary. "Peter Cassidy is no longer an employee of the DID Corporation." Then he hung up.

Peter was into his fourth beer and had just finished rolling a bomber joint when the phone began to ring. He walked from the dining table to the phone table, picked up the receiver and said hello.

"Dr. Cassidy. Mr. Cassidy. Peter, if I may."

It was the good soldier himself. Jesus, thought Peter, they are just not messing around with this one *at all*.

"We have a meeting we must ask you to attend. As a consultant. The subject under discussion falls within your particular area of expertise." Friendly but professional, thought Peter. Forceful but not forward. "It is a Class One situation. You'll be given temporary clearance. Eight o'clock tomorrow morning, in the conference room at the S and S Building." A slight pause. "Would you like an escort?"

The clarion call of national security. "No thanks," said Peter. "I'll settle for the one I've already got."

An even slighter pause. "Excuse me?"

"Eight o'clock," Peter said. "The S and S Building."

"We appreciate that," the colonel said.

* *

Peter sat through many beers at his dining room table.

He was an investment, of a kind, and the quitting didn't change that. Singlehandedly, he had once solved the random glitch problem for them. As singlehandedly as it gets these days. It happened three years ago, and it started with a Class 1 meeting, just like this. He solved the problem for them. He found the culprit. He looked long and hard in unlikely places, and fuck the monkey if he didn't find it. It was a nice piece of work.

The problem had cropped up as a disturbing rise in the incidence of data loss through the upper levels of the SEEK network. Bits of digital information — tiny bursts of electromagnetic energy — were disappearing, or becoming garbled, on the satellite bounce. The DID systems people and the NSA Guardians — the government's computer sleuths — ran traces all along the nodal points of the SEEK network, testing and sampling, probing the thousands of computer terminals and telecommunication lines and satellite frequencies, finding nothing.

Peter and his colleagues at the Research Physics Building charted the minute exchanges of electrical energy through the millions of subatomic pathways in the SEEK chips themselves. Everything tested out. The chips were fine. But the number of reported glitches was increasing rapidly. Mild panic; a palpable surge of distress. Hypotheses raised and hypotheses dashed. Experiments, calculations, simulations. Dead end.

Peter was convinced that a tiny excess burst of electricity, some unaccountably random fragment of charge across the chip, was the subatomic event they were looking for. He had a feeling about it,

14

and he trusted his feelings. The culprit, as it turned out, was a lowly bit of business called an alpha particle, emitted in respectable numbers from the fingernail-sized packaging material around the naked chip itself. It was a case of bombardment from within. The electrically charged alphas were being released by the spontaneous radioactive decay of trace amounts of thorium in the metalloplastic circuit packages. The packaging and production people hadn't caught it. Too minuscule, too subtle. Peter caught it.

It was very simple, in principle. Every now and then a single charged alpha, emitted by the packaging, would collide, for a most inopportune microsecond, with a single atom of niobium at a specific microsite on the chip. Electrons at that site would begin to leap madly from lower to higher orbit; a cascade of unwanted energy exchanges took place as a result of the increased excitation. You had electronic chaos, bits of information caroming out of control like billiard balls at the crack of the break. At the systems level, as you were seated in front of a terminal, the result came out as a "flipped" bit, a "soft" error, a dropped transmission, a random glitch, whatever you wanted to call it. A fuck-up. Like an ant starting a landslide. A germ felling a two-hundred-pound man. Unreal.

With some judicious redesigning of the new packages, they were able to shield for the alphas. But while everyone was hailing his "solution" to the supersensitivity problem, Peter couldn't help wondering, at the same time, whether there might be other, more deliberate ways of producing a similarly disabling effect. If something as insignificant as chip packaging could turn the SEEK system upside down for a while, then the alpha problem was very likely just the beginning. He had said as much in his first memo, three years ago, and in subsequent ones ever since. But nobody wanted to hear it.

They have no hold over you that you cannot break. Go up to Buster's, right now, before ice-in. Learn to play the guitar. Rob a Brink's truck. Practice your roll cast.

When it was very late, Peter dialed David again. He let it ring seven times. The problem, he decided, was that you had to keep track of so many levels, so many extra dimensions, at once.

"David."

"He's out," David said. "It's late."

"With regard to tomorrow's overtime. I've been papered."

"No kidding," David said. "No shit."

"And I really don't care *who* hears about it."

"Be kind," David said.

"My question remains the same as before. Who do I have to screw," Peter growled, "to get *out* of this business?"

David chuckled dryly. "This is a techno-physio-philosophical question. Which is to say a personal problem. I myself am more or less happily employed."

"David."

"What."

A deep round lake, ice cracking off glaciers, trout rising. "They can't have me. I'm through. Finished. Unfit for service. I'm out."

David paused politely.

"Pure research," Peter pleaded. "I was in pure research, remember?"

"See you," David said, "at the doughnut table."

Peter went to the kitchen nook and finished his last beer standing up. The Greeks, namers of everything, had a name for his condition. Enantiodromia — an instinctive, polar reversal at the apex of a one-sided quest. Well, he told himself again, and what did you think? You're an insider, one of the elite. You're anointed. Better than that: a seer. Better than that: a sage. They need you. You should be proud.

No, he thought, I'm out, I'm blind, good-bye. I make no plans or promises. Only this: After tomorrow, it's over.

Presumably, if he didn't show tomorrow, they'd call out the hounds. He took a long unpleasant drag on another stale cigarette from the drawer. The colonel had the muscle to do it. The colonel was old school. Fair enough, Peter thought. Show me someplace in the rules where it says anything about fair. Show me where it says anything about *rules* in the first place.

TWO

ALL ALONG THE walkways of the DID Corporation, groves of lichen-wrapped oaks and big-leaf maples were losing their foliage to the wind. A portion of the corporation's automated sprinkler system was running full blast, spewing out great arcs of water that hit the already saturated lawn in sickly, rhythmic splats. It seemed, in some lopsided way, perfectly fitting. A set of underground moisture detectors was supposed to prevent this sort of thing from happening. The grounds crew no doubt had Saturday off, he thought, like civilized employees. Fucking A.

Peter Cassidy trudged slowly across the green, sodden grounds, his hands deep in the pockets of his Eddie Bauer Fish-Jac, squishing methodically, deliberately, through several clots of moldering leaves. He was hatless and cold. The wind swirled his hair and he absently stabbed it back into place with the fingers of his right hand. A few large drops began to fall. There was nothing for him now but this forced march to the Systems & Security Building, and the rain coming on. He had no idea what to expect. The word for the day is *unraptured. Unconsolable. Watchful.* The word for the day is still out.

From somewhere overhead came the muffled drone-roar of a jet, its position indeterminate, lost in the gray. Sheets of rain formed and broke across the company's sprawling headquarters complex near Portland. Oregon on the cusp of winter — grays and greens, a shrouding mist, a feeble sun. And steelhead. But not today.

As he neared the S & S Building, Peter strained to make out the high hill behind it. A thick stand of Douglas fir blanketed most of the slope, except for a flat, stump-riddled patch at its crest. In the middle of the clearing stood an enormous satellite receiving station, its antenna and dish clearly visible, in better weather, from almost anywhere in the DID complex. Peter took a last look at the sky as he darted for the shelter of the brick-and-redwood portico. Nothing whatsoever was revealed there.

Inside the lobby, Peter removed his jacket and shook it vigorously in the general direction of a large potted plant. Beneath a high, beamed ceiling there were several glass tables surrounded by canvas chairs. On each table were a white telephone and a neat stack of trade magazines and newspapers — *Industry Week, Aviation Week, The Wall Street Journal, Defense Electronics, Electronic News.*

Peter took his place at the security desk, where a bored guard sat reading a copy of *Soldier of Fortune* magazine. Peter stated his business, flashed his ID badge, and signed the nondisclosure forms. The guard picked up a telephone and called for a house escort.

Peter strolled across the lobby and gazed at three backlighted display panels on the far wall. High above the guard desk, a small black camera swiveled in a gentle following arc. The first of the panels held a full-color blowup of the corporation's legendary niobium microchip. It was a rectangle six feet high by four feet wide, with a small red dot at bottom right to indicate its true size. It looked like an aerial shot of a dense, fuzzy city of three-dimensional structures.

Peter knew it well. It was the current champion, the reigning brainbuster in the SEEK memory and logic chip family. A useful little unit with storage density of some ten billion bits of binary information per square centimeter. It wasn't what you would call an off-the-shelf item. It was used exclusively in DID's SEEK system.

It was one of his scary favorites. If you worked with Alejandro's chips long enough, he was thinking, they began to take on personalities, despite any better judgments you might make about that sort of anthropomorphic tilt in the work. Picture one now, a dancing, thousand-dimensional lattice of niobium molecules on the head of a pin, constantly, invisibly in motion, shifting and reorienting; mutating in a picosecond according to the dictates of specific forms of resonant input.

Through a complicated, little-understood process of laser irradiation, Alejandro Hunt had found it possible to increase the storage capacity of memory and logic chips a thousandfold. Where conventional silicon chips could store a single on-off bit of binary information at a specific site, Alejandro's could store a thousand, all of them accessed simultaneously by a thousand different users at a thousand different terminals. It was like storing the *Encyclopaedia Britannica* on a mote of dust. Ten billion binary bits per square centimeter. The numbers numb, Peter thought. We should weave them for their own sake. We do.

The second wall panel consisted of a large portrait of Alejandro Hunt himself. How touchingly archaic, was Peter's thought. A portrait of our founder. A curious dark fish dredged up from the sea floor, only to escape the net. A living member of an extinct species — the lone inventor. Peter envied him that. There was even something in the look of him that suggested a throwback. The precision of his hawklike features, his drawn mouth, the stiff tilt of his head, even his diminutive size seemed to hint at the innocence and rectitude of the nineteenth century.

In his formal portrait Alejandro looked preoccupied, possibly absentminded, in that quaint manner of our scientific forefathers. As with so many of our scientific forefathers, Peter reminded himself, appearances can be deceiving. It was hard to guess how old the portrait was, or what Alejandro looked like now. Nobody had seen him in the flesh for six and a half years. Alejandro had abdicated the throne. His Howard Hughes number, David called it.

The final wall panel, the other frame for Alejandro's portrait, was a stylized map of North America with insets for Europe, Japan, the Middle East, and elsewhere. Forests of twinkling light were scattered across the map. Upon closer inspection they were revealed as individual pinpricks, tiny red LEDs, each one indicating the location and status — on or off — of every authorized upper-level SEEK terminal in existence. The locations of lower-level SEEK terminals were too numerous to bother with. They were everywhere — hospitals, universities, state and local governments, utilities, transportation systems — wherever there existed information suitable for digitizing.

There existed, in the world of the early eighties, very little information, very few modes of work or play, that did not fit that category. SEEK was everywhere, and every part of SEEK was connected to every other part. Peter bent close and read the explanatory paragraph at the bottom of the map, a slight smile playing across his lips.

"Niobium circuitry," it read, "developed by Dr. Alejandro Hunt, forms the heart of the DID Corporation's revolutionary SEEK system — the most advanced computer network in operation, and the last word in communications security."

True, thought Peter, as far as it goes. Just about exactly that far.

* *

You couldn't do SEEK in a paragraph. You couldn't do SEEK in a lifetime. Journalists and congressmen couldn't seem to "do" SEEK at all. If SEEK was an acronym for anything in particular, Alejandro, who coined it, wasn't saying. Perhaps it was a joke.

SEEK had its origins in the late fifties, when the insatiable code-breaking and information-gathering demands of the National Security Agency — the Pentagon's quasicivilian right arm in matters of state intelligence — had begun to outstrip the computing capabilities of its relatively primitive equipment. The amount of raw data pouring into NSA headquarters was truly staggering: idle chatter from Soviet transport planes, a Chinese businessman telephoning Thailand for spare radio parts, tapes of a Cuban diplomat discussing matters of state in the privacy of his own home, not to mention (and nobody ever did) the monitoring of each and every overseas cable, telegram, and telephone call originating stateside. The DID Corporation, for reasons of secrecy, was the SEEK project's sole contractor. Alejandro was its primary architect.

The project grew, then split. The lower levels became a commercially available network for information storage and manipulation. Most of the data that traveled on it were efficiently routed through the NSA snare, there to be combed for useful tidbits. Peter was constantly amazed at the fact that many lower-level users seemed to be unaware of this. The upper levels were a different story altogether. Authorized, DID-produced terminals only. Positive user identification required. Every move a client made on the upper-level net was traceable, accountable.

Level 7, the highest level, was added to the network much later in the game.

Peter studied the map again. It was impossible to tell which blinking lights indicated seventh-level terminals. Level 7 was the place where the secrets were. Each authorized seventh-level terminal was equipped with a microcomputer-controlled rubber eyepiece for purposes of flesh and blood vessel identification. Moreover, each terminal was equipped with a slot into which the user inserted his hand at a specified point in the access transactions. The SEEK central processing units, wherever they were hidden, took the would-be user's pulse, galvanic skin response, and a host of other biometric parameters, then compared these readings with the user's basal norms, updated monthly through rigorous medical examinations.

If the readings fell outside the norms, indicating duress, illness, extreme agitation, panic, or other abnormalities, the system cut off the applicant and notified the NSA Guardians, the most elite cadre of technicians and analysts ever assembled for the purpose of computer-system security.

One choice story that had made the rounds of the SEEK community had to do with a drunken general in Europe who had attempted to report unusual Soviet tank movements on the Polish border, only to find that his five-martini lunch had rendered him unsuitable for Level 7 admission. Other abnormalities registered by the palm slot included extreme fatigue and excessive drug use.

Certain of the Guardians had even suggested that a tiny electrode be implanted in the skull of every seventh-level user. When hooked to the terminal itself, the implanted electrode would give an instant EEG readout — brain-wave identification as well as a further guarantee against psychic abnormalities. The powers that were had decided that this piece of razzle-dazzle was perhaps a step too far at present. Even in this day and age, even in the military, people still harbored some rather antique notions about personal privacy.

There were other safeguards for upper levels 5, 6, and 7. Any attempt at divining the secrets of the upper-level circuitry by dismembering an authorized terminal would set off a small explosive charge that the DID Corporation had implanted therein. There was such a charge in Peter's own fifth-level terminal, which he had moved to his house since his departure from DID. The charge was said to be sufficient to blow up the circuitry, and quite possibly the tamperer as well. Nobody knew for sure. Nobody was foolish enough to want to find out.

There was only one way around all this, and it was known as the Hunt Code. It was a secret form of emergency access designed to be used only in the event of war. With the Hunt Code, the usual restrictions limiting upper-level clients to that portion of the network for which they had been cleared did not apply. Employment of the Hunt Code yielded access to absolutely everything the upper levels had to offer. No checks, balances, or barriers. No restricted files or procedures. Perfect computer democracy. This much was official corporate lore. This much was common knowledge among DID employees.

* *

At long last Peter heard a buzz, and then a familiar answering buzz from the guard desk. A terminally cheerful young woman poked her head through the door to the inner sanctum, motioning for Peter to follow. Suppressing an urge to bolt for the door and the hills beyond it, he followed.

The last thing he saw on the way in was another small display panel by the door, containing only the company's logo — a black circle broken by a curved red line — and its motto: CAN DO. DID. Peter fell in behind the staccato clack of the woman's high heels as she led him along the maze of S & S hallways. In the case of SEEK, he was thinking, they did indeed.

From time to time, people wanted to know what was stored in SEEK. In the upper levels. It was extremely hard to say, in twenty-five words or less. Politics. Business. Industry. Education. Economics. The arts. Science. Philosophy. Religion. Theosophy. The Akashic Records. The many hydra-headed faces of God.

What else. Ah yes. The central control circuitry for the "smart" missile system known — how lovely this is, he thought — as the Peacemakers.

Control Center was in there. Of course.

Awesome works, the Peacemakers — move like a butterfly, sting like a bee, stone fact. Only the most case-hardened Luddite could fail to see the elegantly lethal aesthetics at work here.

Take a bow, Alejandro. You've earned your place in the hall.

From time to time, people wanted to know whether or not there was still a "human element" in the seventh-level circuitry that controlled the Peacemakers. "A human element" — this was the exact term employed. Like it made any difference.

The job of the human element, so named, was to respond to a simple question. Yes or no. Go or no go. If it was yes, if it was go, the missiles did all the rest. Every last little bit of it. Yes or no. You could teach a termite to do that. Better yet, flip a coin. Statistics, game theory, operations analysis. Better yet, just set them off. They'll do the rest. Let them *think* for you. Why? Because they know how.

Enough, he told himself. Let's shake this off. When this is over, we break out the rod and reel. We resign our consultancy commission, forfeit our benefits. We step out of the loop and close it behind us.

In the meantime, stay awake. And be aware of subtleties.

The problem, he decided, was that there were always too many subtleties to keep track of at once.

When they arrived at the conference area, the woman opened the blue door of the reception room and held it ajar for him. Inside, there was another security guard, this one ancient. His wispy, thinning hair rose from his head like the first frail shoots of some delicately primitive plant. A smoked plexiglass hood obscured the top of his desk, and his body below the elbows. "I've got your papers," said the ancient one. "Sign in, please." Peter did so, and the guard buzzed him through to the conference room.

Peter took to the safety of a rear wall, leaning up against it while he conducted a brief survey of attendees. The conference room resembled a small movie theater, carpeted in the deepest blue, with rows of plush orange chairs and swiveled work desks arranged in a semicircle around a raised stage and podium. Behind the podium was a large video screen. People were milling about in small groups, coffee in hand.

He spotted several people he knew. It appeared to be the usual mix — engineers, technicians, project managers, systems analysts, programmers, designers, researchers like himself. A fair sprinkling of unknown quantities. A few corporate fellows. Colonel Core. And Ada Stibbits from Cal-Berkeley. Something of a surprise there. Ada the whiz. Ada who sat at the very feet of Alejandro, gazing up with love in her eyes. Or something. So it is said. They must have some very woolly numbers on the agenda today, Peter thought.

And David Atwood. In his loafers and soft-shouldered sport coat and too-skinny tie, with his impossibly large hands and feet, towering a foot or more above everyone else in the room, David was hard to miss. Every inch the Stanford basketball standout, some ten years after the fact. Lean and muscular. Strong bones. Gingerly, Peter fingered the mysterious bulge around his waist. Had the pro scouts slavering, did our boy David.

David spotted Peter and strolled over, three doughnuts in hand. "You're late," David said.

"Let's just say I have a hangover."

David peered closely at him. "You don't *get* hangovers, do you?"

"Let's just say."

They scanned the thirty-odd professionals in attendance, as an S & S functionary called from the podium for people to take their seats. "A token female," David reported, with evident interest.

"That's Ada," Peter said, "and she's no token. I have had occasion to collaborate with her."

"No kidding," David said. "In some near-biblical sense? If this is who you want to screw to get out of this business, then — "

"Please."

"Really quite a looker," David said appreciatively, inclining his head toward the front of the room, where a thin, attractive woman was engaged in conversation with Colonel Robert Core and another man. She was wearing a tastefully expensive dark green suit and low-heeled black pumps. Her dark brown hair was piled neatly above her long neck. She had a wide mouth, and in profile, just a hint of an overbite.

"What would you say?" David inquired. "Early forties? Late forties? She's still got that model's build. Kind of the *Vogue* look."

"Who's the other guy?" Peter asked.

The dark-haired man could have been anything. An IBM salesman. A project manager in an ill-fitting suit.

"Anton DeBroer," David said. "He's National Security Agency. A field man, of sorts. We're not supposed to know this."

"Do you know him?"

"Haven't had the pleasure."

They took aisle seats, well back from the front. The chairs were thick, enveloping models, crushed velvet soft, with wide, comfortable armrests. The colonel mounted the stage and spread a stack of papers before him on the podium. He tapped the microphone twice and issued a stiff welcome, including apologies for the hour and the day.

The colonel was a distinguished-looking man, broadly built, with a wide, blocked face to match. He wore his hair closely cropped in the manner of his former profession, and the color of it rather neatly matched his charcoal gray three-piece suit. The colonel played tackle, light-years ago, for Army. He had a low center of gravity, making him a very hard man to knock down. The colonel, in Peter's opinion, was something of a four-star, all-around prick.

"The purpose of this meeting," the colonel announced, "is to effect a simulated incursion into the SEEK computer system, at the seventh level of the network."

David leaned slightly in Peter's direction. "An emergency fire drill," he whispered. "War games of some sort."

Peter groaned — not audibly, he hoped.

"This exercise is being conducted under the auspices of Interagency Directive Four Five Nine and at the request of the NSA. The signatories to Document Four Five Nine, may I remind you, include the DID Corporation, the NSA, and the Defense Advanced Research Projects Agency."

Peter sat back in his chair, thinking that a simulation hardly seemed like something worth calling out the hounds for. He knew what to expect — they would run a simulation with the SEEK computers, and certain circuitry would "fail." Certain precautionary measures would be suggested. Then they would all sit around and figure out how they did.

For himself and David, who was a circuit designer, it would boil down to a matter of fielding queries. Could this or that chip theoretically incur this or that transient voltage, thereby causing this or that processing error, programming failure, network inconsistency as a result of the simulated violation of system integrity? Yes, maybe. No, probably not. Peter had been through these terrorist scenarios before. It was best to reply in monosyllables. Those systems people were impossible.

Colonel Core nodded curtly toward the back of the room. The lights grew dim, and an image swam into view on the screen above the colonel's head. It showed the profile of a man in a plaid sport shirt, seated at a small computer terminal, eating a carrot.

"The following," said the colonel, "is a filmed mock-up of the unauthorized incursion. We will be taking it as the starting point for the day's activities. At its conclusion we will be assigning specific intergroup Task-Goal-Resolution structures. A representative of the NSA Guardians will be a member of each group. The specific goals of the exercise are to ascertain the method of violation, to locate and apprehend the violator, and to retain data base integrity in the interim.

"Assume that the terminal used in the violation has not been traced or otherwise discovered. Assume, also, that the extent of the penetration is not fully known. We will distribute printouts of certain technical data pertaining to the incursion.

"As you will see, this exercise has a seventy-two-hour deadline. Assume, at the end of the seventy-two-hour period, that another unpleasant event will occur." Here the colonel managed a weak smile. "Class One security rules will be in force during this period. However, in recognition of various practical matters, we will take tomorrow off, reconvening for the second half of the exercise Monday morning." The colonel's smile at this juncture was not something Peter was anxious to see again soon.

"Under the rules of this exercise, we must be prepared to submit an interdepartmental resolution report in draft by Monday evening."

The colonel's preamble ended. The videotape ran on. Nothing happened for several minutes. The man appeared to be intent on finishing his carrot. There was a digital readout of the time in the upper right-hand corner of the screen, and a close-up shot of the man's computer screen superimposed below that. READY, said the screen-within-a-screen. SEEK SYSTEM, 7TH LEVEL. 13 DECEMBER. LOOP REQUEST?

Peter thought of the black box high on the wall behind him, behind Peter, filming Peter as he watched the film of the man eating the carrot. So many levels to keep track of at once. It got positively unsettling if you let it.

The digital seconds ticked by. Then a new message appeared on the man's terminal. He placed the nub of his carrot on the table beside him and leaned toward the screen.

PRIORITY INTERRUPT, it said. The digital clock read 5:49:59. The man reached for one of the telephones and cradled the receiver between cocked head and shoulder while he jabbed at the keyboard of his computer.

"George," he said to the telephone, "something's come up. There's an interrupt on — "

A bleeped deletion momentarily cut off his voice. "What's going on?" The man listened, nodding constantly, rocking lightly back and forth in his chair. He was considerably overweight. Still listening, the man gave out a long, low whistle. "In that case," he said, "who the hell's on-line here?" David chuckled quietly. "Because," said the man, "I'll tell you. It isn't me."

A new message appeared on the terminal. This is how it read: FIRST INCURSION.

"George," said the man. "Are you getting this? Can you see this?" His hands flickered across the keyboard. "I'm not in control here. What the Jesus is going *on?*"

The man was a very good actor. The same thought kept running through Peter's mind, like a broken record — Why me? Why am I here? What's my role in this dog and pony show? Why bother to call me in at all?

The message vanished from the screen. "Wait a minute," the man said, holding his hands still now, several inches above the keys. "Wait a minute." There was a blurry, high-speed scan of data, and then the computer screen went blank. The man worked his computer console vigorously. Nothing happened.

The computer screen blinked to life again, yellow letters against a glowing green background. FILE PURGE COMPLETED.

Which could mean anything, Peter thought. Theft of data, alteration of data, destruction of data. How much? Which files? I'll leave for Buster's first thing Tuesday morning. I'll go up to Buster's for Christmas.

The man slumped visibly in his chair. "George," he said again weakly. "For God's sake. Somebody's dumping memory."

Time passed. A minute and a half by the digital clock. Another line of text appeared on the screen. A standard display, all caps. DISMANTLE SEEK, it read.

Easier said than done, thought Peter. Rather wishful thinking even for a so-called terrorist.

"George, please tell me what's going on."

More text appeared. DISARM THE PEACEMAKERS, it read. David chuckled again.

Another laudable sentiment, Peter told himself. But a little far-fetched. A typically simplistic personality profile. Not that it mattered. Motive was immaterial.

Then something began to grow and billow in Peter's head. A feeling. With only the slightest shift in thought patterns, triggered by a rumor he'd heard long ago, he began to ask himself: Why this movie? Why do it this way? Why not just give them the ground rules, the nut of this faked violation, and set them to work on it? The false dramatics. Filmed set and setting. What was the point? If Level 7 were so unbreakable, so impervious to unauthorized entry, why run any terrorist scenarios at all?

Another message took form on the screen; a line which struck Peter as so unlikely, so oddly undecipherable, that he could not imagine who could have come up with it, or how it could possibly figure in the exercise.

PRESERVE EGG LOGIC.

Pure obfuscation, perhaps. Pure poetry, even.

There was a sixth line. THE ALTERNATIVE IS PULSE.

Three things came to Peter's mind simultaneously as he read it: the threat of system-wide disruption, his memos on just such disruptions, and the increasingly bizarre nature of the film. There was something mushy about the proceedings, something that didn't quite jell.

Be aware of subtleties. Think. For what *reason* do you offer a sensory stimulus like this? The comfortable chairs, rumors about certain company psychologists. . . .

To provoke a response.

A visceral, semiconscious response. A "good plot," as the technicians might say. A direct metabolic response to these filmed activities. Some tempting anomaly spewing out on graph paper. Peter became aware of the cool, enveloping texture of his body-molded chair, as if for the first time. He had it. He was sure of it. Somehow, professional people had come to trust various forms of remote polygraphic sensing far more explicitly than the evidence warranted. It was hard to say why.

Peter pushed his thoughts forward. Go further, he told himself. What use are covert polygraphic plots in a proceeding such as this?

You do it to find out how people are *reacting*. To find out whether they *believe* what they're seeing. Whether it makes them *nervous*. Whether they *know* anything. No different in principle from the practice among certain African tribes of placing a red-hot poker briefly on the tongues of those suspected of some crime. Only the dry-mouthed culprit would react with a howl of pain. Or so it went in theory.

You do it to find out who's guilty.

At length, a line composed of one word appeared on the man's computer screen, beneath the rest of the message. It could be taken as a signature. And when he saw it, Peter could not help thinking immediately, disturbingly, of his friend and former partner in crime, the illustrious computer hacker known as Captain Crash.

KLAATU.

It was a name Peter knew.

The computer screen went blank again. The man pushed himself up and out of his chair, turning to the camera, looking directly, without expression, at his audience.

There was a humming sound, and abruptly, the images dissolved as the film ended and the lights in the conference room came back up again.

Peter tried it out silently in his mind, like a mantra. His word for the day. *Klaatu.*

A fleshless advance, he thought, feeling slightly dazed and lightheaded. That was it. A prankster, a madman, an insider who's been turned, an outsider who's been turned on.

Someone's loose inside the net. So what do the security people do? They lowball it. They present it as a fire drill, hoping to catch the culprit without anyone ever knowing for real that it happened. Hoping, perhaps, that the culprit or an accomplice is in this room, among this handpicked crew of specialists.

It can't happen. You can't break seventh level. It *can* happen. Every lock has a key.

Someone had picked the lock. It was the likeliest conclusion, though Peter wished desperately that he could back away from it. Someone was running loose in the seventh level. They wanted to know who.

He was quitting. They wanted to know why.

He should have quit a long time ago.

THREE

"THEY'RE BURNING," David yelled. "'We need water. Fire control. Med techs."

"What?"

"They're burning."

Alison emerged from the A-frame and walked over to her husband, holding a platter. David bent low, squinting through the smoke, jabbing with a long-handled spatula at several flaming burgers on the grill. A sliding glass door rattled open and Peter Cassidy, casting a worried glance at the sky, joined the two of them on his redwood deck. The Willamette River, just visible through a rough perimeter of hemlock and pine at the back of his property, was losing its luster as a skein of clouds moved across the sky.

"Picnic's off," Peter announced. "Called on account of a counterfeit sunset." David sawed determinedly at the remains of a burger stuck fast to the grill. Alison abandoned him and took the salvaged ones inside. With Peter's help, she ran a quick shuttle from the picnic table on the deck to the dining table inside the A-frame — paper plates, silverware, napkins, chips, salad bowls, beers, assorted condiments.

Peter stood on the deck and watched her through the glass as she reset the table indoors. David, having sacrificed the final hamburger on a pillar of briquettes, caught him at it. "She's looking very fifties tonight," David said. "Don't you think?"

As Peter looked on, Alison unknotted a sweater from around her neck, poked her head and arms through it, and tugged it over her swollen belly. Nothing had changed but her middle, and the way she carried herself — the same wide mouth, the prominent, sharply angled nose, the wavy, rust-colored hair falling just short of her shoul-

30

ders in a simple and sensible cut. A faint patch of freckles were scattered across her face like an afterthought. A fleeting image of her naked crept across his mind.

"The white shirt is mine," David said. "The black tennis shoes are anybody's guess." On his way inside David mercilessly mimicked Peter's perennial skyward squint, saying, "It's just as well. The Blazers are on the tube tonight."

Peter lingered momentarily on his deck, affirming the arrival of a new storm front. The TV was on, sound off, by the time he entered the house. Alison and David were in the kitchen nook searching for salad oil and fresh beer, respectively. "I never got around to asking," Alison was saying. "What was all the overtime about today?"

"We're troubleshooting," David answered, glancing at Peter. "We're on call."

There was an uncomfortable pause. She said it very evenly. "Classified."

"We'd love to talk about it," David said. "But we can't talk about it."

Peter sat down at the table and watched the game while he buttered a few buns. "Portland trailing by fifteen," he told David, "late in the second period."

"Not to worry," David said, bending cleanly at the waist, storklike, to retrieve a fallen bottle cap. He took a long set shot at the garbage sack, and sunk it. "You watch."

"Any money on this contest?"

Alison was tossing a salad and pretending not to have heard. "Not really," David muttered. "Pocket change."

Oh boy, Peter thought, wrong question.

Alison looked directly at Peter. "I thought you were unemployed," she said. "I thought you were a free man in Paris."

"What's the bit about Paris?" David asked.

Peter knew it was a line from an old Joni Mitchell tune. "There's some glitch with the SEEK system," he told Alison. He always felt uncomfortable about the way they danced with Alison when it came to the work. Alison detested it.

*   *

They ate dinner in relative silence. It was halftime. Outside, a chipmunk scaled the redwood deck and skittered across it to the glass doors. Peter's cathedral in the pines occupied a sandy patch of land southeast of Portland, twenty-five yards from the bank of the Willamette and not ten minutes from the Interstate. A small, triangular

31

house, room for one. Two, if they were close. David called it Izaak Walton Chic.

The house rose from the middle of an expansive lot, separated from the river by a grassy, tree-dotted slope. A short side yard, visible through the windows of the kitchen nook, was hemmed in on three sides by a stand of third-growth Douglas fir. The adjoining lots on either side were vacant, overgrown with weeds and wild morning glory.

The neighborhood was strictly working class, with a large population of retired mill hands. Peter had the money to live in a tastefully landscaped premier Portland bedroom community, like Beaverton, like David and Alison, but he much preferred to be right where he was, in this unincorporated cluster of riverfront homes and trailers. Out of town, out of sight, out of mind, here with his river and his mismatched furniture, his two lofts fore and aft and the deliciously high-ceilinged living room in between.

The sloping side walls of the living room rose a full thirty feet before meeting to form the peak of the roof. The larger of the two lofts was Peter's bedroom, doubling as a ceiling over the kitchen nook, the bathroom, and the map-decorated hallway. A dusty skeleton of two-by-four studs abutted the bathroom — Peter's den-in-the-making. The smaller loft, at the opposite end of the house, was his office at home. Facing the backyard and the river, it was accessible only by means of a steep ladder. Peter had a desk and file cabinets and two computer terminals up there. The view of the river from his desk chair was never disappointing. He hadn't been up there in over a month.

The Blazers behaved despicably throughout the third period.

When the three of them had finished eating, David went to the stereo in search of anything by Little Feat. Alison flopped down on a brown velvet couch near the wood stove and stretched out on the cushions, her head propped against one of the armrests. Peter was wondering how long it would take for her to fall asleep. No doubt David was thinking the same thing. They had not spoken since the morning's meeting.

Peter brought her a cup of coffee, which she declined. He handed it to David, who had punched up a tape and was now sitting on the floor, leaning against the end of the couch nearest the television. He pulled a small metal canister from Alison's yarn bag and handed it to her. "Here," he said, "hand this to Ranger Rick over there."

Alison executed a slow sit-up and Peter leaned toward her in his leather chair. "I feel like a beached sea lion," she said. Peter opened the canister and pulled out a red velvet pouch. Inside the pouch was a curled, leafy bud of marijuana. He held it by the stalk, put it to his nose, and sniffed. A mold smell, earthy, but with a tartness like lime.

"No TV for the Ace," Alison said. "And no dope either. Not until he's at least twenty-one."

"It's Asa, then," Peter cut in. "Is that for sure?"

"Asa it is," Alison said, as Portland muffed another fast break. "Unless it's a girl. Then it's, I don't know. Asette."

Peter joined David on the floor for the last few minutes of the game. Alison slid slightly more upright on the couch, pulling the beginnings of a reed basket from her yarn bag. She executed a smooth marriage between a strand of reed and a cobalt-colored strip of raffia, then looped the raffia several times around the stiff reed and cinched it tight.

The game ended without a miracle. David scuttled around to the front of the couch, staring at the burning logs through the hinged glass doors of the wood stove. Peter could see the fire reflected in David's glasses. He was thinking about how David was going to react to what Peter had to tell him.

In short order, Alison put down her basket and slid back again on the couch, the fire burnishing the tip of her nose. Peter watched her surrendering to fatigue, knees bent, hands tucked up underneath her sweater for added warmth. Hazel eyes to the fire, lashes lowering. The Dixie rhythms of Little Feat chugged steadily along in the background. He was thinking about the face she presented to the world, the way she kept to herself. The nature of her dealings with David. Her effortless voice, her voice the way it sounded on the telephone, confiding to him, worrying for him, teasing him.

These friends, this fire, David's dreamy dope — he wished it could last.

* *

When Alison had fallen asleep, they filled two snifters with brandy and adjourned up the ladder to Peter's work loft. Alison was motionless in the light of the fire, fourteen feet below. Peter propped himself in his desk chair and pushed with his feet until the chair rocked up on two legs, bumping solidly against the wall behind him. Thus angled, he checked the view toward the river. The evening's moon was nowhere in sight. The sky was closed. David, in the rocker opposite the desk, silently examined a potted ficus.

33

"This is not a test," Peter said quietly. "This is not a game. This is the real bloody thing. Someone's loose inside the system."

David held a leaf in his hand, turning it toward the lamp, examining it closely. "One mighty fine plant, no thanks to you. Poor girl's cramped, aren't ya, love?"

"It was real."

"I heard you," David said. "There were people on my team today who shared your opinion. When they weren't scrutinizing chip topographies through electron-beam microscopes."

"And you?" Peter kept wondering about the fact that they'd asked so little of him today. A few straightforward calculations. Routine procedures any moron could do. Many did.

David looked up. "It doesn't," he said, "really make any difference."

"The break was genuine. Some sort of terrorist attack on the SEEK system. Maybe whoever did it can do it again. They want me because they're scared about some form of induced disruption — a frequency pulse. The supersensitivity principle. There was a reference to that, right?"

"Yeah," David said. "It was very poetic."

"They had us hard-wired in those goddamn polygraph chairs, looking for suspects."

David sighed. "There is no method of gaining on-line access to the seventh level without eyeball identification through an authorized seventh-level terminal. Not from fifth level, not from anywhere else. Mathematically, the odds against a genuine seventh-level break are astronomical. The Hunt Code would be the only way to do it. Nobody even *tries* to break the Hunt Code anymore."

"Somebody stole it."

"From *who*?"

"Some Hunt Code insider gone rogue."

"Like *who*? The president? One of the joint chiefs?" David sighed again. "Why are you getting so exercised over this? All it cost you was a couple of poison blowfish."

"Steelhead," Peter muttered absently. "It's steelhead season."

"Whatever," said David.

"It must have happened Thursday night," Peter said, thinking about his phone machine. "Jesus, I forgot to call Sandy."

David leaned forward in the tall rocker until he could place his bony elbows on the desk across from Peter. "You know," he said, "I can appreciate how you've been *moved* so deeply by the activities of

34

the day, but if this thing was for real, a reign of terror would descend upon the already neurotic minions of Systems and Security. They'd be shoving bamboo splints under fingernails."

Peter leaned slightly forward until his chair came back down on all fours with a crack. "You're being naive," he said. "Look at it from their point of view. They can't *afford* to handle it any other way. I mean, if word got out . . . data lost and destroyed . . . think of it. There would be a run on the bank like you've never seen. Black Thursday. Literally. I mean, start with that. World Bank transfers, the IMF, that high-wire act known as international currency futures — almost all of it is conducted on SEEK nowadays. OPEC transactions. Other things. Anything suitable for digitizing. The family jewels."

David looked at his watch.

"The Consolidated Research Consortium uses the net almost exclusively," Peter continued. "The Bell Labs–IBM–DID Corporation melange. The Axis powers. How do you suppose CRC is going to feel about a seventh-level incursion by party or parties unknown? A piece of it belongs to the NSA and the Pentagon. A subroute on the network that nobody seems to know much about. Control central for the Peacemakers — "

"Your problem," David interjected, "is that you got called in for a security meeting after you quit, and you're losing your brains over it. You thought you were out and they called you back for one last go-around. Big deal. Just run your numbers for them and forget it."

"Assuming you could break into the system," Peter said, "assuming you were inside to the extent that you had the run of the upper levels, there exists the theoretical possibility of inducing a resonant wave at a specific frequency — an induced pulse, a wave of electromagnetic energy, impressed upon the data of your signal. It's a function of certain particle-particle interactions across the surface of the doped niobium. It was all in my memos. Now, to the extent that you can model these disturbances mathematically. . . ."

David looked at his watch, looked at the ladder.

"Well, forget that. The point is, you could create and broadcast a certain resonant frequency that has an *affinity* for high-density niobium chips. It might be possible to broadcast a specific frequency pulse that would *seek out* these chips, inside whatever equipment they were found. Like a lightning bolt streaking through metal. Short the fuckers out like a bunch of fifty-cent circuit breakers. Disrupt or destroy all the memory and logic registers."

35

"I may be crazy," David said, "but aren't we wandering a little far afield of your specialty? It's a pretty long jump from alpha bombardment to premeditated sabotage. I mean, what kind of equipment to produce this signal? Who's gonna build it? What the hell are you *talking* about?"

"I have no idea what kind of equipment, what kind of signal. It's all theoretical. Or it was. But you can't believe how sensitive these newer chips are."

Below them, Alison stirred and sniffled. David walked over to the slatted railing at the edge of the loft and looked down at her. "You're viewing this whole thing as some sort of professional *coup* for yourself," David said over his shoulder. "You want it to be genuine for that reason. Fine. A little weird for somebody who just quit, but fine. Supposing it is real. Doesn't make a bit of difference to you or me. Here's what you do, either way. Leave it to the spooks, the people who draw a paycheck for it. If it's live or if it's Memorex, that's what you do. Just run your numbers for them and forget it. Christ, don't go plowing around on this thing. We're on call for a couple of days, there may be a little follow-up, then everything's back to normal. Including your savings account. Don't go stirring things up. Don't *prolong* this little episode."

As David disappeared down the ladder, Peter called out: "I think I'll call up Captain Crash," knowing full well what the effect of his pronouncement was likely to be. David's face reappeared through the rungs of the ladder. He was apoplectic. "That's great. Give Reddy Kilowatt a buzz while you're at it, why don't you. They share a certain cartoonish quality."

"The captain — "

"The captain is a prick," David said flatly. "A slightly larger-than-life prick, but a prick all the same. You can't tell him anything, anyway. The phone taps will run until they declare the simulation over. They always tap for these security meetings. Security checks might be the whole *point* of this fire drill."

Peter let it go. "I wonder," he said, as David began to vanish down the ladder again, "if you've ever heard of the name Klaatu. Before today, I mean."

David appeared again, wearing a look of extreme patience. He said he hadn't.

"Klaatu is a character in a science fiction movie."

David registered only mild interest.

"*The Day the Earth Stood Still.* Michael Rennie and Patricia Neal. You never caught it on television?"

"Nope."

"Michael Rennie plays an alien named Klaatu who comes to earth in a flying saucer and lands it in Washington, D.C. On the grounds of the Washington Monument, I think. Klaatu was a peaceful man from a peaceful world. He looked a little bit like Abraham Lincoln in a jumpsuit, without the beard. Klaatu and the galactic federation he represented had a message to deliver about the perils of meddling with atomic power. This is the way it comes back to me, anyway."

Through the glass wall of his aerie, Peter could see a line of dripping hemlocks in the light thrown out by his deck lamps below. There was light rain now, or blowing mist, Peter couldn't tell which. It was a night for staying inside. For hot sake and a warm body in the bed. "Klaatu ordered his robot — they always have a robot — ordered his robot, Gort, to perform a kind of object lesson. Something that would really get everybody's attention. So Gort neutralized all electrical power on the planet. For one hour. At high noon. You can imagine what happened. Klaatu was humane enough, if that's the word, to exempt hospitals and airplanes in flight and other critical situations. Still, I mean, think about it."

"Con Ed must have been furious," David said, still clinging patiently to the ladder.

"Think of all the places in the SEEK system where DID's newer chips are being used. Hospitals, airplanes in flight, nuclear power plants — "

"So what happened? How did it end?"

"Klaatu delivered his speech about the follies of modern science. I don't remember how it went over. Then he turned the lights back on and left."

"Jeez," David groaned. "That's why I never watched those old movies. They were always so lame."

Peter suddenly had a vision of a beautiful spring day, the sun beating against the red-tiled roofs of campus, a layer of filamentous cloud moving slowly across the sky. He and David were sprawled in the tall grass at the edge of the Stanford golf course, watching a foursome of professors working their way past.

David wanted something from him then. A vow of change? Did we read Nietzsche? Did we believe it? Peter had a clear picture of David turning to gaze at him for the longest time, both of them

37

rotoring along behind approximately five hundred micrograms of lysergic acid diethylamide #25. David was wide-eyed, guileless in Gaza.

"What do you think, Pete?" he had said, indicating the players on the course with a sweep of his hand. "Do you think, in your heart of hearts, that this is any time to be working on your *golf game*?"

All the pacts and the vows. We are different. We are special. We are exempt. There are no holds we cannot break.

Downstairs, they had a hard time rousting Al. Peter walked with them to the Porsche, along a curving pathway of redwood stepping blocks, Peter's mudless link to the driveway. A slug the color of a bad banana oozed across one of the steps. They stood by the car for a minute, ignoring the insistent drizzle like good northwesterners. David planted his hands around Peter's waist and squeezed. "What's the word I'm looking for? *Cuddly*, I believe."

Peter slapped his hands away. "Get out of here."

"You need a program. Falling head over heels down riverbanks twice a week just isn't going to do it."

Peter stood in the driveway and watched them pull away. He suppressed the familiar, wrenching feeling, and when the red taillights faded out around the corner, he went inside to make a phone call.

*   *

Leonard sat motionless in the car, his hands resting idly against the steering wheel. From the radio came the muted strains of classical music. It was Schubert.

Leonard didn't recognize the piece. He watched the taillights fading away down the street. He could see two-thirds of the A-frame beyond a thicket of azalea, and a lighted window just above the orange porch lamp. Several pieces of masking tape had been placed neatly across his dashboard clock. The clock was only a nuisance. He concentrated on the smells coming through the open vent. A wet, marshy odor from the river behind the dingy row of houses. Rhododendron. Pine. That much came through, even in the rain.

Leonard knew how to wait. Most people couldn't do it. When you ceased expecting things to happen, that was frequently when they did. It had to do with something more than patience.

Schubert was one of his favorites. It had been Vivaldi, something quite forgettable, when he had spotted the station wagon, a nondescript Chrysler, some distance behind him. Leonard, his four-foot-ten-inch frame pressed against the seat, his head no higher than the back of it, had seen them some time ago, courtesy of an abominably

38

stupid cigarette. So unprofessional. Personal weakness and nothing more.

There was a briefcase on the seat beside him. Inside it was a slim gray touch-tone receiver. The Schubert ended. He hoped subsequent selections would prove as tasteful. Leonard was waiting for a phone call.

*　*

Peter dialed the captain's unlisted number. After two rings he heard a click, followed by the Strauss flourish used in the opening of 2001: A *Space Odyssey*. "No human is home," said a pretentious voice, in overdub. "Feel free to leave a message." Peter waited for the beep tone, then gave his number and hung up.

He placed a quick call to Sandy, in order to break their amorphous date. Sandy had broken it already. She wasn't home. He was thinking about the internal memos he had written. He was thinking about the captain. He made a brief visit to the chair by his bedroom window. He could make out no station wagon, no dark figures.

He tried to stay cool. The captain would know what was up, if anyone did. He was getting the cart several leagues in front of the horse. He forced himself to focus simply on the matter of the upper-level break. A cancer at some nodal point on a multidimensional web of electronic connectedness. A blizzard of lawsuits. DID would have to cure it or go bankrupt. They'd been vague today about the extent and nature of the data loss. There were any number of possibilities. . . .

Under strict licensing agreements and NSA-sanctioned protocols, thousands of companies and other interested parties had become affiliates of the Consolidated Research Consortium. For a price. A really astounding price, in some cases. Whatever the traffic would bear. Just a glance at certain trade secrets, confidential reports, and R & D work secured in the upper-level memory registers of the SEEK system was enough to bestow upon any affiliate a vaulting lead over nonaffiliate competitors in electronics, computers, telecommunications, and sundry other specialties.

The alternative is pulse. He couldn't shake that line out of his head. The concluding supposition of his first memo kept floating back to him: "On the Implications of Supersensitivity." The captain was no stranger to the principle. Long before the memos, Peter and the captain had often speculated on the possibility that there existed a certain resonant electrical vibration, which, when broadcast through the communication channels of SEEK or any other electronic network, would erase or obliterate every memory and logic chip it encountered as it coursed like a tidal wave through the system. A lost chord, maybe. You couldn't say for sure.

Remembering the captain's usual nocturnal habits, Peter climbed to his work loft and pulled the dustcover from one of the two computer terminals on his desk. He powered up and punched in, accessing a widely used personal computer network. It was an information service owned and operated by Bell, and both he and the captain were subscribers. The captain, in fact, had played a hand in setting it up. Did it for Ma. The captain and Ma went way back.

He typed in a sequence of commands, telling the computer that he wanted to leave a "tickler." If the captain was at his terminal, a blinking white dot in the corner of his screen would tell him there was a message waiting. CHECK YR FONE BOX U FAT FREAK, he typed, and then logged off. He went downstairs and waited to see if his phone would ring. It did. He let it ring twice, picked it up and said hello.

"Who the hell is this?" Long pause. "Cassidy?"

"Yeah," said Peter. "I was wondering — could we talk?"

The captain sounded immensely relieved.

* *

David sat on the spacious bed in his jockey shorts, watching Alison's back as she hung her clothes in the closet. "All I'm saying is this. The basics of it, the child-care aspect — "

"The basics of it," she said, taking over for him as she reached for a hanger, "are *my* problem."

David sighed. "I don't know why you'd want to look at it as a *problem*."

Alison put on a nightgown, making no move toward the bed. The room was done completely in white, very spare — white quilt, white drapes, white dresser, white futon in the corner. "There are all kinds of possibilities," she said, without turning to look at him. "Assuming you were interested. You could work at home a little bit. Pete does it all the time."

"Moon Bird Crafts barely broke even last year. What more can I realistically say?"

"How much *did* you have on the game tonight, since we're on the subject of personal finances?"

"Ten bucks."

Liar, she thought. Without a word, he clicked off the light and they crawled into bed. They didn't touch. The standard standoff,

40

twin slow burns six inches apart. Ten minutes passed, as she judged it, before she felt him roll her way. He reached across her and cradled her breasts and tugged her gently until she rolled over to face him in the dark. He put an ear to her stomach and listened, his head rising and falling slightly with her breathing. "You must have been a beautiful zygote," he crooned, in the stagiest whisper he could muster. " 'Cause baby. . . ."

Alison felt herself drifting. We'll work it out, she thought. Me and the Ace. We'll put it right.

There were no encores for David. He was snoring.

FOUR

COLONEL ROBERT CORE of the DID Corporation, accompanied by Anton DeBroer of the National Security Agency, threaded his way through a scattering of low wooden tables en route to a corner booth at the Lewis and Clark Tavern. It was their habit to meet here whenever Anton was in town. There were no other patrons except for a line of loggers at the bar rail. Fifteen miles the wrong side of DID headquarters, away from Portland, the L & C never caught much company traffic. None at all on a late Saturday afternoon.

Anton took one side of the booth and the colonel slid onto the opposite bench, wincing as he positioned himself. Anton looked at him and raised a questioning eyebrow. The colonel shrugged. "Hemorrhoids," he said.

Anton clucked in sympathy. "Tough break," he replied.

The colonel extracted a twenty from his wallet and laid it on the lacquered surface of the table.

"You should exercise more," Anton suggested.

"I should have surgery. I've been putting it off."

The bar girl, a young nifty, came and took their orders. Scotch and soda for the colonel and Jack Daniel's, neat, for Anton. Anton's black hair was combed straight back against his head and shone brightly even under the meager lights of the bar. He was waiting for the colonel to speak.

Colonel Core stared at the fogged, unrevealing window beside the booth. "We don't have much to go on," he said, his tone of voice becoming more urgent. "As I pointed out last night."

The waitress returned with their drinks. "Outside of channels, you mean," Anton replied, as she was leaving.

The colonel took a long, loving swallow of his drink. He was silent for a moment. "The lid has got to stay on," he said. "And we've got to move fast. Above all else, we have to forestall the possibility of a recurrence."

Anton nodded his head in agreement. "We do the simple things first. We want to start at the simple end."

The effects of last night's scant sleep showed clearly in the frown lines around the colonel's eyes and mouth. "We can't afford to wait very long," he said irritably. "I must admit that today's exercise brought forth very little in the way of edible fruit. No leads, no chance avenues. No polygraphic clues, either. No useful spikes from any of the occupied chairs. Not from Cassidy or anyone else." Deliberately, through an act of will designed to keep himself below the boiling point, the colonel folded his hands together on the table in front of him, and squeezed.

"You can't trust that gear, anyway," Anton observed.

"It's remarkably sensitive." A slight sheen of moisture formed on the highly polished wood beneath his hands, and the colonel watched it spreading, like some living thing. "You get galvanic response, pulse rate, oxygen intake — clothing doesn't influence it."

"The mind does," said Anton. "We've had a number of misfires with the very same setup back at the shop."

The colonel leaned slowly back against the bench. Outside the tavern, the sky suddenly grew lighter as the sun, with stubborn good grace, broke through the clouds for a last-minute show of color. Using a spiral motion, the colonel cleaned the window with a cocktail napkin until he had created a porthole to his liking. Pavement sparkled in the slanting light. In a cow pasture across the highway, against a field of chartreuse, a trio of Black Angus stood motionless under a mushroom-shaped oak tree. In his off-hours, the colonel dabbled immaturely in watercolors. He had a knack for colors. It was supposed to be good for his heart.

Anton sensed an opening. "All we know for certain," he said, "is that Peter Cassidy's personal ID code and terminal number were somehow involved in the attempt to make the incursion appear legitimate on the daily activity logs. Since the Guardians cannot locate the source of the transmission, we have nothing else to go on. We can't trace."

"Yes," said the colonel darkly, "and one is tempted, again and again, to ask why."

"Too much frequency hopping," Anton replied. "Not to mention

43

a seventh-level violation by means of a fifth-level terminal — an un-authorized, unidentifiable one in the bargain. A pirate terminal." A bootleg, Anton was thinking. The electronic signature, its frequency characteristics, didn't match up with the stored signatures for any of the thousands of authorized terminals in use — meaning DID didn't build it. From a technical standpoint, they were looking for a needle in a haystack. "I wouldn't count on the Guardians putting all the pieces back together again."

"The Guardians," said the colonel, "are supposed to be the very best at what they do."

"There's always somebody better," said Anton. He let it go at that. Anton didn't push.

" 'The alternative is pulse,' " the colonel quoted. "I don't know for certain what it means, and I'm not in the least bit anxious to find out. I don't want Mr. Klaa-*two* on-line again."

"It strikes me," said Anton, "as the kind of rant you might expect from someone like Frank Holsa — or from Alejandro, in the event he's gone completely around the bend. He threatens to incapacitate the SEEK system unless we shut it down and mothball the Peace-makers. Quite clearly, neither of these demands is going to be met."

"There was another puzzling reference — "

"Egg logic," said Anton. "I have no thoughts on that. I recommend we dismiss it."

"I'm not so sure."

"Does it mean something to you?"

"No, but I can't help thinking that it means something to its author."

The colonel drained off the remains of his Scotch, ran a forefinger along his lips, and signaled the waitress for another round. Then he raised his glass slowly, as if for a toast, and shook it until the ice rattled.

"Here's to Alejandro," he said. "Father of us all."

The colonel and Anton went way back. Too far, the colonel some-times thought. There were very few secrets between them, profession-ally speaking. They'd both been present at the creation, sitting in the Pentagon at the same table as Alejandro when the forerunner of the SEEK system had first been proposed and approved. It was like Yalta, only with less hot air and more permanent results.

"It's ironic," said the colonel.

"No it isn't," said Anton. "It's not ironic at all." There was very little doubt in Anton's mind about the nature of Klaatu: Find the right string, and pull it carefully enough, and it would lead, inevitably, to Alejandro. But Anton did not push. "What's ironic," he said, "is that there are times when the bottom line is, either somebody gets hurt, or else everybody gets hurt." Anton finished his drink. "I presume you're still attempting to contact him."

"Of course."

"The place is a fortress, electronically and otherwise."

"You've seen the aerials, then."

"Five hundred miles of Guatemalan jungle in every direction," said Anton. He paused a moment, as he eyed the colonel. Alejandro the Magnificent, he thought, come back to bust our balls for good. Between the guerrillas and the death squads, Alejandro had honed his survival skills to a keen edge. He was Guatemala's only professional philanthropist. He gave away money to both sides, all sides, lavish amounts. So naturally, very few Guatemalans thought seriously about killing him, or kidnapping him. Or even bruising his check-writing hand. "What I'm hoping," Anton said, "is that I don't have to worry about you undercutting my authority, if push comes to shove."

Way too far back, the colonel was thinking. "I don't want the intelligence aspects of this case to overshadow what's really at stake," he said. "I want you to realize the utter gravity of what is going on here, DeBroer. The inherent potential for harm."

Indeed I do, Anton was thinking. You can bet on it, Colonel. If Alejandro proved to be Klaatu, the colonel would want to have him jailed, Anton knew. But Anton, on the other hand, wanted to do business with him. Anton would have to do business with Alejandro, and then either sell him or kill him, to avoid a similar fate himself. This was a harsh fact of Anton's life that he was not anxious to share with the colonel. Anton realized that the same conditions might, in time, apply to the colonel, as well. It was too early to say.

"For exactly two minutes," said the colonel steadily, "this interloper had complete control over the entire SEEK system. Every channel, every terminal, every stored piece of data — every piece of equipment linked to the system. It all went down, DeBroer. There are localities which use the lower levels of the system for everything from tax records to traffic control. Traffic lights went out. There were accidents. Go from there — let your imagination run all the way up to the seventh level — do you have any idea what the *death toll* would be if — "

"Our prime suspect remains the same," said Anton, cutting him off. "Alejandro invented the Hunt Code, among other things, and quite clearly he has become . . . unstable. We have two possible routes of approach, at this point. We have Frank Holsa, because he's neurotic and he specializes in system penetrations, and we have Cassidy, circumstantially, on the basis of his ID. One leads to the other, which leads to the other, believe me."

"If it's true," said the colonel, with force, "then we should bring both of them in — right now. We're wasting valuable time."

Anton cut him off again with a shake of his head. "Let's see what Cassidy does, shall we? And anyway, Holsa is well wired. The phone company sees everything that goes in or out on his terminals. They can hear a flea fart within a mile of his living room."

"I'll warrant that half the people in that meeting this morning were able to put it together instantly," said the colonel, his voice rising. "An interrupt of unexplained origin. Temporary failure of certain circuitry in the network. How long can you expect any of that to hold up?"

"It's just an age thing with those two," Anton said hastily. "They speak the same language. They tend not to trust authority figures."

"Cassidy's twenty-nine, Holsa's what, thirty-two? My God, they're hardly kids." The colonel reached into a coat pocket, extracting a Bic lighter and a pack of cigarettes. "I don't like it," he said.

Anton fished through his pockets, found a lone kitchen match, and struck it on the underside of the table. He held the match upright, and briefly studied the flame. Then he blew it out. He looked at the colonel and attempted a smile. "Aversion therapy," he said. "I'm a former smoker."

"We *need* them, DeBroer. If, for any reason whatsoever, these two should elude you — "

Anton flicked the match expertly into the ashtray. "We can get Cassidy anytime we want him," he said. "And as for Frank Holsa, well, we already *have* him, in a sense. The phone company has him. He's a peculiar case, as you know. He's living out on the coast, under something approximating house arrest. We'll get nothing from him if we question him formally."

"Explain to me why he isn't still in prison."

Anton peered across the table at Colonel Core, as if examining him for visible signs of naiveté. "The phone company wanted him out," Anton said. "Holsa does favors for them. And for us, sometimes. I'm surprised he doesn't do any for you."

"We tend not to employ very many convicted felons."

"A pity. Speaking of felonies, at least you can be thankful that your client banks were insured to the limit for all those garbled credit records on sixth level. Some of those transactions with the Consolidated Research Consortium, with CRC, were represented implicitly in SEEK logic and memory, and nowhere else. They're unrecoverable financial — "

"For God's sake, it doesn't *matter* right now," the colonel sputtered angrily. "The money is not the goddamned point. Look, if these are the two guys you want — if you can link them verifiably with Alejandro — then fine; *then we've got to get them, and end this.* They're not going on-line again — ever. We must simply foreclose that option."

"Colonel," Anton said tersely, "that's not the way I have it planned."

"A young man like Cassidy, with a recent record of achievement like his — he just wants to go fishing. We're supposed to settle for that. We're supposed to file that somewhere and say good-bye."

"Perhaps Cassidy's an unwitting accomplice," Anton persisted. "Perhaps he's being run. We don't know. The only thing we know for certain is that he's a fucking amateur. I'm only asking for twenty-four hours."

"There will be demands for thoroughgoing explanations by Monday morning. Rash suggestions will be winging our way from the East."

"Let me do it my way, Colonel. I've got a blank check from the home office on this one."

"I'm going to have to ask you to bring them in."

Anton raised a placating palm. "I intend to, Colonel," he said, as he got ready to leave. "You can have them on Monday."

"Christ almighty!" the colonel exploded. "You've *got* to!"

Anton stood up. "Not just now, Colonel," he said. "Look at it this way. Somebody always hangs at sunrise, but it's never you. And it's never me."

Colonel Core watched Anton walking away, and said nothing. The colonel already had decided to have Cassidy monitored visually as well, using the colonel's man, Leonard. Leonard was sometimes suspected of answering to a higher calling — there were rumors that he was Alejandro's hot line to the front — but he always got the job done, and he had sufficient autonomy at DID Security to come and go as he pleased.

The colonel would have to be leaving soon, himself. The last line of Klaatu's message kept coming back to him, haunting his thoughts. It was the one line that had been deleted from the day's exercise; the one line the colonel did not want to reveal. Standard block capitals, like the rest of the messages, appended after a seven-second delay:

PULSE DECEMBER 21.

Less than a week from now, the colonel was thinking, as he watched Anton disappear through the door of the tavern. Friday next. The last thing he wanted to deal with at the moment was Anton's private agenda, whatever it might be.

Because it was impossible, the colonel desperately wished that he could go home for dinner that night.

Bright and *hopeful* were not the words the colonel would have chosen to describe his mood that afternoon.

FIVE

B Y EIGHT O'CLOCK Sunday morning, Peter was packed
and out the door. He put Fish Dog in the pen
and said good-bye, sorry, some other time. The black Lab whined
and paced, executing a series of doleful postures that had gotten him
out of tight spots in the past. No luck. Peter laid it out for him: "It's
for your own good. You wouldn't like Ajax."

Peter drove the freeway to Portland at a steady sixty, trying not to
think about the Alsea River and other lost opportunities. As he approached the outskirts of the city, he branched off the Interstate and
looped west on a connecting thoroughfare, catching glimpses of the
Jantzen Building, a few tall banks. Spidery cranes loomed from the
shipyards along the Willamette. To the north, unseen, lay the Columbia River. Columbia II, Peter called it. In honor of the river it
once was. Electricity was cheap in the Northwest. With an engine
like the Columbia on hand to generate the power, small wonder.
You had low utility rates or you had salmon. It didn't really come
down to that in truth, just, more often than not, in practice.

A few minutes later he was out of town and headed for the ocean,
the traffic thin, a reminder that it was early Sunday. He gunned
around an old truck, its trailerful of thin plywood veneer stacked like
baklava.

He took a long look in his rearview mirror. No station wagon.

Steering with his knees, he filled a Styrofoam cup with thermos
coffee and settled in for the twisting drive over the forested spine of
the Coast Range. The two-lane highway had pullouts along the worst
hills and yellow signs warning drivers about the dangers of underes-
timating the curves. Not a log truck in sight.

Peter paced the Scout cautiously through the bends. He had been

49

a freshman, still finding his way around campus, when he first met Holsa. The captain-to-be was smoking cigarettes and belting down Cokes while he played Space War on a terminal in the campus computer center, pitted against some other warrior across campus. Holsa was already pedigreed in Comp. Sci. but was still hanging around campus, running out the string on some tenuous grant-in-aid. T & A, Holsa called it. Teaching and assistance. This strange, hairy fat man proved to be a specialist at performing very advanced and expensive operations on other people's very advanced and expensive computer systems. God forbid that Frank should have to pay for it.

Eventually the university felt obliged to kick him off campus. In a memorable act of vengeance, Holsa the hacker brought down the entire campus computer system in a massive, cross-wired snafu that took university officials some thirty-six hours to untangle. Ever after, he was known in hacker circles as Captain Crash.

As Peter remembered it, Holsa left a Master's twisting slowly in the wind and opened a one-man computer consultancy in Palo Alto. The captain's personality and drug-fueled, anarchistic politics left him with a somewhat abbreviated list of clients. Late one evening, on a stroll around town, trying to do some sharp thinking about where his next nickel was coming from, Frank Holsa walked past a large local supply office belonging to Pacific Bell Telephone.

In an alley beside the building he spotted three large industrial trash bins and couldn't resist having a look. Twilight, and the alley was empty. The captain poked around in the bins and fished loose a coffee-stained document entitled "Bell System Policies and Practices." More probing and grunting and out came another manual — "Bell System Plant Operating Instructions." Something in that vein. There were other manuals and guides, as well as discarded billing sheets, internal memos, and inventory lists. A cornucopia of procedural documents. Evidently a house cleaning of some sort. Unbelievable. Holsa carted home the lot and faithfully filed everything in ring binders.

After careful study he made a wonderful discovery. Buried in one of the manuals was a nugget of information that did not escape his notice — the regional access codes for dialing into Pac Tel's computerized inventory-control system. Further study revealed equipment specifications, ordering procedures, and drop-site codes that Pacific Bell used in the greater Palo Alto service area.

It was that easy. In the end, the captain borrowed some money and bought a used Pacific Telephone service van. Bought it from Ma herself at a vehicle pool auction. Got a great price on it. The captain was touched. Thanks, Ma. Then, summoning up his courage — major felonies were still relatively new to him at the time — Captain Crash dialed into Bell's inventory system, using a computer-telephone hookup in his basement flat, and placed an order for thirteen thousand dollars' worth of computerized telephone switchboard equipment. At the appointed hour he drove to the designated warehouse in his company van, signed a fake name to the bill of lading, and watched with nervous awe as three hard-hatted workers nonchalantly stuffed his van with crates. It was that clean.

The captain drove home afterward and got drunk. The next day he ordered a few more items, no sweat. The next week, a few more. Computer parts. Phone parts. Keyboards, multiplexers, memory units, switching devices, circuit boards. All kinds of toys. When he found that he could order a hundred of something just as easily as two or three, he folded his consultancy and rented quarters in a ratty industrial loft in East Palo Alto. He repacked Bell's equipment in boxes marked Released for Resale and started moving the goods at a near-perfect profit to various interested parties in the Stanford environs — electronic parts distributors, small computer supply houses, gray-market profiteers. The captain had friends. There were never any queries he couldn't answer or dodge. He offered a whopping discount. Buyers rarely asked why.

And that was how the captain became briefly moneyed. He threw it in forty directions at once. Soon a loose coalition of computer freaks and drug dealers was operating out of the captain's dingy loft. There were Leno and Hardware Hal, and there was the Niobium Kid. And, for one exceedingly brief period, even David was there. David had fallen away quickly. He and the captain were at each other like pit bulls most of the time.

The Niobium Kid was both fascinated and horrified by the scene around him. Disemboweled electronic gear on the formica table, switchboards in the bedroom, Baggies in the hall, people tripping over yards of multicolored wires. The wires were everywhere, like a cobweb strung by some huge, unbalanced spider. Half-eaten ketchup and bologna sandwiches, an open bottle of wine, a frayed yellow copy of the I Ching, a lit candle melting slowly into the countertop. Garbage everywhere. A litter of kittens doing their business in the bathroom. Ponytailed Leno injecting a combination of vitamin B_{12} and methamphetamine into some coed's upraised ass. The captain on one of his illegal, unregistered phones, cutting a deal for a piece of minicomputer development software stolen from a major semiconductor house.

Giddy, lawless days. They built computer systems and state-of-the-art blue boxes for ripping off long-distance phone time. With a phone and a computer terminal, you could do anything, go anywhere, in the early seventies. They assaulted every time-shared computer system within reach, leaving cracked calling cards like "I am the phantom glitch. Catch me if you can."

They did this on the strength of an ethic which said that if you can find the data, you can have the data. By breaking into a computer system, the captain held, you showed the designers and programmers of that system how little they knew about keeping you out. Maybe they'd do better next time.

The captain and his band bartered goods and traded information with computer and phone freaks all over North America. This activity resulted in the passage of several landmark pieces of legislation having to do with the security of telephone and computer systems.

Once they even arranged a nationwide conference call — for free, of course — linking up some twenty-five underground geniuses of the day, for the purpose of disseminating a new means of piggybacking Ma Bell's trunk lines. When one of the group's members left to take honest employment with the Intel Corporation, he sent back some of the first microprocessor chips ever to roll off the production lines, with a complete set of testing and debugging data in the bargain. They incorporated the microprocessors into customized sound equipment for forward-thinking rock bands like The Grateful Dead.

One night there was a knock at the door and in walked the legendary Augustus Stanley Owsley III, formerly the most prolific manufacturer of LSD in the known world, a master electronics freak who learned his trade in the army. In walked Owsley, unannounced and uninvited. He'd heard they were doing some interesting things. He and the captain circled and sniffed each other warily, two of the most raging egomaniacs in life. They compared notes on their separate schemes to liberate the sleeping citizenry. They talked about computers as electronic handmaidens for the military-industrial complex. They talked about how they were the new Minutemen, taking up the new muskets. Computers for the people. They talked sabotage, systemwide crashes. They were greatly cheered by the ramifications of the great New York blackout. They wanted to see about arranging something similar for Stanford and the Silicon Valley.

For the Niobium Kid, it was the last dance minus one. It turned out that the guy wasn't Owsley after all, but it didn't really matter. Alison hated the whole business. She asked him — she begged him — to get away from it, to stop going to the captain's. He tried to explain to her the nature of the attraction, the pull that kept him orbiting on the fringes of this flying technological wedge, these brilliant heads assembled in the captain's loft. Dark, dangerous deeds. Guerrilla mentality. Hit and run, learn and discover. Pass it on. They were not alone. There were others, everywhere.

You could pick up more expertise in three all-nighters at the captain's than in fifty years of conventional class work. They were flying, untouchable, he told her. He wasn't sure he even believed it, but that was the way it *felt*. She was afraid for him. She saw it as puerile, doomed. She could not conceive of these grotesque people as actual friends of his. Perhaps she saw it as some deep, central flaw in his character. It will all blow up in your face, she told him. I don't want to be around you when it does. She told him that her foster father, a Stanford professor, was making vague rumblings about the activities of one Frank Holsa. And she started seeing David.

He should have seen it coming. But he continued to circle the captain's flame, now working with some of the newest niobium circuits in production. The captain procured them. He wouldn't say how. This put them in very deep — niobium circuitry was the special province of the phone company and the Department of Defense. They were overplaying their hand. People began dropping out of sight, the nocturnal traffic through the captain's quarters thinning drastically. The captain began developing a clinical case of rampant paranoia. But the Niobium Kid hung on, entranced by the work, spooked by the inner knowledge of what was inevitably going to come down. Finally even the Kid began pleading with the captain, telling him to pack it in for a while. Bank the fires. Shut down and move away.

On the final night, he was alone with the captain, except for Short Circuit, little Pons Grozniev, a pimply-faced freshman at Palo Alto High who had an awe-inspiring affinity for computers and codes. He seemed to have been born with it. He was building personal computers for himself and his friends before anyone even knew what a personal computer was. Pons had braces and a rich father. He was devoted to the captain.

The Niobium Kid was pleading with the captain anew. The captain wasn't listening. The captain was elsewhere. Holsa was seated in front of his favorite switchboard, the one with multiple line-tie capability, built with operational amplifiers of his own design. Ten pulses per second, near-perfect frequency and amplitude tolerance. Better than anything the phone company put out commercially.

It was three o'clock in the morning. The captain had just completed a complicated stack of connections, with the help of long-distance operators in New York, London, Brussels, New Delhi, and Tokyo. He was holding two black telephone receivers, one to each ear. "Hello," he said into the mouthpiece of the receiver in his left hand. "This is the captain speaking." Thirty seconds later a dim, tinny echo of his voice came back to him through the earpiece of the receiver in his right hand. The captain was holding a conversation with himself by sending his voice completely around the world. The captain only did this when he was feeling morose. It was his own special brand of metaphysical therapy.

The Niobium Kid was sitting right next to the captain when it happened. Suddenly there were flashing red lights playing off the curtains. Muffled shouts, loud knocks at the door. Something about a search warrant.

The Niobium Kid was running through the kitchen toward the bathroom, little Pons right behind him, when the front door splintered off its hinges, falling inward with a crash. The Kid made a high flying leap out the bathroom window as Pons dove into a foul laundry basket.

The Kid tumbled into the bushes two stories below, spraining his ankle severely, gimping madly through yards and alleys to the safety of a weed-choked railroad right-of-way and hiding there, gasping for breath, his ankle throbbing wildly, thinking over and over this one overriding thought: This isn't any fun anymore. Thinking: No more cops and robbers. Thinking: You always lose. When you go to prison, you lose. Thinking that he had already lost something else, someone far more precious than any of this.

The captain got caught. Shortly thereafter, he was on Ma Bell's payroll as a consultant.

*   *

Peter neared the coast and hooked up with Highway 101, heading south. He drove steadily, giving wide berth to a lumbering Winnebago in the opposite lane. There were mercifully few of them on the road today. It wasn't tourist season any longer. He shot through Depoe Bay and Newport, past clam bars and driftwood shops and tacky seaside motels. He stopped twice, once for gas, once for a bag of cinnamon taffy. The sun was a hard white disk against a metallic haze, and the open ocean was the color of mercury. He would make the captain's by eleven.

At a point just north of Florence the highway skirted the oceanside edge of a jutting headland, climbing steeply until there was only a low rock retainer between the highway shoulder and the water below. The Specific Ocean, David called it. In honor of who knew what. Peter spotted the bobbing heads of six or seven sea lions just outside the surf line. They caught a wave in unison, looking like a line of fat brown cigars, and when it broke they were gone.

Peter came to the girdered bridge marking the cutoff to Holsa's and slowed for the turn. The captain lived along Little Creek, a clear, shallow stream that flowed to the ocean through a deeply wooded cleft in the coastal hills. He drove leisurely along the first few miles of blacktop, noting the muddy ruts at roadside where anglers had parked that morning to work the pools. The road cut away from the stream and steepened, and Peter downshifted the lugging Scout as he kept alert for landmarks.

After passing a grassy meadow and a forlorn sheep pen with no tenants, he slowed at the sight of a red-white-and-blue mailbox affixed to a stiffened piece of chain. As soon as he veered off the blacktop into the captain's dirt lane, he felt the wheels of the Scout losing purchase. He hit the brakes and fishtailed to a halt in the muck. The rains had transformed the half-mile lane into a sluggish river of mud and loose gravel — the captain's first line of winter defense.

Peter stepped out of his car and switched the steel rings on the front hubs to their four-wheel-drive settings. Colonies of bright orange mushrooms had exploded through the gummy clay of the road cut. Sword ferns blanketed the floor of the surrounding woods, and the whole forest seemed to be dripping, splattering, and seeping. Winter in the cold Pacific rain forest, ten leagues under the sea. He crouched and sighted down the roadway, arms resting lightly on his thighs. The lane was alive with a furious migration of tiny green frogs, all moving left to right. Peter got back behind the wheel and gunned the Scout confidently ahead. "Sorry, boys and girls," he muttered, his breath forming a visible cloud of moisture inside the cab. "It's a frog's life."

The rest of the lane was easy. He parked on a muddy patch of loose rock between an old Volvo and a rusting pickup. A peeling bumper sticker on the back of the Volvo informed him that Nature Bats Last. An odd sentiment, that. Peter had never seen any evidence that the captain believed it.

The captain's house was in need of far more than a simple coat of paint. The picket fence that surrounded it had wilted to the ground and the roof bulged with several years' worth of accumulated moss. Sheets of clear plastic had been tacked to the windows. Three long boards laid end to end constituted a sort of floating walkway across the captain's swampy yard.

Peter stepped quickly toward the porch, arms out straight for balance. There was a growl, and Ajax came hurtling off the porch like a furry bullet. Immediately Peter crouched low, holding out his hand, murmuring endearing homilies in the sweetest tone he could muster. The captain's weird mongrel halted just in front of him and began yipping happily as Peter stroked its head.

Peter continued on to the porch and knocked on the captain's door. The porch was strewn with old automobile parts and empty cases of Olympia. Dozens of clay nursery pots were piled haphazardly in one corner, empty of plants but full of mud. Peter banged the door again, loudly, and was preparing another salvo when it opened. There stood the captain — huge, hairy, and completely naked. Holsa grunted and waved him inside. Peter felt a surge of warm air as he entered. He couldn't help noticing that the captain's penis was covered with a slick coat of semen.

"Terrific timing," said Holsa, by way of welcome.

"Looks like it could have been worse," Peter replied.

Across the room a curtain parted and a dark-skinned girl emerged, wearing an oversized gray sweatshirt and nothing else. She tossed a bathrobe to the captain and padded off to the kitchen. She was short, and vaguely Asian, and could have passed for fifteen. It occurred to Peter that the captain must have outweighed her by as much as two hundred pounds.

The captain threw on the robe and stepped into a pair of mukluks. He opened a drawer in a battered armoire, removed a small cylindrical device, extended a short antenna attached to the top of it, and began waving it at his visitor.

"You worried about hijackers?" Peter demanded.

"Don't fuck with procedure," the captain growled as he completed the electronic frisk. His eyes were bloodshot and his stomach protruded grotesquely through the folds of his corduroy bathrobe. His tangled hair curled over his ears and his shoulders, blending with a full, untrimmed beard. "I had a very bad night." Over the years, he had come to look less like Jerry Garcia and more like Rasputin the Mad Monk.

Peter shoved a stack of newspapers off the sofa and sat down. Across the cluttered living room, the captain piled into a red barber's chair, pumping a lever until he had gained a foot or two in elevation. "So, pal," he said. "Whaddaya know?"

"Not much," Peter freely admitted. "No more than I ever did." He glanced at the newspapers by his feet. "Peter Pan almost got killed in a traffic accident in San Francisco. Mary Martin."

The captain snorted. "Good career move."

The girl returned from the kitchen and set a plate of bacon and a cup of steaming coffee on a tray next to the barber's chair. The captain jacked himself down a foot.

Peter watched the captain devouring his bacon. "I was thinking about the old days while I was driving over here. Do you think there's any qualitative difference between the old days and the new days, Frank?"

The captain concentrated on his bacon. "Hard to say." He thought for a minute. "Money," he said.

"Money?"

"Money. The world's in a shit fit over money."

"Anything else?"

The captain thought about it some more. "I'm not doing as many drugs as I used to," he said. "At a certain age, you gotta start thinking about damage control." The captain let go with a ripping belch. "Which reminds me. Remember Pons Grozniev?"

"Who could forget Pons? The only twenty-six-year-old I ever expect to meet who's worth a hundred and three million on paper. How's Tangerine Dream Computer Corp doing these days?"

"Who gives a shit. What am I, your broker? Pons is putting on a rock festival next week in Marin County. You know about it? An open-air thing. Better than anything Wozniak's ever done. Invitation only. He's making a last-minute stab at reuniting The Who as headliners. Two-hundred-foot Eidaphor video screens flanking the stage. Worldwide satellite feed. Niobium amplifiers. He's gonna burn up enough juice to light California for a week. He was smart enough to contact me for some technical assistance."

Peter gazed around the room, noting the cluttered bookshelves, the row of record albums stretching for ten feet along the baseboard of one wall, the Fillmore poster tacked to an upright steamer trunk. "Where's *your* money, Frank? In the basement? Down in the lab?"

"I have invested wisely. I own property."

"Real estate?"

"As real as it gets."

The young lady returned, carrying a hand mirror and a short length of glass tubing. She handed these carefully to the captain. On the mirror were two fat white lines of cocaine. The captain put the tube to his nose and bent his head to the mirror and snorted up one of the lines. He looked questioningly at Peter. Peter nodded thanks, no thanks. So he snorted up the other one.

"I have a question," Peter said. "Of a technical nature."

"Save it."

"I was wondering whether Hardware Hal might be able to answer it for me."

The captain glared at him. "I have this thing about talking business in the living room," he said. "Indulge me."

"Okay, what shall we talk about? Your real estate?"

"I'd love to," the captain replied, but instead of doing so he rose abruptly from his barber's chair and lumbered out of the room, his loose robe swirling in his wake. With the captain, you just had to put up with it.

When Holsa returned, he was wearing a beige pair of chinos and combat boots, with a buttonless flannel jacket thrown over a black T-shirt. "Let's go out back," he said. "I've acquired several new hobbies since you were here last."

The backyard was in no better shape than the front. Most of it was taken up by amorphous mounds of firewood under black plastic. As they slopped toward a low metal shed the captain said, "Not too many people know Hal's around."

"Is he still operating his listening service?"

"Hardware Hal, poorest man alive, who barely owns a bar of soap, has about a million bucks' worth of telecommunications gear up there."

"Up where?"

The captain smiled sweetly. "Up where he lives now."

"My question," Peter said, as the captain pulled open the door to the shed.

"Fucking Atwood shorted Hal five hundred dollars once. For a modem."

"Oh yeah? Where did Hal get it in the first place?"

The captain looked offended. "That's hardly the point," he said.

Inside, under two naked light bulbs, rows of squat cages were stacked against one wall. The floor was littered with straw and flecked with the unmistakable signs of bird life. Low coos and murmurs issued from the cages.

"Pigeons," said Peter, with wonder.

"Pigeons," the captain agreed.

"Beautiful," said Peter. "Unbelievable."

The captain checked a thermostat and made a slight adjustment. "It's very hard to bug a pigeon," he observed. "Now — you have a question for Hal?" He pulled a tiny tape recorder from the pocket of his flannel jacket. "We'll take a little walk in the swamp there, out beyond the fence. Keep it brief."

*   *

Anton DeBroer was sitting alone against the edge of a desk, speaking quietly into a gray mobile telephone while he picked at the remains of a burrito wrapped in tinfoil. The office, a well-equipped room in the Systems & Security Building, was on loan to him for the duration of his stay. The DID Corporation was kind enough to do this for him whenever he was in town.

"He has a question," Anton said. "The man has a question."

He stared idly at a bank of TV screens mounted above him on the wall, settling for a raven-haired receptionist, lower right screen, bending over a storage cabinet. Wouldn't mind sinking my dick into that one, Anton thought.

"Everybody has questions."

Anton had a few of his own. He was thinking again of that curious mixture of feelings that had come to him two nights ago when he was first notified of the SEEK incursion as he was driving urgently back to Fort Meade on the Baltimore-Washington Parkway, watching the NSA complex looming into sight as he cut off onto Savage Road, the great nine-story central building, the green **A**-shaped annex, the roof of the headquarters tower sprouting parabolic microwave dishes and log-periodic antennae.

He found himself longing for the simplicity that had marked his last visit to the West Coast. A Cal-Berkeley student had devised a very clever trapdoor computer code, a subtle and useful piece of work. Dozens of commercial computer firms were ready to break down the kid's door. The press was beginning to swarm around him like flies on dead meat. Anton's job was to assure everyone that the best minds and computers at the agency had been unable to break the code. Congratulations all around.

In point of fact, a team of agency programmers had broken the code wide open inside of seventy-two hours, with the aid of approximately ten acres of computer systems in the agency's basement.

The receptionist spun around and started walking down a corridor.

A voyeur's paradise, he thought. She faded out down the hall and there was a slow pan back to the electronically locked file cabinets. Anton listened awhile longer. "If they had any sense," Anton said into the phone, "if they knew anything at all about surveillance, they'd go to the beach."

*   *

After snipping the tape of Peter's message and tucking it into a tiny tube affixed to the leg of one of the captain's helpers; after the pigeon had spiraled up and away from the shed, wheeling north, winging through the thicket of electronic smog surrounding the captain's little corner of the wilderness; after all that had been taken care of, Peter turned to the captain as they were walking back to the house and said, "That's quite the stream down behind your place. Looks very promising for steelhead."

"I wouldn't know," the captain responded. "I'm not into that shit."

At the captain's insistence, they drove to the beach.

Heavy breakers curled and crashed in the half-light as they stood at the edge of the parking lot. Holsa stared fixedly out to sea, contemplating some quarry far less tangible than a mound of blubber for the harpoon. Just call me Fishmeal, Peter thought.

Call me Fishmeal and wish me luck.

They skipped the beach and crossed through a picnic area, past outhouses and trash cans lined with brown plastic, heading off on a trail that snaked up a rocky headland at the northern boundary of the state park. The trail led to a Park Service viewpoint overlooking the surf; nothing more than a flat piece of rock hemmed in by guardrails and chain link and decorated with signs saying Warning, Do Not Venture Beyond This Barrier.

They had a splendid view of the coast in both directions. The broken land line, serrated by other headlands and resistant islands of basalt, looked feathered, slightly blurred, in the haze. Two perfect half-moon bays, split by the peninsular arm of rock upon which they were standing, lay left and right of them. There was no apparent route down the headland to the north beach, visible only as a dark strip of land against the hills. A few beachcombers were working the south beach near the parking lot.

The captain produced a torn red booklet of tidal charts, consulted it briefly, and returned it to his pocket. "Let's have a cigarette," he said, "and then we'll take a hike." He assumed a deep crouch, mo-

60

tioning impatiently to Peter, intending to use the skirts of Peter's fishing jacket as a temporary windbreak. "Everytime I see you, you're wearing this thing," he said. "What is it, a lucky coat or something?"

*　*

"The guy's going *down* on the guy," Marlene moaned, leaning forward in the car seat until her field glasses cracked up against the windshield. "I *swear* it."

"First it's pigeons," said Eddie, from the driver's seat, "and now this."

With a look of distaste, Marlene shelved the binoculars on the dashboard and lit a cigarette. She cracked a vent and the wind howled through. Across the parking lot a little girl was dragging a huge curl of driftwood toward a VW bus. "What do you think, Eddie?" she said, blowing smoke in his face. "Are we too old for this?"

Eddie drummed his stubby fingers on the steering wheel. "Depends on how you mean it," he replied.

*　*

The captain stood at the railing, smoking, cupping the cigarette inside his fist between drags. When he finished, he flipped the butt oceanward over the fence.

"Shame on you," Peter said.

"It's organic," said the captain. "It's a Camel."

He led Peter to the front of the viewpoint, where the drop to sea level was less forbidding. Someone had cut a hole in the chain-link fence where it faced the open ocean and the captain slipped through it, Peter following. They ramped halfway down the headland, weaving through crumbled boulders, slipping on loose clay, angling back underneath the viewpoint in the direction of the dark beach. After a steep scramble they intersected the geological feature that made the trek possible — a long horizontal cleft along the face of the headland, forming a narrow trail to the northern beach. The captain proved quite nimble on the ledgeway. He was humming a tune Peter couldn't quite recognize.

"What song, Frank?" Peter kept a wary eye on the ledge, listening to the crunch of Holsa's combat boots on the rubble underfoot. The captain stopped and turned around. Beads of moisture clung to his beard. He was smiling his conspirator's smile. " 'Take Me to the Pilot,' " he said. "You remember it?"

"Yeah, Frank, I remember it. Elton John."

"I'm taking you to see the Pilot," Holsa said. He turned sharply, not waiting for a reply, and continued along the ledge. Very dramatic. Multo mysterioso. With the captain, you just never knew.

Near the black-rock beach the headland leveled out and the trail broke away from the ledge, executing a series of switchbacks up and over a loose hump of rock. They fell once each scuttling down the back side of the slope. Underneath the hiss of the surf Peter could hear the beach pebbles tumbling and clicking, tugged oceanward by the receding wash of each wave. The captain surveyed the dense line of vegetation that stood between the beach and the rise of the coastal hills behind it.

"This is where it gets interesting," he said.

They hiked steadily for half an hour under a canopy of twisted shore pine. The surf sound faded as the captain picked his way along the murky hillside, branching confidently from trail to trail. "Where are we?" Peter asked. "National Forest?"

Frank nodded. "With a few private holdings thrown in."

Peter peered at the latticework of branches over his head. "This is amazing," he said. "I don't have the slightest idea where we are."

They paused for a breather in a blackberry-choked clearing. All around them were the remnants of some long-forgotten logging operation — rusting spools of cable, a huge winch, an engine block. Peter was surprised to hear the muted hiss of the ocean again. They were roughly two air miles northwest of the parking lot, as he judged it. There was no way to tell for sure without asking, and he wasn't about to give the captain the pleasure.

They continued on, following a trickle of water into the mouth of a dogleg canyon. The blackberries gave way to moss and liverwort, and there were bursts of maidenhair fern on the walls. They scaled a ledge and stood facing a hidden valley, a very small one, bounded by willow thickets. A browse line showed along the willows where the deer had eaten all the tender shoots they could reach. In the middle of the valley stood a simple cabin made out of plywood and plastic, sitting several feet above the ground on a precarious set of log pillars. A thick black cable ran from the roof of the cabin, disappearing into the trees behind it.

"Quite a hideaway," said the captain. "Eh, Hernando?"

Peter whistled. "Unbelievable," he said, for the second or third time. It was beginning to sound like a strong candidate for word of the day. "How did you find this place? Whose cabin is it?"

With a dramatically phony flourish of his hands, the captain said, "Allow me a *few* little secrets."

The interior of the one-room cabin consisted of a bunk bed against the back wall, three mismatched windows to the front, and a large wooden table flanked by padlocked cabinets. A plank had been toe-nailed across one corner of the room, and it held a greasy Coleman stove, a coffeepot, a box of canned goods, and a litter of burnt matches. Peter sat down on a high stool near the table while the captain pulled a bottle of Southern Comfort from his musette bag and began prowling the room, searching unsuccessfully for anything resembling a cup. He took a pull from the bottle and handed it to Peter.

"Who knows about this place?" Peter asked. "Hal?"

"Hal helped me build it," the captain answered. He unlocked one of the cabinets and withdrew a steel firebox encased in a waterproof plastic bag. He placed the box on the table without a word, then bent to the cabinet and drew forth three similar ones. The first box yielded a desktop computer module housed in a molding of blue plastic, with a mounting at the back for a display terminal and another one at the front for a keyboard. With practiced ease the captain unboxed a keyboard and a display unit and some memory attachments and set about jacking everything together.

The components bore no logos or other identifying marks. Peter figured it for a custom job, although it was impossible to tell without pulling a few circuit boards. The captain ran an extension cord to an oversized wall socket. He had his computer up and running within fifteen minutes. READY, said the screen, in yellow letters against a glowing green background.

"Meet the Pilot," said the captain, as he dragged a stool into position before the keyboard. He was beaming like a kid with a new train set. "The programmable independently locatable outlaw terminal," he said. "Pilot. I built it myself."

Peter looked on approvingly. "Where's the juice for it?"

"I patched into a power line about a quarter-mile away. And I've got a dish on a rock about five hundred yards from here."

A dark thought occurred to Peter. "Couldn't we have just walked the power-line cut from the highway?"

"Sure," said the captain, wounded. "If you like walking through three miles of blackberry thorns. In six inches of water. It's all gone to brush."

"All right," Peter responded. "So what are you running here? A listening service, like Hal?"

63

Another arrow to the captain's heart. "I am not a peep artist," he said soberly, "as is our colleague Hal."

"Well, what then? What do you use it for?"

"You're just busting with questions today, Jackson."

"You love it."

The captain chuckled quietly. He squared himself in front of his computer. From behind his ear, hidden beneath the shaggy tangle of his hair, he produced an enormous joint rolled in yellow paper. He lit it and sucked deeply, then remembered his manners and offered it perfunctorily to Peter. Thanks, no thanks. The captain sucked some more and then parked it on the lid of a tin can. He cracked his knuckles and placed his hands on the keyboard, like a pianist about to bang out the opening strains of some sonata. He looked at Peter impatiently.

"Do you mind?" he said, jerking his head in the direction of the front windows. "I'd rather you didn't see this part."

Peter walked to the windows and looked out at the willow patch across the valley. It was, in most cases, impossible to deal straightforwardly with the captain. The captain didn't have it in him.

Holsa began punching keys, entering a series of commands and responses. "You want to know why I come here, Cassidy? You'll appreciate this, you really will. You want to know what I use the Pilot for?" The captain punched a few more keys. "C'mere." A message came to life on the screen. SEEK LEVEL 5. MAILBAG REQUEST?

"I go fishing," the captain said. "That's what I do."

Peter walked over and stared dumbly at the terminal. It took him several seconds to fully comprehend what he was seeing. When he had a grasp on it, he stared at the captain, just as dumbly. "You unbelievable bastard," he said at last, with grudging admiration. "It's a bootleg SEEK terminal. It's not possible."

The captain beamed and basked.

"A counterfeit fifth-level terminal."

"Right."

"This gives you as much upper-level SEEK clearance as *I* have," Peter said.

"There isn't," replied the captain, "anything very *cleared* about it at all." The captain's terminal flickered. SUNDAY MAILBAG OPEN. NEXT UPDATE 5:00 E.S.T. LIST FILES OR BULLETIN BOARD?

Peter stood beside the captain, looking over his shoulder. "Well, Frank," he said, "you really did it this time."

"Thank you," the captain answered crisply.

"How the hell did you beat the verification procedures? You'd have to steal a personal ID and an access code. You'd have to impersonate a registered terminal. I don't suppose you plan to tell me how you did it."

"I'll spare you," the captain said nervously. He had an unfocused, faraway look on his face.

Peter tried another tack. "Why are you showing me this, Frank?"

"Because," Holsa responded, "I have a slight problem."

Peter was stunned by the captain's unexpected reply. It just wasn't possible. He felt certain that the captain would not be foolish enough even to try. But he could not disregard one salient fact: A bootleg terminal, a technically unprecedented feat of electronic engineering, would be the perfect anonymous launching pad for a seventh-level incursion.

Assuming you knew of a way in. Fifth level was a long, long way from seventh level. You couldn't get there from here. Alejandro had seen to that. There wasn't any bridge. No, wrong. There *was* a bridge. The Hunt Code. Alejandro had seen to that, too.

Peter had come to the captain's on a surreptitious mission, hoping to verify the reality of the seventh-level break through the services of Hardware Hal, the premier electronic eavesdropper on the West Coast. Hoping for clues as to why they were involving him in this business in the first place. If the captain had somehow broken seventh level, it was all too patently obvious. The captain was a friend of his. Possibly they knew it. And here was the captain, blithely offering himself up as a suspect.

"Hold on a minute," Peter said, feeling somewhat dazed. "Let me think." The captain said nothing. "I was wondering," Peter said. "Don't jerk me around on this one, Frank. It's too important. Have you ever heard of the name Klaatu?"

The captain looked puzzled. "Sure," he said.

Peter licked his dry lips and waited.

"Klaatu was the name of a rock band a while back," the captain said. "Everybody thought they were the Beatles, going incognito. They weren't. What kind of squirrelly question is that?"

Peter took a deep breath and plunged ahead. "What do you know," he asked, "about the Hunt Code?"

At first, the captain didn't act as if he had heard the question. He appeared to be shrinking, collapsing on the stool. All the usual bravado seemed to have leaked right out of him. "I don't know fuck-all about the Hunt Code," he said, with a curious, shaky lilt in his voice. "How about you?"

"Frank, answer me straight. Were you on-line with this terminal on Thursday night? Did you access the fifth level this past Thursday, about six o'clock?"

Holsa cocked his head and eyed Peter for an uncomfortably long time. "Whose side are you on these days, anyway?" he said. "Are you the priest or the private eye?" The captain typed in the standard fifth-level exit message, then reached underneath his computer console and flipped a switch. The screen went dead.

Thrust and parry, Peter thought. The captain could fence like this all afternoon. Peter had no choice but to break security and drop the bomb. "They pulled me in yesterday for a classified meeting. Somebody broke into the seventh level Thursday night, Frank, I'm sure of it. They set it up as a simulation, a dry run, but — "

"Who was there?"

"Robert Core, David and I, a guy from the NSA named DeBroer, a bunch of other — "

"Stay away from Anton," the captain said, with surprising force. "Anton can be very bad medicine."

Caught off guard, Peter said, "You know him?"

"I know *of* him."

"Whoever broke seventh level did it from a fifth-level terminal. A fifth-level terminal, Frank."

"You're a team player now," Holsa broke in. "Is that it? I thought you quit."

"I don't know what I am," Peter said, and he meant it. "Just tell me, Frank. Tell me whether you were on-line with this terminal Thursday evening. Tell me that much, and then we'll discuss your problem." *Clear* yourself, Peter was thinking. Do that much for me.

The expression on Holsa's face was utterly foreign to Peter. "All right," said the captain, "here it is." Then it came to Peter. Pure fear. That was the look. Nothing but. "I *was* logged into the fifth level with this terminal," the captain said. "I *was* on the fifth-level net, Thursday night. And that *is* my problem."

"Did you do it, Frank?" It came out as a shaky whisper. "It's treason. You've *got* to tell me."

Slowly, the captain raised a hand and held up his thumb and forefinger, bringing them together until they almost touched. "I was that close," Holsa said. "That's how close I came." The captain appeared to be in danger of losing the thread.

"Close to *what*, Frank?"

The captain's eyes were puffy and his voice drifted dreamily as he spoke. "A broken twig. A spot of blood on a leaf."

"Close to *what*?"

"To Klaatu."

Set and match.

"Tell it, Frank," he said weakly. "Tell it however you want to, but tell it."

Holsa looked away. "I'm sitting here," he began, "and I'm reading this working paper on niobium circuit design. You know how it works — you power up and type in your request for fifth-level access. The request reaches the SEEK central processing units, wherever the hell the CPUs are hidden, and your screen asks you for proper identification. I type in my fake ID set, right? The screen says okay, access granted, you're in. Everything smooth as a baby's bottom. The screen asks me what I want to do. I never get fancy, I just ask for the mailbag. The screen gives me the mailbag menu. So I pick this working paper some clown was floating through the net for comment. Of course, I wasn't planning to do any commenting. I was planning to make like Hal. Hal just listens. He never speaks.

"So I'm reading this paper on the screen, just scrolling along, and suddenly, out of fucking *nowhere*, man, I swear to you, there's some sort of interrupt or override. The screen starts flashing me a set of code I can't read, and then it says, REQUEST FOR OFF-LINE EXCHANGE.

"Pay attention to this part. The request was *input*, man. This wasn't coming from the system. This was coming from my terminal. Only, I didn't type it in. I didn't do anything. I didn't even touch the keys. But somehow, my own terminal is requesting an off-line exchange.

"This is all happening in about half the time it takes to tell it. The next thing I know, the screen clears, and then it says, OFF-LINE EXCHANGE GRANTED. And then it clears again and there's nothing at all for a couple of minutes.

"I'm thinking fast. The first thing I'm thinking is, I've been bagged. Piggybacked. Somebody bagged my terminal. Somebody knows the frequency and signal characteristics of my secret terminal, and they've taken control of it. Now, I've pulled that stunt a time or two myself, so I'm fascinated.

"And then I remember what 'off-line exchange' means in the SEEK system, and suddenly I'm scared shitless. The only time you get an unrecorded exchange, a dialogue between terminal and CPU that isn't copied into the maintenance listings for routine record keeping, is when somebody employs the Hunt Code for emergency access.

"It takes me a couple of minutes to put it all together. Whoever bagged me was counting on this. If I'd have just pulled the plug immediately, it would have all been over. But I didn't. For one thing, if you just shut down like that, without using the formal sign-off procedures, it gets listed on the maintenance logs as a glitch, an abnormality. It goes to the Guardians and they trace the terminal and call you up and give you shit. Now, I don't think there's any way they can trace this terminal, I'm careful about that, but I don't really want to give them a reason to try. I keep low-profile going in and out of the fifth level.

"I'm putting all this together, my terminal under somebody else's control, this apparent request for Hunt Code access to the upper levels, and I decide that discretion's the better part of whatever, decide to sign off and take my chances, when all of a sudden the screen starts flashing green hell and it says SEEK SYSTEM, 7TH LEVEL. It says, LOOP REQUEST? My terminal is telling me that I'm in the seventh level, but I can't believe it. No way can I believe it. I don't know what's happening. I don't have a clue. All I know is, I have to get out of there, and fast. All I know is, I'm a dead man if the Guardians trace this terminal. I don't want to give them any more signal time to work with.

"So I shut the whole works down, like I should have done before. But it's too late. Whoever took control of my terminal must have used the Hunt Code to ride on up to seventh level. They're already inside. The terminal they're using is impersonating mine, and they're already in there. Doesn't matter now if I shut down. They're inside the gates, still impersonating my now-dormant terminal. The Guardians are not gonna know that it was a bag job. I have no idea whether they can trace this terminal if they get really motivated. It's obvious to me that they're gonna be really motivated. I mean, a seventh-level violation.

"I didn't know what to do, so I packed everything up, and popped a couple of Vals, and went home. I sat around waiting for the shit to rain down on my head. When it didn't, I got cocky. I stayed that way until your call. That's when I figured maybe something was up."

* *

Colonel Robert Core was sitting in his den, monitoring a boring football game, sound off. He was listening to Frank Sinatra singing "New York, New York" on the radio. He loved that song. Never mind that the Nelson Riddle Orchestra came crashing in with a covering flourish every time Ol' Blue Eyes reached for a high note. None of us, thought the colonel, is getting any younger.

The phone rang and he picked it up at once, listening for several minutes without comment.

"You're sure?" he said. "They accessed the fifth level from the pirate terminal? The signal characteristics match exactly? That's it, then. My God. I want you to bring Holsa in. Privately. No authorities, no publicity. And then I want a dozen people combing that coastline until they find that terminal. I don't want you to wait until we find out what Holsa is willing to tell us about this escapade. Everything fits now.

"And try to get a fix on this Hal character. If he actually gets into the maintenance listings, like Cassidy asked him to, then we'll prosecute him formally. If you can locate him, then have him arrested. My God, the noms de plume these people dream up."

The colonel listened awhile longer. "I don't care *what* DeBroer says," he shouted angrily. "Anton DeBroer does not set policy for the DID Corporation. We'll play ball with him on Cassidy for a little while longer. But as soon as Cassidy leaves, you get out there and pick up Holsa. Pick up Holsa and bring him to me."

A child entered the room as the colonel was hanging up the phone. The colonel's third, his twelve-year-old. The accident. "Hey," he said lovingly, "what say we go out in the yard and play some football?"

"Daddy, I *hate* football."

The colonel reached over and chucked the child under the chin. "Where's that fighting spirit, tiger? Just a couple of scrimmages. Go get your coat."

The colonel watched the child trudge resignedly out of the room. Three kids, he thought. Margaret manages three kids and every blessed one of them turns out to be a girl.

*   *

By the time they returned to the house, so had the captain's pigeon. Holsa took a piece of film from the tube on its leg and slid it into a hand-held, battery-operated slide projector. They took another walk in the swamp. Above them, a twin-engine Beechcraft soared lazily across the gray sky. Holsa stopped and leaned against a tree,

69

holding the tiny projector to his eyes with one hand. "I'll para-phrase," he said. "Hal sends his best. Looks like he wrote us a book."

Peter stayed silent. He was busy fuming.

"You wanted to know whether Hal could get a peek at DID's copy of the maintenance logs for SEEK Level 5. Turns out he can. I'm surprised I didn't think of it myself. So anyway, let's see. Hal takes a peek. A pretty low-level peek. They only hold the logs for forty-eight hours, unless something doesn't clear."

"I know," Peter said. "That's why I asked."

"Hal checks out the Thursday list. Average stuff, a few technical miscues, routine entry errors, everything straightened out and checked off and put to bed. Except for two glitches. Guess what time they were added to the list."

"Five-forty-nine," Peter said in a monotone.

"On the nose," said the captain, eyes glued to the eyepieces of the tiny projector. "Funny thing is, they're listed as seventh-level abnor-malities. Seventh-level glitches on the fifth-level glitch list. The en-tries are flagged ten ways to Sunday so Hal gets a little panicked and signs off. More than that our boy cannot say, bless him. Wait. There's a postscript. The two entries give ID numbers for the terminals in question, so Hal takes a stab at calling up the fifth-level inventory list, figuring maybe it's lumped in with the routine maintenance list-ing on DID's internal network. It is. One of the terminals is un-listed." The captain read on silently. He took the projector away from his eye and looked directly at Peter. His face was drained of color. "That one must be mine. The other terminal is yours, pal. It was your terminal."

Shocked, Peter blurted out, "I'm not Klaatu! I was out fishing. I was sixty miles from my terminal!"

The captain was about to say something, then appeared to change his mind.

"This Klaatu must have used my terminal! My ID! He used my terminal to bag your unlisted one. Jesus, double cover. Core and DeBroer, they must think — "

The captain looked into his projector once again. "Hardware Hal wants to know how you did it."

SIX

ALISON ATWOOD, having counted up the day's meager take, wrote a check for the utility bill and locked up the glass display case behind the counter. It was a few minutes past five. The sign on the front door of Moon Bird Crafts said Open Sunday Till 6, but there didn't seem to be much point in honoring the promise. The only bright spot in the day had come early, when a customer bought the pathetic-looking ceramic sculpture Alison had taken on consignment from a local lady who also painted childlike seascapes and signed everything "Patti." Alison had been happy to see the thing go. It was an abstract, presumably. David said it looked like two dogs fucking.

Alison's own work occupied two walls of the little shop. One browser had sniffed for a while in the general direction of the large quilt with the raised white-on-white design, but no go. No one had even glanced at her cloth-and-fiber wall hangings featuring pine trees and rising moons and stylized birds. She hadn't sold a basket in two weeks, despite price tags that barely covered the materials she special-ordered from a supply house in Ohio. She flipped idly through the flimsy stack of sales slips before locking them away. Lots of dried sand dollars at a dollar-fifty apiece.

Her shop was located on the far outskirts of Portland, on a main highway to the coast, and she could move almost anything with some sort of sea motif — the sand dollars, lacquered driftwood sculptures, even a few of Patti's dreadful little oils. It all added up to slightly less than what she needed each month for rent on the place. Times were tough.

Alison heard the crunch of tires on gravel and leaned across the counter as far as her belly would allow, peering out the front win-

71

dows in time to see Peter's Scout rolling to a halt in the parking lot. He often stopped by on the way home from one of his weekend fishing forays; they chatted, they had coffee, they talked about David. They reminisced, skirting the edges of certain shared moments. A string of Tibetan temple bells jangled as he came through the door. He barely glanced at her as he crossed to a bench near a rack of Art Cards for All Occasions. He sat down heavily. Alison noticed that he wasn't wearing his fishing boots. He didn't have that fishing look.

Peter shifted uncomfortably in his chair and looked out the window at the highway. "Where the hell is David?" he said, as she was about to ask him what he was doing here, not that she minded, but —

"Where is he?" Peter demanded.

Alison made a face. "Try not to be thick," she said.

"The conference doesn't start until — "

"He's down at Tahoe," she said. "He left early. He's at the tables."

Peter closed his eyes. "I'm in trouble," he said quietly. "I'm in some very deep shit. It's possible I may have to drop out of sight for a while. It's possible I may get arrested. Or worse. I want somebody to know it. Where's David staying? What casino?"

"He didn't say. Pete, what's going on?"

Peter stared hard at her, an unusual thing for Peter to do. With other women, he was a shameless starer. In her case, she had noticed, he had a tendency to overcompensate. "How much do you know," he asked her, "about the SEEK computer system?"

"Not much," Alison said uncertainly. "No more than anyone else who doesn't use it, I guess. I've read some magazine articles. David never tells me anything."

"Somebody broke into the most secure data channels in the SEEK system. A terrorist of some sort. A loony. The original designer. I don't know. Apparently they used an emergency access procedure that only two or three people in the world are supposed to know. It's only supposed to be used in time of war. Whoever did it apparently used my authorized terminal. I don't know how. I was out fishing. I'm putting this all together on the rebound. DID thinks I know something, they're stringing me along. The whole network may be compromised. It's supposed to be impervious to this kind of crime. The missiles — "

"What missiles?" Alison said helplessly. "What's *in* the SEEK system that makes it so special? Did somebody steal something?"

"The enabling codes for the Peacemakers. Secure data links for military command, communications, and control. Military C Three." Peter took a deep breath and continued in a flat, uninflected tone, like a doctor recording the results of an autopsy. "Major research breakthroughs from the largest corporations and think tanks in the country. Strategic planning. New technologies. Mathematical discoveries. Money. Government records of behind-the-scenes historical events. Secret amendments to public treaties. A list of intelligence activities around the world. Things I don't know anything about.

"You worm your way in there, it's like turning on your headlights on a dark night. All the secret operations of government, the military, big business — it all goes into the seventh level. Plus whatever the National Security Agency culls from the lower levels. It's not even heavily coded. The authorized terminals, the ID requirements — they keep the riffraff out that way. No teenage hackers can break into *this* setup. It's all so . . . it's centralized in such a way that . . . shit. Forget it. I just want somebody . . . I want you to know that it wasn't me. This thing may break wide open any minute. Data was taken, destroyed."

Alison's frightened, uncomprehending look brought Peter up sharply. "Surely," she said, "they would know that you didn't — "

"Let me try an analogy," Peter began. "Say you're a banker, a very prestigious banker, and all the richest, smartest people in the world want to put their valuables in your vault. They want to use your vault for storage, for exchanging messages with each other. They want to use it as a secret clearinghouse, a place for pooling their resources beyond the public view. The vault is called the seventh level, and they want to be very sure that your vault is safe. Most vaults aren't. All the other computer networks in use today are the very worst places to try to hide the good stuff. They're the very worst places to put secrets. Absolutely abysmal. Like trying to hold water in a sieve.

"So this seventh-level vault has to be absolutely safe. Safe against anything. Safe against the deadliest burglars and lock pickers in the world. This banker is sitting there at his desk one day, and in walks this dotty old guy with some kind of super combination lock. That's Alejandro Hunt. That's the Hunt Code. Nobody can break this lock because the combination changes every day. There's a trick. It's related to a problem in mathematics called the knapsack problem. You have a large number, any number, and you have to find a set of smaller numbers which, when added together, are equal to it. But only one set of numbers among an infinite list of possibilities will do

73

the trick. It's as if you have a knapsack full of rocks, and all you know is the total weight of the knapsack. In order to unlock the vault you have to guess how many rocks are in the sack, and exactly what each one of them weighs. Only, the weight of the sack, the number of the rocks, changes every day. The dotty old guy is the only one who can open this lock. He's the only one who knows how it works. He and the president and a few other people. There's a system whereby the banker — DID and the NSA — can put things in, and take them out, but even the banker doesn't know how to open this special lock and get all the goodies. It's a self-protecting system, it's all in the circuitry.

"So the dotty little guy takes payment for a job well done, and then splits. Just vanishes. Rich and powerful people start pouring all their valuables into this safe. The banker's happy, so are all his customers.

"Years later, the banker comes to work one morning and the door of the vault is standing open. Valuables are missing, destroyed. Not all of them, not even the most secret ones. But whoever did it left a note in the vault, a warning, saying they're going to come back and do it again, on an even grander scale. Saying they may just blow up the whole goddam thing. It's blackmail. They want the vault dismantled. Now — who's the likely suspect?"

"The dotty old locksmith. But, Peter — "

"Right. He's the prime suspect. It begins to look like he set the whole business up for the purpose of executing a massive burglary. It begins to look like he gulled everybody. But the authorities can't find him. They know where he's hiding, but they can't get at him. Now comes the kicker. There's a twist. The locksmith, if he did it at all, didn't do it alone. There's a set of fingerprints on the lock. They don't belong to the locksmith."

"You mean — "

"They belong to me," Peter said tonelessly. He spread his hands in front of him, palms pointing upward; a gesture of resignation, supplication, something Alison couldn't read. "They're my fingerprints."

*　*

David Atwood plunged down a hill midway between Lake Tahoe and San Francisco, pushing the speedometer needle of the rented red T-bird toward seventy. His ears were ringing, and had been ever since he stepped off the plane from Portland that morning. He wasn't

74

scheduled to give his presentation at the San Francisco Solid State Circuits conference until Tuesday, but the meetings started tomorrow, on Monday.

This had been his one and only run at the tables, and he had blown it badly. He checked out the license plate of a truck ahead of him on the freeway, and wiggled his toes. A Corvette whizzed by him in the left lane and he recorded that license number, too. Left toe down twice, right toe up one, down one, left toe down again. Practice, practice, practice.

Taped to each of David's big toes was a tiny gold-plated switch, connected to a minicomputer strapped across his chest by a series of wires running up his trousers. The device on his chest was about the size of a transistor radio. It contained all of the read-only program memory, random-access data memory, central processing capability and input-output circuitry required to handle all possible combinations of unplayed cards at the blackjack tables. Plus programmed options for splitting or doubling down.

Input was not really the problem; he could untie knots with his toes by now. The problem was output — the row of pin-sized light-emitting diodes along the inside frame of his thick black glasses. They were too closely spaced for his peripheral vision. Since his computerized counting scheme tipped the odds in his favor only by a percentage point or two, the occasional misread had been quite enough to screw things up. He would have to redesign the glasses, using three or four different colors of LEDs to indicate output. That's what he had learned for his lost ten thousand dollars.

David spotted a sign for a rest stop and began easing off on the accelerator. More seed money, he thought. He was going to have to recapitalize. Interest time was fast approaching — interest at the bank and at his bookie's — and it was going to take a rather intricate series of financial transactions to square everything. Just the thought of it made him slightly nauseated. It had all become much too confusing.

David parked, unlimbered from behind the wheel, and entered a stall in the rest room to unhook his rig. He took off his fake glasses and packed the whole works in a small leather shaving kit. Then he washed his face in the sink, combed his hair, and looked closely at his face in the mirror.

If he could get out of the hole this one last time, he'd give it up cold. He vowed to turn over a new leaf, thinking, at the same time, that this would be his twenty-seventh new leaf this year. . . .

* *

David drove straight from the rest stop to the Hyatt Regency near the wharf in San Francisco. He took his suitcase to his room, figuring to catch dinner in the revolving restaurant up top; the one that used to have the stunning view of old San Fran prior to three new generations of high rises. There was a phone message for him. He didn't recognize the number. He dialed it, and the voice of Anton DeBroer came on the line.

"I knew you were an idiot," said Anton, "but Jesus."

* *

Pons Grozniev, a.k.a. Short Circuit, founder, president, and chief executive officer of Tangerine Dream Computer Corporation, sat in a private suite adjoining the Carnelian Room on the fifty-second floor of the Bank of America Building in San Francisco. Seated before him in a rough semicircle were his personal banker, his investment adviser, and a venture capitalist who ventured with Rockefeller money.

Through the floor-to-ceiling window Pons could see that the evening's bloom was off the skyline; the TransAmerica pyramid no longer blushed pink, and the swollen band of smog against the Berkeley hills across the bay was losing its dirty orange glow. Below him, the clean wide diagonal of Market Street was now lit by yellow-white globes, and the clock on the Ferry Building at water's edge was illuminated as well. Beyond the clock loomed the curving arc of the Bay Bridge. The bay itself, no longer sullied by the day's stiff winds, slept blue, broken only by the lights of a freighter creeping past Treasure Island. A few dark triangles — laggard sailboats — sought berth along the shoreline.

"Pons," said the banker, "if I might reiterate — while specific cost projections are clearly speculative at this stage, I see no reason why the opportunity to maximize a significant return on investment could not be realized in — "

"Lots of bands," said Pons. "There's less than a week to go, and we've still got some open slots. I'll take care of the rest."

"Right," said the banker politely. "You're absolutely right. Lots of bands. Of course. But if I might just direct your attention toward the risk-reward ratio inherent in a venture of this kind — "

"Lotsa kick-ass rock and roll," Pons broke in again. "Grateful Dead. The Starship. The B-52s. Tom Petty. Santana. And don't forget The Who."

"Who could?" said the banker, smiling thinly at his little joke.

"The Who *can*," Pons corrected him firmly. "I'm still hopeful.

76

I'm getting a special little surprise together for them. See, like, the important part is, let's just do it. Let's not worry about the money."

A series of droplets, like clear beads, formed on the banker's brow, at the point where his hairline used to be. "You know, Pons," he said, in an even, tutorial tone, "we really ought to start back at square one, with regard to this whole concept. In the sense that it would be wise to try to nail down certain matters of accounting for the — "

"I figure I'm willing to drop, oh, I don't know, what? Say five or six million."

Tenderly, with a shaking hand, the banker patted his brow. "If I may," said the investment analyst, coming to the banker's rescue, "I'd like to inject a thought here. I feel strongly — and I think Dennis would back me up here — that for any number of impeccably good reasons we should attempt to conduct this operation in a distinctly for-profit mode. And I'll tell you why — "

"It isn't the money," Pons said. He took a slurp of his drink, spilling some on his *Star Wars* necktie. "I've got the money. And I've learned one very hip thing about money."

"Yes?" said the banker, a trifle overeagerly. "What's that?"

Pons smiled, showing two rows of perfect, gleaming teeth. "It just comes in the mail," he said.

The banker leaned slowly back in his chair, apparently in great pain.

"You let me know how it goes," Pons said.

*　*

By the time Peter left Alison's shop, the stupidity of his visit to the captain's had become completely clear to him. His fifth-level terminal, the one in his work loft at home, was somehow involved in the Hunt Code violation. They were watching him, waiting to see what he would do. And he had done something. He'd gone slinking off to Frank Holsa, one of the premier computer criminals in America. Which made them both suspects.

Assuming the captain was telling the truth, Klaatu had used Peter's terminal as a post from which to bag the captain's unlisted one. Perfect double cover. Possibly, Klaatu was someone Peter knew; someone who had gotten Peter's ID and access code. Someone who also knew about the captain's little hideaway.

There was only one possible route out of the whole mess. A slim one, but better than lamming it, which would make him seem guilty beyond all doubt. He would go home, and call three very good lawyers, and tell them everything. He would try to squirm his way off the hook by telling the truth. Maybe it would even work. If he came clean, before they closed in on him, it might go in his favor, help establish his innocence. If they had just leveled with him from the first, none of this would have happened. But that was too simple. That wasn't the way the world worked. Not the world according to DID.

Halfway home, Peter pulled off at a phone booth and worked a coin through and called the captain collect. No human was home. And no answering machine either. He had made the captain promise to sit tight until Peter figured out what they were going to do. Apparently the captain hadn't seen fit to take his advice. So be it. There was nothing to do but drive home and call some lawyers. Tell all. It wasn't me, you bastards. Peter just hoped it wouldn't take everybody too long to find that out.

When Peter arrived home, he went inside and started to put kindling inside his wood stove, intending to call the colonel as soon as he was through. He heard a cough from somewhere above him. A slight, involuntary scream escaped him as he looked wildly up toward his work loft. There was a figure there, looking down at him from the railing.

"Evening," said Anton. "Have a nice day at the beach?"

Peter said nothing, waiting for his heartbeat to return to something approximating normal. That was that, he thought. I'm too late.

By all indications Anton had made himself very much at home in Peter's absence. As Anton stared down from the loft, he took a leisurely sip of something from one of Peter's brandy snifters. Peter was amazed at the swiftness with which major decisions seemed to have been taken out of his hands.

Anton glanced back at the fifth-level terminal on Peter's desk. The plastic dustcover had been removed. "You ought to have that thing bronzed," Anton said. "As a monument to your stupidity."

"What are you doing here?" Peter said. It sounded noncommittal enough. Peter bent to the stove and finished with the fire. Play it cool. He assumed Anton was far enough away not to notice that his hands were shaking as he struck a match.

"You ought to pour a little charcoal starter on it," Anton said, as he climbed down from the loft. "That's what my old man used to do whenever he took me camping. He called it instant Boy Scout."

Peter straightened up and faced Anton. "I didn't do it," he said evenly.

78

"I don't think," Anton said slowly, "that we *know* that for sure. Not just yet."

"I figured out from yesterday's meeting that the violation was for real, that's all. My first thought was Holsa. I went out there to see if he knew anything. He didn't."

"I don't think we know that for sure, either."

Peter realized he had talked out of turn already. Now he would have to finger Hal. That hurt. "All I found out was that my terminal was somehow involved."

"Yeah," said Anton. "We know. Your boy Hal is already in custody."

So much for Hal. Everything was happening too fast. "Somehow this Klaatu got hold of my fifth-level ID set. To throw off the scent. Then he — "

"You're not too smart, are you?" said Anton, peering closely at Peter. "Or else you think *we* aren't. Holsa's the one who used your ID set. That's how he was working the scam with the bootleg terminal you two went off into the woods to play with. We have that on record."

Peter remembered how he had stood by the windows while the captain accessed the fifth level. How utterly idiotic of him not to have figured it. The captain, not Klaatu, was using Peter's ID set. Which meant that the captain and Klaatu were quite possibly one and the same. It couldn't be.

"That's news to me," Peter said. "Holsa made me look away while he tapped in. That was the first time I'd ever heard of his bootleg. That's the truth."

"Funny thing is," Anton said, "I believe you. I'm not sure it's going to make much difference, though. Personally, I don't think you're crazy enough to try to get hold of the Hunt Code. Holsa is. He and Alejandro have a long and curious history of correspondence."

"Also news to me," Peter said.

"Maybe so. What *isn't* news to you, I'm betting, is the matter of where Holsa's hiding."

"What?"

"He went AWOL right after you left. We were supposed to pick him up. Colonel Core was, anyway. He's gone. Are you telling me you didn't know that, either?"

Peter kept quiet, his mind racing. The captain's muddy lane had saved him. Anton seated himself in Peter's leather chair. "The colonel wanted to have you arrested," Anton said. "I nixed that. It didn't seem appropriate. I was thinking you'd want to cooperate with us. In a few days, some very important people are going to start putting this thing together. Pentagon people. DID investors. People who like things cut and dried. In a few days, these people are going to start hollering for blood. It's possible that this whole Klaatu act was a one-shot deal. Right now you're the closest thing we've got to a culprit, my friend. If we can't get to Holsa, can't get to Alejandro, we may just have to throw you to the lions. Give them something to chew on."

"Go home," Peter said. "Get out of here. You want my help, make it official. Call me in. Quit threatening me and make it official."

To Peter's surprise, Anton rose from the chair and walked over to him. "Okay," Anton said. "Let's shake on it." Peter extended his hand. It happened so quickly that Peter had no chance to draw back. Anton's thumb flicked and something shone brightly and Anton stabbed the flaring kitchen match into Peter's palm.

As Peter howled, Anton hit him, very low, very hard. Peter doubled over and dropped to the floor. Through a haze of pain he watched as Anton strode purposefully across the living room. He watched as Anton took the cane fly rod from its hallowed spot against the wall. He watched as Anton broke the fly rod neatly into three pieces across his knee.

"I know more about you than your mother," Anton said to him. "Our data banks are remarkably thorough. All your little outlaw friends, your secret alliances, every cunt you've ever plugged. Your dear dead father. The Niobium Kid. That black hooker in New York. Alison Atwood, the basket weaver.

"You've led a pretty sheltered life, haven't you? Things just seemed to break your way, didn't they? You breeze through Stanford on daddy's hard-earned orchard money, you wander around after graduation, seeing the sights, wetting the line, beating your meat. Then you slide into a high-paying job with the most prestigious electronics firm in the world. And what do you do? You whine about it. You quit. It's so tough for you. All you want to do is go fishing. I'm going to give you a chance."

Anton walked over and looked down at Peter. "I'll tell you what I think," he said. "I think you've got a *thing* for your best friend's wife. Am I warm? I think that, underneath it all, you're just the kind of spoiled little shit who would pull a stunt like that. She ought to exercise better judgment. She could get hurt, hanging around with you two."

Anton straightened up, and brushed his tie back into place. "You go fishing with us," he said. "Am I coming through? You find Holsa, and I'll find Alejandro. We're partners now."

As Anton started for the door, he added, "By the way, you're due in the colonel's office tomorrow after the meeting. That would be the time to bring us all some good news."

* *

Pons Grozniev parked his motorcycle in the garage of his three-story house overlooking the sea near the Golden Gate Bridge. It was three o'clock in the morning. He had been barhopping with friends. As he walked toward the house he suddenly spied a hulking figure seated on a large stone in his front yard. Pons leaped three feet backward, struggling for the Swiss Army knife he carried in his jeans pocket, before he recognized the form at rest there. "Hey, Captain," he said happily. "What a surprise. You scared the piss outa me. How goes it?" Pons trotted over and stuck out his hand, arm angled skyward at the elbow, as if intending to arm wrestle.

Captain Crash thrust out a paw, recognizing in the nick of time that Pons intended not a conventional handshake, but the long-forgotten Revolutionary Fist Grip. The captain adjusted his hand in midflight and they met in a sort of fumbling compromise. "I was wondering if you could put me up for a few days," the captain said. "Quietly. I ran into a spot of trouble up north. I'll tell you all about it."

"Sure," said Pons. "Feel free. My crib is your crib. We can work out a few details for the upcoming festival while you're here. I've got some new ideas for the sound system."

"You wouldn't happen to be holding," the captain inquired as they walked toward the door. "Would you? I had to leave in a hurry."

"Got some primo weed," Pons replied.

"That'll do," said the captain.

81

P A R T

TWO

SEVEN

O N THE AFTERNOON of Monday, December seventeenth, shortly after the conclusion of the second Class 1 Security meeting on the subject of the Klaatu incursion, Colonel Robert Core, having bolted a hasty lunch, took the elevator to the seventh floor of the DID Systems & Security Building near Portland. The colonel was still smarting over the way he had been forced to go before the assembled technicians and admit that the Klaatu threat was real; that the simulation concocted for them on Saturday had been nothing but fiction. Too many inside people had found out, and now they knew the truth, and, very soon, so would everybody else. As he walked down the well-lit hallway, the colonel caught himself wishing desperately for the presence and companionship of Alejandro Hunt.

The colonel walked into his office and seated himself behind his massive glass desk. Anton and Ada were already there, Anton slouched on the couch to the colonel's left, Ada sitting in a glass-and-canvas chair to his right.

The colonel's desk held only a computer module, a bank of telephones, a yellow legal tablet, a single sharpened pencil, and a framed photo of three skinny girls in purple football jerseys. His graying hair, though neatly combed, was feathered slightly over each ear, betraying the absence of his customary morning shampoo. Hanging on the wall behind his desk was a photo of the colonel as a crew-cut young flyboy in the cockpit of a vicious-looking fighter plane.

The colonel greeted his two visitors. It occurred to him that if you added Alejandro — the missing fourth — it would be like 1959 all over again. The meeting in New York; the last time the four of them were together in the same room. But that was years ago, and this time there was no Alejandro, only his ghost.

Ada Stibbits was thinking the same thing. The child had been there, too. Ada was thinking: And baby made five.

And Anton, over on the couch, was wondering, as he had wondered back in 1959, just what Ada was doing here in the first place. People never leave the business, he thought. They always surface. Anton looked her over. His gaze was casual, appraising. He was momentarily captivated by her legs, so artfully crossed. A lean run of calf showed between hemline and boot. Anton would have liked to have seen more. He didn't see her very often. They weren't exactly friends.

Robert Core folded his hands together, placed them on the desk top, and sighed. "There's been a leak," he said.

"I assumed as much," said Anton. "Judging by your candor downstairs with the troops this morning."

"Additional misdirection would have served no useful purpose," the colonel replied.

"I've also been asked to make an arrest," the colonel said, realizing that this, too, was the same as it had been in 1959, except that in '59 it was Anton who had said it. Those may have been Anton's exact words to Alejandro that night, the colonel realized. It was a discomfiting thought. Anton's exact words. Ada would remember.

"These would be our Pentagon friends," Anton said. "The ones doing the asking."

The colonel nodded. "Early this morning we were approached by most of the major networks and news agencies. Some of them were brandishing copies of the first Klaatu communiqué. They were given to understand that they were on dicey ground from a national security point of view. Nonetheless, we can expect speculative headlines by this evening. In order to forestall their worst excesses, a press conference has been scheduled for tomorrow afternoon. In the event that we do not have Klaatu in hand by then, I have been asked to come up with *someone*."

"What about the leak?" Ada asked.

"I don't know," the colonel said. "I don't have time to care. In less than one week, someone is threatening to shut down the SEEK system. This coming Friday. That's all I have time to care about."

PULSE DECEMBER 21. The colonel held the image in his mind almost constantly now.

"The Pentagon," added the colonel, "gets very nervous when the

Guardians are stumped. I am being asked to assume that Klaatu can do what he says he's going to do."

"Who is this Holsa?" Ada asked.

"A very tenuous link to Alejandro," the colonel said bitterly.

Anton contented himself with a hard glance in Ada's direction. "Frank Holsa would have made the perfect Guardian," he observed, "if he wasn't crazy. His mind is a bowl of shredded riboflavin." He turned to the colonel and said, "I really, I have to ask. What is she *doing* here?"

Ada let the colonel answer for her. They always enjoyed that.

"Ada is here," the colonel said steadily, "because she's been placed in charge of the statistical analysis effort. She's reconstructing the record of SEEK transactions over the past year. She's looking for anomalies. I want her input."

"Her input on what? Cassidy and Holsa are the only statistical evidence of interest at the moment. Ask her how she's doing with that."

"The reconstructed records," Ada responded, directing her remarks to the colonel, "show no prior usage anomalies, in the case of Peter Cassidy."

"There," said Anton. "Terrific."

"However," said Ada, "we have discovered a related anomaly — "

"If you put Cassidy away," Anton said to the colonel, ignoring her, "we're shut down. He's *still* our only line to Holsa."

"I think I'm going to have him arrested," the colonel said.

Anton gazed at the ceiling. "Your media circus doesn't go off for twenty-four hours yet. Pick him up later. Better yet, find someone else."

"In that respect," Ada put in, "the related fifth-level anomaly to which I am referring — "

"We risk losing him," said the colonel, with a pointed glance in Anton's direction, "as we lost Holsa."

Fuck you, Colonel, Anton thought. *It was a bad bungle. You think I'm* happy *about it?*

The colonel picked up one of the telephone receivers on his desk. "Find Peter Cassidy," he said, "and tell him to come to my office."

"If he's guilty," Anton persisted, "give him twelve more hours to prove it, before he starts stonewalling in court. If he's innocent, give him the day to reestablish contact with Holsa. Pick him up late tonight. I'm telling you, that's the way to go."

The colonel picked up his phone and said, "Get Security."

"He can't talk to Holsa from a jail cell," Anton said acidly. "I'm asking you to reconsider."

"If I had a fallback candidate," said the colonel, "I might. No readily available stand-in comes to mind."

Ada Stibbits said: "We have reconstructed an event which suggests that there has been one other fifth-level violation involving Peter Cassidy's ID sequence. Based on available logs, the indicated source is a SEEK terminal registered to a DID employee named David Atwood."

Anton, taken completely by surprise, focused all of his attention on the need for exuding a semblance of outward calm.

"Are you sure?" the colonel asked.

"We're working on it. It appears to be traceable."

The colonel pushed himself back in his chair. "Good Christ," he said. "Does *everybody* have Cassidy's ID?"

Anton decided to take a chance. "It's very tenuous," he broke in, loudly. "It's flimsy. All you've got on the face of it is a fifth-level entry violation."

"A violation," said the colonel, "using the same cover Klaatu used. I'm going to arrest him just to find out what the hell he was doing."

Anton backed off, feeling scorched.

A light began blinking on the colonel's telephone console. The colonel pressed a button and said, "Two minutes." He leaned forward in his swivel chair, adjusted the keyboard of his computer module, typed briefly, then leaned back again, studying the results as they appeared on the screen.

"David Atwood," he read aloud. "Joined DID in 'seventy-seven. Debugs SEEK circuits for production. His father is an insurance executive in Philadelphia. Good grades in school, minor disciplinary infractions. Psychiatric sessions nineteen sixty-five, 'sixty-six."

Anton stared at Ada, while Ada listened intently to the colonel's recitation.

"Graduated from Stanford with honors in 'seventy-four."

She hates my guts, Anton thought. She's hated me for twenty-five years, but she can't possibly know. It's coincidence; nothing but ill-timed stupidity on Atwood's part.

"Married Alison Eiler," the colonel continued. "An art student."

Ada had a vision of herself with Alejandro, the child crying in the front seat between them.

"Base annual salary in the midseventies, less benefits, bonuses, and expenses." The colonel paused. "His bank accounts fluctuate wildly. As of last month, he was nearly broke." Colonel Core looked up. "Perhaps he's being paid to do something."

"He was all-conference rebound champ on the Stanford basketball team for two years," said the colonel, still reading from the screen. "And then he quit. He just walked out of the gym. I will never understand these people."

The door to the colonel's office opened, and Peter Cassidy walked in.

Anton was nervously and methodically straightening the seam in his slacks and did not look up when Peter entered the room. Peter saw him instantly, and thought of his shattered fly rod. Peter turned to the colonel and said, "I don't deal with this guy."

Anton shrugged helplessly, for the colonel's benefit.

Peter caught the gesture out of the corner of his eye. "He's not too well adjusted," Peter said. "Basically, he's an asshole."

Anton stiffened. The colonel rose to his feet and was about to deliver himself of a splendid invective when Ada spoke up instead.

"Boys," she said.

Her voice was delicately laden with just the intended amount of satire. Anton relaxed. The colonel closed his mouth and sat down. Peter took the chair beside Ada that the colonel indicated for him.

Amazing.

The colonel, frowning, studied his legal tablet in awkward silence for a few moments. Peter smiled — meaningfully, he hoped — in Ada's direction. Good old Ada, he thought. What's she doing here? Does she know that I'm being set up?

On several past occasions the DID Corporation had called Ada away from her Berkeley professorship as an outside consultant, and Peter had had the pleasure of working with her. Ada was a cool one. Her effect on Peter was never short of extraordinary, and while she had never acknowledged this, tacitly or otherwise, Peter had always harbored the notion that he, in turn, represented a tantalizing im-possibility in the eyes of Ada Stibbits. If the disparity in their ages had not been so daunting, he might have tried to sleep with her. She might have agreed. There was something about the mouth, the eyes . . . David was right. Something about Ada got to you.

When the colonel finally looked up from his tablet, Peter prepared himself for the worst. The way the colonel had leveled with every-body at the morning's meeting had not brought Peter a great deal of comfort. And later, in his work group, calculating circuit threshold levels based on a fresh flood of data the Guardians had coughed up, Peter had concluded that the word on Klaatu must have gotten out, meaning publicity, lawsuits . . . arrests. The colonel might have decided that now was the appropriate time to reel in his only extant scapegoat, Anton's interest in Holsa notwithstanding.

Nodding curtly in Peter's direction, the colonel said, "Take the rest of the afternoon off, Cassidy. If Holsa tries to contact you, arrange for a meeting, then call me immediately at this number." The colonel shoved a small card across his desk.

Peter stared at the colonel. It was not at all what he had expected to hear.

"Don't call that number," the colonel warned him, "unless you have something to *say.*"

"I've got something to say right now, Colonel. There's no reason at all to think that Frank Holsa is going to check in with me." Try his mother, Peter thought. Get me out of here.

"People have been using your SEEK credentials right, left, and center," the colonel said. "You could very easily go to jail for that."

Peter picked up the colonel's card. Prison had always been the one inconceivable option in his life. "I think it's time for me to very publicly retain some competent legal counsel," he said. It was humbling, in a particularly brutal way, to be this scared.

"Go home," the colonel said. "Consider yourself lucky, for the time being. And no more crap about lawyers."

The colonel made a gesture of dismissal. Peter rose and headed for the door. This is your exit, he told himself. Don't screw it up.

Check with Ada, then go.

After the door had closed, the colonel turned and faced Anton once again. "It's two o'clock," he said. "Pick him up in eight hours, DeBroer. He's all we've got, and I want his wings clipped for the duration. This ends it. Am I understood?"

At that moment, Anton was more concerned with David Atwood. Ill-timed stupidity, Anton thought again. I will have to cure him of that.

Without comment, Anton nodded his assent.

* *

Peter loitered restlessly in the vicinity of the seventh-floor elevators while he monitored the traffic along the connecting hallways. The colonel's reprieve had been wholly unexpected, and Peter intended to take maximum advantage of it. He had been hoping all along that the end of the day would not see him in prison, and he had even installed Fish Dog in the back of the Scout as some sort of ritual, some talismanic gesture, before leaving the house that morning. It was unfair to the dog. It was Peter's way of pretending that this was going to be a normal day. It was ridiculous.

As he waited by the elevators, it struck Peter that this was the time to ask himself whether or not he could trust Ada Stibbits. They first met three years ago at a circuit conference in Houston, and they had worked on a couple of projects together since then. They'd taken each other out to dinner several times. He'd been fascinated by the knack she seemed to have for drawing him out, while giving so little of herself away. He'd noted the wrinkles at the corners of her eyes, and had decided they made her look sexy. Professionally, she was dazzling, but seemed content to remain more or less in the shadows.

Ada will level with me, Peter decided. She always has.

He spotted her the moment she came into view, striding purposefully along the left hallway. He had to admit that she fascinated him precisely because she was so inaccessible; so classically unobtainable. She was such an unknowable quantity. It was weightless fantasy; no one could get hurt. In many ways, Peter thought, as he watched her coming toward him, it was the perfect love affair.

Peter angled toward her theatrically, like a deprogrammer about to bag a Moonie. With a firm grip on her elbow, he steered Ada away from the hall traffic, toward a trio of silver drinking fountains.

"Hello, Peter," Ada said. "Is this your way of asking for a few minutes of my time?"

Embarrassed, Peter let go of her arm and took a nervous sip of water. Ada bent for a token drink of her own.

"I saw you at both Security meetings, but we never got a chance to talk," Peter said. He glanced over her shoulder and down the hall. "Have you been huddled with those two psychos all weekend?"

"It feels like it," Ada said.

"Then you know my predicament."

She studied Peter thoughtfully for a moment, drawing a tapered finger across her eyebrow. "To a degree," she said. Her look was frank, searching. To Peter, it felt like being x-rayed. "But this is hardly the place to discuss it. Just do what they tell you, Peter."

"DeBroer tells me to find Frank Holsa. I can't do that."

Ada hesitated. She could do something on Peter's behalf, if she chose to. How would he react, she asked herself, if he knew the truth?

91

She turned toward the elevators. "I'm going back to my hotel for a nap and an early dinner," she said. She named it. "We could meet there, in the downstairs bar, in an hour and a half."

"Ada," Peter said, "you don't drink. You're a teetotaler."

She smiled. Peter felt very young, and immensely relieved.

"I like to watch," Ada said.

* *

In the parking lot near the Systems & Security Building, Eddie Moran warily circled Peter Cassidy's Scout, groaning and cursing at the barking dog in back. Just his luck. Perfect. Eddie hated dogs. Eddie held his breath, reached inside the car through the open vent, and unlocked the front door. Big surprise: The dog quieted down, and sat on his haunches, tail wagging madly, while Eddie did his bit of business for Anton.

Then Eddie was struck by a burst of inspiration. He walked around to the back of the Scout, picked the lock on the tailgate, and took a firm grip on Fish Dog's collar. "Nice pooch," Eddie said. "Good dog." Then Eddie did another bit of business with the dog, relocked the tailgate, and walked away.

EIGHT

FOR JUST AN INSTANT, Ada Stibbits caught herself
dozing during the taxi ride back to Portland. She
snapped her head upright, forcing herself to concentrate on the
downtown skyline as it floated into view across the river. The driver
ramped up an overpass and onto the bridge. The oily night-light wink
of the Willamette was visible below them.

Ada felt the lack of her customary centering time, an interregnum
she created every morning of the workday week on the long walk
across the Berkeley campus to her office. She missed it acutely. She
would concentrate solely on the cut of the clouds that day, the grass
beneath her feet, the spires of San Francisco glimpsed from the heights
of campus, hanging innocently above the blue-gray of the bay. She
would concentrate on these things, on the several objects of her several senses, and for a split instant she would succeed in extinguishing
everything else — the classrooms, the faculty meetings, her lonely
apartment, the endless parade of numbers that composed the null set
of her professional life. For a split instant she would imagine herself
a part of a different world. A world less designing, less prone to excess. Less naked in its greed. . . .

As she stared out the window of her cab, Ada strove to create a
version of this special morning moment with the materials at hand.
She failed. She reached for that special feeling of promise, and could
not achieve it, coming back instead with the memory of another bridge
and another dark skyline, larger, more brutish, many years ago. So
many years ago.

She first met Alejandro when she was nineteen years old. He was
twice that. Her own father was — would have been — the same age.
The two of them were in her mind now almost constantly, their

93

memories blending and mixing in curious ways. The Rabbi and the Scientist, protopatriarchs in the image of Moses.

Picture the two of us, she thought, giving in to it at last. A thin, intense Jewish girl from a succession of boroughs and nowhere else, watching Alejandro Hunt, the half-Guatemalan, half-mad State Secret delivering a lecture at MIT on the future of solid-state electronics. She remembered very little of what he said. It was all glorious and vague to her now.

She was a mediocre math student at the time. Call her a prodigy *in potentia*, unaware of her powers, suffering every stale form of gender abuse imaginable in the year 1958. Alejandro was president of the DID Corporation, with a private research laboratory in upstate New York, where he did classified research on electronic computer systems. All manner of stories were floating around about Alejandro in those days — how he had been involved in a number of daring intelligence operations during the war; how he could close his eyes and quote long ragged bursts of *Faust* from memory; how his experiments had led him to propose in private a bold new method of using the force of electricity.

It was winter, and the panes of glass in the windows along the wall of the lecture hall were frosted over on the inside, and it was dark beyond the windows. Sitting there, taking him in, she could feel his weight, even at a distance. She attached herself to him, recklessly and invisibly, as he delivered his talk.

She met him afterward in the faculty lounge, as was the postlecture custom. People always expected Alejandro to be a foreigner, which, in every important way, he was. His accent was Spanish. His hair, against all genetic odds, was a dull crimson. He had precisely chiseled features and a trim, well-muscled body. He was wearing a belted woollen sweater with patches. Ada's was cashmere. They stood there admiring each other's sweaters. Alejandro spoke to her at some length about the mathematics of computer programming while the two of them silently attempted to fathom the depth of this mutual attraction hanging so palpably and unexpectedly in the air between them.

At the close of the dreary reception, Ada wangled an invitation to a private party at the home of a professor she knew, after hearing that Alejandro planned to be there. The house was small but comfortable, with a clubby front room in which Alejandro held court. He was pointedly nonspecific about his work. He spoke of his Guatemalan childhood, his early interest in mechanics and electronics, his belief in undiscovered forms of electronic communication. He held himself in reserve, never courting the flattery and approbation that came his way.

Great cracks in the foundation of physics were opening up, he declared. "Gaps," he called them. The wilderness of the electromagnetic spectrum opened up to scrutiny only with the greatest reluctance, like the essence of the atom.

He was in town for several days, and they arranged to meet again. They kept meeting, and finally — it was so difficult then — they arranged to meet in his hotel room. An assignation, as it used to be called. She remembered steam heat and pull-down shades, a kind of mournful elegance wholly absent from her present quarters in Portland. . . .

She felt the taxi slowing, swerving into an open lane beside her hotel. She paid and stepped out of the cab, allowing the doorman to guide her through the revolving doors and into the warmth of the lobby. She walked noiselessly across the thick carpet, under high chandeliers, and took the elevator to her floor.

Her room was stuffy, overwarm, despite the fact that the help had thoughtfully ratcheted open the windows an inch or two. The room was nondescript, distinguished only by a full-length mirror and a dusty bowl of fruit. All the light switches were in unexpected places. Ada removed her coat and sat at the dressing table near the window, allowing the sinuous breeze to stir the brown hair at the back of her neck. Vacantly, she unpinned her hair. . . .

She had been a virgin, of course. Alejandro had seemed surprised. She had simply assumed that he would know.

She rode a fine line between pleasure and pain that night. When he entered her, she felt overpowered and slightly ashamed. And in love. . . .

Ada rose from the dressing table and paced the lime green carpet, pausing at the wall mirror to examine her face for a moment. The moment became another, as she calmly took in the lines around her eyes and mouth. Tired clear through to the marrow. She removed her pearl gray cardigan jacket, her contrasting pink blouse, her bra. Turning slightly, she said hello to herself in the mirror. Saying hello to what he had known of her, through this reflection of her other self. . . .

There had been no way of knowing the truth about Alejandro; that when your life intersected with his, everything about you became changed. You might remain unaware of it until one day you woke up and realized that huge pieces of your life were no longer under your direct control. . . .

Another half-turn in front of the mirror, a cascade of unpinned hair. She stepped out of her narrow skirt, removed the boots that met the skirt at midcalf, discarded her panties and hose. Still turning, she watched her double in its rotation through space, smooth belly, hands holding slim waist; hips, flanks, now breasts in profile. . . .

There were other assignations. Three months after Alejandro left, she discovered she was pregnant. She heard the sound of her Orthodox parents rolling over in their graves. "Watch out for schmucks," was her father's sole piece of concrete advice on the romantic front. Well, yes. But Alejandro Hunt was different.

She did not panic. She did not contract for the services of the off-campus butchers. Within three weeks, she quit school and went to join Alejandro at his laboratory in the Adirondacks.

Alejandro rented a nearby cabin for her, and arranged for visits by a local physician. It was a lovely setting, in deep pine forest, but it would have been the dead heart of the wilderness without Alejandro.

On the night of her arrival, after she had gone so eagerly to his bed, he told her that there would be no marriage. He did not want her to be associated openly with either himself or his work. For her safety, he said.

Actually, Alejandro had two secrets. Ada, for a time, was one of them.

Alejandro's research grounds consisted of a large two-story barn and three double-wide trailers in a weedy clearing. The solitude of the surroundings was marred only by the rumbling arrival of trucks bearing electronic equipment and assorted research gear from New York City. It was May of 1958. Summer was coming, and Alejandro was planning to settle in.

It was a strange, anonymous life she led there, pleasant but constricted. Despite his reluctance to involve her in the work, or publicly acknowledge their liaison, Alejandro came to depend upon her keenly analytical mind and her prowess with numbers. She found herself working side by side with his lab assistant, Leonard.

There were no complications, when the time came. The child was lovely. When Alejandro held Rachel for the first time, he made a joke about a skinned rabbit with an old man's face. She started crying, for the three of them. For what might happen, and what might not. . . .

Ada turned once more in front of the hotel mirror, noting where the neck flowed to soft shoulder, where the ear met and caressed the side of the face. She thought of a shower but went, instead, to the hotel bed. She stretched out and did not move for several seconds. And then, with her hand, she began proving that this corpus of smooth curves and soft recesses still belonged to her. . . .

Night after night of love; Alejandro leaving her bed and stealing down the path to the converted barn, where he would work until daylight before stumbling back to the cabin, red-eyed and worn, for pancakes and sausages and strong black coffee with milk. This was how she chose to remember it. It was right, it was fair, to remember it that way. . . .

Ada fixed her gaze on the blank white field of the hotel ceiling, her hands idle now. She felt like taking a shower, but couldn't summon the strength for it. She was supposed to meet Peter in half an hour. She would be late, and he would forgive her. . . .

The research, their exile, lasted only a year. In retrospect, she did not find it difficult to account for Alejandro's interest in the research project that was quietly taking shape inside the barn. So little was known about electromagnetic theory in those days, for one thing. That was the kind of landscape Alejandro liked best.

In the summer of 1959, Alejandro made arrangements to conduct an experiment. On the night of the test, other than herself and Alejandro and Leonard, the only other witness was Major Robert Core, whom Alejandro had sworn to silence. Rachel was too young to count.

Crickets and a smattering of fireflies. . . .

Ada rose from the bed, naked, and made her way to the bathroom for a scalding hot shower. The steam rose and enveloped her, and the water hissed, and no matter how hard she tried, she could not cleanse herself of the memories that kept drawing her back.

Go ahead, she told herself. Go through the rest of it for the thousandth time. . . .

When Ada was finally ready to leave the room, she realized, by the time she reached the elevators, that she was ravenously hungry. She planned to risk indulging in a plate of grilled salmon at the downstairs restaurant. She glanced at her watch. She was not looking forward to her meeting in the bar, because, Peter being Peter, he was sure to resist her advice. In all probability, she would have to lie a little, in order to make sure that he took it.

But in the end, she was certain, Peter would forgive her for that, too.

NINE

PETER WAS WAITING for Ada at a window table. The bar was nearly empty, as if the onset of the December rains had somehow quenched everybody's thirst. Peter knew better. On days like this, good northwesterners stayed home to drink.

On the street beyond the window, a small black kid in roller skates and yellow rain slicker was cutting shaky circles through the drizzle. Peter stretched out his arms and leaned forward on the round cocktail table, studying a small hors d'oeuvre menu encased in plexiglass. He had ordered a martini, for no good reason he could think of. Fern bars, they were called.

Very deliberately, he placed thumb and forefinger against the menu and flicked it neatly across the table, where it teetered on the brink for an instant before skidding off the edge. What the hell.

Ada Stibbits joined him at seven-thirty, having eaten alone in the adjacent restaurant. Peter inquired politely about the fish. Brutally overcooked, she told him.

She sat facing the light from the street, her forearms cool and silvered in it, her face pale. Another trick of the wet winter neon. She was smiling, and he found it disconcerting.

"Can you keep a secret?" she asked him.

Peter considered the question, taking it quite seriously, however it might have been intended.

"The complexity of your question astounds me," he said, shaking his head slowly. "The many levels of it." He watched as two businessmen entered the room, taking seats at the cedar bar.

She laughed. It was a marvelous, full-throated sound. "I was only going to say that I cannot stand working with either of those . . . with those two men. I hate it."

"Careful, Ada. The very walls have ears."

"I am free to meet with you, presuming that you go home like a good boy afterward. Nobody is bugging public places at the moment."

"Aw, Ada, that's *touching*."

"You're a little off today."

"I admit it. A little frayed." Peter felt a sourness rising in his stomach. He licked his lips. "Ada," he said. "Who are we all looking for?"

"I should think it was obvious."

Peter was on the verge of telling her that nothing, at the moment, was obvious to him on the face of it.

"We're looking for Alejandro Hunt," she said. "As always."

"And Alejandro, I take it, doesn't want to be found."

"As always."

"There's no way of getting at him, short of armed invasion?"

"Very likely it's being considered."

Peter sat silently for a moment, staring out at the street. The kid in the yellow rain slicker had vanished. "It was inevitable," he said firmly. "Something like this was bound to happen."

"Perhaps," said Ada.

Peter studied her features carefully for a moment. "And you're sure it's Alejandro."

"Yes," she answered.

"Why?"

"Because he knows how."

"When was the last time you saw him?"

"Many years ago."

"I thought you two. . . . I mean, there were rumors that. . . ."

"Yes," she said again, without hesitation. "Many years ago."

Peter paused again, toying with his empty glass. "It might not be such a bad idea, really. This thing Alejandro has in mind."

Ada made no reply.

"He's intent on destroying his own creation. He's throwing in with Victor Frankenstein. Do you suppose that's the way he's looking at it?"

"No," said Ada, slowly. "I don't."

"An act of ecological terrorism. Like blowing up a dam on the Colorado River, only far more effective."

"I don't think so," Ada said.

"Well, *what* then?"

"You'd have to ask *him*," said Ada. "I haven't seen him in twenty-odd years."

Peter said, "I'd very much like to do that."

Ada ignored him.

Another drink materialized for Peter. The euphoric flush, the relaxation of tensed muscles, was, by the second martini, giving way to a slight numbness in his limbs. Better watch it, Peter told himself. This stuff is like Pentothal.

"Did you know," Peter said, "that I am no longer an employee of the DID Corporation? I quit about a month ago."

Ada looked surprised. "I had no idea."

"I walked. I have the feeling you might not find that so terribly difficult to understand."

"What are you planning to do?"

Peter answered, "I don't know yet."

"You must have plans of some sort."

"To tell you the truth, Ada, I was planning on going fishing."

Ada looked bemused. "For the rest of your *life?*"

"I don't know. Possibly."

"Peter — "

"It goes nowhere, Ada. It's so *pointless*. All we do, Ada, is speed things up. We speed things up — and nobody benefits." Peter leaned toward her in his chair. "How do I get out of this? *Tell* me something, Ada."

Ada said, "They need a scapegoat."

"I *know* that. They've got one. Me. And if they can get hold of Holsa, they'll have another."

"I cannot help you in the way that you think I can."

"Sure you can, Ada. You can help me any way you want to. You're a big girl."

"They feel compelled to make an arrest."

"Something *concrete*, Ada."

When she did not immediately reply, he said: "If Frank Holsa doesn't fly into my lap very soon, your friend the colonel and that twisted sidekick of his are going to reel me in. How are you going to feel, Ada, when they put me on the front page as suspect numero uno? Are you going to feel *good* about that?"

Peter waited expectantly. Come through for me, Ada.

Ada's lips quivered slightly. "First of all," she said, "you should know that the colonel was not entirely candid at this morning's meeting."

"Par for the course."

"There was more to the Klaatu message than he was willing to reveal. A date. Klaatu is threatening to shut down the SEEK system on December twenty-first."

Peter gaped. "That's just a few days away."

"You should also know that someone has been using your fifth-level ID set."

"Thanks, but I already know that much. Holsa."

"No," Ada said. "Forget about Frank Holsa. Someone else."

"Who?"

"I can't tell you," she said.

She told him anyway. She pulled out a pen and wrote it on a cocktail napkin and pushed it across the table toward him. Peter turned the napkin around and stared at it.

David Atwood.

She had curious, looping handwriting. The curve of the capital *D* in David's name was thrown wide to the right, and all the other letters of the first name were written inside this sprawled first initial.

He stared at her in shocked surprise. "Are you sure?"

"I was the one who discovered it in the records."

Peter could not fit David into the picture. David *used* me, he thought, just like the captain. They both put me in jeopardy. Nobody knows what anyone else is like. The mask never slips. Best not to know, best not to inquire. Nobody knows, nobody owes. Strangers all.

Christ.

Ada looked at Peter, noting his tense curiosity, his uncombed thatch of blond hair, his broad shoulders bunching as he leaned forward against the cocktail table. She flushed slightly, and shifted in her chair. She tried not to think of Peter in that way.

"Colonel Core has scheduled a press conference for tomorrow afternoon, Peter. Do you understand what that means?"

There was no need for her to spell out the rest. She means an arrest, he thought. If not me, if not Holsa, then David. The colonel wasn't likely to go onstage empty-handed.

Ada leaned against the table and folded her hands in her lap. "Peter, you have become involved in a game which you cannot possibly win. It has to do with things that happened years ago. Before the SEEK system even existed. This is . . . this is Alejandro repaying old friends and smiting old enemies. People you've never even heard of."

"That's fine, Ada, that's just great. I'm all for repaying and smiting, but I don't *care* what kind of grudge match is going down between Colonel Core and Alejandro. It's not my event. I'm just an insider looking for a way out."

She reached across the table and took his hand. "You want me to tell you something concrete." Her voice, her tone, was fiercely serious. "Very well. Here it is. Run away from here. Go hide somewhere, and don't come back until all of this is over. Until it's finished. Go fishing, Peter, and don't leave a forwarding address. Vanish without a trace. This is my concrete advice to you."

A series of unpleasant peristaltic contractions wracked Peter's lower regions. It's that bad, he thought. "There's one other thing," he said. "If they had Alejandro, they'd call off the dogs, am I right?"

"Peter, forget it."

"Are you in sympathy with him, Ada? Do you know where he is?"

Ada smiled, a little sadly, and shook her head. "You're not the first person to ask."

"I think that maybe you wouldn't tell anybody," he replied, measuring her reaction carefully, "even if you knew."

"I see. And why, then, would I tell *you*?"

"Hell, Ada," he said, " 'cause I'm cute."

She laughed.

"Cute and innocent."

The laughter stopped. "Being innocent," she said steadily, "does not make you exempt."

"I'm not sure how to take that."

"It means that I like you just the way you are — unharmed."

"Tell me how to get a message to him," Peter insisted. "Tell me how to try. Holsa is one route, or so Anton thinks. Is there another?"

She drew back, marveling at his hell-for-leather, barnstorming proclivity for folly. Something programmed deep in the genetic wiring. . . .

"Tell me how to get through to him," Peter said.

"You should go now," she said, and Peter was thrown off track by the sudden remoteness in her voice.

"Okay," he replied. "I'm leaving." He stood up.

He needs to be protected from his own worst instincts, she thought. "People who wish to contact Alejandro generally attempt to do so through Leonard."

Peter frowned. "Who's he?"

"He's with DID Security. Robert Core thinks that Leonard works for him, but that is not the case. Leonard works for Alejandro." Ada found it difficult to say this.

"How do I find him?" Peter asked. He sounded grateful.

She smiled again, but there was no tenderness, no sense of comradeship in it this time. "Leonard," she responded, "is in charge of finding *you*."

"Ah," said Peter. He knew it was time for him to leave. Ada's look told him as much.

There was more she wanted to tell him. A good deal more.

Peter was about to say something.

"Don't tell me," she urged. "Tell Leonard."

It seemed like a sensible suggestion.

Dearest Ada.

*   *

Driving slowly homeward, Peter conducted a mental survey of the contents of the Scout. The sum total of its holdings at the moment, excluding Fish Dog, consisted of a pair of boots, a single work glove, a well-masticated chew log, a ratty sleeping bag, some fishing gear, and three crumpled McDonald's sacks. A quick check of the glove box revealed a jumble of cassette tapes, the title to the car, a flashlight, and three screwdrivers — standard, Phillips, and broken.

Oh, man, he thought fervently, if only I was flying down the trusty old highway on any other errand than this. Interstate 5, his thin ribbon of sanity in days long past, route of escape from his Wenatchee youth. If not for Interstate 5 he'd have ended up as a framer working for his old man's uncle, making lousy money, nailing studs all day and dying of too many Chesterfields.

He tried to imagine this highway as it had been for him then, and not the way it was for him tonight. Fine line there. A sidestepping sluiceway out of town, any way you cut it. Hurtling downvalley, you could imagine you were headed for San Francisco, San Diego, Cabo San Lucas . . . or you could loop north and head for Buster's, where the porcupines gnawed holes in the handle of your best canoe paddle and ate your boots for the salt. . . .

He had reached the point just south of Portland where it was possible to view Mount Hood maybe one day in ten. He punched his tape deck out of habit, and music flowed over him. Snatches of something by The Police.

David, the captain, and me. One of us gets to play the sacrificial lamb. We're all three of us twisted up in the same net, and December twenty-first is only four days away.

He caught himself thinking of Alison, and tried to make the thought go away.

Then he thought of Ada, who had surprised him by giving out the same advice the captain had already seen fit to put into practice. *Run away. Do not pass Go.* Take that good woman's advice, he told himself, and split. This is what you get when you try to live in two worlds at once, giving exactly half of your brain to each. You get careless. You fail to see it coming and you catch it right in the face.

Briefly, and without much enthusiasm, Peter considered the prospect of lawyers, and fighting a false charge in the courts, in the event of his arrest. No, he told himself, it would be suicide. Guys in dark suits and shiny black shoes, a tape recorder on the table, a videocam whirring away nearby. . . . Is there such a thing as bail in a Class 1 proceeding?

They could never make it stick. They must know that. If Klaatu struck again, the whole frame-up would crack of its own weight. Peter could fight it.

David could fight it.

They could try.

Jesus.

Peter pulled slowly into his driveway. He was taking a chance coming home at all, but there were six hundred dollars' worth of crisp twenties wrapped up in a pocket of his old suit — no burglar was ever going to steal a cheap suit — and he would need it. He had a grand total of three dollars and fifty cents in the pocket of his jeans, and the credit cards in his wallet did not strike him as the most far-thinking means of financing his quiet departure from the scene.

There was only one other thing that he planned to do before leaving. It was a long shot, and it was not likely to be worth the trouble, but the car was out there in the street. He'd very definitely spotted it on the way in. It might be Leonard.

Peter pulled the Scout all the way into the open garage. He would grab the money, and throw the portable catalytic heater into the Scout, and then he would drive to the nearest grocery store, which happened to be three miles away in the middle of an enormous shopping plaza, surrounded by uncounted acres of foggy parking lot in which to ditch whoever it was that might be tracking his whereabouts that night.

But first he sprung Fish Dog, counting on him to bound off toward the street, in the direction of the nearest automobile tires. Happily, Fish Dog cooperated. Peter followed.

Peter walked up to the one car in the street that he did not recognize. He tapped lightly on the passenger window. After an uncomfortable minute, a very small man leaned across the front seat and opened the window a crack. Peter leaned toward it.

"Are you Leonard?"

There was no reply. The little man's face gave away nothing.

"I need to get in touch with Alejandro," Peter blurted out.

The man's expression never changed.

Holy Mother, Peter thought, suddenly panicked. Now he whips out the cuffs. . . .

"That can be arranged," Leonard said. "If you do exactly what I say. . . ."

Peter bolted up the stairs to his bedroom and transferred the money from the suit to his jeans pocket. He thought of another twenty dollars in the drawer of the phone table, and went downstairs to get it.

There was a single call on his phone answering machine. Peter took a deep breath and blew it out slowly. Shit piss corruption. No time. He decided not to answer it.

A few seconds later he answered it anyway.

It was a recorded sales pitch for condominium real estate in central Florida. Only minutes from Disney World and Cypress Gardens, said the voice. There was the tinny sound of waves breaking on the beach.

Peter was reaching for the off button when he heard music being cued in above the surf sound. "Take Me to the Pilot" by Elton John.

"This astounding offer," said the recorded voice, "is brought to you by Ozone Enterprises, a division of Short Circuit Limited." There was a toll-free 800 number for further information.

Nice, Frank.

Peter filed the number in his head and turned off the machine. He quickly checked the time and was preparing to leave the house when he had second thoughts. Holsa's message was only twenty minutes old, according to the phone machine. Who could say when he would get another chance to connect? The captain was trying to signal him, find out if Peter was still in circulation. Peter picked up the telephone. If the captain had gone to this much trouble to set up a blind call, he would likely hold to the cover in the event that Peter called him back. Peter was just desperate enough for information to take the chance.

Peter hesitated, then put down the phone. The captain had screwed him over once already. Why give him a second chance? Suppose, in the end, that Holsa was Klaatu?

Peter picked up the phone again. He held his breath and dialed the number. Come on, Frank, he prayed. Be *discreet*. Just a little hint as to your whereabouts would do just fine.

There was a long pause, then a series of clicks, followed by a high-pitched whistle. Another series of clicks. Static. By the sound of it, the captain had arranged a towering stack of connections.

"Ozone Enterprises," said a voice.

"I'm calling in regard to your real estate offer," Peter said, picking his words with great care. "I don't like being solicited by recordings over the telephone. I want my name removed from your computerized dialing lists. And I want to send a letter of complaint to your home office. Where might that be?"

There was another pause. "Just a minute," said the voice. After a moment, a new voice came on the line.

"So, pal," said the captain.

"Are you the one handling complaints about solicitations over — "

"Forget about it," the captain said matter-of-factly. "Forget the cover."

"Listen, uh, this is not the time for — "

"We're live, right? I wanna set up a little conference call here. I want DeBroer in on this."

"Frank — "

"Shouldn't be so hard. Anton DeBroer, please. Frank Holsa calling. I'll accept the charges." The captain let loose a dry, booming chuckle.

"Frank," Peter said warily, "you're fucking up. I've got to go."

"Caught you at a bad time, right? Bummer."

As Peter was debating whether or not to hang up, one minor piece of the puzzle suddenly fell into place for him. It was last New Year's Eve, some weird bet having to do with the four-color map theorem, Peter seated at his fifth-level terminal which he'd brought home for the holidays, drunkenly punching up some reference paper on the subject while the captain and . . . who else? Someone else. While the captain and . . . David, that's right, while the two of them looked over his shoulder . . . and memorized his ID sequence, the goddamn sneaks. David already *has* fifth-level access. Why use another one?

"You used my ID, you bastard."

"I was gonna tell you about that," the captain said uncertainly. "Water under the bridge, right?"

Peter closed his eyes, the telephone receiver held limply to his ear. "I don't suppose you plan to tell me where you are."

Long pause. "That'd be smart," said the captain.

Peter pulled out his pocket watch and frantically checked the time. "That's it for me, Frank. Gotta go. Oh, and hey, thanks just *carloads* for dragging me into all this."

"I didn't do it!" the captain whined. "It's this friggin' Klaatu. We *both* got boxed, pal."

"Five more seconds, Frank. Are you in touch with Alejandro Hunt?"

Peter could barely make out the captain's response. "I wish," Holsa mumbled. "I was once, you know. And I will be again, real soon. More than that I cannot say."

"Frank — "

"If you thought about it a minute, you'd figure out where I am."

Peter was about to reply when he heard the other voice.

"Holsa," barked the new voice on the line.

"That you, DeBroer?" Holsa asked.

"Yes. Where are you?"

Silence.

"Cassidy, where is he?"

"Forget it, DeBroer!" Holsa screamed. "You oughta be *nice* to me, for a change!"

"Cassidy, one more time. Where is he?"

"I don't have the slightest idea," Peter answered. There was a humming silence, as if the three-way connection had suddenly gone dead.

"You blew it," Anton said.

He means me, Peter thought.

"He means he can't trace," Holsa sneered, as if reading Peter's mind.

"Holsa, I'm telling you. Don't force me to make you my personal hobby. Understand? We want to talk to Alejandro. You open that door for us and you might even survive this."

"Let me tell *you* something, DeBroer. Let me *disabuse* you of a few notions about Alejandro. I am only his instrument, you dig? We are not fit to kiss the hem of the man's robe. We are not fit to look upon — "

"You're all done, Holsa. You're the deadest cocksucker alive."

"I pity you, man. I really do. Me and Peter, we didn't have any-

107

thing to do with this. You oughta be able to see that. That's all I wanted to tell you. More than that I am definitely not gonna say."

Two events occurred simultaneously as Holsa finished delivering his diatribe. Holsa abruptly hung up, and Anton DeBroer opened Peter's front door and marched straight into Peter's living room. Anton was holding a slim portable telephone to his ear. He was followed through the door by a stocky man in a rumpled sweater.

I'm just another hick Mick, Peter thought. I'm the slowest thinker alive.

"It seems," said Anton, "that we've been cut off. Which more or less wraps it up for you, my friend."

Since Peter had not yet returned the receiver to the cradle, he was forced to experience the disagreeable sensation of hearing Anton's actual voice in one ear, and his telephone voice in the other. The captain would have loved it.

They put down their telephones in unison. Anton leaned casually against the kitchen counter, looking bored. The man in the rumpled sweater came up to Peter and held open a wallet. Shakily, Peter reached out and angled the wallet so it would catch the light from the lamp on his telephone table. The badge from the county sheriff's office was visible enough without the light. Peter wanted to get the name.

Eddie Moran took back the wallet and handed Peter a search warrant.

"Congratulations," said Anton. "You're under arrest."

"For what?" Peter demanded. He was beginning to sweat profusely.

Anton shrugged. "Depends." He nodded at Eddie.

"I'm leaving," Peter said. He took a step forward. With great delicacy, Eddie placed the fingertips of one hand against the front of Peter's chamois shirt. "We like it better when the resident is present for the search," he said apologetically. "Sometimes residents make the mistake of thinking that we planted something."

"It's been known to happen," Anton observed.

All traces of moisture had vanished from Peter's mouth. He was experiencing the kind of fear that can either galvanize or paralyze. He would have given anything to be free of it. As acute as migraine, worse than the flu — that kind of fear.

Eddie produced a Miranda card and a pair of plastic handcuffs.

"Wait," Peter said thickly.

"No," Anton replied. "This wraps it."

With a deep, knowing sigh, Eddie moved in on Peter. Peter held him at bay, desperately, and turned to face Anton.

"I know how to contact Alejandro," Peter said.

Anton looked at Eddie. While Eddie deftly pinned back Peter's arms, Anton walked over and stood in front of him. Anton took a handful of Peter's hair and pulled it slowly, steadily, backward against his scalp. A flood of hot tears washed away Peter's vision.

"I would do it, then," Anton said quietly. "I would do it right now."

TEN

"Y OUR PROBLEM," Pons was saying, as he delicately positioned a huge telescope between the twin colonnades of his third-floor porch, "if I may say so, is that you take the solar system for granted. You've blinded yourself to the music of the spheres. So to speak."

The captain, in response to the charge, simply grunted. He was standing at the edge of the porch, nursing a Heineken, trying to pick out the milky froth and boil of the dark surf below. Through the open French doors of the porch came wafting a jagged, blasphemous musical assault. Pons had given the captain the run of his record collection, and the captain had opted for some seasonal material — Jimi Hendrix doing a free-form instrumental rendition of "Silent Night." Not for the fainthearted.

"We should be able to get a bitchin' Mars," said Pons, as he made minute adjustments to the focus screw.

Other than a few nasty barks to the shin, Captain Crash had survived his helter-skelter bailout quite intact. By the time he crossed the swamp and intersected the old logging road where he'd stashed his spare pickup many moons ago, the captain was puffing and hacking like a dying steam engine. He supposed it had something to do with the relative cross-toxicity of various controlled substances, not to mention his daily diet of forty Camel straights.

Wonder of wonders, the decrepit battery had possessed just the requisite number of amps to turn the engine over, allowing him to make the Eugene airport with a complete absence of fanfare.

All through the drive, Peter Cassidy had flickered guiltily across his mind. Peter was a big boy. Peter would cut a deal. They both had to stay clear of the cross hairs until the Klaatu business was resolved.

Happily, the House of Pons was open to the captain for an indefinite period. Pons was nothing if not noble when it came to bestowing favors on deserving others. Ordinarily, rich people bored the captain. But Pons was different. Pons Grozniev had always operated under the fundamentally blissful assumption that if you did what you sincerely wanted to do, the money would come. It had worked for Pons, and it had *almost* always worked for the captain. So it must be true.

Pons fiddled and twiddled some more, then turned to the captain with a satisfied look. "There," he said. "Have a look. The fog's screwing things up a little."

The captain walked over and bent down for a noncommittal peek.

"The planets and the moon give off a sort of food," Pons explained. "It's a form of nutrition that human beings need."

The captain looked at him scornfully. "You *buy* that?" he said.

Little Pons just arched his eyebrows and shrugged, looking for all the world like Moochie on the old Spin and Marty shows. "It's all a matter of keeping an open mind, you know? Our internal fluids ebb and flow with the sea tides. Solar flares and lunar cycles affect human behavior in unfathomable ways."

The captain returned to his perch against the railing. He took a last swipe at his beer bottle and pitched it over the edge.

"Aw, man," Pons said, grimacing. "People *sunbathe* down there."

"It's all right," the captain assured him. "It'll float harmlessly out to sea."

They stood for a while longer in the harsh chill of the moonless night, silently facing the hills of Marin. It was the captain who chose to break the silence. "I want to have another look," he said, and Pons knew the captain wasn't talking about the planets.

"Suits me," Pons said. "Help me carry this unit back inside the house."

Together, they stashed the telescope in the master bedroom. Pons opened a wicker basket and brought forth a black kimono with a bright red dragon on the back of it. He pulled it on over his clothes and the captain followed him down the curving stairway to the main floor, past a line of Escher originals depicting the permutational possibilities inherent in the laws of form — animal, vegetable, or mineral. The captain followed Pons across the ornate parquetry of the entranceway and into the kitchen at the side of the house. There was a butcher block counter, long enough to serve as a landing strip, strewn with assorted comestibles.

The captain paused and rummaged among the pâté and Brie and dried figs, until he had managed to secure a handful of Ritz and an aerosol can of Cheez Whiz. "Hey, Pons," said the captain as he wolfed down his crackers, "who cleans up this mess, anyway?"

"It always disappears on Thursday," Pons explained. Every Thursday a trio of housekeepers took over the place, headed by a black woman named Bessie. Bessie and her aides-de-camp were very nearly the only women ever to set foot in the place. Women had never been a part of the House of Pons to a noticeable degree. Not for lack of trying, Pons might have added, had someone asked. Pons had a problem. Pons had once suffered from a case of acne that was not to be believed. His parents had run him through every faddish cure that ever came slithering out of the medical pipe. The worst of it was over, and the scarring was minimal, but it had taken a new wonder drug to beat back the scourge. There were side effects. His lips were constantly chapping and peeling, and to combat it he always carried with him a small jar of Vaseline. He was forever pulling the jar out of his pocket and smearing some of the goo around his mouth — not the best of ploys at the neighborhood singles bar. Still, the thought of *buying* female companionship appalled him. Pons wasn't that kind of guy.

Pons had been the captain's right-hand man for some years now, and he enjoyed the role. It was Pons's money and manpower that had enabled their pet project to get off the ground in the first place. It was all very secret and a little bit scary, but if the captain was right, they would soon be as famous and respected as Edison, Marconi, Bell. Plus, they would be accomplishing something that was good and right and true. Pons felt this very strongly, because he shared the captain's awe and enthusiasm for the untapped wonders of the electromagnetic spectrum. The captain had been visiting the House of Pons regularly now for three years, overseeing the work, sharing the problems, and now they were *so close.* . . .

When the captain had finished his snack, he pointed to the basement door and nodded at Pons. Pons reached for the key ring on his belt — the big silver kind that janitors wear — and unlocked the door, revealing a long steep flight of stone steps. The captain paused at the basement door. Last night had been another rough one, and there had been altogether too many of *those* lately. Last night, first thing after getting high, the captain had demanded access to the basement, and Pons had led him down these selfsame steps. Sorrowful, sorrowful. . . .

They reached the bottom of the stairs and ducked under an arch-
way and entered a huge workroom, part laboratory, part pied-à-terre.
The House of Pons had been built into the sloping face of the sea
cliffs by some turn-of-the-century spice baron who had cleverly anticipated the advent of the split-level concept. A separate double-doored
entrance, some twenty feet high, connected the basement work space
with a rear driveway along which two semis could easily have passed
without touching. One wall of the work room was dominated by a
neat rack of oscilloscopes, board testers, digital voltmeters, and sam-
ples of the latest Tangerine Dream computer systems. A large refrigerator and a pup tent held taut at each of its four corners by cement
blocks occupied one corner of the room.

The captain stood and stared at the apparatus in the center of the
room, scratching absently at his tangled beard. It was thrilling to be
a part of history. The captain was not ashamed to admit this. History
was an odd beast, anyway; a game played with the football of truth.
History, as the captain had discovered by dint of his own painstaking
efforts, was, almost always, something quite different from what you
thought it was.

From a distance, the machine which dominated the center of the
room resembled a gleaming silver dunce cap; a strange conical tower
standing almost twenty feet high, flared sharply at the base and wrapped
tightly with hair-thin wire. Inside the cone, hidden from view, was a
maze of niobium circuitry, connectors, junctions, amplifiers, and assorted microscopic devices.

The coil.

This is what the captain had come to see.

It began roughly six years before, with a series of fan letters. Mash
notes, really. What distinguished the captain's correspondence was
the single-pointed nature of Frank's ardor. The captain didn't much
care about Alejandro's aboveboard history. He wasn't impressed by
Alejandro's multimillion-dollar corporate enterprise. He was grateful
for the niobium circuit but he knew that if Alejandro hadn't refined
it into something wonderful, somebody else would have. And while
the captain knew that the SEEK system was a peerless achievement,
he was also hip enough to know what SEEK was *really* about, and
he did not shy away from pointing this out to Alejandro in his letters.

SEEK wasn't about electronic banking or air traffic control or missile guidance. No. The truth about SEEK's history was something
altogether different. The SEEK system was a monument to the modern art of surveillance and control. The secret of SEEK was that

there were no secrets at all. The captain had said as much, many times, to anyone who would listen. And of course, nobody would. If you couldn't finesse your way into the SEEK network undercover, then there wasn't any point in being on the network at all. Each and every scrap of data ended up in the basement of the NSA. Everything. SEEK got it all. SEEK was the answer to the riddle behind the NSA's growing hegemony among American intelligence operations. And nobody seemed to know it.

The CIA: Bumbling cloak-and-dagger clowns with poison pens, strictly from the nineteenth century.

The FBI: A gaggle of professional wrestlers who didn't have the wit to keep from tripping over their own shoelaces.

The NSA, though, they had it all: thanks to SEEK. The NSA held the keys to your kingdom, whatever it might be. If you were a congressman, or a general, or a Fortune 500 capitalist, and you wanted more than your share of the pie, well . . . the NSA was your baby.

Frank could only conclude that Alejandro, visionary that he was, had somehow been innocent of SEEK's true intention, or had been coerced into the project.

Frank didn't believe that networks of electronic surveillance and information gathering were Alejandro's bag. Frank had read everything that had ever been written by or about Alejandro, and he was convinced that Alejandro's true interests were decidedly more esoteric and thoughtful. Frank knew of the turn-of-the-century work of his own illustrious countryman Nikola Tesla — he knew about the concept of the coil, and he could read between the lines. He *knew* what Alejandro had been after, at least at one point in Alejandro's life. In letter after letter, the captain soared eloquently on the subject of the coil, and indignantly on the subject of SEEK. To these letters Frank appended sketches, diagrams, theories, equations — rather good ones, he thought.

Alejandro never answered.

A week after the captain's last letter, Anton DeBroer showed up and had a talk with him. They'd been reading Alejandro's mail. Of course.

Lean times for the captain.

But Frank kept the faith, and was eventually rewarded. After several years, Alejandro came through — but not in person. Frank well understood the necessity for a go-between. Alejandro, by then well ensconced in his jungle hideaway, could no longer hope to carry on the research by himself. Frank had heard rumors that an entire transponder on one of the NSA's satellites was dedicated solely to Alejandro's surveillance. If Alejandro so much as flicked on a light switch, the agency would know about it at once. Any perturbation of the electromagnetic field near Alejandro's home would be immediately known, and analyzed. The chances of Alejandro's building and testing a coil without NSA interference were nil. It was not hard to understand why Alejandro had chosen Frank as his agent in this work.

The captain, under phone company surveillance which he grandiosely fancied to be every bit as tight as Alejandro's, had to wait almost two years before an opportunity to actually try building a coil presented itself, in the form of Pons Grozniev. Pons had the money and the technical resources and, in the spirit of technological adventure, was willing, once the captain had explained to him the nature of the undertaking.

The rest would be history, or so the captain hoped.

Maybe once in a lifetime, if you were earnest and right-minded and diligent enough; if, above all else, you were objective enough to recognize it, truth would come strolling up and bite you on the ass.

This coil was the truth. The truth *in potentia*. Captain Crash felt humbled in its presence. He felt himself part of some grand design, some chain of transmission begun long before his birth and destined to continue long after he'd become meat for the worms. I am only an agent, the captain thought. An instrument.

Pons crossed behind the captain and slipped through the flaps of the orange pup tent, emerging with a tattered yellow hardback book, the Wilhelm-Baynes translation of the *I Ching*. The captain groaned inwardly, viewing Pons through slitted, disbelieving eyes. From time to time Pons fancied himself a Taoist. Many people believed, mistakenly, that Alejandro fancied himself one, too. This conclusion had been erroneously drawn from the fact that the DID Corporation's logo was the yin-yang symbol of unity done in red and black — a circle neatly bisected into two equal regions by a line resembling the common sine wave. People who viewed this as proof of something spiritual in Alejandro's nature were sorely misled, lacking sufficient grounding in industrial history. Alejandro had simply appropriated the symbol from the Technocracy movement of the thirties and forties — a doomed soviet of technicians, dedicated to science in the service of human needs, who had, in turn, appropriated the age-old symbol from Lao-tzu and his cult of Chinese necromancers, fortune-tellers, and filthy voodoo artists.

"You wanna throw one?" Pons inquired, nodding in the direction of first the captain, then the coil.

"No," the captain answered tersely, "I don't."

"You used to."

"I know."

There are no secrets, the captain was thinking. Nothing there for the divining. Nothing inside the box. No one's hiding anything. There is only current and undercurrent, major chord and minor chord. No one's hiding anything but this — everything you know is a lie. Master that one fact, and the secrets unlock themselves.

Pons disappeared back inside the tent. In a moment the captain could hear the sound of coins clinking and falling. He thought of telling Pons that the Creator was a mechanic, now retired, who wouldn't come to the phone anymore.

Captain Crash turned to face the coil once again. He resolved to remember to take photographs soon. Pons probably hadn't thought of it. Too young to know. The captain wanted photographs; some pictorial culmination he could add to his tattered scrapbook. Thank God he'd secreted all of Alejandro's diagrams and notes here at the House of Pons some months ago. Yes, photographs. Something to slip in alongside his photos of the century's earlier, misdirected adventures. There weren't many. A fuzzy black-and-white of Nikola Tesla, putting the finishing touches on his own antique curiosity in Colorado Springs, a memorable gambit in its own right in those pretransistorized days of yore.

And there was an even fuzzier shot of the crude coil built by the German known as Conrad, photo courtesy of Alejandro Hunt. And another print, this one in true Kodak color, of Robert Golka standing before *his* version of the coil in an abandoned Air Force hangar in Utah. Project Thunderball. Nice try, Air Force. But you weren't privy to the *papers*. No way to make a go of it without them. Lost files, redirected and misdirected . . . shunted who knew where . . . forgotten. Destined, from the official viewpoint, to become just another paranoid's wet dream, another Air Force Blue Book. A source of endless speculation, a magnet pulling every conceivable brand of crank and crazy out of the woodwork.

What would the Sage of the Southern Yucatan give to be standing here with the captain, admiring this conical gleaming monument to his dreams? What was SEEK compared to this? The captain thought of himself and Alejandro as soul mates. Alejandro Hunt, if he was

116

still alive and sane, would have to read about it in the papers like everybody else. Shameful.

Little Pons crawled out of the tent and faced the captain triumphantly, brandishing his yellow book. "Hexagram eighteen," he announced breathlessly. "Decay. It means, 'Work on what has been spoiled.'"

The captain, taken aback, tried not to show it. Work on what has been spoiled. Geez Louise. Too close for comfort. The captain took a Snickers bar from his pocket, unwrapped it, and stuffed it whole into his mouth.

" 'What has been spoiled through man's fault can be made good again through man's work,' " said Pons, reciting from The Judgement. " 'It is not immutable fate . . . that has caused the state of corruption, but rather the abuse of human freedom.' I'm excerpting here. 'We must not recoil from work and danger. . . . Decisiveness and energy must take the place of the inertia and indifference that have led to decay, in order that the ending may be followed by a new beginning.' "

"Are you through?" inquired the captain acidly, but it was no good. Pons could read the effect of his recitation very plainly on the captain's face.

"We'll get it right, Captain," Pons cheerily assured him. "Just you wait."

ELEVEN

PETER RAISED the chair over his head with both hands and threw it with all his might. The sound of breaking glass was music to his ears. In the instant before he jumped, the ridiculous truth flashed through his mind. It had been ten disgusting years since the night of his ignominious flying exit from the captain's quarters in East Palo Alto. And now, tonight, once again, he found himself leaping desperately out a second-story window.

He aimed for a tall thicket of azaleas, and missed. He flexed his knees and rolled upon impact, and did it badly. Just like the last time. Some things you never learn.

He scrambled to his feet and tore around toward the back of the house, just as Anton burst through the front door in pursuit. Fish Dog was at Peter's heels, wondering what was up.

Ignore what hurts. Just fly it.

Peter sprinted to the end of his backyard, where the river began. Without looking back, he jumped, and Fish Dog jumped with him.

Telling the big lie had been a mistake. Even so, Anton had immediately released his grip on Peter's hair. When Peter had managed to blink away the tears, he said, "It's not so easy to do. If there's even a hint of surveillance, he'll spook."

There was no reply from Anton. Peter was locked in his fixed, immutable stare for what seemed like a lifetime. A wave of nausea cramped him. *He doesn't believe me. He isn't going to bite. Why should he?*

His only hope was that Anton had already pumped Ada and Leonard and Holsa, and had come up dry. His only chance lay in the possibility that Anton *needed* to believe him, however much logic dictated otherwise.

"Alejandro's been interested in my work for a long time," Peter said, nervously filling the gap. "It all started when I — "

Anton cut him off. "Just do it," Anton said.

Peter tried to still his trembling knees. What was it the rock climbers called it? Sewing-machine legs.

"I can do it over the phone," Peter said. "I have to get something out of the bedroom first."

Anton looked at him suspiciously. "What might that be?"

"A phone number."

Anton cocked his head, saying, "You don't have it memorized?"

Peter's mind raced. "It changes," he said.

Anton nodded curtly to Eddie. "Go with him," he said.

Eddie followed Peter to the base of the steep bedroom steps. Peter hesitated. "After you," he said weakly.

"That's okay," Eddie answered. "Be my guest."

Peter climbed the stairs slowly, conscious of the need to have Eddie as close behind him as possible. When he was three steps from the landing he stopped, turning to look down at Anton.

"There's one other thing."

Anton, now leaning against the phone table, looked up at him questioningly. "Yes?"

Peter shifted his gaze to the ceiling. He appeared to be deep in thought. Without looking down he cocked his right leg and kicked Eddie squarely in the chest. Eddie's hands flew off the banister and clawed frantically at the air. His body hit the living room floor with a solid thump, and Peter heard the air go out of him. Peter took the last three steps in one leap and sprinted out of Anton's line of sight. He picked up the chair next to his bedroom window, and when he was certain that he heard Anton's feet rattling the banister in pursuit, he let it fly.

Peter was swallowed up and sealed over by tons of pluming water. He had intended to swim underwater as far as his held breath would take him, but that did not happen. Instead, he surfaced almost immediately, sputtering and shell-shocked, panting as he tried to force air into his lungs.

Nothing had a right to be this cold.

The current swept him swiftly away from the shore, out of sight of

Anton and the A-frame. He felt paralyzed, and his mind held only a single thought: Hypothermia, and good-bye.

Don't *die* for this.

He rolled helplessly, sucked along by the powerful pull of the river. He smashed up against something solid and saw a star-burst of white light, followed by red and purple streamers, like comets. His right knee throbbed. He was underwater again. Another sharp object collided with his right elbow as he surfaced. He fought back the retching, and sculled frantically with his arms until he had managed to get himself over on his back, leading with his Frye boots, hoping he could fend off any further rocks or snags with his feet. He was a good swimmer but smart enough to know that it didn't make any difference. Once, when he was thirteen years old, he broke through the ice of a lake and spent sixty seconds dog-paddling in shock before his father fished him out. It was nothing like this.

So cold. Got to stay conscious. Got to get out.

The midstream darkness was nearly total. Shadows floated by him on the shore. There was no sound except the surge of the current and his shallow, labored gasps.

Something loomed up ahead of him to his right, just back from the water's edge. When it was almost too late, Peter recognized the shape as Sig's grape arbor. It dominated the whole of the Olmos backyard, one very long block downstream from Peter's own house. Peter rolled over on his stomach and struck out for shore, his numb right leg trailing uselessly behind him.

When he reached the shore, he forced himself to crawl upward through the weeds and rocks until he reached the wet grass that marked the beginning of the Olmos backyard. He collapsed on his belly and lay there gathering strength for a final surge toward the house.

He did not know how long he lay there, only that at some point he rose, coughing and spitting, and lurched toward the back door of Sig's house. He pounded on the door until the yard lights came on. He heard the click of the screen door opening and then Sig was peering out at him in astonishment.

Peter looked at him gratefully. "Fell in," he gasped. And then, without further ado, he fell down.

TWELVE

W HEN PETER came to, he was stretched out on a couch belonging to Sig and Tillie Olmos, his neighbors down the block. He was swaddled tightly in an old army blanket. He felt naked, and he was.

He sneezed. It was a major sneeze, but only a prelude. Six or seven sneezes later, his nose began to flow copiously. Mrs. Olmos handed him a Kleenex and a hot cup of tea in a powder blue cup as fragile as an eggshell. He sat up slowly in his blanket and flexed his right leg. Bruised badly but not broken.

"Take her real easy," Sig advised him from across the room. Then Sig walked over to have a look-see, his absurd house slippers making a sad shuffling sound on the threadbare carpet of the living room. "Take some deep breaths."

Feeling a little light-headed at that, Peter did what Sig suggested, and it helped. The feeling of weightlessness began to drop away, but the price for it was a swift and wrenching headache. Peter arched his back and stretched, causing a great popping of joints and crackling of cartilage.

Sig was peering down at him. Anxiously, Peter wondered whether either of them had called a doctor. The more he watched Sig, the more he thought not. Sig was a tough one. Thirty-five years in a shake mill, running cedar slabs past a high-speed band saw, and missing two fingers to prove it. Sig wouldn't call anybody, not for a little impromptu dip in the winter Willamette. Peter tried to relax.

He told Sig and Tillie that he had been trying to get the Scout started, when Fish Dog took off toward the river in pursuit of a beaver. When Peter went down to chase the dog off the scent, he slipped and fell in, and banged himself pretty good, and couldn't make the bank of the river until he reached Sig's place. The lie came easily to his lips. It was not a comforting discovery.

Peter knew he had to hurry. Anton was probably working the whole row of houses right this minute.

"Sig," Peter said, "I have to ask you a favor. The alternator's shot on my Scout. Won't hold a charge. I'll miss work tomorrow unless I get over to a friend's house and pick up a new one. He's only going to be home a little while longer."

Sig said, "You sure you're feeling up to it?"

"No problem," Peter said, with as much false heart as he could manage. "I was wondering if I could borrow your car for a half hour or so." Peter noticed a neat pile of Sig's work clothes beside the couch. Tillie's doing. "I'd be real appreciative." It was the kind of do-it-yourself-on-the-cheap logic Sig could appreciate, Peter figured.

Sig didn't look convinced. "I'll drive ya over," Sig said.

"No need," Peter said quickly. "Really."

"Happy to do it," Sig countered, with a firmness that did not admit of argument.

"Great," Peter said tonelessly. He pointed at the pile of clothes. "Where can I get dressed?"

Peter gave directions from the passenger's seat, making them up on the spot. He felt the fear rising up his spine again. Amazingly, Fish Dog had followed Peter on his river odyssey, and was now happily sitting in the backseat, over Sig's mild objections. As Sig rolled the Buick out of the garage and into the street, Peter ducked beneath the dash, feigning some minor adjustment to the work boots Sig had loaned him.

Peter selected a route that would bring them near the big shopping center near the freeway. As they neared it, Peter said, "Would you mind pulling in by the Rexall, Sig? I've got a splitting headache."

"Don't doubt it," Sig replied, obligingly turning in at the mall entrance. He parked in front of the drugstore, then turned and looked at Peter, waiting for him to exit. Peter smiled sheepishly. "No money," Peter said. "I left it all in my pants." What an idiot he was. He'd been too groggy on the couch to remember.

Sig didn't seem to mind. He turned off the ignition and stepped out of the car. Go, Peter urged him silently.

Sig ducked back inside. "You just want aspirin," he said.

"Aspirin would be fine."

It was undoubtedly his imagination, but Peter could have sworn that he saw Sig's eyes alight casually on the key ring in the ignition. "Excedrin would be better," Peter said hurriedly. "If they're still open."

Sig walked to the door of the drugstore and disappeared inside. Peter counted ten and then slid across the seat. He started the Buick and pulled away, feeling like a first-class asshole. Sig was a nice guy, a friend. Peter made a left turn at the end of the mall complex and lead-footed it around to the back, bouncing horribly over a trio of speed bumps. Sorry, Sig. Forgive me.

Peter cruised the rows of parked cars near the rear entrance to Penney's, cursing the feeble power of Sig's defroster, until he found what he was looking for. Out-of-state plates. Wisconsin numbers on a Ford station wagon. He was crazily confident that Sig was the kind of man who would carry tools in his trunk. He was right. He found a screwdriver right away, and the whole operation took less than five minutes. It wasn't likely that Mom and Dad and the kids from Wisconsin would notice the switch in the dark.

Sig would report the vehicle stolen, and that pained Peter. But the fresh plates would be enough to confound the local constabulary for the time it would take him to get clear of town. There were plenty of Buicks on the road. He could switch plates again, later that evening.

It might even work.

Peter roared through the sleepy suburbs of Portland, trusting to luck and statistics to keep him free of a speeding ticket. He veered sharply off the freeway at the first Beaverton exit, knowing that what he had in mind was foolish and dangerous — and worse than that.

"Stupid," he muttered. "Stupid, stupid."

He told himself he was on a mission of mercy. But the truth was, he hadn't decided precisely whom he was intending to save.

In downtown Beaverton, there were deep puddles at the intersections where fallen leaves had clogged and diked the street drains. It was like driving through a succession of shallow streams, and Sig's bloated boat of a Buick was exactly the wrong car for it. Rain, rain, never goes away. Cabo San Lucas. Mazatlán. He didn't know a word of Spanish. Check that. *Hasta la vista.*

If Alison knows how to contact David, Peter thought, then I will warn him. That way, Anton and the colonel will be blanked out completely. Three strikes, and no pinch hitters.

Is that what you really intend to do?

Alejandro's our man, Peter thought. Would it matter to Alejandro if he knew how badly he was chewing up innocent lives? Did he know already?

David's phone will be live, just like yours. Warn David, and you give yourself away.

He knew he was not thinking clearly now, but he didn't care. He realized, finally, what it was he intended to do.

David's a big boy. We're all big boys now. Even her.

*   *

Alison was sitting in her living room, waiting for David to call. When he didn't, she migrated back to the kitchen, hoping to find something there that would divert her attention. When nothing clicked, she tried a small glass of Amaretto. She appreciated the sharp bloom of the liquor at the back of her throat, but it made her feel slightly nauseated and she put down the glass unfinished.

She tried the couch again. Asa had the hiccups. They swallow some amniotic fluid and then these little rhythmic hitches go on and on. It was the weirdest feeling.

In another few minutes, she wouldn't care whether David called or not. That was bad.

She stared fixedly at the Paul Klee on the wall across from her — little triangular animals, like baby chicks, against a red background. She stared at them until her eyes watered and they were still little triangular chicks against. . . . *What's the matter with you?*

It isn't all hormones.

She scrunched down on the couch and let her gaze travel across the living room. A baby grand piano on a polished wood floor, surrounded by a bare minimum of furnishings, dominated the left half of the large room. David played well, in a self-mocking way. It was something he picked up from his parents and he didn't take it seriously at all. He was always quick to dismiss the things he was good at. Take no praise and give no quarter; always full speed ahead. Always looking for trouble.

Alison felt both tired and restless at the same time. Whenever she turned her head or shifted position on the couch she felt slight twinges of discomfort in her legs and her back. It didn't help when David was late in calling. She didn't know where he was, what he was doing, when he was coming home. In the past, whenever she'd found herself bottled up like this, she had often gone for a walk, or to a movie alone. She vowed to do just that, as soon as David called.

This wasn't the way she had imagined it. You staved off the impulse for years, putting up with the pills and devices, the jellies and foams, all the bodily insults you longed to forgo, waiting for your lives to come into proper balance, and then when it happened, and the new life inside you began to grow, things went from bad to worse. The worst they'd ever been. She knew David was in deep — she could read a bank statement.

There was a time when she'd taken the gambling as a personal affront, an insult to *her,* as if it were nothing but a symptom of some deeply rooted insensitivity. She knew better now. David needed to season his life with the Big Risk. David needed to push beyond what he had. David could not trust what worked.

"I'm afraid of falling asleep." David's words. The gambling was his way of injecting an eye-opening measure of darkness into his life. He'd been spiraling downward for months now: frenetic bursts at the tables and the track, hushed dealings and midnight phone calls from someone named Anton, David growing more sullen and unpredictable every day, his sense of humor flagging, almost quenched. The tension had been piling up for too long. It all came through; Asa shared in everything. It was placental conspiracy.

She needed a thick, layering blanket of calmness in her life, and couldn't muster it.

It should have been so easy. This mundane miracle within her should have changed him.

She didn't know what to expect, so she found herself expecting the worst.

Killing time, Alison got down on the floor and began running through her prenatal exercises. She could see pieces of herself in one of the window bays. David had wanted glass block everywhere, but Alison had resisted. She didn't want the whole place looking like a doctor's office. Any more of it and you'd begin to smell the alcohol.

She tried to concentrate on her exercises, but was only partially successful. My life, she thought, has become a soap opera of veiled intentions, covert side steps. If you know what you want, she told herself, you should go and get it. Okay: I want surcease. I want it for Asa and Asa wants it for me. Me and the Ace, we have to win this in the end.

She started out with a few easy warm-ups in her gray sweat suit, following with some mild yoga postures — asanas for the gravid. Her foster mother had done hatha-yoga in a black leotard every morning of her life because Gloria Swanson, her celluloid heroine, had written a book about it.

Alison finished with the exercises and started practicing her La-maze breathing. So what does it all add up to? she asked herself. The strain is getting to be too much. All of her impulses were pulling her inward, and all the forces in her life were pulling her outward. Some sort of breaking point was inevitable. . . .

She was huffing her way through the transition breath when she was startled by a loud, impatient pounding at the front door. She had not even managed to pick herself up off the floor when Peter burst into the living room unheralded. His timing was less than adroit.

"Jesus, Pete! Where do you get off making an entrance like that? I thought you were a — " Seeing his taut face, the grim set of his features, she stopped. Not again, she thought. No more intrigue, please. When David calls, I'll put these two together and let them thrash it out.

Peter looked furtively around the room as if he expected to see someone else. She saw that slight glaze of disapproval on his face. She saw it almost every time he came to the house, and looked at the appointments. It's so hard for him to understand about David and me, she thought. He doesn't know. He takes it all at face value. Peter could live in a cardboard box, as long as there was room for his dog.

"Grab some things, Al," Peter said curtly. "We have to leave. I'll tell you about it on the go."

She stared at him, puzzled by his cryptic command and at the same time awed by the insensitivity of it. Alison knew Peter like she knew David, and they were both something else. Both damaged in almost imperceptible ways. Incapable, most of the time, of anything resembling sustained forward motion. All the running-in-place spe-cialties her boys concocted! The fishing and the gambling. How did it all get started? Where, she wondered, in silent imitation of her foster mother, did all the nice boys go?

She said, "What is *that* supposed to mean? Go where? Tell me about what?"

"Big trouble," Peter said. "Pack some things." He watched her closely, trying to gauge the strength of her resistance, weighing it against the pounding pressure of his own fear.

She bristled, saying, "You're just like David, you know that? You fly by now and then, drop me a few crumbs of information, not enough to make any *sense* out of, mind you — "

"We're going to make a hasty exit, stage left. I'll explain later."

"Explain yourself *now*."

"No time."

"All the time in the world," she said firmly. "I've got my own problems, you know? Yours are just not that interesting to me at the moment. David's going to call any minute, and when he does — "

"They're going to arrest him, babe," Peter said. He had not wanted to reveal this until the two of them were safely out of town.

A flush of uncertainty rose in her cheeks.

"They're going to frame him for sabotaging SEEK. It won't stick, but that doesn't matter at the moment."

She said, "He didn't do it."

He marveled at that. "Of course not. You have to understand that it doesn't make the slightest bit of difference."

Her eyes never left his. "Then we have to warn him," she said.

"We can't help him unless we find the person they *really* want. And we aren't going to be able to do that unless we stay clear of trouble. If you stick around here playing the brave little wife, they will crucify you, Al. They might even throw you into the pot as an accomplice. Is that what you want? How are we going to help David get clear of this if you and I get arrested as well?"

She continued to study his face, his eyes, and he was forced to look away. He felt her groping steadily toward the truth. "I thought *you* were the suspect." She said this slowly, drawing out the words.

Peter felt his heart rolling over. "I was," he said. "Now it's him."

"I'm not going anywhere," she said.

"Yeah," he said roughly, "you are."

She was shaking badly now. "We have to stay cool," she said. She walked deliberately to the couch, measuring her steps, and sat down. "We have to think."

"Get your things," he said again.

She did not move.

"The only way to help him is to get the hell out of here. We have to stay clear of trouble. By tomorrow morning, maybe before that, there will be a hundred reporters and photographers at your door. That's assuming they don't just bust you, too. There's no time."

The telephone rang.

Peter turned and headed for the kitchen extension. With surprising swiftness, Alison ducked around him and grabbed the receiver off the wall.

It was David.

"David," she said frantically, her back to Peter. "Pete's here. He — "

Peter reached around her and yanked the phone cord out of the wall socket.

She stared dully at the dead receiver. "He trusts you, Pete," she said. "You're supposed to *know* that."

Peter had the sensation of falling down a dark, airless shaft. "It's bugged, Al. The only way to help him is to find the person they *really* want. That's absolutely our only chance."

She wasn't listening. "I want you to leave," she said, biting off each word with finality. "Don't come back here again."

"Okay," he said quietly.

He asked her for money. She got some out of her purse and handed it to him, wordlessly.

"Does David have a gun in the house? A pistol?"

She hesitated a moment too long. "No."

"Go get it."

Another painful pause. "No."

Peter ran upstairs. He checked the bed stand, checked the closet, and found a .38 in David's underwear drawer. It was loaded. There was a pile of change and several crumpled bills on the dresser, and he pocketed those as well. He went back downstairs and found her on the couch again. She did not look at him. Peter spotted David's portable home computer in its case by the door. He carried it out to the car, and then he returned.

Peter had no recollection of having decided to do it. As if in a dream, he found himself walking Alison down the front sidewalk, holding her in a light arm-lock. She did not resist, which only succeeded in making him feel worse than he already felt. This was as low as it got.

He wrenched open the door of the Buick and pushed her inside.

"You're sick," she told him. For just one instant, he considered letting her go. She did not attempt to flee. Everything she did made it worse. There's still time to stop this, he thought.

As he stood by the open door, he heard the sound of a car turning hard into the Atwoods' cul-de-sac. As the headlights bore down on him, Peter jammed one shoulder against the side of the car to steady himself and pulled David's pistol free of his jacket pocket. He held the pistol with two hands. The car slowed, Peter illuminated in its headlights. Peter fired twice and the headlights winked out with a hiss of broken glass. With the lights out, he could see that there was only one man in the car. He fired twice more, into Anton's windshield, passenger side. There was the squealing sound of tires chewing madly against pavement, Anton swerving in reverse, sideswiping a parked car.

Alison screamed. Peter leaped behind the wheel and grabbed Alison by the back of the neck, jamming her down low in the seat. He spun the Buick around and jounced over the curb. Anton was in the process of executing a three-point turn. Peter drove across the Atwoods' lawn, and two adjoining lawns, until he was past Anton's vehicle. He cornered hard at the intersection, and floored it, and did not look back.

THIRTEEN

ONLY TWO MINOR incidents had conspired to mar David Atwood's otherwise ebullient mood that Monday — the abrupt manner in which his phone call to Al had been cut off, and the front-page headline he'd caught in the evening *Oregonian*: "GLITCHES IN SEEK SYSTEM LINKED TO COMPUTER TERRORIST-AT-LARGE."

For the moment, he was willing to forgo any morbid speculation about the phone call. He was sitting in a roadside restaurant near Salem, only about fifty miles from his home, and with any luck he'd be pulling into his driveway in an hour or so. David felt he could afford to sustain the theory that sometimes a dead phone was nothing but a dead phone — nothing more sinister than the phone company screwing up. It had been known to happen. Yes, thought David, and sometimes a cigar is just a cigar. But not very often.

He was also willing to rein in that unpleasant feeling that had surged through him when he slid a quarter into the newspaper rack and read the first few paragraphs of the lead article: "A troubling series of malfunctions and irregularities on the SEEK system, the nation's premier computer network, appears to be the work of an unidentified computer criminal, according to highly placed sources at Portland's DID Corporation."

I'll be damned, David thought. Score one for Peter. Curiouser and curiouser, to quote Alice, who was almost always quotable when the subject was the SEEK system. This is going to translate into one hell of a shake-up. I will have to ask Anton about this.

"On at least one occasion," the story continued,

sensitive financial transactions carried on the SEEK system, ranging from IMF loan transfers to corporate bonds trading, were temporarily disrupted. Additional reports indicate that confidential patent and research material belonging to the Consolidated Research Consortium may have been erased or stolen from the SEEK memory files, and there have been unconfirmed reports of information blackouts at the highest levels of military command.

The disturbing incidents have cast a pall of doubt over the SEEK system's reputation as the most reliable computer system in the world, experts say. No arrests have been made in the case thus far, according to. . . .

David tried not to let this news dampen his spirits. He would allow no dark stains on his newly stitched fabric of optimism. Every possible complication in his life paled in comparison to the giddy joy of getting himself out from under DeBroer at last. The SEEK redesign had been halted — there would be no more exchanges after tonight.

This ends it, David thought. Whatever heat Anton applied, David was prepared to deflect it. Anton was one spooky piece of work. So long, pal, David thought with a shudder. It's been real.

David had stashed the goods in a U-Store-It several days ago — getting them out had been only a minor logistical problem, as usual. It was so much easier than anybody was willing to admit. When Anton had slipped him an unexpected and peremptory request for this meeting, David had not been angry, or nervous or scared, because he knew it was the last dance. Best to get it over with, even when it meant canceling his scheduled paper the next afternoon on grounds of illness and hopping a plane to Salem and renting another car for the drive upvalley. This abruptness on Anton's part was puzzling, but no doubt Anton had his reasons. David didn't know what they were, and he was just too happy to care.

David sat at the counter and sipped his coffee, waiting for Anton to show. He idly scanned the nearly empty restaurant, wondering what sort of mad psychologist had been in charge of decor. These stools at the counter — puce?

Outside the windows of the restaurant a solid curtain of water cascaded off the roof — the never-ending winter rain. Half the sod on the lawn out front had been washed away. The roof had no rain gutters. Nobody had thought of it; some contractor had put the place up, and hadn't remembered that you needed rain gutters in Oregon. David was fascinated by this. He was a collector of willfully stupid incidents.

It was so easy, sometimes, to lose faith in the possibility of change. Even to accept it as a working hypothesis — that change was possible — was sometimes asking too much.

It had been one very weird and revelatory weekend. First, there was his latest disaster in Tahoe. There would be no more of that, no more high-tech enhancements. He had thrown away the whole works in a fit of disgust — the glasses, the minicomputer, the toe switches — all of it. The slide he was on had finally come clear to him. You get caught once with that kind of gear, and any casino in Nevada is going to want to make a very visible and costly example out of you. They were all very scared about all that brand new wizardry anyway — people out there breaking every slot machine in sight with gizmos of one kind or another.

Another revelation, a related one, had struck him forcefully in the past couple of days as well: his attempted embezzlement on the SEEK lines, courtesy of Peter's ID sequence. Peter didn't deserve that. Never again.

And when you piled those two stunts on top of his escapades on Anton's behalf, it added up to nothing more noble than straight crime, and for that you got straight time, and that was one giant step over the line. You *do* grow up, David was thinking. You don't have any choice. That's biology for you.

David knew exactly why he had done these things — no mystery there. He had been able to achieve, in each case, a glorious magnification of that fine wailing thrust of adrenaline that had always been his at the tables. It was the one drug he could not live without. He needed that boost, in order to ward off the enervating sense of flatness that seeped in and surrounded his life whenever he wasn't looking. Peter understood it, a little. David wished he could do it Peter's way. Just quit and go fishing. Wouldn't that be sweet.

In the face of all this, the cause of David's happiness was simple: his unbelievable luck. He was no believer in omens but it was hard to ignore the solid fact of his good fortune. The computer-aided gambling, the embezzlement, the thefts on Anton's behalf — safe on all counts. He'd pushed himself far enough out on the limb to get good and dizzy, and now he was ready to pack it in. The ceaseless adrenaline buzz had turned into a nightmarish headache instead of a high.

David sipped his coffee and tried to stretch his limbs sufficiently at the cramped counter. He was anxious for Anton's arrival. Well, he told himself, these are noble thoughts, fine sentiments, but I don't know. I just don't know.

It was frightening to contemplate all the instances when he had made exactly this vow. Because it was frightening, he banished the thought, and remembered the Ace, and was happy again. This last exchange with Anton was destined to be a lucrative one. He owed the money ten times over, but tough shit. The first thing was to lay it all out for Alison, as soon as he got home, and then he would have to borrow some money from Pete in order to stay afloat for the short term. Pete would oblige. His money simply piled up in a savings and loan; he was a financial primitive and he didn't care.

Yes, David thought, Asa makes it different — and so does this chance to get out from under Anton. This is where it starts.

Anton DeBroer was scowling, as usual, when he entered the restaurant at a few minutes past ten. That was all right with David. He'd seen Anton smiling once or twice, and it was an appalling sight. In Anton's case, the joke was always on somebody else.

Anton took a seat at the counter beside David. "Hey, Anton," David said jovially, "you ever hear about the shy bride and the frustrated groom?"

"Let's go out to the car," Anton said.

David signaled for the waitress. "The guy says to his new wife, 'Honey, I know you don't like to talk about it, so I've worked out a code. When you feel like making love, just pull once on my pecker. And when you're not in the mood, just pull on it like, say, ninety-nine times.'"

Anton's expression did not change. David shrugged. "I'd like a great big coffee to go," he said to the waitress.

"We only got one size," she replied.

"Okay then," David said, "large." He burst out laughing, then turned to Anton. "Lighten up. Why so glum? This is celebration time. I'll explain it all to you in the car."

"I'll bet you will," Anton said.

David got his coffee and followed Anton out of the restaurant. They walked toward David's car under the ghastly light of the mercury vapor lamps that lit the parking lot. David yawned, feeling quite exhausted at the end of a long and problematic day. He was weary, as well, of the carrot and the stick. Anton always brought both. As they neared the car, David flagged his good spirits back to life and began rehearsing his swan song.

Anton reached the car, opened the door, and slid inside without a word. David got behind the wheel, his head just grazing the ceiling. Anton twisted around and took a small cardboard box from the backseat. The silvery light from the parking lot was giving him a headache. He placed the box on his lap and opened it, giving the contents a cursory glance. With their gold connecting pins buried in the Styrofoam liners of the carrying case, the niobium microchips in their multicolored plastic packages resembled a child's neatly arrayed collection of Lego blocks. The very latest SEEK chips, a bargain at any price. Anton was the first on his block, as usual.

David had no idea what Anton did with them, had never asked, hoped never to find out.

Why do you do it, DeBroer? This is what David had sometimes yearned to ask him, but he knew he never would. Always better not to know. Perhaps, thought David, our man Anton has his own share of fiduciary indiscretions to contend with.

Out of the corner of his eye, David caught Anton looking at him. Waiting. David smiled broadly, reaching into his pocket and handing Anton a small roll of film. "Documentation and testing. If you follow this, you get those."

Anton took the film without comment, then reached down and idly scratched his crotch. He turned and faced David squarely. "You have a little problem," he said quietly, "in the area of self-control."

David felt a slight tightness in his throat. *He hasn't handed me the money. He wants to squeeze.*

"You seem to have come to just about everybody's attention," Anton continued, in the same quiet, tutorial tone. "You seem to be the only one left standing in the pumpkin patch."

David had no idea what he was talking about. To David's complete amazement, Anton said, "I don't think I can continue to do business with you."

Fine by me, David was thinking. Never had a feeling been so mutual. David was about to tell him that the SEEK redesign work was over, that they were finished, when Anton said, "If you wanted a raise, you should have come to me. You shouldn't have decided to moonlight."

"I'm not following this."

"Your little fifth-level escapades have come to light. Congratulations."

"Impossible," said David, with all the false confidence he could muster.

"That embezzlement you pulled at DID. Your timing was remarkably injudicious."

"I experienced a temporary shortfall. Somebody's — "

"Shut up and listen. You used Cassidy's ID. So did Klaatu, as it happens. When DID caught somebody with his fingers in the pension till, they traced it to your terminal. Then they started combing back through all the SEEK transaction records, going back for months. You turned up as a statistical sore thumb. All those highly irregular fifth-level transactions you engaged in for the purpose of supplying me with testing data — they've all come to light. Nobody knows what to make of it yet. Nobody knows about our dealings. Your job is to make sure that things stay that way — after your arrest."

"My *arrest*? Anton, I can't believe I'm hearing this from you. All I did was, I jived my pension and benefits account a little bit. It was like a loan. I was only stealing my own money. I don't expect to live until I'm fifty-nine and a half."

"Not at this rate," Anton said.

David turned in his seat to face Anton, and started firing very coyly with both barrels. "Anton, you'd be blowing a big opportunity for both of us if you let this deal go down. I mean, what are you saying, my reputation's tarnished? You're a fixer, are you not? A man of affairs. A man of influence, no? You mean to tell me you're going to stand by and let them pop your business partner over a minor piece of gerrymandering like this? Dive in there and *square* it, Anton, I swear it won't happen again. We're a team, are we not? I always had you pegged as a realist, a pragmatist. We're great back-scratchers, you and I. Very talented rollers of logs, true? I can't believe you want to let this thing break up a winning team."

"You don't get it," Anton said. "They're going to charge you with the Klaatu incursion. Seventh-level breaks. That's treason, my friend. They need a suspect, and you're it."

David recovered, flashing Anton his most winning smile. "That's crazy, Anton. You mean to tell me you don't have any say in this? No clout at all? I thought that at least some portion of this investigation was in *your* hands."

Anton did what David hated to see most. Anton returned David's smile. "Your friend Cassidy, his hands aren't so clean right now, either."

When David made no reply, Anton said, "Actually, Cassidy just skipped town — *and he took your wife with him*. So when I bust

135

him, maybe I'll have to bust her, too. Maybe that would interest you. Just deserts, right? It's a crazy world, right?"

David felt like he'd been slapped. He's lying, David thought. He goes too far.

"Anton, let's just forget about all this. Find some deserving third party. I'll tell you, when you and I started out together three years ago I thought to myself, This Anton, I don't know if I can trust him. That's how foolish I was. Jittery, you know? That night you approached me in Vegas, when I was down a few tens of thousands — "

"Atwood," Anton said wearily, "you're an even more outrageous bullshitter than your friend Cassidy."

"Anton, have I not been, at all times, the very soul, the very epitome of discretion? Have I ever asked you what you do with this stuff I bring out for you? Have I ever pressed, kibitzed, reneged, nosed around? Ever done anything but play it straight for you?"

"That's enough," Anton said icily. "I *can* get you out of this. I'm the only one who can. But not right now. I was asked to assist in your capture, here on neutral turf, so as to avoid advance publicity. I told them I called you and let it be known that I had information pertaining to your embezzlement. They presume that you agreed to meet in the hopes of blackmailing me." Even Anton saw the irony in this.

"Here's what you do," Anton continued. "Simply advise your lawyers of your innocence in the matter of Klaatu. Tell them that your embezzlement was an attempt to clear yourself of certain hazardous gambling debts. That way you'll be telling the truth, and all the polygraph artists will be happy with you. DID will presume that your earlier fifth-level forays were in some way related to your recent theft."

David laughed, and it took Anton by surprise. The laugh ballooned up from somewhere deep inside him and swirled around in the space between them. All the shoes had dropped at once. It wasn't what David had expected — it was far worse — but he was determined to be free of it all, just the same. "You're afraid, aren't you?" David said. "This is going to be very interesting."

Anton did his best to appear as if he were ignoring David's remark. "As for this matter" — Anton touched the box on his lap, lightly. "Say nothing. You will not mention my name. If you so much as *breathe* in my direction, you'll go down in espionage history as Klaatu."

David laughed again.

136

Anton thought very seriously about hurting him, but then, with great reluctance, allowed the feeling to pass.

"You're scared," David said, "just like me. You're scared that they might shut it down. Close the whole circus."

"It should be clear to you that you're in no position to fuck with me over this."

"If they shut down SEEK because of Klaatu, your whole enterprise goes up in smoke. If they redesign everything to eliminate whatever flaws this Klaatu capitalized on, all the circuitry I stole for you becomes worthless. It's really very funny when you think about it. Whoever it is you sell to might not think you've been all that candid with them. You're supposed to be in the know, DeBroer. All your deals would end up looking like one giant con."

Anton began polishing his thumbnail.

"What's my guarantee in all this, DeBroer? How do I know you can get me off if I play ball? If you can't keep them from popping me in the first place, how the hell are you going to — "

"For your information, Klaatu happens to be none other than Alejandro Hunt, and when I get him I will take you off the hook."

"*If* you get him."

"Cassidy is going to lead me to him. But if you insist on talking out of turn while in custody, well . . . I will no longer feel obliged to serve as your benefactor in these proceedings. Alejandro will be dealt with quietly and you will go down in history as the most famous saboteur of the century. If the SEEK system can't be salvaged, then neither can the Peacemakers, in which case we might even be able to press for the death penalty."

"You are. You're scared as hell, DeBroer."

"You're forgetting something, my friend. You're about to go to prison for a spell — *and I know where your wife is.*"

David suddenly felt very cold.

"She's pregnant, isn't she?" Anton's voice was soothing, confidential. "You have to realize the delicacy of your position here. You're nothing to me, or to anyone else."

David was still looking out the windshield. His eyes were slits.

Anton said, "Are there any questions?"

David shook his head carefully, to indicate that there were none.

"Fine." Anton gestured toward the dashboard. "Turn on your headlights."

"What?"

"Turn on your headlights."

David reached past the steering wheel and pulled the knob. The headlights flared. Anton looked satisfied.

Nothing happened for several seconds. Then David saw them: three cars moving in unison across the parking lot. He heard the wail of sirens, and there was a wash of twirling blue lights as the squad cars wheeled expertly into position, one in front, one to the left, one to the right.

"If you hurt her, DeBroer — let me put this in terms you'll understand — if you so much as *breathe* in her direction — I'll blow your whole enterprise wide open. You'll be finished. Make sure you leave her alone."

Men climbed out of the cars, some in uniform, some not. Things were shaping up nicely, considering. Atwood was a risk that Anton would have to take. "That's your cue," Anton said. "You're on."

The car doors opened. Someone grabbed David roughly and hauled him from behind the wheel. A second man spun him around and jammed him up against a squad car, and a third man cuffed his hands behind his back.

"You have the right to remain silent. . . ."

David turned his head in time to observe Anton handing over the box of circuits to someone. In time to hear Anton say, "This was going to be his bribe." In time to notice that Anton had not handed over the roll of film.

Anton looked over at David sadly, the twisted smile once again in place.

They hustled David into a squad car and peeled off across the parking lot, the other two vehicles forming a convoy in front and behind.

David leaned back in the seat and tried not to notice the wire mesh all around him. His hands were trembling, and through a deliberate act of will, he stilled them. Over and over again, like a litany recited under his breath, he told himself: This is my lucky day. My luck runneth over.

And Anton's has run out.

THREE

FOURTEEN

DAWN WAS BEGINNING to show as an indistinct smudge of color against the hills at treeline. Peter pulled the Buick to the side of the road and parked near a snarly growth of low brush. Ahead of him the road climbed steadily, cutting across a high saddle, while far below him he could see a strip of brown marking the road they had taken at lower elevation. Alison walked into the bushes for a quick pee and Peter made a hasty check of the Buick's vital fluids. Low but not serious. Barges like this weren't built for hill climbing.

Peter took a pair of battered binoculars from the trunk — Sig, I'll make this up to you someday — and sat down on the hood of the car, balancing his elbows on his knees to form a steady viewing base. There was no sign of traffic on the main road below. It was just dark enough for Peter to doubt his own eyes.

To the best of his recollection, there were three Forest Service haul roads, marked only by numbers, branching off the road above them, just beyond the saddle. Exactly one of them would get him where he wanted to go. Let's hope memory serves, he thought, taking a last look downslope through the glasses. He could see no movement of any kind. Even if they were following, even if they had maps, they would have no way of knowing where Peter was headed.

It wasn't me, you bastards.

Peter got back in the car and gunned the engine. He watched Alison hitching up her sweatpants as she emerged from the bushes. The lack of sleep showed as a slight puffiness around her eyes. They had rested once, waiting for daylight, but they hadn't slept. They hadn't talked much, either. It had been a quiet night.

In a few miles Peter found the road he wanted. It was muddy but

141

passable. They would be entering the Red Zone any time now. He had his excuses ready but didn't expect to need them. The mountain had been silent for months, and the hundreds of geologists who had stumbled up and down its slopes in the wake of the first big explosion had long since returned, for the most part, to their labs and offices. Even so, Mount St. Helens was in no danger of being understudied.

Peter had been up in the Red Zone, where the real damage began, only a few weeks after the old girl blew her top. He'd hooked a ride with T.J., his old high school buddy who worked for the U.S. Geological Survey out of Vancouver, Washington, and who had a pass to go wherever he wanted. Peter remembered standing there with T.J., surveying the smoking barrens that had once been Spirit Lake, where the two of them had taken many trout, and gawked at many sunsets. "Jesus," T.J. had said, humbled by the aftermath of that magnificent belch of nature, the way it had taken everything and everybody out, just like that. "Jesus, it was beautiful." Freaked everybody out. Mountains only did that in the movies.

There was ash in the air then, like having a bag of Portland cement cracked open on your head. The ash was gone now, but as Peter swung the Buick into yet another dirt road, this one leading in the direction of the base of the mountain itself, very little else about the landscape seemed to have changed in the years since the eruption.

From their vantage point halfway up the wall of the main valley, they had the eagle's view of the reclamation work in progress along the river channel below. Dozens of yellow bulldozers and earth movers were beetling back and forth across the flats, rearranging the flood-driven soil, making mounded debris piles, gouging a new channel for the old river. It had been going on for years and there was no end in sight.

Farther up the valley, the landscape had not changed much, either. He drove slowly through acre after acre of dead forest; trees blown flat like matchsticks, their stumps encased in caked gray silt. It was eerie proof of both the force and direction of the blast. Only the stocky base of the mountain itself was visible in the distance, the gouge of the new crater swathed in a thick layer of low-lying cloud. Alison was curled inside an old cotton sleeping bag, another item from Sig's bottomless cache in the trunk. She leaned against the door, surveying the wreckage as he drove. There was nobody else around, and no sound but the engine of the car.

"It's kind of unsettling," she said.

Peter was startled to hear her speak. "I know that feeling," he replied.

Alison stared at him. "I was talking about the trees."

Peter heard the rhythmic churring of a helicopter overhead. He rolled down the window and stuck his head out until he spotted it. A Bell Jet Ranger, helicopter of choice for geologists everywhere. Still, he did not relax until he had seen it disappear over a ridge.

"How long are we going to be staying?"

Buoyed by the prospect of actual conversation, Peter was quick to respond. "Until we locate Frank," he said. "We'll be safe up here for as long as that takes." He had told her this twice already.

Alison did not look convinced.

"Everything hinges on contact with the captain," Peter told her reassuringly. "Holsa really does have something to do with this. He all but admitted it over the phone."

She looked at him again. "And you're surprised?"

Peter wasn't sure how it would actually go, when he finally got to Frank. Find the captain and maybe you find Klaatu; you end the whole episode before anybody gets badly burned. You come out of this looking like a prince, and everybody lets you go fishing. . . .

"I'll wring his neck," Peter promised, as he guided the Buick through a muddy curve. "But first I will get the story out of him."

Alison leaned her head against the window until Peter hit a bad bump, causing her to bang her head against the glass.

"I keep hoping that you're going to forgive me," Peter said, after a pause.

"You're forgiven," Alison said. "I'm not injured."

It was Peter's turn to stare. "I was talking about last night."

Alison thought about David's pistol, and the unhesitating manner in which Peter had used it. She was still astonished by the way he'd gone sailing right off the edge with that gun. It added a certain factual gravity to the weight of Peter's arguments, she had to admit.

"I keep thinking about that guy," she said. "The one you shot at."

"I didn't shoot *at* him," Peter reminded her. "Those were in the nature of warning shots."

"It was pretty close range," Alison said, observing him carefully.

"You're saying the distinction may have escaped him." Peter checked his rearview mirror, then shrugged. "People are playing this for keeps," he said. "I feel obliged to follow suit."

They rode in silence for a while. At length, Peter found the last road he needed to find. He bore left, past a field of broken rock dotted here and there by lichen and shoots of alpine grasses, and accelerated rapidly up a long incline. There were tire tracks, none of them recent. He was relieved, having half expected to find company. He gave the Buick even more gas.

"David in jail," Alison said at last. "You keep saying it, but I just can't picture it. You didn't give me enough time to get it straight."

"Al, there wasn't any."

"Yeah," she observed, rumpling her hair angrily with both hands, her characteristic gesture of distress. "Everybody's been in a *real big hurry* lately. You and David have truly outdone yourselves."

I know these two, Alison thought. They want me safe, they want me happy. They don't mean to hurt. She shifted uncomfortably in the front seat. "He does need you, Pete. I wasn't kidding when I said that."

Peter watched the road ahead, as the Buick gained elevation under protest. "We go way back."

Twenty-nine going on eighty, she thought. "It's more than that. I'm not saying it right, Pete. What I mean is, I'm scared."

Peter was glad to hear it — glad to have it out on the table for both of them. He could use the company.

"My old man had a line for that," he said. For the first time since leaving Portland, a slight, wry smile twisted his features. "If you ain't scared, then you ain't payin' attention."

Alison made an effort, not a very good one, to grin back.

When they reached the end of the road, Peter parked on a grassy patch in front of a spacious post-and-beam bunkhouse belonging to the Forest Service. He got out of the car and leaned against the hood, momentarily surveying the bunkhouse, the work shed, the woodpile, the enclosing woods. The place looked serene as hell. It didn't look like the most promising cockpit from which to launch a search for Captain Crash.

Doesn't matter, Peter told himself. The captain was a pattern of electronic pulses to be located in space and time. A computer and a telephone are all you ever need.

Peter opened the back door of the car, freed Fish Dog, and grabbed David's portable computer. Fish Dog dashed to the porch and returned, crowding Peter's leg and nuzzling frantically, attempting to herd Peter toward the intoxicating new smells issuing from beyond the closed door of the bunkhouse.

"I hope this is good," Alison said, gesturing at the computer in

144

Peter's hand as she climbed stiffly out of the front seat. "I really want this to work."

Peter wasn't sure how to answer that. "What's important," he said, "is that we're all on base. We're all safe at the moment."

That word again, Peter thought. As in safe haven. As in fragile respite. . . .

"Except David," she said.

"Nobody's going to hurt him." And please, Peter silently begged her, don't ask me why I think so.

The key was hanging on a nail in a rafter of the porch, right where T.J. had found it the time the two of them had stayed here. Peter unlocked the door and peeked inside, waiting for his eyes to adjust to the gloom before entering.

The inside of the bunkhouse smelled musty and unused, like old army blankets, like dead rodents in the wall work. Peter threw open the window shutters and took a quick survey, while Alison walked into the kitchen and pulled open a drawer at random, frowning with distaste at the sprinkling of mouse droppings among the knives and forks. Other than the kitchen, there was only a large living room and a dormitory with matching rows of iron bunk beds along two walls. Alison looked around. Ashtrays overflowing with J-shaped butts; the obligatory pile of well-thumbed beaver magazines. Evidently an all-male enclave.

In the center of the main room, ringing a potbellied stove, were four evil-smelling armchairs, one of which had apparently caught fire at some point. A cribbage board and a greasy deck of cards sat atop a card table by one of the windows. An old black-and-white Zenith television set was perched on one of the chairs, yards of aluminum foil sculpted around its antenna.

Alison sat down heavily in one of the chairs by the cold wood stove, causing a massive discharge of stuffing from several rents in the fabric.

Peter left the bunkhouse and walked out back to inspect the gasoline generator beside the toolshed. The fuel tank was empty, so he took out a pocketknife and cut a length of garden hose from a coil on the wall, then went to the Buick and siphoned a couple of gallons into an old tar bucket. He lugged the bucket back and filled the tank, and when the generator still did not respond he pulled the cowling off the engine and poured a dollop of gasoline straight down the carburetor.

He yanked on the crank rope again. The engine spurted blue flame, coughed grumpily, and died.

"C'mon, honey," he muttered absently. "Don't be difficult." David's computer didn't happen to run on batteries.

He tried again. And again. He tried for quite a while, and the result was the same. "C'mon, you whore," he grumbled. Machinery was almost always female — especially when it crossed you up. Alison would have a field day with that.

He paused and stood with one foot on the generator, surveying the cloud-mottled flanks of the mountain. He felt the first ticklings of a short, dark slide into despair, and he desperately wanted to head it off. He was tired of skating delicately across the surface of his own anxiety. From firm resolve to utter hopelessness in seconds: It had been that way for the whole damn drive.

Peter found a wrench in Sig's trunk, then went back to the generator and extracted the spark plug. As he studied the plug, he reminded himself that he would have become involved in the Klaatu affair one way or the other, whether he had quit or whether he had stayed. It was scant comfort.

I always head for the mountains when my life gets sticky. Get high and go far away.

What is it going to cost all of us to get out of this?

As he cleaned the spark plug, he found himself wishing, perversely, for a dose of whatever weird, apocalyptic fervor burned in the heart of Klaatu. Egg logic, indeed.

The screen door banged open, and Alison, wearing a baggy wool sweater from the trunk of the Buick, joined him beside the work shed. She peered at the generator, then at Peter, and frowned.

"We're down," Peter said soberly. He finished cleaning the spark plug, and reinstalled it.

"Can you fix it?" she asked.

Peter gave the plug a last twist with the socket wrench. "The racial memory of hand tools," he said, as he readjusted the choke and gave the carburetor a critical jab.

Alison stuck her hands inside the ample pockets of her sweater and watched him, so earnest, so absorbed in his labors. Peter loved to work these mechanical margins. Even David reserved the right to change his own spark plugs.

Peter gave the rope a good yank and the engine turned over immediately, offering up four good coughs before dying. "Hah," he said.

Alison turned and looked distractedly toward the woods beyond the bunkhouse yard. The trees were part of a sloping forest which the eruption hadn't touched. "I feel really sluggish," she said. She felt a good deal worse than that, actually. "I'm going to take a walk, see if I can recharge. You go ahead and get set up."

"Just a short one, okay?" Peter braced himself for another series of pulls. "This is no place for getting lost."

Reluctantly, he watched her go. She was no expert in the woods, but she made her way through the undergrowth with a certain unaffected grace. Just to watch her move, he thought. Cinnamon hair on gray sweater. Freeze that for later.

After a hundred more pulls, by Peter's rough and exasperated calculation, the generator finally rumbled to life. He stood back and let it warm up, and when the engine was humming properly, he throttled down the choke and went inside the bunkhouse to try all the switches and outlets. Everything was in order, including the telephone.

He hooked up David's computer and modem, and started accessing the Bell personal computer network. The odds of getting an instant response were not high, but it had worked with the captain once already, and there was a way of doing it that did not require giving away either of their locations, if they were *careful* this time.

It took Peter some time to design a computer message he could live with. He stared at the luminescent screen and tried to invoke the muse, the White Goddess — whoever it was who fitfully bestowed inspiration upon needy postulants. The message had to be nonspecific, yet pointed enough to catch the captain's attention in the event that he happened to scan the Bell network bulletin board. Public message centers of this kind were inevitably flooded with every manner of bark and plea imaginable — harebrains searching for a kindred loony, people selling used equipment or bartering software, even guys looking for computer-oriented dates. To catch a message in the midst of all the usual dross, the captain, who was an inveterate browser, would have to be looking for it. Just possibly, he was.

The computer screen glowed on, waiting with endless metallic patience for Peter's entry.

If you ain't scared, then you ain't payin' attention . . .

Peter leaned forward in the folding chair, and rubbed his eyes. He couldn't think back to anything in graduate physics that quite covered his current predicament. It went back to his involvement with Holsa. It went back to the contents of his mind.

Peter finally settled on a message: CRASH! LOST IN THE OZONE AGAIN, AND I DON'T MEAN FLORIDA. BIG DOINGS. WHERE ARE YOU? REPLY SOONEST GENERAL BULLETIN BOARD.

He would have signed it "The Niobium Kid," but Anton was already hip to that. "Crash" was bad enough.

I want out of this alive, Peter thought fervently. *You bet I do. I want to be home again on a Friday night, fucked up in front of the fire with my friends.*

Peter typed in his message and shut down. The power of one mind, he thought.

Sometimes it didn't seem like a hell of a lot to go on.

* *

Alison tried to focus her senses on the colors as she walked. The cloudy morning light was like white chalk on slate. Muted earth tones and tarnished silver; she'd made a basket once that looked exactly like these woods.

The three of us, she thought. Can it be true that I met both of them on the very same day, in my own living room?

She headed for a break in the trees, a small clearing, in a vain attempt to encounter some sunshine. The occasion had been her foster father's Thursday night seminar on the philosophical history of science, no less. Thomas, her father, was a balding, emphatic professor of philosophy who sported the requisite goatee and who, when he waxed particularly eloquent on the subject dearest to his heart — Hegelian phenomenology — was capable of generating less personal warmth than any other human being she had ever met. She used to sit in a corner of the living room on Thursday nights, watching everybody trying not to spill Cokes on the rug, and wondering about their sex lives, if any. There were always two or three coeds, harried-looking and a little furtive.

She was an art major herself, and held the appropriate view of scientists: There was nothing you could do about them. They seemed, in the aggregate, so different from her own friends, who mostly worked odd jobs at diners and car washes and majored in Art History or English Lit. when they majored in anything at all.

She had no trouble remembering the night that David and Peter first showed up. They sat there on the floor, trying to look casual, hemmed in by Thomas's favorite form of encounter-group agony, the Meaningful Dialogue. Alison sat in her corner, wearing off-white painter's pants. In those days she wore her hair long and tightly curled, flying her auburn flag proudly. The two of them were intelligent, funny, deferential to her father — and obviously turned on by her. After class, Thomas finally told her to cut it out. If she wanted to attend the seminar she could take Philosophy of Science 304 and get two credits to boot.

Her art friends had a good deal of difficulty decoding the significance of Alison's sudden interest in these two admittedly handsome representatives of the Double E set. It was simple: They were fun, and eager to please, and while they were rather obvious about their affection for her, they were just as relentlessly *cool* as everybody else back then. Which meant, basically, that you never knew exactly how you stood with them.

They were both freaked on electronics, but they never gave off that whiff of maladjustment and neurosis she later detected around the likes of Frank Holsa and those other monsters, the deep and devious hackers like Leno and Hardware Hal. Which made Peter's dalliance with that crew all the harder to fathom.

She took up with Peter, in the beginning, if only because he was an ounce more aggressive about it. She wasn't really certain how she felt about either of them at first. She just knew that she felt a peculiarly pleasant tug in her abdomen on both counts.

Eventually, it began to seem obvious to her. It *did* seem obvious, then. A gradual, growing certainty — and David knew it, too. Nobody ever knows how these things happen, she thought. David was content to let her settle things in her own way.

And when she did, she was amazed to discover that Peter did not have a clue. Some willing form of blindness had been Peter's signature disease. They were walking along the edge of campus, late at night, past bookstores and coffeehouses. There were leaflets tacked to poles, leaflets blowing down the middle of the street. Save this, off that. Right up until the moment she told him, Peter didn't know. Peter had made assumptions, and then turned those assumptions into fact. He had taken things for granted. . . .

He thought she was making a mistake, and he said so.

Alison crossed her arms on her chest for warmth as she walked, squinting appreciatively but cursorily at the textures of the mountain forest. She flinched as a raven suddenly squawked in the branches overhead. God, she thought, what am I doing here. I should be with David, knitting booties in front of a warm fire. Wouldn't that be the life.

The trouble was, you never knew which David would be home. Peter was here now, and David wasn't. Peter was always the third. David was floating away from her on a sea of bad debts, and Peter, caught on the hooks of some personal and professional crisis he was unable to resolve, was watching her from the outside, waiting to see how it would all turn out. . . .

Peter was always the third, and yes, she had always liked it that way. But now, Peter wanted to quit, and start all over again somewhere else. And yet he hadn't done it. He was still here. And she had wondered, more than once, whether she, in fact, was any part of the reason for it.

The three of us, she thought again. Lately, it seemed more like the one of us, all too often.

Alison stopped walking and sagged against a splintery deadfall of pine, turning in the direction of the cabin to get her bearings. Her legs tired easily when she walked, and seemed to cramp just as easily when she sat. The doctor said her blood pressure was fine, said it was okay to be tired, but to be honest, she hadn't felt quite with it for weeks. David hadn't been around enough lately to notice. Her pregnancy hadn't seemed to sink in with David. The Ace remained an abstract entity for him — a concept. He had a commitment to make, and she didn't know how long she should wait to find out if he was going to make it.

Three months and counting, she thought. From the abstract to the real. That's when she would know about David.

As she leaned against the downed tree, Alison felt a slight rippling sensation across her abdomen. An elbow, or maybe a little hip. The baby kicked again, and when she pressed down gently with her hand, Asa obligingly pushed upward against her palm.

I don't care about any of it. We'll all go live in Mexico, or somewhere. . . .

Blame it on whatever you want, she thought. Me and the Ace, we're old-fashioned, we can't help it. We need a hug from Poppa right about now.

She stood up and brushed the pine duff from her sweatpants, and started to head back for the cabin. She suddenly felt very tired, from the lack of sleep and the hours of tension. She was ready for some food, some rest, and some reassuring words from Peter.

Halfway back to the cabin, Alison suddenly stopped walking. She reached for the trunk of a nearby sapling, and steadied herself against it for a moment. Then, without any warning whatsoever, she bent double, and began to vomit.

In a few moments, when there was nothing left but the taste of bile, she straightened herself and, slowly, began walking again.

* *

When he had a steady fire going in the wood stove, Peter went to the kitchen to begin working up an omelet from the groceries he'd secured during last night's freeway stop. He glanced continuously out the kitchen window, keeping a nervous vigil on Al's behalf. The large round thermometer outside the window verified the obvious. It was getting colder. A better-than-even chance of snow by nightfall.

He'd give the captain an hour or two, for starters. If there was no reply, he would switch to another network and continue the hunt.

He searched the kitchen cabinets, and found a half-empty bottle of rum under the sink. He examined the clear liquid, splashed a little into a tin cup, and tasted it, tentatively.

Well before the hour was up, he checked David's computer. No such luck. Which was only to be expected — on a normal day, the captain wouldn't be out of bed yet. Peter was just assuming that this wasn't going to be a normal day for the captain, either.

Well before the omelet was done, he checked the computer again. Still no reply from Frank. The sooner the better, Peter thought. People are never as well hidden as they think they are.

He was putting the finishing touches on the meal when Alison finally returned. She headed directly for the chair by the stove.

"Feeling better?" Peter asked.

She had a peculiar look on her face. "Sort of," she answered.

Sort of, Peter thought. The word for Alison is *noncommittal*.

They brunched on Peter's omelet. Gradually, Alison regained her color.

Peter cleaned up the dishes and started bouncing nervously around the bunkhouse, arranging their gear, keeping the fire stoked, keeping his mind occupied until it was time for the noon news.

Repeatedly, he checked his computer. This is worse than waiting for your dealer, he thought. The captain has what I need.

151

Alison was curled in the burned chair by the stove. She had gathered her hair into a short, haphazard ponytail. "Pete," she said.

Peter was stuffing logs into the stove. He looked at her over his shoulder. "What?"

A good loom, a little money for yarn, and a steady poppa for the Ace. . . .

"Let's all go live in Mexico. Do I sound serious?"

Just before noon, Peter turned on the television and started fiddling with the antenna. A blizzard of snowy interference raced across the screen. After considerable coddling and positioning, he managed to bring in a single station, just barely. A network affiliate in Yakima. Alison left the armchair and came over to the table for a better view.

It was the lead story on the noon newscast. The correspondent delivered it in the somber tones traditionally reserved for the deaths of heads of state.

"Good afternoon. They said it could never be done. But early this morning, in a surprise press conference, officials from the DID Corporation and the Department of Defense revealed that the SEEK computer system, the nation's largest and most secure channel for electronic communication, has been seriously compromised by a troubled young computer genius who may also have been involved in an attempt to steal the system's most secret microcircuitry."

And there was David in handcuffs, being hustled up the steps of the Portland courthouse for arraignment. He was surrounded by swivel-necked geeks who had wires running out of their ears. "Oh, no," Alison whispered.

David, his hair perfectly combed, his sport shirt miraculously pressed, impassive except for a slightly bemused twist to his features.

"Atwood," said a correspondent, in voice-over, "has been charged with numerous counts of security violations, espionage, and grand theft. Authorities believe that Atwood managed to disrupt the SEEK system on at least two occasions, and had threatened to shut down the system entirely. At this point, there is no way of knowing for certain whether or not the threat could have been carried out. Neither Atwood nor his attorneys have issued a public statement thus far."

There was David, pausing at the top of the steps, accompanied by a federal marshal and surrounded by a bristling field of microphones.

Guilty by reason of those handcuffs, Peter thought. Whether he screwed me or not, it's my doing.

And then David made a gesture toward the camera, in the great tradition of Patty Hearst. Peter gave out a short laugh. It was the most uplifting gesture he'd seen all week.

"The SEEK penetration involved access to the highest levels of secured computer data, and it is not known whether threats of further strikes have been received. At the Defense Department, a major user of SEEK communication channels, officials have scheduled an emergency meeting to discuss the effect of the SEEK penetrations on national security. Meanwhile, in Houston, the Consolidated Research Consortium has gone to court in an effort to force the retrieval of data which it claims are missing from its computer files as a result of the incursion.

"When a network as vast and complex as the SEEK system goes down for even a few seconds, the lives of millions are affected, from pedestrians waiting on SEEK-controlled stoplights at the crosswalk, to military commanders monitoring reports from the nation's remote defense outposts. . . ."

Peter felt the onset of the short, dark slide again, as the talking head on the television reminded him of the stakes.

There was a shot of the Atwood residence. Peter could picture the reporters and photographers trampling the bushes out front; the miles of coaxial cable snaking across the lawn from news vans to videocams. Another voice-over. It was inevitable. Atwood's wife, Alison, unaccountably missing since shortly before her husband's arrest.

From the abstract to the concrete, Alison thought with dismay. Television made it real. It was supposed to be the other way around.

There was a jump-cut to a local correspondent in Portland. Poor little rich kid. Psychiatric sessions. The sickness of compulsive gambling. Followed by a short piece of film showing David's father leaving his Philadelphia home, a briefcase held in front of his face. No comment.

"God," Alison moaned. "They couldn't resist."

Finally, the scene shifted to a videotape of the press conference itself. Peter recognized the room as a large lecture facility on the ground floor of the S & S Building. And there he was, Colonel Core, the good soldier. None other. Peter ground his teeth together until his jaw began to ache. All in a day's work for Colonel Core. The colonel stood at attention behind a podium, flanked by flags, no less.

The United States of America, port and starboard. Peter looked in vain for Ada.

A reporter asked, "Can you tell us exactly how the violations were accomplished?"

"We have reason to believe," said the colonel steadily, "that a minor but previously undetected flaw in the operating system was exploited. We have already rectified this technical loophole."

That's it, Peter thought — just the right seasoning of national security basso profundo. Good show, Colonel.

"Can you guarantee users of the system that this sort of thing will not happen again in the future?" said the disembodied voice of another reporter.

"Yes," said the colonel briskly, "we can."

Great question, thought Peter. What the hell did they *think* Core was going to say?

"Was Atwood acting alone?"

"Yes," said the colonel. "There is every reason to think so."

The questions droned on:

"Did Atwood gain access to any sensitive material pertaining to the Peacemakers?"

"Atwood did not. Data loss was minor."

"Are any major changes in the SEEK system being contemplated as a result of these violations?"

"Definitely not. The system is as secure as ever."

The colonel nodded perfunctorily at another reporter. "It's been widely rumored, sir, that the Peacemaker missiles are controlled by means of a top-secret data link in the SEEK system. Can you comment on reports that the safety of this missile has been jeopardized by — "

"I will not dignify that report with a comment, except to say that it is absolutely false."

When the questions ended, DID's general counsel took the stage. You schmuck, Peter thought. You get paid however it goes.

When the story ended, Peter walked over and turned down the sound. Yes, he thought, right, that'll fly. Give the colonel credit.

Yes, Virginia, there is a Santa Claus.

It was so easy to make people believe it.

FIFTEEN

THIS TIME, it worked.
Captain Crash had put in one of his notorious
all-nighters, and by the time Tuesday's dawn had put the first pastel
touches on San Francisco he was ready and eager for another trial
run. All through the wee hours the captain had alternated between
total immersion in the notebooks, and total concentration on the
figures that scuttled across scopes and screens as he tested and retested
and reset the delicate circuitry of the resonating coil.

Alejandro's gambit, in the captain's view.

When he was convinced that they were ready for another go at it,
the captain marched resolutely up the curving stairs to Pons's bedroom and roughly shook him awake.

Pons moaned, burying his head under a massive feather pillow.
"Gimme a break, Cap'n."

"No breaks, little pal," said the captain gruffly. "Today's the day.
I just feel it." He went to the windows of the bedroom and yanked
open the blinds. "He who snoozes, loses."

Pons was huddled so pathetically against the reality of the daylight
that the captain beat a strategic retreat, figuring to whip up something
guaranteed to light a fire under his diminutive host. Something on
the order of an eye-opener. Into the kitchen blender went raw eggs,
orange juice, bananas, mangoes, wheat germ, bran, lecithin, brew-
er's yeast, a dash of cinnamon, a dollop of yogurt, a level teaspoonful
of sifted Lebanese hash, and three fingers of Southern Comfort.

The captain poured the mix into two tall tumblers, drained one,
and rinsed the blender thoroughly. If you didn't rinse, the stuff would
bloom into a thick green mat inside of three hours.

He went back upstairs and hovered nearby until Pons had managed to gag down the soupy brew. Then the captain dragged him down to the basement where, without any ceremony whatsoever, he shoved Pons's nose into a particular page of the dog-eared ledgers, the Sacred *Grimoires* of Alejandro the Sage.

"See?" said the captain excitedly. "You had the tolerances all balled up. That's why we weren't getting resonance!"

Pons, frowning, studied Alejandro's hastily scribbled equations. "Maybe," he said noncommittally. "Lemme look at these for a minute, will ya?"

The captain backed off, every inch the diplomat. He knew he was right. He was willing to wait until Pons knew it too.

"Take your time," he said. The captain walked over to the tent in the corner, nudged the flap aside, and settled himself on the canvas floor. He picked up an ancient Zap comic book and browsed through it, but he wasn't interested in the adventures of Mr. Natural or Wonder Warthog.

The captain gave Pons a few more minutes and then emerged from the tent to see what was what. Pons had finished with his preliminary investigation, but he still didn't look entirely convinced. "Well, Cap'n, it's this way," Pons said. "I think we oughta just run a detailed computer simulation first. That way we can find out if a signal of this strength is likely to — "

But the captain wasn't having any. "Caution's for losers and faggots, Pons-boy. I got a better idea. I already made most of the adjustments. It's time for a trial run. Let's just turn the sucker *on*."

It was clear to Pons that the captain was in no mood to be denied this scary pleasure. Pons tried anyway; a tiny voice of reason in the eye of the captain's manic hurricane of expectations. "Even if it *does* work, we might tip our hand, Cap'n. Besides, what if the thing — "

The captain wasn't listening. Marvelous dreams, visions of sugarplums, were dancing through his head, and the captain danced with them, executing a goofy shuffle that fell somewhere between Stepin Fetchit and Curly of the Three Stooges. The captain was ready to bring IBM and the telephone company to their knees. Power and information to the people. The captain was ready to *broadcast*.

Pons looked at the captain, looked at the gleaming pyramid in the center of the room, and knew that he'd lost.

Taking up position near the coil's control panel, the captain stared beneficently down at the switches and said, "Let's have a moment of silence, my friend. In honor of our mentor."

After he had gone over to stand prudently in the captain's bulky shadow, Pons complied. Frank was lost in thought, and Pons left him to it.

At length, the captain looked over his shoulder at his partner, grinning like a man possessed. "What is it, Sancho? You look a little green around the gills."

"I have to tell you, Captain, I'm a little nervous," Pons replied. "I always am, when it comes to throwing that switch."

The captain could sympathize with this. He stifled the urge to pat little Pons on the head, like a favorite puppy. Wouldn't be seemly. Pons had once been on the cover of *Time* magazine.

"This is no time to pussy out on me, Pons." The captain laid his right hand carefully on the bank of switches. "Nothing ventured, nothing gained."

Pons was definitely nervous. "Do me a favor, then, will you? Keep it at ten percent of full power. That's enough for a test."

The captain considered this. "Fair enough," he responded. The captain made the required adjustments.

Having done so, the captain proceeded to plug in.

*　*

Danny Zorn was slouched on his parents' downstairs couch, ignoring the fact that it was a school-day morning, catching the latest MTV videos on the family home entertainment system. On-screen, a young man with pomaded hair and a gleaming stiletto in his hand was stalking a hot blonde in skimpy lingerie.

His mother, a deeply religious woman who was proud to tell anyone who would listen that she lived only a few doors from Pons Grozniev the computer maven, was yelling at him from upstairs. If Danny did not go out and get into the taxi *this very minute* there would be no television, no computer games, for *one whole week, buster.* And wait till his father got home. And look at the way Danny treated her. And oh, and woe.

"Hag," Danny muttered. "Bitch."

His eyes never wavered from the screen. The kid with the stiletto had just slit the blonde's bra neatly into two pieces.

At that point, several vases of inestimable value crashed off a shelf near the television.

As Danny's mother ramped angrily down the stairs to confront her son, the family's entire home entertainment system — TV, VCR, the whole works — suddenly burst into flame.

Danny fell out of his chair and was only peripherally aware of his mother's caterwauling pronouncements. She began to ululate so violently that little flicks of spittle flew from her lips.

Danny sat up on the floor and stared vacantly at the burning ruins that had formerly been his pride and joy, his sole nameable reason for living.

"Unreal!" Danny said, conferring upon the proceedings his highest accolade. "Un-fucking-believable!"

SIXTEEN

T HEY SPENT the rest of the afternoon indoors.
There was nothing for Peter on the computer,
and it made him furious. It made him feel like a fool. His presence
here on the mountain was becoming a holding action. He was no longer
certain that he felt like staying the night, but it was already too
late in the day for going anywhere else, without some needed sleep
first.

Peter stayed by the computer, sitting at the rickety card table, trying
this and that, getting steadily bolder with his messages and not liking
it. Alison was killing time in the kitchen, mechanically putting away
a few dishes. He wondered whether it was possible that the cold blue
fact of David's incarceration, as seen on TV, actually might work as
a source of comfort for her. It meant that David was findable. Perhaps it was better than not knowing.

At length, Peter got up from the table and started searching for
some bedding. He made up two of the bunks in the back room,
figuring on a two- or three-hour nap before tackling any major decisions. He had come up with three options, none of them very en-
thralling. First of all, he could try signaling the captain more urgently and conventionally. Or, failing that, he could call the colonel,
and tell him . . . what?

Or, finally, he could choose to take the strange, street-side advice
that Leonard had given him last night.

Peter mentally replayed his conversation with Leonard again, and
ended up as puzzled as before.

— *I need to get in touch with Alejandro.*

— That can be arranged. If you do exactly what I say. Go directly to Frank Holsa's shack out by Florence. Stay there until Alejandro arrives.

It was a titillating idea, but it seemed far too easy.

— *I could never find the place again, Leonard.*

— You walk the power line that comes out at the highway. A fifteen-minute hike through wet grass. Holsa led you on a wild-goose chase. You'll be safe there, until Alejandro comes. But you must be patient.

Leonard didn't give him anything else. Basically, Peter had decided, Leonard didn't add up. A true wild card. Peter had opted for the anonymity of St. Helens, instead.

Peter showed Alison to the bunk he had prepared for her. "Try to get some rest," he said. "If we're forced to signal Holsa more energetically, we may have to try taking his answer on the move." Alison curled herself into an **S** shape on the bunk, and he covered her with an unzipped sleeping bag.

Back in the living room, Peter sat down at the computer and enrolled himself in a refresher course on chain-smoking while he took up the hunt for the captain again. On the strength of several bogus telephone numbers he had memorized years ago, Peter traveled to New York, Atlanta, Vancouver, Tokyo, São Paulo, and Rome, among other destinations, in his search for the captain. He thought of every bulletin board the captain had ever used, above ground or under, and he pinned a note on every one of them he could reach. It was a slow process.

"C'mon, baby," he said quietly to David's computer. "Do your stuff. Go fetch."

This time Peter waited for two full hours. When he started checking again for responses, he found himself losing track of all the message centers, rekeying so many entries that it made him nervous. Too much time on the air. He shut down again in disgust.

He heard bedsprings creaking in the other room. He walked over and peered through the door, into the half-light of the windowless dorm. He had assumed that she was sleeping, but Alison was stretched out on her side, her head cradled in her arm, and she was studying Peter intently.

Peter leaned against the door frame. "Can't sleep?"

She kept looking at him. "Peter," she said. "Why did you quit?"

Peter frowned. It took him completely by surprise. He walked into the dormitory and sat down on the other bunk, facing Alison. He didn't know which answer she was looking for, or how she intended to apply it.

"You mean the actual reason," he said, feeling certain that she wasn't going to be satisfied with any of the usual dodges. He lit a cigarette. "I quit because I'm not a bookie," he said.

"I was wondering whether it was something David should have done. Whether it would have helped."

What could it hurt, Peter thought. The short version of a very long story. "It's supposed to be a big secret," he said. "I have this specialty, it's called radioactive shielding. I happen to know a hell of a lot about the process of shielding computerized networks against various kinds of electromagnetic disturbances. My field is highly classified."

"I know," she said.

"I can't tell you how it happens, Al, it's just that one thing leads to another. The numbers take you there. It's almost amusing, because when the numbers go under wraps, you have two choices. You can kiss the work good-bye, or you can follow it wherever it leads."

Alison tugged the sleeping bag more tightly around her shoulders.

"So, for a while, I followed," Peter said. "And what happened was, I took the research farther than anybody wanted to see it go. I took it into a very scary and speculative arena called supersensitivity. I wrote a series of memos about it. I've been sending updates ever since. Very highly classified, these memos. For exalted eyes only. It's completely illegal for you and me to be having this discussion about them."

Peter broke off while he went to the living room and hunted down an ashtray. When he returned, Alison was sitting slightly more upright on the bunk. "I strongly suggested that systems like SEEK have a giant Achilles' heel," he said, when he sat back down. "They suffer from a form of vulnerability that Klaatu is apparently attempting to exploit. But they don't want to discuss it. They locked away my data, and they airbrushed all my papers before publication, on grounds of national security. The memos themselves — I don't know. I think the memos are confined to some arcane file that circulates mainly to Colonel Core and a few of his cronies. That's the gist of it, Al. That's where it stands. Beyond that, I don't have a clue."

Alison shifted again under the sleeping bag. "So you quit," she said.

There was a long pause from Peter's shadowy side of the bunk room. He was thinking about what David had said to him: *You're viewing this whole thing as some sort of professional coup for yourself. . . .*

"Fuck 'em, Al. I decided that my job was not to feed findings of fact into the paper shredder. If they don't want my help, so be it. I can't take the work anywhere else, either — I'm boxed out of that option. I signed some very heavy paper."

Peter sat quietly on the bed for a moment, remembering how he had laughed his way through the signing of every legal form the DID Corporation had thrown his way. Take their money but don't take them seriously — an avalanche of signed documents, growing larger as he went deeper into the work. He'd been busy, as usual, at the other end of the telescope; too busy bringing himself to everybody's attention; being rewarded with rarer and rarer forms of peep-show wonders — the circuits, the blueprints, the works. The special feeling of power that came with the accumulation of all that insider's knowledge. All the strokes, the pats, the perks. . . .

Admit it, Peter told himself, you loved it. Always going for the trophies. Always wanting those big fish.

"Al," he said, "the people at DID do not view supersensitivity as a scientific question at all. It's not a technological issue for them, and it's certainly not any kind of ethical dilemma. It's a simple matter of supply and demand. Anything that might affect client traffic is taboo. They don't want the finger pointing back at SEEK."

Alison shifted again, in a seemingly endless search for a more comfortable position on the bunk.

"Bad times, Al," Peter said quietly. "Cracks in the edifice. Brush fires everywhere. You see the cracks and you learn to paper them over. You discover the little fires, but after a while, you don't put them out. We build these systems, and then we hang everything of value out there on these fragile pieces of lacework — "

Peter broke off, and stubbed out his cigarette. "Riding for a fall, it's called." He stretched out on his bunk, with his hands behind his head, staring up at the springs of the topmost bunk. I should sleep, he thought. I wonder if that's possible.

"What about the rest of it?" Alison said. "You had other plans. You wanted to go to Buster's."

"Yeah."

"But you didn't go."

Peter didn't answer.

"You keep talking about making a clean break," Alison persisted.

162

"You even wanted to sell the house. But for a month, all you've done is go fishing, and invite us over for dinner. And now, with everything so . . . I mean, what do you want, Pete?"

Experimentally, Peter closed his eyes. Alison had seemed to understand about the quitting, all along. Trust Al to cut right to the heart of the matter, when the matter was the heart. "I just want out," he said, with finality. "That's all." He opened his eyes, and looked over at her. "But it's harder to find the exit than I thought it would be."

Alison could no longer see Peter clearly in the gathering darkness of late afternoon. "You thought it was going to be all sweetness and light," she said. "All hail and farewell."

Peter thought about it, on as many levels as he could manage to hold in his mind at once.

"So did you," he said.

Alison put her head on the pillow and rolled toward the wall.

For several minutes, Peter thought she was finally falling asleep. He stared at a rip in the mattress above him, and during the long silence that ensued, he stopped pretending that there could have been any other reason for his actions over the past few weeks. Alison was the reason. It was a dangerous thought, and he vowed to handle it carefully.

After half an hour, Peter could hear Alison beginning to stir again. He said something to her, but afterward, strangely, he was never able to recall what it was.

Long afterward, he was never able to remember precisely how the rest of it had come to pass at all. He remembered only the act of rising from his bunk, and walking over to hers, and massaging her shoulders, like he used to do. The tension in her muscles was palpable, and he dedicated himself to relieving it.

Alison turned over on the bunk to look at him. She caressed his face, and kissed him. In the end, that was what surprised him most of all.

This shouldn't be happening, he remembered thinking. But he didn't believe it.

The kiss, like the ones that followed, was neither urgent nor matter-of-fact. Peter did not know what compelled her, or what it signified. He simply accepted the fact that logic, so useful in its many spheres of influence, was playing no part in this. David hung in the air between them like the last notes of a distant symphony, and it didn't matter. Not now, in this awkward bunk on this cold mountain, with the rain coming down and the wind whistling at the corners of the cabin and only the field mice to bear witness.

This is how you make your escape, Peter remembered thinking. This is how you stop the clock. Not the quitting, not safe haven at Buster's. Just this. You're awake for as long as it lasts.

They came together and explored each other gently, becoming acquainted anew. The softness of her body, and her breasts fuller, more sensitive than before. The taut and distended curve of her belly, smooth, authoritative, alive. He experienced a moment of hesitation, when her pregnancy became a visible truth, but she willed it away. She consented, she designed it, raising herself on her knees and elbows as he came into her from behind, half-fearful of her condition. He cradled her breasts with his forearm, and gave in to the blind sensation of touch.

They made love slowly; so slowly it was a torture and a revelation to him. Legs between legs, chest to back, the swell of her belly adding a cautious tenderness to their motions that he could not have imagined.

They made love slowly. This much is on record.

He tried not to let it end quickly. Slowing, and slowing, not ready to let it end. . . .

Just this one time for both of us, Peter thought. Take your time, it's all you've got. Don't ask for more. . . .

And ending it, just the same. . . .

And remembering so little. . . .

Dreams die hard, he realized. Only the faithful can afford to let them go.

And later, as he held Alison, his face hidden in her hair, Peter said something else to her. This time, the memory of it was not lost to him. "I love you," he said.

It seemed like a lifetime since he'd allowed himself the full measure of that sweet-and-sour thought.

They snuggled together for warmth, and they didn't speak. Alison felt the pressure of Peter's weight at her back, and it felt exactly right. It felt like what she needed. Succor and sympathy, the language of the body. . . . Is it cruel? Is it crass? Ten years like it never happened, like it couldn't happen again, and now that it finally has, are we free of it?

I have seen this coming, I have seen it coming for years. . . .

All the men and boys in my life, forgive me. . . .

And gradually, they felt themselves drifting toward an uneasy sleep.
The captain would have to wait.
They forgot to put Fish Dog out.
And they missed the seven o'clock news.

SEVENTEEN

ALL THINGS considered, it was not Anton's lucky day. Tuesday, December eighteenth. He would remember it.

Thus far, Anton had spent the entire day, and most of the previous night, at the DID complex, listening to Eddie's periodic summations of nothing in particular, courtesy of the goddamned dog. Eddie had a habit of leaving a pair of ears almost everywhere he went. It was like a reflex by now. Wire-crazy Eddie gets his gold star this time, Anton thought.

Shortly after Cassidy had escaped with the girl, Eddie had called Anton in the car to inform him that the dog was on board. The girl was actually a useful touch, Anton had realized. It would keep things verbal. Anton knew where Cassidy was, and the colonel didn't. Anton was willing to keep it that way for another twenty-four hours or so.

Exercising remarkable self-restraint, Anton had decided to hold off. The colonel had made it clear that David Atwood was going to be arrested eventually, Klaatu notwithstanding, so Anton had chosen to deal with that, instead. Anton was steering clear of the colonel, for the time being. Let Cassidy do the other work, Anton had reminded himself. That had been the plan all along.

The son of a bitch really *was* trying to do the right thing, Anton had to admit, with grudging respect. Peter Cassidy was trying not to trust anybody.

Anton was pissed at Cassidy, nonetheless. Very definitely and undeniably pissed about those potshots.

As the day passed, Anton had continued to monitor Cassidy and the girl as they set up shop on the mountain. In addition, he requested and received the DID files on Holsa's bizarre former correspondence with Alejandro. The letters were full of Holsa's crank theories about electromagnetism, and Anton reread them all. It was hard not to think back to the old days, before SEEK, when everything was so much simpler; when Alejandro was off doing pet projects in the mountains. . . .

SEEK had very quickly taken precedence over everything else back then, but who really knew? Perhaps Alejandro, masquerading as Klaatu, had revived a pet project of yore, and Holsa knew about it. If Alejandro had cooked up something special, after all these years of being the good trained seal in exile, Anton wanted to know about it. As much as Anton had made light of the messages left by Klaatu, he had, in fact, paid earnest attention. PULSE DECEMBER 21.

If Alejandro actually thought he could bring this one off, Anton wanted in on the ground floor. If it involved some new kind of electronic weapon, or a resurrected old one, Anton planned on sharing in the largesse which inevitably accompanies such advancements.

If Alejandro had put together some sort of special surprise for December twenty-first, Anton, in short, wanted a copy of the blueprints. Anton knew a terrifically dependable buyer of things like that.

Moreover, Anton was not immune to speculation over the possibility of sole ownership of some pricelessly dirty little secret. He might have to kill Alejandro after all. That part wasn't clear yet.

Providing Atwood did what he was supposed to do for seventy-two hours, all avenues remained open for exploration.

Anton remained at his desk all afternoon, taking bulletins from Eddie. By late afternoon, as Cassidy began threatening to exceed the self-imposed limit of Anton's patience, Anton soured demonstrably, and Eddie started to avoid him. But when Eddie came charging back in a few minutes later, grinning triumphantly, Anton perked up. With an impudent flick of the wrist, Eddie tossed a microcassette into Anton's lap. More tape from the dog, via satellite replay. Anton popped it into the tape player and listened intently for a minute or two. Methodically, he began pushing back the cuticle of his right thumb, using the nail of his left.

On the tape, the soft murmurings intensified. Anton looked at Eddie. "So he dicked her," Anton said. "Is this a joke? If I wanted a tape of the two of them screwing, I would have — "

Eddie raised his hand in protest. He looked disappointed. "That was just for fun."

The tape ran on. "I love you," Peter said.

Anton lit a kitchen match. Very slowly, he blew it out, watching as a thin line of gray smoke needled its way toward the ceiling.

The sound on the tape was as fuzzed and crackly as an old phonograph record. Anton scowled. "What's the problem?"

"Fleas," Eddie said. "The dog won't quit with the scratching."

"All I can say is," Anton commented, "they better not put Rover out for the night."

* *

When Peter came awake again, it was unremittingly dark inside the cabin. It took him a minute to remember where he was. And when he did, he wasn't pleased. He rose unsteadily, and gathered his clothes from the floor. Alison, her face to the wall, continued to sleep.

He dressed in the living room, then turned on all the lights. He was starving. He crept back into the bunk room to check Alison's watch, and discovered that it was almost ten P.M. I stayed in the bunk room too long, he thought. That much was for sure.

Peter checked his computer, and there was nothing for him there. He decided not to wait very much longer for the captain to come through.

As he crossed to the kitchen, he caught himself wondering why she had allowed it to happen. He thought of asking her. And then he thought not. He even thought of asking her whether it would ever happen again, and he counseled himself against that question, too. The answer would have to be no, he realized, for all the reasons that were prompting him to ask in the first place.

For dinner, Peter cooked up a towering platter of broiled tuna and cheese on buns. Despite his efforts to be catlike, Alison appeared, just as he was sitting down to it. She came to the table and squeezed Peter's shoulders just once, briefly, before sitting down. Not a word passed between them.

Peter hovered solicitously nearby until she had eaten as much as she could manage. It was his lifelong culinary specialty, very filling, and not especially tasty. Fish Dog ended up with three buns all to himself.

A few minutes before eleven, Peter clicked on the television. As it turned out, there was nothing new or revelatory in the network's late coverage of the Klaatu affair. They watched David's arrest again, sit-

168

ting side by side at the card table, and neither of them felt compelled to offer a comment on the specter of David in handcuffs.

When the coverage switched to a replay of the press conference, Alison left the table and went to the kitchen for a glass of water. She was experiencing the onset of an unpleasantly familiar spasm at the back of her throat.

Peter stared at the television. Colonel Core was showing the magician's flair for misdirection, but there were two visible edges the colonel had not managed to file off, and their names were Frank and Peter. No mention at all of the captain and the Kid. Why not put out a bulletin, turn up the heat? Anton did not seem like the type to forgive and forget.

"There's the guy who showed up at your house," Peter said over his shoulder, as he pointed to the television. "Standing just to the left of the colonel."

On-screen, Anton looked smaller and tweedier. It was the colonel's barrel chest that came through. Alison came out of the kitchen and stood behind Peter's chair. "Who?" she said.

"Three heads to the colonel's left," Peter said. "Agent DeBroer. That's Anton."

Alison brushed the hair from her eyes, and studied the screen quizzically. "Did you say Anton?"

"Yeah, Anton. Surely you don't know him."

Alison studied Anton's taped image. "David gets phone calls from somebody named Anton," she said.

"Coming up next," said the newscaster, "Boris the Iguana fights for its life."

Peter reached across the table and turned down the sound on the television. "Shit," he said. "Are you sure?"

"Usually late at night," Alison said. "David doesn't like it when I overhear. I always figured him for a loan shark, or for someone who happened to share David's particular disease. A midnight tipster or a fellow track rat."

"I don't get it," Peter said uncertainly. "Anton DeBroer is undoubtedly the one who arrested David in the first place."

Alison frowned, and walked over to the torn chair by the stove. "How many Antons can there be in the world?"

Peter mulled it over. Anton and David, he thought. Another odd couple. Another Anton altogether? "I don't know," he said. "Maybe they've got something going. I can't imagine what." He paused. "Maybe Anton set him up."

169

"I don't know, either," Alison said. "I just thought it might be helpful."

Peter hesitated again. Bathed in the glow of the silent television, he watched as the news of the day flipped across the screen in thirty-second bursts. He tried to trap and freeze the conflicting contents of his mind for examination. Plans, countermoves, lines of action and intent. "You might be right," he replied.

* *

At a quarter past eleven, Eddie returned with another batch of tape. He offered it to Anton without comment. Anton punched it up and listened.

"*I always figured him for a loan shark, or for someone who happened to share David's particular disease. A midnight tipster or a fellow track rat.*" Anton listened with care.

"I don't get it," Peter said.

Maybe not, Anton thought. But I have a feeling you'd be willing to look into it.

"*How many Antons can there be in the world?*"

"*I don't know. Maybe they've got something going. I can't imagine what. Maybe Anton set him up.*"

Gradually, Anton sat back in his chair. He was a perfect study in nonchalance. He remained in his chair with his feet on the desk, his suit coat hanging open. Eddie stood waiting.

"We're going to pick them up," Anton said quietly. "For private interrogation."

Eddie brightened.

"We're going to do it unofficially," Anton added, in the same low voice. "And we are going to do it right now."

Sometimes, thought Anton, the world is just too small for everybody's good health.

* *

Peter leaned closer to the television, and squinted. After all the familiar faces on-screen, the last thing he had expected to see was another one. He reached across the table and turned the sound back up. Alison was still in the chair by the stove. Fish Dog padded over and plowed his head into her lap.

With his hand resting on top of the television set, Peter watched the promo for the Mount Tamalpais rock concert that Pons Grozniev was sponsoring in Marin County. The station was running a prerecorded interview, with Pons sitting in a studio next to an impeccably coiffed entertainment correspondent.

170

"So, Pons," said the woman, all flutter and sparkle. "Tell me. In all seriousness. How did you manage to reunite The Who for your upcoming rock concert?"

Little Pons squirmed excitedly in his chair, his Vuarnet sunglasses flashing under the studio lights. "Wasn't hard," he said. "All I did was ask 'em."

"Is it the money?"

Pons frowned. "It's never the money," he said. "We added a little extra incentive of another kind."

That other voice on the telephone, when Peter had last spoken with the captain: Ozone Enterprises. It was Pons. Little Short Circuit. None other. I missed it, Peter thought. Terrific.

The woman leaned conspiratorially toward Pons, and winked in the direction of the camera. "Can you tell us about it, Pons?"

Pons beamed, then remembered himself and shrugged modestly. "I'm only gonna say one thing. This is gonna be the loudest rock 'n' roll show anybody's ever heard. Five million people are gonna hear this show live. More than that I'm not gonna say."

"Pons," said the woman, "what do you think of Peter Townshend, The Who's charismatic but elusive — "

"I think they oughta carry him around London in a sedan chair for the rest of his life."

There was no use trying to call Pons on the telephone, Peter realized. Pons would have a thousand secretaries; a thousand people would be calling for Pons.

On the TV, Pons mentioned the date of the concert again. This Friday, the twenty-first.

Peter remembered that the captain had always been big on what he called meaningful coincidences; the way two seemingly discrete events sometimes conjoined in a thought-provoking way. December twenty-first. The date of the Mount Tamalpais show. The date set by Klaatu for blacking out the SEEK system.

The interview ended. "Coming up tomorrow," said the newscaster, "a tortilla that some say looks like Jesus!"

Alison was scratching Fish Dog's head and neck with nervous, jerky strokes, when Peter clicked off the set and told her it was time to leave. He tried not to make it sound like an order this time.

Alison raised her eyebrows. A peculiar look came over her face.

Peter did not want to tell her where they were going until they were actually under way. He didn't want to spark another round of resistance on her part. Alison wasn't crazy about long-haul driving, even in the best of times. He was planning on allotting eighteen hours for it, start to finish. Fear would see him through, but he didn't know about Alison. "I figured out where Holsa's hiding. I'll tell you all about it in the car, okay?"

Alison stopped scratching Fish Dog, and bent down to examine Fish Dog's collar.

Wouldn't it be nice to take a plane, he thought. Drive right up to the Portland airport. . . . "What's the matter?"

"I don't know," she said. "A burr or something." She continued probing with her fingers. "Maybe a tick. Peter, what is *this*?"

Peter walked over and took a look. Attached to the leather under-side of the collar was a tiny, lozenge-shaped object, like a miniature flattened football. Peter removed it, and held it in the palm of his hand for several seconds, and felt slightly sick. Then he dropped it on the floor.

He was about to grind it savagely under his boot heel, until all the transistors, resistors, capacitators, and whatnots became nothing but metallic sawdust, when he changed his mind. Instead, he put a finger to his lips, which was unnecessary. Alison had already guessed what it was.

They were out the front door and back in the Buick, all three of them, before Fish Dog could comprehend what was happening.

By the glare of the headlights, Peter could see that the afternoon's rain had metamorphosed into big, blowsy snowflakes. The mud on the roadway was already hardening into ice. As they pulled away from the cabin, Peter was forced to slow the Buick to a near-crawl in order to stay out of the ditch. There were still no signs of life on the mountain, but Peter no longer found that consoling.

Twenty minutes later, when the snow flurries had abated momentarily, he stopped the Buick and stepped into the roadway for a quick look backward. There were lights in the sky behind them. The bunk-house yard was about to become a landing strip. He got back in the Buick, and turned off the headlights.

They would arrive on Wednesday night, if they were lucky — and all the action was scheduled for Friday. They were cutting it way too close.

It was not going to be an easy drive to San Francisco.

EIGHTEEN

DAVID ATWOOD sat on the bunk in his small cell, his feet propped against the back of the nearby toilet. He had just returned from being led out for his shower, but he already smelled stale again. He was alone. It was his first experience with prison, and he hadn't found it edifying.

It was Wednesday, and the morning had been punctuated by the sound of barred doors sliding open and shut, the banging echo of footsteps on tile and concrete, the relentless neon of the interrogation room. The endless and pointless questions.

— What about Klaatu?

— What about my *wife*?

He would have welcomed a cell mate. The loneliness was the worst. David was busy rediscovering things like that.

He missed her acutely. The feeling was tangible, like an open wound. From time to time, in the seclusion of his cell, he would find himself in the grip of some diseased fantasy which always ended with Alison pinwheeling off into oblivion; Alison dead, or worse. David Atwood had always felt that there was room for one great disaster in his life. This was surely it.

I'm going to lose her, he thought. I really am. This time I pushed it too far.

Ever since his arrest, David had been trying to work up an alternative vision; a leavening way of putting Alison's disappearance in the best possible light. Peter had been at the house when the phone went down. So if Alison was gone, Peter must have done it, like Anton said. The why and how of it was, as always, another matter.

David knew all about Peter and Alison. That was fine. The only person likely to get hurt over it was Peter himself.

Hold that thought, David told himself. It's a pretty good one.

When she had her bicycling accident in college — when a car hit her, and she knocked out her two front teeth on the pavement, leaving her dizzy and disoriented from a concussion — who was it that showed up to help, as two very shady-looking punks got ready to split the scene? A good thought, a very good thought. They were a very good pair.

David raised his hands to his face and placed the tips of his long fingers along either side of his jawline. He deliberately tried to relax his clenched jaw, feeling his facial muscles slacken. He took several deep breaths in the manner prescribed to him by his former therapist, who had been very big on biofeedback machines — a little dab of conducting cream, electrodes at forehead and temple, and a continuous tone in a set of earphones, the tone rising in pitch with an increase in muscle tension. David spent most of his time under the headphones listening to a high, shrill scream, like a teapot gone berserk. The problem with stress reduction was that it was all in the mind. It was its own placebo effect.

He flexed his arms and legs, trying to compensate for the small cell by performing a few stationary calisthenics. His fear was overwhelming, and motion was always so falsely soothing. He thought back on all the years of compulsive, repetitive training, and he concentrated on his right leg, noting the smooth hinging of the knee joint, the lack of any bump or catch despite the off-season surgery while in college.

All of a sudden you walk away, he thought, for all kinds of very good reasons, none of them having to do with knees. You go cold turkey, but the need for it does not go away. It does not. You discover that you've got to feed the hungry monkey, and that in the absence of his customary fare, the bastard'll eat anything.

People think it's so easy to quit. Or else they think you're a moron.

Three weeks after David quit being an athlete, he laid his first bet. The tables came next. Whenever he tried to stop gambling, he drank. Whenever he stopped drinking, it was back to the tables again, with the stakes a little higher every time. He had the basic pattern down pat by now. He knew it by heart. Runaway oscillation, in cybernetic terms. A feedback system gone out of control.

And he knew the cure, too. It was the basic addict's pledge: A power greater than yourself can save you. The answer, the way out, was supposed to be faith. And faith, for David, was the sticking point. It was asking too much. God's not on-line, David thought. No higher powers, no secrets. Alejandro banished them from the kingdom.

Curiously, David had discovered over the past two days that he wasn't up to making the effort lying would have required. His trio of appointed attorneys didn't look like they cared much, one way or another. Creative lying would have been lost on them. It didn't take a law degree to see that they'd been cued in advance. They were stalling, content to hobble the proceedings, marking time. David told them nothing. He was watching very carefully for an opening, and so far, none had developed.

He knew what that meant. Sooner or later, he would have to create one of his own.

The next time he was escorted down the hall to see his lawyers, David gave them only one statement. One last big bet, David thought — the kind you make when you're already beaten.

"I want to talk with Robert Core, privately."

He hadn't committed himself yet, but he was experiencing the ineffable tug toward the unlikely wager. "Tell the colonel it's about Anton DeBroer."

One last big bet, laid very carefully, after due and proper consideration, on the head of Colonel Robert Core. Double or nothing. No one but the colonel was in a position to help Alison now.

When he was back in his cell, David sat very still this time, and breathed very deeply, and drank lots of water. From time to time, his jaw would begin to work furiously. He knew that Alison would call it the gambler's fallacy; the belief that a long run of bad luck is always followed by a hot streak. The sad but unmovable truth of statistics was on her side.

If he went with his bet on the colonel, he knew what he would have to do: He would have to tell the truth. It wasn't the kind of gamble David was used to taking.

If the colonel doesn't trust Anton, he thought, then I have a chance. If they've got their hands in each other's pockets, then I'm finished. And so is Alison.

It was possible, he decided, that faith, or something very much like it, was a part of this after all.

* *

That afternoon, David was escorted to the interrogation room once again, but this time there were no lawyers. There was only Robert

Core himself, sitting ramrod straight, his hands folded in front of him on the table. He was dressed in a dark blue suit and a rather stylish yellow tie.

David seated himself at the long table, and waited.

"Son," said the colonel, observing David intently, "you mentioned Anton DeBroer to your attorneys. I would like to know why."

Good, David thought.

The colonel sighed and tapped out a cigarette. "I must note," he said, "that our polygraph people did not do a very good job with you. No hint of this prevailing streak of larceny in your makeup."

Less than four hours ago, the colonel had been sitting in his office, awaiting the arrival of Anton and Ada for a scheduled morning meeting. The colonel had waited in his office until almost noon. Anton did not show up. Neither did Ada.

David chose to go with a technical reply. "Anybody can beat a formal polygraph test, Colonel. I thought everybody knew that."

"Actually," said the colonel, "no."

"You put a big nail in your shoe, and when you hear a control question, you tense down on the nail, so that your graph plottings are skewed from the start. That's one route. You really ought to ask Anton about this. You better believe *he* knows."

"If you have something to tell me about DeBroer — "

"Colonel," David said, "where's my wife?"

"We're looking for her," the colonel said.

"I'll bet you are."

"I think we can assume that we both want her safe."

"In Anton's case," David said, "I don't think we can assume that at all."

"And why not?"

"He's looking for her, Colonel. He wants her just as badly as he wants Peter Cassidy. If you want to hear about Anton, you have to keep him away from Alison. Can you do that?"

"As I said, we haven't even found her."

"You can find Anton," David said.

The colonel did not take David's request completely in stride.

"If necessary," the colonel said.

"Oh, it's necessary, Colonel," David said. "Believe me."

"In that case," the colonel said briskly, "you have my word."

The colonel was thinking back to his last telephone conversation with Anton: "You've lost them, DeBroer," the colonel had said.

"They're both gone, and I am now officially in charge of this investigation." At which point Anton had hung up.

David sat back in the chair, and studied him for a long time. It was written all over the colonel. It was in his tone, his look. The colonel was hungry. He didn't trust DeBroer at all.

The colonel was giving his word. The colonel belonged in some other century.

"You can start with the matter of your SEEK transactions under Cassidy's ID," said the colonel, "Anton or no Anton."

"I was attempting a premature dispersion of a portion of my retirement benefits," David explained.

"Lord," said the colonel.

"For technical reasons, I couldn't use my own ID to jive my own fund. I used Peter Cassidy's. It didn't work so well, as it turned out."

"It distresses me to deal with someone so callous about multiple felonies, but we don't have time to go into it."

I'm not callous, David thought. I just don't know how to come back in again.

"Colonel," David said, straightening himself in his chair, "if you're ready to listen, I have a series of stories to tell you about Anton DeBroer. Just for the record, they happen to be true."

NINETEEN

A S HE DROVE south along the Oregon coast, leery of
Interstate 5 now that it was daylight again, Peter
noted with dismay that the Buick was beginning to develop a disconcerting wheeze. The Specific Ocean was only a dull, blue-gray blur
in the periphery of his vision. It seemed like several lifetimes since
he'd driven this route the last time.

He looked over at Alison, who was trying to achieve a semblance
of comfort for her aching back. Alison was not feeling well. Peter
could always tell, even in bad light. When she was pale, her freckles
tended to disappear. Whatever ailed her, a grueling balldrive to the
Bay Area was obviously not going to be the cure.

The captain was down there somewhere, making preparations for
a rock and roll show. Pons would know where to find him.

It had taken Peter several precious hours' worth of close-order driving, most of it at a slow crawl, to get back down the dark mountain
undetected. He was glad to have it over with. He glanced in the
rearview mirror as he drove, and saw Fish Dog sitting innocently in
the backseat.

Anton is still waiting for me to find Holsa, Peter thought. He's
going to be very disappointed in me for not sharing Frank with
him.

Peter pressed the Buick down the highway for all it was worth,
ignoring the likelihood that the water pump was going going gone. A
positively baroque piece of razzle-dazzle, that. No doubt the bug was
Anton's. Anton and the colonel. . . . Picture a length of recording
tape rolling slowly past the heads of the machine . . . did they get
it all? Did they love it? Picture a bunch of grinning ghouls, listening
in. . . . Did he cry out? Did she?

Alison turned around and reached into the backseat for the grocery sack. She handed him an apple.

"How are you doing?" he asked.

"Pete," she said, "I don't know. I'm carsick."

Peter checked his mirror again. It was becoming a habit. "What would help?"

Alison craved a hot shower, a hairbrush, and a change of clothing. "Walking seems to," she said. Six hours, seven hours and counting, she was thinking. San Francisco was still a full day's drive away, and there was no way of knowing what to expect when they got there. As the Buick jounced and swayed through the coastal curves, Alison bit into an apple, feeling the familiar gulpy feeling at the back of her throat. She was beginning to wonder, very seriously, whether she could make it that far.

As they rounded Cascade Head, Peter reached across the seat and gently angled Alison's wrist, so that he could see her watch. She wasn't giving him much choice. "I can offer you a fifteen-minute hike through wet grass," he said. Leonard's words. In two hours or so, they'd be passing through Florence. Holsa's shack was on the way.

Intermittently, through the course of the morning, Peter had been wrestling with the subject of Leonard again. Specifically, Leonard and his advice about Alejandro. It was such an improbable story, Alejandro at the shack, why bother with it? If Leonard's intent was to do Peter harm, there had been plenty of opportunities. Leonard had been following him around for days.

All morning long, the questions had been nagging Peter: What if Leonard was telling the truth? And if he was, why tell it to *me*?

Alejandro at the shack, Peter thought again. Alejandro waiting for the twenty-first. Picture driving right past him.

He looked over at Alison. "Can you stand the Buick for another two hours?"

Alison nodded.

A very short stop, Peter decided. Just sniff around a little bit, and if nothing turns up, leave.

Near Florence, Peter stashed the Buick in a dense pine grove across the highway from the power line. He grabbed a blanket for Alison, and a grocery sack, and David's gun. Fish Dog ran off to prowl as Peter and Alison crossed the asphalt. The swath of cleared ground beneath the power poles was just as Leonard had described it; an easy

179

hike, blackberry thickets encroaching on both sides but not too dense in the middle for walking.

As they plowed along, Peter thought back to his hike with the captain, playing Hardy Boys through the coastal hills, all for the sake of effect. Simple revenge on the captain's part, perhaps. Peter had taken Frank camping once, in the autumn foothills of the Sierra range. The captain didn't have friendships in the usual sense — he had a thousand devious ways of thwarting that impulse — but every now and then, he was willing to give it a go. Frank didn't even think to bring a raincoat that weekend. So naturally, it rained incessantly. The captain spent the entire weekend trying to fashion something suitable out of two plastic garbage bags. When they got home, neither of them ever mentioned the trip again.

You try, thought Peter. What else can you do for people, except take them outdoors?

Peter stopped in the grass and waited for Alison, who was lagging behind. When she caught up with him, she told him that the walking helped, but he couldn't tell by looking.

When they reached the shack, Peter discovered that whoever had been dispatched to pick up Holsa's bootleg terminal had also cleaned out almost everything else, including the Coleman stove. It was unpleasant inside the shack, more dismal than he remembered it. The meadow beyond the warped glass looked pitifully wet and trampled. There was no one home.

Alison tried to stop shivering, and could not.

Peter took a thorough survey around the room. There was no sign of Leonard, no notes or clues, no useful information of any sort. He refused to actually look for a bug. Being aware of subtleties was one field in which he'd been doing a lot of falling down lately.

I don't know what I expected to find, he thought. An easy way out, maybe.

To his dismay, Alison wrapped herself in the blanket and crawled wordlessly into the captain's bunk.

"Al, there's nothing here," he said. "Let's go."

Alison's eyes were already closing. "Not . . . just . . . now . . . ," she said. "Just . . . a few minutes. Go check the Buick or something. . . ."

Peter's impulse was to fly, but he knew it was impossible for her to sleep in the car. And she was right, the Buick had asthma. It might save them some time later on. "Half an hour," he said. "Okay?"

Alison curled herself tightly into a ball.

Peter left the cabin and walked across the meadow to the power line, where he began retracing his steps through the wet grass.

He walked steadily for ten minutes or more. He started looking for birds, signs of wildlife, along the path. It was an old habit. He didn't see any birds, but all the looking was useful, even so.

Peter saw the man coming before the man saw him.

In the shack, Alison slept fitfully, and dreamed. There was a man standing in front of her. Some kind of uniformed guard, and he was staring out at her from behind a set of thick glass doors. She was pounding on the doors of the hospital, but the man wouldn't let her in. He opened the doors for everybody else, whole crowds of people, friends and strangers alike, because they were all going to watch.

I'm out here! she screamed, but the people just kept nudging her aside, pouring in through the door, and the guard kept pushing her back.

I want to watch, too! she cried.

We'll film it, said the guard.

It's a boy! somebody yelled from inside.

Big feet, said somebody else.

She pleaded with the guard, but the guard ran a huge chain through the door handles. She could still see the people inside. Their mouths were moving but she could no longer hear what they were saying. They looked like goldfish. She felt herself sinking slowly into the pavement. . . .

And then the Ace walked up behind her, and said hi.

* *

Anton was soaked. His slacks were muddy and his shirt was torn, and he was wincing from the accumulation of burrs in his stretch socks. He was making his own route to Holsa's shack, breaking through the heavy brush a few hundred yards to the south of the power-line cut. Eddie had orders to follow, using the regular route. Anton might need a backup. He didn't know precisely what to expect. Play it safe. Element of surprise. Couldn't hurt.

Anton wanted some time alone with Cassidy before he killed him.

If you say you're going to do something, Anton was thinking as he neared the clearing, then do it. If you say you're going to find Alejandro, find Holsa, then find them. Find *somebody*. If you're going to shoot, shoot. Don't take potshots.

There had been one last snippet of tape from Eddie last night — good news and bad news, Eddie had called it. Cassidy knew where

Holsa was hiding, but hadn't revealed it. And he had made the bug. Anton had weathered a few heavy hours at DID headquarters until Cassidy had been spotted, heading south on Oregon Highway 101, midway between Newport and Florence.

Anton bumped into a low-lying spruce branch, and cursed it under his breath. He was no longer in the mood for Peter Cassidy. Anton was looking forward to removing Cassidy from the field of play. All that remained was one last chat about Holsa's whereabouts and intentions.

The girl, however, was another story. She would be invaluable to him back in Portland. The colonel's jailhouse visit had come to Anton's attention, and Anton was therefore anxious to rekindle David's effort to impersonate a stone wall. He wasn't going to kill the girl — a fact which left Anton free to speculate on a number of far more satisfying options.

In short, Anton hadn't decided about Alison Atwood yet. It all depended upon her point of view.

These were decisions that Anton did not plan to share with Robert Core. Anton was beginning to distrust the colonel. He was just not in a trusting mood.

As he plodded resolutely toward the shack, Anton started thinking about his future. Men like Robert Core and Alejandro Hunt didn't need to cultivate the flexibility of mind that was Anton's special talent. Men like that were on a greased slide to the goodies. No matter what happened, no matter how many screwups they presided over, the promotions, the raises kept coming. Anton had learned that lesson way back in 1959.

Over the years, Anton had been doing business with the Soviets, usually having to do with the SEEK system. It added up. The Russians were obsessed by computers, and small wonder. Their own computers were terrible. Three years ago, when word had leaked of a major SEEK redesign effort, it had become Anton's job to make it available. But with Klaatu had come the threat of a SEEK shutdown. Anton was supposed to know. He was supposed to solve all the puzzles and explain them. He did not want to look like a sower of the seeds of confusion.

Anton slowed his pace as Holsa's shack became visible through the trees. A black dog was prowling around in the clearing, and its ears picked up as Anton approached. It bounded to the edge of the clearing and stopped about six feet away from Anton, letting out with a rumbling growl. Anton looked at the dog, took out his gun, and attached the silencer. He leaned forward, aimed briefly, and fired a single quiet bullet.

Anton had been turned in 1960. It wasn't love of Bolshevism. It wasn't contempt for capitalism. Far from it. It was, as Anton had come to think of it, simply the free market in action.

When Anton broke into the clearing, he faced the shack, and shouted Cassidy's name, and waited for a minute. Then he called out again.

There was a flash of movement past a window. In a moment, the door opened, and Alison came out on the steps. Sleepily, she examined him with great care.

"Take good notes," Anton said cheerily. "There's going to be a quiz."

"You're Anton DeBroer."

Anton nodded. "Where's your new boyfriend?" he said. "I want to talk to him."

Slowly, Alison said, "Peter's not here. He left."

Anton's gaze flickered around the clearing. "Where do you suppose he went?"

"We don't know. He didn't tell us."

Anton took a few steps across the grass in Alison's direction. "David wants to see you." He took a few steps more.

Alison tried to look indifferent to this news. "Get me to a lawyer."

"You're not under arrest."

"Arrest me." As Anton reached the bottom of the steps, Alison ducked back inside. Anton followed warily. There was no one else in the shack.

"I'll talk to a lawyer," Alison said, "and then I'll talk to David, and then I'll talk to you."

"Fine," Anton replied. "You can quote me on that. But first, you and I talk privately."

Alison had recognized Anton immediately. Long afterward, the eyes were what she remembered. Green and deep, like a double eclipse. She stood by the table and he stood by the door, outlined in it, and what she remembered was Anton looking out at her from those borderless pools of green.

"Lady," Anton said, as he shook his head, "what I can't seem to impress on anybody is that we're running really short of *time*. I need to know a couple of things. After that, we're off to see your lawyers, we're off to see Atwood, your mother, Attila the Hun, I don't care."

He began walking toward her as he talked. "I need to know where Holsa is hiding. Cassidy went to a lot of trouble to discover that. I find myself thinking that he must have had a reason for doing it. And I'm wondering, now, what did the two of them have in mind?"

A radio was playing softly in the corner of the room — a tinny FM model Peter had picked up along with the blanket and the food. "Listen," she said, her voice cracking slightly, "back off a little, will you?"

"Alison," Anton said wearily, "honey, do you *want* him, or don't you?"

She knew who he meant. He meant David.

"I'll tell you all about it later," Alison said. "Let's just get going."

Anton smiled. It was different with the kids, Anton figured. It was tough to be a responsible young person these days. All the odds were against it.

"No, see, I'm not coming through," Anton said. "I want to know everything. I want to know where Cassidy went. You can start with that."

Alison gathered herself and broke around Anton.

Anton missed his grab for her arm, but caught her around the ankle from a half-crouch. Her free foot slipped backward on the wooden floor, and Alison came down hard. She experienced a curious implosion of light. Then she was on the floor looking up, one leg tucked demurely under her body, her vision swimming, the FM radio ebbing and flowing around her. "Sea of Joy" by Blind Faith.

Anton came into view. He studied her from above, head cocked, then crouched down beside her. "You're a little overwrought," she heard him say. "Are you okay? It was an accident. I wasn't trying to — "

She vomited.

Anton watched her swollen stomach heaving with every breath she took. She was pale. A frown — almost a look of concern — crossed Anton's face.

Alison came slowly back into her body after the fall. Nothing felt quite right. Am I hurt? she wondered. I want to know. Somebody tell me if we're hurt, me and the Ace.

She felt a tightening, a sharp spasm, across her stomach.

Anton bent over and placed his hand on Alison's forehead. Alison began to talk.

In every way, Anton was unhappy with what he heard.

"I think I'm in labor," Alison gasped.

*   *

Peter ducked instinctively, and painfully, into the cover of the thorny blackberry bushes. It beat jumping out of a second-story window all to hell. Gingerly, bleeding only slightly from the thorns, Peter raised himself just a little, until he could see through the tops of the bushes.

It was Eddie Moran, cutting his way through the tall grass. He had a gun in his hand, and he was pointing it casually skyward, keeping it free of the wet foliage. He was coming slowly in Peter's direction.

So much for Leonard, Peter thought. He held his crouch in the cover as he waited.

So I will just take Eddie. And then we'll see.

He recalled that this was not the first time he'd leaped into a thorn bush. Every seminal event in his life seemed to repeat itself at regular intervals. When he was nine, he'd been stricken with the over-whelming desire to hurl the empty pop bottle in his hand against the side of a passing truck, and had dived for cover an instant later. It'd been tough explaining those scratches to the old man.

Peter studied the gun in Eddie's hand. He had David's gun in his own pocket, but didn't intend to use it. We're all potential targets now, he thought. But we're not all murderers. Everybody pays, no-body knows why. Everybody gets hurt. . . .

When Eddie reached him, Peter let him pull ahead by a pace or two, then rose up and tore loose from the blackberries, surrendering a piece of Sig's shirt on the thorns; a small green swatch of chamois, like a flag, like a billboard proclaiming Watch This Space.

He hit Eddie low, right around the knees. Eddie crumpled, and Peter was all over him with his fists. It seemed to go on forever, Peter pummeling and Eddie covering. Finally, Peter managed to scoop the gun out of Eddie's hand. He stood up, and after a few seconds, so did Eddie. It was not a masterful performance, but it worked. There was a thin trickle of blood leaking from Eddie's nose.

Peter held David's gun on him, and threw Eddie's gun in the bushes. Eddie blanched. "You want to take over," Eddie said, "fine by me. I'm just the hired help."

"The handcuffs," Peter said.

With bitter reluctance, Eddie handed Peter the plastic restraints. Peter dragged him to the edge of the path and hooked him to a myrtle tree. "Where's Anton?" he demanded.

Eddie smiled. "How's the dog, fuckface?"

Peter hit him. He shouldn't have, but he did.

He descended a level, and knocked Eddie out.

* *

Anton, his attention fixed on Alison, didn't hear the door of the shack opening. He was still kneeling beside Alison when Peter put the gun to the back of his head. Anton rose slowly, turning, and saw only the gun, like an exclamation point at the end of a long and clause-riddled sentence.

Alison was quiet, her breathing a series of jagged gasps. "I'm having contractions," she whispered.

"Be easy, Al," Peter said tightly. He increased the pressure against Anton's head. "She needs a doctor," Peter ordered.

Anton took the phone off his belt and started punching in a call.

"A civilian," Peter warned him.

Anton completed the call. "We've got a medical emergency," he said. He described their location meticulously. He put the phone back on his belt and looked over his shoulder at Peter. "How was that?"

Peter forced Anton back down on his knees and pressed the gun hard against the nape of his neck, forcing Anton's chin to his chest. Anton gurgled. "Stay there," Peter said. He went quickly to Alison and knelt on the floor beside her, placing his hand on her taut stomach. "It'll be all right, Al. We'll see this through."

Alison gasped, and, very slowly, under her breath, began to count. She was trying to concentrate, and it was *hard*.

"In about five minutes, Cassidy," said Anton, "the cavalry's coming. And I'm not talking about the chopper."

"What do you need, baby?" Peter said to her anxiously. "What can I do?" He kept the gun trained on Anton.

"You can still get out of here," Anton said.

"It's time," Alison said wonderingly, taking hold of Peter's hand. "I can't believe it."

"We'll get the girl to a hospital. Forget about Holsa. We'll let it ride."

Alison's quivering cadence rose a full octave, as she struggled to straighten out the order of her Lamaze breaths. She was in labor, and it was far, far too early. Little Ace, she thought. It wasn't his fault, and it wasn't hers. It wasn't anybody's fault.

"We will get you out," Peter promised her, as he squeezed her hand tightly. He thought he saw Anton stirring, but when he checked, his eyes were drawn to the window behind Anton's head. There was movement in the meadow. Reluctantly, Alison let go of his hand as he stood up to get a better view. "Be easy now," he said again. "Somebody's coming."

Anton, still kneeling in the prayerful posture to which Peter had consigned him, sensed the possibility of a reprieve. "Put the gun down," he said. "It'll be better that way."

Two figures were walking rapidly in the direction of the shack. One was tall and one was short, and Peter recognized both of them.

Much later, when he had the time and the desire to think about it, he would remember the way Ada looked that day, striding furiously across the meadow, obscured from the knees down by the wet grass, her features set in hard, uncompromising lines. So competent, so unblemished — Ada Stibbits in the raw. For Peter, Ada and Leonard added up to a combination so odd, on the face of it, that he was unable to come up with even a fleeting conjecture as to what it might mean.

Leonard came through the door a moment later, and Ada followed. She gave Peter a long, dimensionless look that told him nothing. She was breathing heavily. Her tapered fingers were bunched into white-knuckled fists. She looked at Anton and muttered under her breath. "Damaged," she said. It was the only word Peter could catch.

Anton turned his head toward the door, and saw Ada with Leonard. Anton was about to speak, but changed his mind.

Ada walked quickly across the room, looking down at Alison with concern. She bent over and smoothed a stray lock of Alison's red hair. The gesture was reflexive, unforced. The kind of thing a mother would do.

With the delicacy of a sommelier, Leonard took away Peter's gun. He pointed his own small armament at the kneeling Anton.

"We've got to get her out," Peter said. "There's a copter coming. Ada, what are you *doing* here?"

"I wanted to help you," Ada said. "I *tried* to help you."

They could all hear the rattle of the approaching chopper, coming in from Florence.

Everything was reaching Alison in snatches now. From her position on the floor, the geometry of the room seemed canted and alien. She felt herself withdrawing, disconnecting from the people and the events that surrounded her. "Oh shit. Another one. Here goes."

Ada stood up and straightened her coat. She looked briefly at Anton. Then she turned to address Leonard.

187

Peter, eager for anything that might resemble an explanation, was prepared to listen carefully.

"Shoot Anton," Ada said.

Peter reached for Ada's arm, but she shook him off. "Wait, Ada, no — "

"I didn't have anything to do with it," Anton said frantically. Ada took a step toward him.

"Ada," Peter implored her, "Ada, for God's sake — "

"It wasn't me," Anton said. "You're thinking New York, am I right? You're thinking Gramercy Park. I just helped bring him in, that's all. I was just a spear-carrier — "

"Please shoot," Ada said.

Leonard, in his silly hat and dripping plastic raincoat, looked crestfallen. He pointed to the front windows, through which the approaching chopper, coming in fast and low, was now visible. "It will make for difficulties," Leonard said. "We're overdue as it is."

"Peter," Alison whispered through clenched teeth, "It's time, it's time." Peter stood his ground uncertainly, midway between the two women.

Leonard reached into the pocket of his raincoat and withdrew a disposable plastic syringe. He removed the throwaway cover and exposed the needle as he walked over to Anton.

"A functionary," Anton said. "You think I dreamed it up? That whole operation — it was Robert Core. He was all over that case from the start." That there could be so much pull left in such ancient events puzzled Anton tremendously. How long, he thought, can these weird torches burn?

"Left arm, please," Leonard said.

Anton seemed about to speak again, but changed his mind. I'm tired, he thought. I'm suddenly very tired of this. He glanced sideways at Leonard's syringe, and closed his eyes. Leonard gave him his shot.

Anton crumpled to the floor without dignity, and did not move.

Peter backed toward Alison and took her hand again, but he kept his eyes trained on Ada. "Who was supposed to come for me, Ada?" Peter said. "Are you going to fill me in, or not?"

"Something concrete, Peter?"

"Who are you working for? What's your stake in this? You've got to tell me what you know." There were beads of sweat on Alison's forehead, and her hand felt cold. Peter felt utterly powerless to help her.

"This time," Ada said vehemently, "I want something very concrete from *you*. It's important, Peter. I need the answer to a concretely specific question. *Do you know how to find Frank Holsa?*"

Leonard kept shooting nervous glances out the windows. "We've got to go," he said.

Peter considered Ada's unexpected demand. He glanced briefly at Anton's still form on the floor, and did not answer right away. A clever but ugly thought occurred to him.

"No," Peter said to her. "I don't know where he's hiding."

"Is that the truth, Peter?"

"I don't know where he is, Ada. That's all I can tell you."

She seemed to be wavering. "That's very lucky for you, then," she said. "You must stay away from Holsa. You have a second chance." She glanced at Alison. "You can't imagine what a lucky man you are."

Ada turned to watch as two uniformed attendants, carrying a collapsible stretcher, burst through the door of the shack. One of the attendants stopped en route to Alison, and checked Anton's pulse.

"He fainted," Leonard said.

The two attendants placed Alison on the stretcher. Out of the corner of his eye, Peter saw Ada and Leonard slipping out the door. He thought about following, but he didn't think Leonard would go for it. And he didn't want to leave Al.

When they carried her out, Peter followed the stretcher. The medical chopper was waiting near a dense stand of brush, and Leonard and Ada were nowhere in sight. A swarm of DID security guards in their distinctive gray khakis was piling into the clearing from the direction of the highway.

Alison dug her nails into Peter's arm. She, too, was watching the rapid approach of the security guards. "You've got to *go*, Peter," she said fiercely, not caring whether the attendants overheard. "When they find out who you are, they'll bust you."

Peter estimated his distance from the guards, and stole a quick glance at the stretcher attendants.

Alison was wracked by the onset of another contraction. "Peter," she gasped.

Three guards with shiny pistols were closing on the helicopter. Peter kept walking. He needed more time, and once again, he didn't have it.

"Please, Peter, go!"

For a long, cold moment, Peter didn't think he was going to be able to.

Finally, Peter broke away from the stretcher and ran for the easy cover of the nearby willows. He took a quick glance backward. Nobody was following. Immediately, he began to work back toward the highway, keeping to the difficult safety of the thickest forest.

As he smashed through the brush beneath the trees, he kept telling himself, over and over, that Alison would be all right. He kept telling himself that this was the right thing to do.

He found the Buick without incident. A squirrel started chattering on a pine bough as he raced the engine. The forest was cold, and the cold had weight. It cut right through.

We aren't going to be there for her. Neither of us. We fumbled it that badly. . . .

Peter cocked one ear toward the dissonant sounds from underneath the hood. He wanted a new water pump, and he wasn't going to get one. He wanted David and Alison home and safe. He wanted Fish Dog, and Fish Dog was lost on the coast.

Peter nudged the Buick cautiously forward, already planning his route through the hills. A two-lane rut connected him with a country road running east. He watched the farmhouses and cabins, everything built from wood, deep brown and rust-colored, weathering to black and orange on the oldest buildings. He watched the road, and he watched the sky, and he kept telling himself there was hope for Little Ace, the premature one. But he wasn't a bookie. He didn't take bets on the future. And the twenty-first was less than two days away.

He wanted to go fishing. And that was becoming impossible to imagine.

TWENTY

B Y SUNSET, the zigzag layers of Douglas fir on the hills had given way to the drier madrone of southern Oregon. Keeping to the time-consuming back roads, and cutting gradually away from the coast, Peter reached the Interstate at last light, and merged south. He sped by a McDonald's with one arch darkened. A log truck roared past him, spitting bark along the pavement. Thick cumulonimbus were boiling up against the Siskiyou Mountains to the west.

Whenever he tried *not* to think about Alison, it was like the old koan about trying *not* to think about the left eye of the camel. The hospital was the only sensible place for her to be. . . .

Welcome to California, said the sign. White letters against a green background. Peter picked an exit at random. The Buick was definitely finished — it lugged and shuddered and occasionally cut out entirely. Peter no longer thought it was the water pump. He didn't know what it was.

More lost time; more grand larceny. He selected a white Vega with keys, on a quiet street, and it was adios to the Buick. He planned to push the hell out of it until the car blew up, or the driver fell asleep, one. Think of it, he instructed himself, as the steady accretion of karmic debt in a less than perfect world.

When he was back on the freeway, trying to adjust to the reduced interior of the Vega, he discovered that the heater didn't work. There were lines of headlights on the freeway now. Within two hours, realizing how tired and jangled he felt, Peter began to wonder about his chances of making San Francisco. He didn't relish the prospect of trying to find Pons in the middle of the night, either.

Peter thought back to the spontaneous lie he had thrown out for

Ada. He was still amazed by the wrathful way she had dealt with Anton — certainly a disturbing new facet of Ada's personality. Maybe Ada was government property after all, Peter thought. Maybe she was just another spook, like Anton. These intelligence wars — who could keep track of the players? Peter tried out his new car radio as he hurled past a line of trailers on a downgrade. He wasn't sure about the injection, and didn't care to know. He was grateful to Ada for cooling the bastard, though. Judging by the way he'd hit the floor, Anton wasn't going to be a menace to Alison or anyone else for a few rounds. Maybe he was out for good.

Simply credit Ada with having a proprietary interest in the outcome of the Klaatu affair, Peter concluded. Maybe she was chasing Alejandro, like everybody else.

Just find the captain, he told himself. And forget about Ada for the moment.

For more than thirty miles, Peter considered the idea of pulling off the freeway, and finding a gas station, and placing a personal call, direct and collect, to Colonel Robert Core. Was it easier for a guy like the colonel? he wondered. Some carefully cultivated blind spot? Just call the colonel, and unload everything onto the good soldier himself. Let the colonel deal with Holsa and Klaatu.

He'll go in with panzers if you do. He'll flush everyone all over again. . . .

He thought about calling, but he didn't do it. And he knew why. If Robert Core is the good soldier, he thought, then Alejandro is the great beast. I don't even blame him, Peter realized. I just want Alejandro to know what he's doing.

I just want to see his face.

Somewhere near Redding, Peter nodded off, weaving across two sets of raised fluorescent safety bumps before regaining control of the wheel. There was no point in pressing his luck. He exited the freeway and followed a series of signs to a Forest Service campground.

In the light of Peter's headlights, it had a deserted, off-season look. Peter recalled the thousand and one times he'd been to California, for business, for pleasure, for education. There was probably a passable view of Mount Lassen from this very campground. In the old days, in the Late Paleolithic, he used to ride Amtrak back and forth, just for the hell of it, and in good weather you could stand between the cars and watch the sun catching the peak of the mountain. . . .

But not tonight. Peter chose a pull-in near the entrance, and parked the Vega. He felt tired and alone and tied up in knots.

The word for the night was *Alison*.

Peter slouched back in the bucket seat, trying to find a position that would pass for horizontal. At the end of the day, he had been promising himself, everything will come together. All the pairs, the odd couples, the provocative dyads: All of this will make some sense. It was time to make good on that hopeful promise.

So he gave it a try.

And it took him quite a while to get it straight. He'd always seen Alison's relationship with David, at bottom, as some sort of marriage of convenience. Some sort of misjudgment on her part. Which had worked out well for Peter, who got to play the part of the stoic martyr — aloof, tragic, doomed. Great part, he thought. There's a certain kind of person who would die for a part like that.

He'd been wrong about all of it. David was the father now. Peter had never managed to allow for that.

We shape other people in our minds, he was thinking, and we always prefer the artwork to the real thing. We are, every one of us, heedless of subtleties.

In the days to come, Peter would look back upon this train of thought as a flawless example of egg logic in action.

TWENTY-ONE

A LISON WOULD always remember the helicopter ride, when she remembered it at all, as the longest and most unpleasant airborne experience of her life. They had taken off with the intention of flying her to the nearest hospital, which was in Florence, but when the fixed rate of her contractions seemed to offer hope for Portland, the pilot changed course. A young med-tech on loan from the sheriff's office hovered over her constantly. He didn't look all that comfortable about the switch in plans. She remembered trying to measure her condition through his eyes, and not liking what she saw.

He gave her headphones to cut the noise, and blankets, both of which were small comfort against the lurching air pockets. Against her protests, the med-tech had insisted on jabbing her with a needleful of painkiller or tranquilizer or both. Somebody had told him to do it, and God, she had to admit, it did help. It did at least half the trick. But she was conscious, and there was still noise and vibration, and the loss of horizon; the vertiginous tug of flight doing battle with the earthbound tug of childbirth.

Doped, she thought. All the hours you spend in contemplation of a natural birth, thinking of how it will go. . . .

The Ace was ready. Never mind that it was at least ten, maybe twelve weeks early. The Ace was up. It didn't matter how any of them felt about it. It didn't matter in the sleast, she thought. I mean slightest. Least. I mean it doesn't matter.

It had been hard, while inside the helicopter, to concentrate on anything very specific other than the wrenching contractions. She remembered an IV needle in her arm. She remembered that they hit a bad bump somewhere over the Cascades, which made her grimace, and the concerned med-tech leaned over to look at her, managing to hook the toe of his boot on Alison's IV tube. She yowled and he had to reset the needle. It didn't hurt much, but the med-tech looked horror-struck.

It just wasn't their day. Alison remembered thinking that it wasn't anybody's day. And then she checked herself. No, she thought. It was Asa's day.

There were lights when they landed, and then corridors of tile, and more lights, and lots of steel. They wheeled her straight to the delivery room, where the doctors and nurses strapped her with monitors and helped her into the delivery chair.

With a wet cloth on her forehead and the voices of six strangers banging in her head, Alison clenched her teeth, pushing when they told her to push. The fetus was stressed, they said. There was no messing around.

Alison didn't have to worry about a C section. The Ace came out fast. Three pounds, nine ounces, according to the digital readout on the delivery room scale. Alive, but not well. His lungs were question marks, and nobody was willing to venture a guess about the rest of him yet. She couldn't catch it all. She was twenty leagues under.

She got one good look at him, maybe ten seconds' worth, before they took him away to the preemie ward. He was pale, birdlike, almost transparent. She stroked his cheek with a finger, and felt the frail, fluttery heartbeat that tickled inside his chest. And that was that. She couldn't remember having held him at all.

*　*

When Alison awakened, she was in a recovery room, alone. She stared at the blue pastel curtain that surrounded her bed. They must have bumped me right off the edge, she thought. Too much medicine.

So many questions; so hard to dig them out. . . . Boy or girl? The Ace, of course of course, tiny wrinkled tube-wracked frog. . . .

Asa's day.

There, she thought triumphantly. Out of the whirling mush of my mind comes a sensible thought at last. . . .

When she woke for the second time, she was in a private room. The first face to come through the door was friendly, and familiar. Sandy something, Alison thought. Peter's old girlfriend, on-again, off-again. Sandy was a nurse. When Alison was thirsty, Sandy took care of it. When the men from DID and the government people started filing into her room to ask questions, Sandy helped fend them off for a while.

The Ace was in the preemie ward, condition unchanged.

She wanted to hold him, but the answer was no.

By late evening, Alison was sitting up in bed, still feeling groggy. Sandy came in and announced that she was punching out for the day. As Sandy was leaving, the phone rang on the table beside Alison's bed. Alison reached over and answered it, holding the receiver uncertainly in her hand as she listened. She smiled, and said hello. It was David.

"Baby," David said, "am I glad to hear your voice."

"It's the Ace," she said faintly.

"Al, I can't talk very long. How is he?"

Alison was terribly thirsty again. "Not so good, I think."

"Alison, listen to me. Are *you* all right?"

"I'm way off speed. They doped me up."

Her thirst was excruciating. She struggled to bring the last two days into focus — and the fleeting image of Fish Dog crossed her mind. "David, is anybody listening?"

"Don't worry," David said. "It doesn't matter. Just hang in there, and I'll be with you before you know it."

"Are you still in jail?"

"You relax."

"Can you come see me?"

"Al, I have to know one thing," David said. "Where's Peter?"

Alison closed her eyes, and lay back on the pillow. There was so much she wanted to say. . . .

"Al," David said, "where was Peter planning to go?"

It could be benign concern, Alison thought hopelessly. It could be a dozen other things.

In the long pause that followed, she sensed the presence of David's listeners.

"I don't know," she lied.

There was another pause. "David?"

"Yes."

She was crying now. "The Ace says hi."

TWENTY-TWO

O N THE MORNING of Thursday, the twentieth of
December, Peter did not drive directly to San
Francisco, as he originally had planned. Instead, less than twenty
miles from San Francisco, he cut across the San Rafael Bridge, heading for Marin County. Pons would be on Mount Tamalpais, Peter
figured, putting the finishing touches on tomorrow's extravaganza.

As he drove the bridge, he had cake doughnuts and a Marlboro
for breakfast. He felt hollowed out and hardened. Sand had permanently ingrained itself beneath his eyelids. Peter had been too tightly
strung last night for anything amounting to honest sleep.

On the other side of the bridge, Peter drove through the residential
hills and valleys of Marin, heading for the base of the mountain.
When he got there, he started driving uphill through the redwoods,
following the sound of snarling semis as they wound their way toward
the peak.

The location of the concert site was fairly evident. Halfway to the
top of the mountain, the semis pulled off and parked in a dusty glade
the size of a football field. Upslope from the glade, on several acres
of cleared ground, Peter could see bleachers and the beginnings of a
huge stage.

Peter parked the car and walked toward the skeletal scaffolding that
marked the location of the stage. The Grateful Dead blared out of
temporary speakers for the benefit of the stage construction crew. He
walked past a green line of Port-O-Sans, angling toward the back of
the stage. He was stopped by a flimsy wall of fiberboard partitions, in
front of which a harried-looking kid in aviator shades and a silk flight
jacket was pacing anxiously.

"I'm looking for Pons Grozniev," Peter said.

"Who isn't," came the clipped reply.

Peter worked along the partition, peeking through the gaps at the crowd of people backstage. Pons wasn't going to be easy to spot, he realized, as he wormed his way through the fence.

Peter asked around, and then he got lucky. Pons Grozniev, standing near a pile of rolled hurricane fence, arguing heatedly with three people at once, spotted Peter instead, and saved him the trouble.

"Pete!" Pons hollered happily. "This is some surprise!" Wearing an oversized navy pea coat, Pons trotted over and laid The Grip on his long-lost buddy. "More crowd control!" a man shouted after Pons. "You gotta beef up! Whaddya think, you're headlining Lothar and the Hand People?"

As Pons and Peter glided out of earshot, Pons would have laid an arm across Peter's shoulders, if he'd been able. When they were a safe distance away, Pons stopped walking, and began scribing a very deliberate circle in the dust with the toe of his tennis shoe.

"Pons, long time no see," Peter said quickly, "but I have to ask you, very discreetly — *where's the captain?*"

Pons contemplated the question as he scribed.

"Pons," Peter said, "it's too late to dodge with me."

Pons looked away. "You don't know it all, man. But you oughta."

"Pons," Peter said wearily. "Take me to your leader."

"Yeah," Pons sighed, gesturing toward the stage. "I could use a break from this."

He led Peter to the spot where his Honda 750 was parked. "He had to see a guy about a part," Pons said, handing Peter a spare helmet.

"Where?"

"The Golden State Computer Fair, at the Civic Center." Pons punched the ignition button, and the bike rumbled smoothly to life. "He wasn't planning to stay very long. We'll go root him out."

"What's he up to, Pons?" Peter demanded, as he climbed on behind.

"Ask the man," Pons answered. "He won't tell me anything anymore. You go try it with him for a while."

Pons roared out of the backstage parking lot, hairpinning his way off the mountain in record time. The Civic Center was no more than twenty minutes away, assuming Pons was doing the driving.

Peter held on and leaned hard, and when they finally missed a stoplight, he started shouting questions. But Pons only shook his helmeted head, gravely. "If you're thinking of strong-arming the captain — with or without my help — you're about six months too late."

"Pons. You're a basically responsible guy, right?"

"Pete," he mumbled uncomfortably, "don't even *start* with this."

Pons checked the intersection both ways, and gunned through the red light before Peter had a chance to reply.

* *

Inside the Civic Center, the computer fair was in full swing — crowded as hell, and nearly as hot. Exhibit-roamers, wearing name tags, toting crinkly bags full of product literature, were swarming the wide aisles of the hall. As he entered, Peter stood on tiptoe and gave the place a quick scan, as was his habit at gatherings like this. Personal computers, software, electronic games, bionics, robotics: visionaries and hustlers in equal mix, judging by the names on the booths. Small companies, mostly. No big names, no mainstream corporate presences, no founding fathers. Definitely the captain's turf.

Miles of aisles, Peter thought. A roiling sea of electronic goods and services. He was reluctant to take the plunge.

"Hang out over there for a minute," Pons said, indicating a registration area with a good view of Aisle 1. "Better let me do it."

Peter stood by momentarily and watched Pons go, intending to tail Pons after giving him a short lead. Nearby, at a large table edged in green-and-white bunting, with comfortable chairs for striking deals, a salesman was displaying a line of microcomputer-controlled organs and blood vessels to a rapt crowd of onlookers.

Peter waited a few more seconds. Convocations of this nature always put Peter off.

Lovingly, the man put together the two ventricles of a shiny plastic air-driven heart.

Deciding that Pons had had enough of a start, Peter took off in pursuit, following Pons unobtrusively through Aisles 2 and 3. They connected up with Captain Crash at the head of Aisle 4. Good thing Pons was in charge of the looking, Peter thought. No wonder the captain wasn't nervous about being at large on the eve of his big day. Peter might have missed him altogether.

The captain, in a three-piece suit and a pair of glasses, was standing next to a video games booth. He was holding a small valise in his hand. The suit was neatly pressed, all fifteen yards of blue serge. His beard was missing, his hair was trimmed, and he had carved his mustache pencil-thin. All his chins were showing.

He looked like Victor Buono.

The captain watched both of them approaching, but gave no outward sign of recognition. He can't be all that happy to see me, Peter reasoned. He must know I'm ready to go for his throat.

People in the aisles were beginning to realize that the legendary Pons Grozniev was among them. The captain noticed this, as Pons drew up beside him. "You're drawing flies," he said quietly.

Peter moved to within grabbing distance, pointing at the suitcase in the captain's hand. "Planning a trip?" he said, as pleasantly as he could manage. He glanced at the captain's name tag. "Are we, *Carl?*"

Holsa turned and gave the hall a quick three-hundred-and-sixty-degree survey, like a submarine captain at the periscope.

"You left Oregon in a hurry," Peter said, with a hint of menace in his voice.

"Same as you, pal."

"You kind of left me in the lurch there, Carl."

"Well," said the captain weakly, "you know."

Peter reached down and stripped off a piece of masking tape that was covering the logo on the captain's valise. Underneath the tape was the signature of the Yoyodyne Company, a speculative little outfit specializing in the development of a personal computer so fast, furious, and unregistered that the Defense Department hadn't even finished tearing it apart yet. As a result, it was absolutely unavailable for public purchase. The perfect tool for a long-term underground stay, Peter thought. No fingerprints. Other than SEEK, you couldn't do any better.

The captain tightened his grip on the suitcase, and gave the gathering an uneasy smile. "It's for a friend," he said.

"I'm in big trouble, Frank. And it all started with you." Peter didn't intend to ask the captain about Alejandro; not until he had the captain safely in irons.

Holsa swiveled his beefy neck, gauging the distance to the exits, and ruining the press in his collar. "Look," he said with exasperation, "do you suppose we could discuss this *somewhere else?*"

"He means my weekend place," Pons said.

"Shut up," said the captain.

"I'll call the cops, Frank. I'll fold the whole tent."

Slowly, with great dignity, Frank Holsa turned and began walking toward the entranceway.

Peter stayed close to the captain, once the three of them were outside, and didn't say anything until they were safely beyond the range of the security guards at the entrance. As they hurried across the teeming parking lot to the captain's pickup, Peter said, "You really should have told me about my SEEK ID, Frank. Big mistake."

Holsa refused to answer as he unlocked the truck.

"You and I need to discuss a few points."

Without a word, the captain threw his valise into the front seat, jumped inside, and locked both doors again, simultaneously, before Peter could stop him. Peter was about to throw himself into the bed of the pickup when Pons started shouting at him not to bother.

"It's okay," Pons said, pointing to his motorcycle as the captain tore out across the parking lot. "He's just a little embarrassed about what he did to you up north. He isn't going anywhere but home."

Peter climbed on behind Pons again. "Hug his bumper, just the same," he said.

TWENTY-THREE

WITH ONE WELL-PLACED boot to the captain's backside, Peter managed to propel Frank Holsa all the way up a flight of six steps leading to the Second House of Pons, in San Rafael. "You asshole" — another kick sent the captain stumbling across the porch to the front door — "I'll break everything in your body that still works."

The house was an ivy-covered cottage set well back from Sir Francis Drake Boulevard, and from the outside, it looked like a shrubbery-shrouded gingerbread house for adults. Pons didn't make it up there very much, maybe two weeks a year, the price he paid for doing well in the real world.

When Peter threatened a third kick, the captain growled and rose to full bearish height on the porch, turning his dilated eyes in Peter's direction. "Cut that shit out," he warned. "The hell's the matter with you?"

"Open up, Frank. Show and tell."

The captain stood his ground, blocking Peter's access to the door. "Okay," he said. "So here's the deal."

"Isn't going to be any *deal*, Frank, believe me."

Pons slipped around the captain and quickly unlocked the door.

"The deal is this. You need a place to hide out? Fine. We can do that for you. But if you just wanna queer the whole works — "

Peter jammed the heels of his hands against Holsa's chest, about midtie, and shoved him roughly through the door. "You should have told me all about Klaatu when you had the chance."

The captain shook his head vigorously in denial. "How *that* shit got mixed up with this, I have no idea. Do I *look* like Klaatu?"

Pons scuttled across the sparsely furnished living room and yanked the latch on a large wooden door by the hall closet. With difficulty, he separated the two combatants long enough to send both of them down a long flight of metal steps to the basement.

The chief feature of the Sub Rosa House was, in fact, its basement. Still under construction, the downstairs room was partially paneled in rough cedar. There were stacks of lumber on the floor, and tools leaning against unfinished walls. Computer gear, oscilloscopes, keyboards, power converters, all the modular microtoys of the captain's trade, were scattered across several workbenches.

In the center of the basement, reaching almost to the ceiling, stood a gleaming silver cone. Moving the coil to San Rafael had not been part of the plan, but after the unanticipated results of the impromptu test in San Francisco, the captain had opted for a strategic retreat from the House of Pons.

Peter's eyes widened when he saw it.

A short, stout antenna was attached to the apex of the cone. At its base, a tangle of wires and multicolored connector ribbons led across the floor to an equipment bank against the far wall.

It did not resemble anything with which Peter was familiar. Anything at all.

"All right," Peter said. "Tell me what it is."

"Yeah, well, I mean, you'd like to *know*, wouldn't you?" the captain said excitedly, noting the mixture of surprise and suspicion on Peter's face. He stepped lightly over to one of his workbenches and flipped on the basement stereo system. Something by The Who. "Just like old times in East Palo Alto."

Peter walked over and flipped it off.

The captain stared at him, openmouthed. "You've lost the vision, Cassidy. That's what it is."

Peter was running very short on patience. As he was debating whether to punch the captain out, and just finish it, so he could sort things out in peace, the captain took a few steps toward the center of the room. "This thing interests you, Cassidy? Alejandro Hunt perfected it a long time ago — and I'm the one who's gonna prove it works. Call it an amplifier. That'll do. I can't pretend to tell you how it works, man. It just does."

It looked benign, slightly ridiculous; a giant dunce cap in a rock-wall catacomb. A section of metal paneling was open on its smooth surface, exposing layer upon layer of printed circuit boards.

"You had help, did you? Alejandro helped?"

"Listen to what I'm saying. Some kind of weird wave action — but proving out. The coil is fuckin' marvelous, Cassidy." The captain gestured grandly at the coil, his face bright with pride. "And tomorrow we pull off the wraps for a surprise demonstration. We're gonna take her out on the gridway, and see what she can do."

Peter stood uncertainly still for a few beats.

The captain gazed tenderly at the coil. His eyes lost their focus, and his whole face seemed to soften. It was eerie to watch. "You have to give in to the beauty of it, Cassidy. Within a radius of maybe fifteen miles or so, almost any electronic component will pick up the signal you can generate with the coil. Televisions, car radios, stereo systems — whatever you got. At real short range, the signal is gonna come beaming into metal of various kinds, conduit and plumbing and circuitry and what have you."

The captain's eyes danced with delight. "Instead of 'Watson, come here, I want you,' it's gonna be 'Won't Get Fooled Again' — *and five million people are gonna hear it live.*"

Peter shook his head slowly. "You need therapy, Frank."

The captain slapped his forehead in frustration. "You don't see what it means? Now, man, you *know* I don't believe in magic, but this little beauty subverts everything we were ever taught about the transmission of electronic signals. Alejandro's known about it all along. It resonates at frequencies that, well, aren't quite on the map."

"He's telling the truth," Pons put in.

"It's a mindfucker, Cassidy. But you can damp it down. You can control the signal. It's an entirely new technology, but it's been suppressed, ever since — "

"I think it's time I made a phone call to Robert Core." Too many lies, Peter thought.

"No way," said Pons, who was leaning against the staircase, applying a gooey patina of high-octane acne medicine. "The captain pulled the lines for the duration." Pons was undergoing a flare-up.

"Look," the captain said hastily, "all I can do is show you Alejandro's notebooks. Just look at the numbers, for yourself. We have to put all this ball-breaking on hold until you've seen the notebooks." He pointed to a dank corner of the basement, where a table had been knocked together out of plywood and sawhorses. A huge ring binder lay open on top of it. "You want to know about Alejandro? How he fits into this? Then read the notebooks. You won't understand the answers to any of your questions until you do."

Peter shot a venomous glance at the captain. In the end, however, the record will show that he did not waste too much time resisting the impulse.

"You don't believe it can happen," the captain called after him. "You've got the blinders on, just like everybody else. All those technologies, all the ones that DID and IBM and Defense have been making fortunes out of for years — do you really believe they're the only ones possible?"

"You stay put," Peter said, as he crossed over to the plywood table. Peter reached down and riffled through the material, working backward toward the opening pages. Pons retreated up the stairs.

The captain looked at his watch. "Take your time," he said.

The Xeroxed sheets in the first section of the binder were yellowed with age. All the figures and graphs looked crude, as if they had been hand-drawn with a ruler. Peter was accustomed to the rectilinear precision of computer-generated graphics. "A Technical Description of the Hunt Resonating Coil" was the heading. There was an introductory passage written in dry, intransitive prose.

The purpose of the resonating coil, as described in the following pages, is to generate and broadcast electrical power and information wirelessly, through the selected use of heretofore untapped frequencies of the radio spectrum. . . .

Peter skimmed the introduction, skipping over the obscure diagrams. The section that followed consisted of nothing but page after page of handwritten notes in German. Someone named Conrad appeared to be the originating impulse. The material was identified as notes taken in Alejandro's hand in 1945. There were sketches, circuit specifications, wiring diagrams — it was impossible to make anything out of it at a glance. Peter was a physicist, not an electrical engineer.

He flipped through a series of long tabular columns of parameters and specifications, and discovered, at the back of the binder, a thoroughly modern section, adorned with bookmarks and paper clips and composed of the latest in computer-generated text and graphics. In this last section, all of the previous technical data had been converted into the language of contemporary microelectronics. There were scribbled notations and revisions everywhere. In place of hard-wired transistors, as in the earlier material, the design of the resonating coil now called for niobium microprocessors and assorted silicon building blocks.

*   *

On these final pages, Peter had no trouble recognizing some exceedingly familiar numbers, in green felt-tip.

He knew those numbers. He knew them better than the captain, who shouldn't have known them at all. They were *his* numbers, Peter's, the fruit of his memos — and they were scattered over every page at the back of the binder.

Holsa turned away from Peter, busying himself with readings and adjustments at the equipment bank.

Peter sat down at the makeshift table, and began to read in earnest.

* *

For more than an hour, Peter immersed himself in Alejandro's notebooks, and long before he finished surveying the material he felt himself breaking through into some zone of exhausted confusion he had never explored before. He had never even known it existed. Flipping back and forth between the sections, watching the equations becoming even more fantastical as they paraded down the pages, Peter couldn't presume to pass any sort of final judgment on the flights of fancy contained therein. A lot of it was airy speculation about wavelengths and transmission frequencies; and the captain was right, a good deal of it wasn't coherent at all. Ten leaps of faith, scientifically, on every page.

Nowhere in the material was there any reference to a design prototype, or an actual test. It was all theoretical. There was no mention of the coil being used as a means of producing a disruptive electromagnetic pulse. It was just a machine, the design of which was alien to him.

Alejandro's research in this fringe outpost of the electronics age apparently had convinced him, some twenty-five years ago, that a dozen or so coils, properly spaced across the face of North America, would be capable of transmitting electrical power and information to any suitable antennalike device within broadcast range, at a fraction of the cost of conventional systems. A single working coil would produce enough electrical energy and broadcast wattage to power an entire nation the size of England. . . .

A world linked by electricity, where information, pictures, voice, all traveled over the same, seamless, invisible web. A vision of an alternative grid. . . .

The specs, in a word, were staggering. Madness, Peter thought, and nothing more — Alejandro's private dream of the ultimate telecommunications device. The files of every patent office in America were overflowing with broken ideas just like it. A perpetual motion machine: Plug it in, and it powers the world with energy and information, resonating at frequencies so off-the-wall that, under any of the known rules of the game, it shouldn't work.

But someone with access to the memos thought otherwise. Someone was trying to fine-tune the prodigious output Alejandro originally had claimed for the coil, using Peter's numbers as the basis for the reconfigurations. If the captain didn't have the memos — if Alejandro was the one with the memos and the felt-tip pen — then the captain wouldn't necessarily see it that way, Peter realized. The captain wasn't in the loop; he was an outsider. He *couldn't* see it that way.

The notebooks, the memos, the Hunt Code: Alejandro had the whole set.

Still, Peter thought, as he read on, the thing shouldn't work at all. There were laws of physics.

But there were also exceptions to those laws: hypotheses to be tested, rules to be broken — there were all the lawless, uncharted avenues that had attracted Peter to the neighborhood in the first place.

Peter glanced over at the captain, who was standing in front of a bank of computers, smoking a cigarette while he watched the readouts on several screens at once. As far as it was possible to tell, the predicted energy output was in the range of what you would expect from a very advanced linear accelerator. If the coil actually worked, Peter could not imagine that even someone as precariously balanced as the captain would be willing to go through with it.

Why does he trust me with this stuff? Is he conning me, or is Alejandro conning him?

He took a last random gallop through the pages at the back of the binder. It would take too much time, and too many questions, not to mention the assumption of straight answers from the captain, to pin it all down for certain. He'd seen enough. Whether Peter believed in the coil or not, the point was, Alejandro apparently did.

Something on the page, a scribbled marginal notation, caught Peter's eye.

It wasn't the material itself, which was nothing but a footnote to a long technical discussion of the coil's properties. It was something about the words themselves that first attracted, and then held, Peter's attention. Something about the heading on that notation: "Design Details."

Look at it, Peter told himself. Look at it again.

"Design Details."

The curiously looped nature of the handwriting. The curve of those *D*'s thrown defiantly wide. . . .

For several minutes, Peter didn't move from the table, or jump to any conclusions. He shuffled hastily back through the pages of the concluding section and, this time, because he was looking for it, the characteristic *D* was everywhere. . . .

As in "David Atwood," on the napkin.

The notebooks' revisions in Ada's hand were recent. Think, Peter ordered himself: If Ada Stibbits did the numbers, what does that mean?

Peter studied the handwriting again, as if by sheer force of will, he could change it back into something unrecognizable. The captain had a helper: Ada Stibbits. Ada working with Alejandro, is what it means.

Peter closed the binder, and swiveled around to look at Holsa. The captain was looking back at him from the corner of one jaundiced eyeball. Peter was relatively certain that the captain wasn't going to offer up Alejandro's whereabouts and exact intentions without a fight. Nor Ada's, for that matter.

So be it, Peter thought. If that's what it takes.

Peter stood up to face Holsa. "Where's Alejandro, Frank? I'm going to give you one chance to get it right."

The captain walked over to the table, picked up the notebooks, and carried them back to his workbench. "He has an emissary," Holsa mumbled. "Alejandro won't be here until tomorrow."

"An *emissary*, Frank?"

"Through an emissary, yeah."

Peter moved away from the table. "Have you ever *seen* Alejandro, Frank? Actually talked to him? Ever looked him in the eye?"

Holsa turned his back on Peter again. He didn't appear to be very anxious to discuss the notebooks now that Peter had finished looking them over.

Peter walked casually over to a nearby closet, where he began appraising a wide selection of work tools. "This emissary, then."

"He wishes to remain anonymous."

"It's not a he, Frank. It's a she."

The captain's face crumpled. Bewildered, he spun around to face Peter. "You mean you *know* about Ellen?"

"I don't know any Ellen. Her name is Ada Stibbits." Go on, Peter urged himself. Play the What If game. Suppose the coil actually works, and suppose, furthermore, that Ada was telling the truth about not having seen Alejandro Hunt for twenty years or more. What then?

"Ada who? I don't know who you're talking about."

Peter found what he was looking for in the closet. "I'm beginning to think you're right, Frank."

"What're you doing over there?"

Peter wrapped his hands around the handle of a large sledgehammer and backed quickly toward the center of the basement. Holsa very adroitly came at him then, bellowing like a wounded rhino, but when Peter raised the sledge, threateningly, the captain stopped dead in his tracks.

"Oh, man," the captain said weakly. "You wouldn't."

When he reached the coil, Peter stood by the open panel and cocked the sledge high above his shoulder. The captain held out an imploring hand, taking an exploratory step in Peter's direction. "Anything you wanna know, just ask," he said. "Just don't be rash, man, *please.*"

"The memos, Frank. Ever seen the memos?"

"Man, you keep talking riddles. Listen, just — "

"You don't know what those numbers mean," Peter said as he held his batting stance. "You can't see them from the other side — from inside SEEK, like I can."

The captain took another step, but when Peter waved the sledge, he took it back. "Pons!" the captain roared. "*Can you come down here please for a minute?*"

Peter measured his distance from the coil. "Here's an interesting fact for you. Klaatu has scheduled an act of sabotage — a blackout pulse — which happens to fall on the same day as the Pons Concert. And Frank, let me tell you, that ain't meaningful coincidence, that's no coincidence at all. Do you really believe that all this machine can do is play The Who singing 'My Generation' through everybody's plumbing?"

The captain shook his head in disbelief. "Jesus, Cassidy, you don't think that's enough? You still don't see it? This is industrial history in the making! Kings are gonna fall! You damp down the coil's output, you can broadcast anything you want — and for *pennies*. Radio signals, computer data, even raw electrical energy . . . You don't need any kind of specialized receiving equipment. It's a whole new science! It's like . . . it's like a new start! After tomorrow, every digital network in the world is gonna be rendered instantly obsolete!"

For an instant, as the captain yammered on, Peter felt almost sorry for him.

"Yeah, you have, you've lost the *vision*," the captain said frantically. "That's what happens when you go to work for an asylum like DID!"

Peter heard the sound of short, fast steps on the metal stairway, and a great crackling and popping of plastic. Holsa heard it, too, and a vicious smile came over his face. It was the sound the captain had been waiting to hear for at least an hour.

All the frustrations and uncertainties of the past week welled up in Peter at that point, and he found it easy, much easier than he might have imagined, to raise the sledgehammer as high as he could, swinging with everything he had. The sledge crashed into the open port on the side of the coil, pulverizing several PC boards and ripping loose a good two feet of metal housing.

The captain screamed.

Leonard appeared at the bottom of the stairs. Leonard and his gun.

Leonard looked at the captain, and he looked at the damaged coil. Then he looked at Peter.

Peter let the sledgehammer drop to the floor with a thud.

"Alejandro can see you now," Leonard said.

TWENTY-FOUR

A T LEONARD'S direction, Peter walked out to the driveway and installed himself in Leonard's car. In a way, he was relieved to have it over with — glad to have the whole thing out of his hands, once and for all.

And then he thought of Ada again. Not too many people had the juice to get their hands on Peter's memos. Ada was one of them.

Even fewer would be able to understand them. Ada was one of those, too.

That I could have missed it. That she could have conned me so beautifully. . . .

Pons came out to see them off. Peter rolled down his window. "Don't do it, Pons," he said. "People could get hurt. The captain doesn't care what happens, as long as it makes a big noise. A high-energy burst of potentially devastating — "

"Not another word," Leonard said, as he climbed behind the wheel.

"The show must go on," Pons stammered painfully. "Who said that? Ed Sullivan?"

Leonard backed the car into the street and accelerated into the traffic on Sir Francis Drake Boulevard. No, Pons, Peter thought. It was P. T. Barnum.

Peter said, "You're not taking me to see Alejandro, are you?"

Leonard passed on it.

"You don't have to kill me, Leonard. I can think of any number of reasons why you wouldn't want to do that."

Leonard held the gun in one hand and steered with the other. "Really," he said.

If Ada had wanted the numerical key to the Hunt Code for some reason, Peter was thinking, conceivably she could have gotten it from

211

Alejandro himself, years ago, when the two of them were thick. The same with the notebooks.

The Hunt Code, everybody's favorite piece of evidence. The perfect vehicle for casting every iota of suspicion onto Alejandro himself.

Peter had a hunch. A strong one. He let it grow.

"Tell me this much, Leonard," he said. "By any chance, are you in love?" Like all the other insights that had come to him in the last seven days, this one struck Peter far too late in the game to be of much help.

Leonard cleared his throat. "Oh yes," he said. "Very much so."

The notebooks, the memos, the Hunt Code: When you added everything up, in order to make the solution come out right, you really didn't need Alejandro in the equation at all.

"How is it supposed to be, after all this is over?"

Leonard only shook his head. "She makes no promises," he said.

Peter let his head loll back against the seat, and closed his eyes, as Leonard drove south toward the Golden Gate Bridge.

Dear sweet Ada. I think I know who and what you are.

Leonard drove across the bridge into San Francisco, and then kept heading south, all the way through town. He parked the car in a small motel court near the Glen Park BART station, about twenty minutes from downtown. A fake palm tree had been placed haphazardly in front of every room. As Leonard cut the engine and pulled on the emergency brake, he looked squarely at Peter and said, "Are you tired, too?"

Peter coughed once, checked the location of the pistol, and opened his door. His mind had failed him, and his fishing pole was broken. His two most prized possessions were in need of repair.

Leonard had a key to Room Six. He unlocked the door and waved Peter inside. "Sit on the bed," he said.

Peter sat. Dying is so stupid, he thought. It would be nice to buy a new rod and reel.

Leonard went to the chipped table beside the opposite bed and placed a phone call. "It's me," he said. "I'm here with Cassidy." Leonard listened for a while, replying in monosyllables.

"Let me talk to her," Peter said, as Leonard was about to hang up. He held out his hand for the phone.

At first, he didn't think Leonard was going to give it to him. "He wants to talk to you," Leonard said. He listened a while longer, nodding absently. A moment later, he handed the phone to Peter.

Peter could hear her breathing on the line. "Talk to me, Ada." He could picture her, poised and purposeful, her hair pinned above her neck and just the hint of an overbite. . . .

"It's almost over now," Ada said.

"Where are you now?"

There was a pause. "I'm with Frank. He says to tell you that he's redundant with respect to most of the circuitry you destroyed."

"I'm betting Alejandro doesn't know about the coil. Not this one, anyway."

She laughed. Marvelous, that sound.

"You kept Holsa and Pons in the dark. You played on all the old myths and half-truths about Alejandro."

"I'm impressed. Really very impressed."

"The captain is convinced the coil is harmless."

"Alejandro convinced everyone, actually. A long time ago."

"I just guessed it through, Ada. I saw the notebooks and played What If."

"Yes," said Ada. She paused again. "You've quite outdone yourself today, Peter."

Leonard, standing nearby, watched Peter vigilantly. He took a step toward the bed, for emphasis. In less than thirty-six hours, Leonard was thinking, we will be through with this. Contemplating the long drive back to Marin, Leonard began to fidget as he tried to decide whether Grozniev's house was a safe place for Ada to be.

Costa del Sol, Leonard decided. He would suggest it, and see how it struck her.

"Who are you trying to hurt, Ada?" Peter asked her.

"No one. I'm trying to protect."

"But the coil — "

"It functions," said Ada, "as an antidote."

"Why do you want to do it? I'll ask you again — who do you want to hurt?"

"Egg is so fragile, Peter. So homeless."

"If you succeed in creating a blackout pulse with this coil, people are going to die."

"Egg is so damaged."

"This is egg logic, Ada? Call it off."

"How peculiar," she said. "I always thought, somehow, that you'd find yourself in sympathy with my intentions."

"I saw the notebooks. I can extrapolate. A peak field on the order of fifty thousand volts per meter, miles away from the generating

213

source. I figure something like Hawaii to Salt Lake City, LA to Vancouver. Am I close? Fifty thousand volts *per meter*, Ada. It's murder. You won't just destroy SEEK circuits, you'll kill a lot of innocent people. You get this huge transient pulse skittering over the SEEK net, like drops of water on a hot griddle, and you don't know what's going to happen."

"You know, Peter, you'd be wrong, despite appearances, to presume that I am working totally at cross-purposes from Alejandro Hunt."

"You wanted to protect me from all this. I don't get it."

"Anton was going to kill you," she said. "I couldn't let that happen. You would have been safe at the shack, if you had gone there when Leonard told you to."

Another insight, way too late. "You don't care about *me*, Ada. You just want my *work*."

"Peter," she said gently, as if speaking to a child. "It's the same thing."

"Don't do it, Ada. You have that choice."

"Now it's time for you to go to bed."

"Ada — "

Leonard took the phone from Peter's hand. He put it to his ear and listened without comment for a moment, then hung up.

Peter sat on his bed, watching Leonard, on the other bed, preparing a syringe.

"Ah, Leonard," he said shakily. "Let's skip it. I'm not like Anton."

Leonard looked up from his work. "This won't kill you," he said.

"You're lying."

Leonard just shrugged.

"Leonard," Peter said frantically, "you don't understand what's going to happen. She's probably planning to kill you when this is over."

"Left arm, please," he said as he approached.

"*Call Alejandro, Leonard.* Tell him about the coil and the notebooks. Don't take *my* word for it."

Leonard leaned toward him, the gun in one hand, the syringe in the other.

Woodenly, Peter rolled up his sleeve. "She's making a fool of you," he said. "*Ask Alejandro.* Can you really be so sure of her love that you won't even do *that much*?"

Deftly, Leonard inserted the needle.

Peter waited passively until Leonard's attention was fixed on the injection in progress. Then he swung quickly with his right fist, hop-

ing to catch Leonard off guard. But Leonard caught Peter instead —
right under the chin with the butt of the pistol, breaking off the
hypodermic in the process.

Peter's teeth clacked together as he fell backward on the bed, the
needle still buried in his arm.

It was his third and final encounter with Leonard Gort.

P A R T

FOUR

TWENTY-FIVE

O N THE MORNING of the Pons Concert, dawn came to Marin as a neat wash of fog the color of a gin and tonic. The fog burned off by late morning, revealing a cloudless sky. By noon on December twenty-first, the multicolored flags ringing the concert site on Mount Tamalpais were fluttering smartly under full sun. The temperature, Pons noted, was in the sixties. You didn't always get days like that, in December in Marin.

The parking lot had filled rapidly, and by midday thousands of invited guests, mixed with an equal number of hopefuls and hangers-on, were trudging slowly up the path to the Pons Arena, carrying coolers, blankets, and hats. From his perch on the railing along the uppermost row of the bowl-shaped arena, Pons could see them all coming. They were raising a good bit of dust. Pilgrims on the road to the Kaaba, thought Pons. On the road to the holy stone.

Pons turned away from the crowds and looked down at the concert site, his kingdom for a day. Half the seats were full already, and Huey Lewis wasn't scheduled to start the show for at least another hour yet. The scaffolding and speakers were all in place, and among the semis and transportation gear scattered across the cordoned area behind the stage there was one particularly high-backed van, wired and ready, serving as command central for the captain and his coil. The captain had stocked the van with plenty of Heineken and bologna and was planning to remain sequestered there until shortly before nine P.M.

Earlier in the day, Pons had been quick to mark the presence of increasing numbers of law enforcement types in mufti. A few of the more official-looking ones had already hit him up on the subject of Holsa's whereabouts. One of them had petitioned Pons on that subject while the two of them were standing not forty feet away from the Mack truck-and-trailer that housed the captain and the works.

And if that weren't enough — as if his whole life and business and fortune didn't hang in the balance already — the stage crew had been hectoring him all morning about one imagined oversight or another. It was too much. Pons didn't like ducking the law, and putting on a primo rock concert, and fretting over the matter of the coil, all at the same time.

The repairs to the coil had proven fairly minor, but Peter's rampage had managed to get Pons worried. Ellen had shown up shortly after Leonard had taken Peter away, and when the coil was intact again, Ellen and the captain ran a simulated test, firing up the coil for less than sixty seconds. When they started picking up a weak signal on test equipment at the concert site, they shut it down. The frequencies checked out perfectly, and nothing got broken this time, but who could tell at ten percent power?

Early this morning, they'd managed to get the coil on-site without any major hassles — nothing broken there, either.

The walkie-talkie on his waist crackled to life, and Pons winced. He didn't want to answer it. He craved insulation. Life, someone once said, is only one damn thing after another, and that, thought Pons, just about covers it for today.

Pons had made a vow, early that morning, while the fog was still in: Nobody gets hurt at my show.

Pons was willing to go with the agenda, as it stood, with one added proviso. Using the coil, they would augment a portion of a single number by The Who for three, maybe four minutes. No chance for anything untoward in four minutes, even at full power. The captain and Ellen wanted eight minutes minimum, but Pons was planning to nix that. It was too risky, and he wasn't going to bother arguing with them about it.

Pons was accustomed to being liked and used by people simultaneously. Everyone always came on to him with such a well-oiled combination of affection and greed. The captain had always been that way, too, but Pons believed that the affection, in the captain's case, outweighed the greed. Just a little. Just enough.

As for Ellen, Pons didn't trust her at all. He hadn't seen her all morning, either, which was fine. She was supposed to show up later, according to the captain. After the last test, she'd started making herself scarce.

Pons wouldn't argue with either one of them about it. He would just station himself next to the switch, and *do* it, when the time came.

Nobody gets hurt at my show.

The radio on his belt started crackling again. This time, Pons answered. As he listened, he cupped a hand over his eyes and admired the lustrous rise of the red-and-purple moon-shaped stage down below. For his big day, Pons had chosen simple, understated attire: a white-on-white suit with white bucks and an orange rose in the lapel, plus wraparound beatnik shades. With a little hair on his face, he could have passed for a gnomic George Harrison.

The Who were scheduled to arrive in four black stretch limos at seven o'clock, but now the lady on the radio telephone was telling Pons that the band had gotten to town early. At least two of the band's members were heading over for a quick look at the layout.

Pons took the steps three at a time.

They would stick with the original schedule, he decided. The band would go on at seven-thirty. Pons and the captain would augment their act at exactly nine o'clock.

The rest of the day went extremely well, considering. The bands played on, and Pons was graciously allowed to take three or four strums across the frets of Peter Townshend's very own guitar backstage. He spent most of his time dodging the press.

And as the sun began to go down behind the mountain, after approximately seven hours of the concert had elapsed, Pons moved to his private viewing box, stage right. His sunglasses sparkled as the stage lights came on. Pons threw himself into the music, thinking that the music could cure his jitters, if anything could, and for a while, for Pons, it did just that.

There were twenty thousand people in the audience. Pons hadn't invited them all. Who cares.

Attached to the low front wall of the viewing booth was a remote switching mechanism which would activate the coil. Pons had insisted. The captain had wired it under protest, but Pons was adamant: The coil would be switched on, and off, from the Pons box. He wondered how much of the show the captain was catching, out back in the trailer.

At exactly half past seven, as promised, The Who took the stage.

Pons had sweated this reunion for so long, that when it finally came, he allowed himself a sweet measure of release. He'd done it. Who'd have believed it. The Who.

> People try to put us down,
> Talkin 'bout my generation
> Just because we g-get around,
> Talkin 'bout my generation . . .

The sound in the arena was as clean and hard as sheet metal. Lasers sprouted from risers on either side of the stage, lolling crazily on flexible necks, firing streams of steel blue light over the crowd.

Pons closed his eyes, smiling into the teeth of it. This should have been the most perfect moment of his life. And it almost was.

The only thing that marred it was his knowledge of the captain's impending arrival. The captain was going to show up in the booth very soon — much too soon for Pons's liking.

And spoil everything.

Which was more or less how it turned out.

✻ ✻

Ellen stood with one hand on the open door of her Mercedes, looking down on the illuminated city of San Francisco.

From her panoramic vantage point on Mount Sutro, not far from Golden Gate Park, she could see both of the city's bridges. Between them, downtown was aglow, and Market Street was a long clean diagonal through the center of town. It was the week before Christmas, the stores were open late, and everywhere, the lights were on. Headlights glided along the streets below her; many windows beckoned.

Lost in the trees at the foot of the hill, a car backfired distantly, the sound carrying to the nearly deserted parking lot as a series of muted pops. A slight wind worked across the hill. Ellen turned and could just make out Leonard as he trudged resolutely toward the back of the hill, in the direction of the massive Sutro transmitter tower. He was carrying an army surplus entrenching tool and a fireproof steel file box. Ellen checked her watch. It was a few minutes past eight.

The night was clear except for thin wisps of fog trailing from the spires of the tallest buildings. Ellen saw that streamers of fog had attached themselves to the blinking red crown of the Sutro tower as well. She could barely discern Leonard's form, crouched near the base of the tower. There was nothing left for her to do.

The necessary adjustments to the coil apparatus had proven quite minor. The simulations had been so unblemished, the short test so conclusive, that Ellen had felt free to spend most of the past twenty-four hours attending to the details of her coming departure. The captain's work was impeccable. If the coil's affinity for niobium circuitry was even half as fatally acute as Peter Cassidy had predicted in those useful papers of his, the final pulse from the coil would do more damage to the SEEK system in an instant than Ellen possibly could have accomplished in several lifetimes of concerted individual effort.

She could never have dealt the system any sort of finishing blow by means of the Hunt Code. The coil was more direct, and proper, and final. In Ellen's mind, the blame for everything that had happened in 1959 resided not so much with the faceless perpetrators of the scheme to place Alejandro under quiet NSA custody, but with the original and abiding reason for their actions: the SEEK system itself. Over the years, it had become obvious to her — to anyone who cared to look — that systems like SEEK, when they reach a certain size and complexity, acquire direction, momentum, intent: the faculty of self-preservation. They devour to connect, and Egg is helpless against them. Family is anathema to them.

Ellen had every reason to expect that, after eight minutes of operating time, the coil would emit a pulse capable of flashing across fully half of the North American SEEK network, destroying nearly every SEEK chip through which it coursed, and creating, as a by-product, a widespread blackout. Through one channel or another, the pulse might carry all the way to the NSA's basement. This was Ellen's fond hope.

The colonel and Anton were finished, but the colonel and Anton would be replaced by word-perfect copies.

As they wished: Ellen had the coil.

For the sake of precision, what Ellen had was the sole extant copy of the notebooks. The coil itself would self-destruct at the end of its performance. Leonard, ever resourceful, had assured this through the surreptitious implantation of explosives. The coil's ephemerality is its strength, Ellen thought. It has not existed long enough, in either of its two incarnations, for anyone to understand what it is.

Ellen thought back to the explosion that had jolted her awake in the Adirondacks, so many years of nights ago. Alejandro Hunt had unwittingly inspired her actions in more ways than one. It was because of Alejandro that she had adopted the name Klaatu. Surely he had guessed by now. Surely he had seen the movie, as she had, with Michael Rennie as Klaatu, his chiseled features set in an expression of worldly concern, bearing the most uncanny resemblance to Alejandro himself, as she remembered him. Surely he must have seen it. . . .

Summer, 1959. Crickets and a smattering of fireflies, the Big Dipper spilling its contents in the direction of the North Star. Ellen remembered dandelions, whole fields of them, dancing in the moonlight.

The coil itself, housed in the barn, looked ungainly and improbable — a roughly conical machine with miles and miles of wire wrapped around it.

On the night of the test, after a battery of monitoring devices had been secretly arrayed all across the county, they used a phonograph record as the experimental broadcast signal. Alejandro turned on the coil, and it worked.

Alejandro was ecstatic. *Think what you can do.*

For three or four minutes, it seemed to work.

Then something began to happen. There was nothing in the design of the coil to account for it. The physics of it eluded even Alejandro. No one could have foreseen the exponential increase in the strength of the coil's output.

From Pennsylvania to Maine to Ontario — blackouts, tripped circuit breakers, screeching radios, dead phones. . . .

For hours after the test, they huddled in the barn near an emergency radio set. They learned that a small private plane had crash-landed near Lake Placid, killing the pilot and three passengers.

Think what you can do. . . .

Just before dawn, she remembered being awakened from a fitful doze by the shuddering thump of an explosion. Rachel began to cry in the crib at the foot of the bed. She wrapped Rachel in a blanket, threw on a nightgown, and was halfway down the path to the barn before she realized what Alejandro had done. When she emerged into the clearing with Rachel in her arms, she saw him standing upwind of the burning barn, his sharp features in profile, lit by the soaring flames. Robert Core was standing beside him.

Alejandro stared steadily at the fire as she approached. Hail Mary, full of shit, she heard him swear quietly. Bloody puta. Whore. . . .

He sent her back to the cabin, and spent the day with Robert Core. That evening, after removing his clothing and personal effects from her cabin, Alejandro and Core left for New York City. The barn ruins were still smoldering.

Two days later the investigators arrived and began combing through the wreckage of the barn. Alejandro had warned her of this, but she was frightened all the same. She had searched the cabin one more time, as Alejandro had requested, which proved fortuitous. In the back of the closet, encased in a fireproof file box, was a smudged but complete copy of the coil notebooks. Alejandro had apparently forgotten about it. She knew she should destroy her find as Alejandro had destroyed all other extant copies in the barn fire.

Instead, she put the notebooks back in the firebox, took a shovel from the storage shed, and buried the notebooks under a scraggly spruce tree near the cabin. It was harder work than she had anticipated, and while she struggled against the rocks and roots, Rachel cried on the blanket beside her.

The man who knocked on the door of her cabin was young. He had thick black hair and an air of intensity about him which she found unsettling. He said he was an arson investigator in charge of interviewing the neighbors, of which there were few, because of the deliberate isolation of the work site.

Some sort of lab fire, she told him. Her vacation home, she said. She did not invite him inside.

He did not press. Except for a series of hot and cruelly appraising glances at her body, Anton did not seem to harbor the slightest interest in her personally. She disliked him immediately.

The day after the investigators finished sifting the wreckage, she left for New York City with Rachel. Alejandro had not called, had not contacted her in any way, and she was desperate to find out what had happened.

Alejandro owned a nondescript frame house on Long Island, not far from the DID offices. When she met him there, she searched his face for a hint of his mood. He seemed remarkably transparent. He did not tell her everything, but he told her enough. He had informed the Defense Department's research people that he was abrogating all contracts between DID and the Pentagon. Pure, unfettered research. No more SEEK development, no more disastrous secret projects like the coil. . . .

He must have known all along that it wouldn't be that simple, Ellen thought, as she watched the glittering San Francisco skyline. He must have known how badly they wanted him by then. . . .

Just before they left home for dinner out, Alejandro received a phone call. He returned to her looking mildly puzzled. Robert Core

225

urgently wanted to meet with him at seven o'clock that night. He had no idea why. All he had was an address.

She guessed it would be somewhere near Gramercy Park. They cruised randomly in Alejandro's Studebaker, one-year-old Rachel tired and cranky from all the activity, Alejandro craning his neck as he tried to read block numbers. He refused to stop and ask for directions. They always do.

It was twilight when he found the house. Alejandro parked down the block and volunteered to carry Rachel, who fell asleep the instant she hit his shoulder. She was wearing a white summer frock Alejandro had bought for her, Ellen remembered. There were goose pimples on her legs.

A stranger answered the door, and they followed him down a long hallway to a sitting room at the back of the house. The house had an oppressive, cloistered air — embalmed Victorian, malignant with doilies and chintz.

Alejandro entered the sitting room ahead of her, and she saw the muscles in his back bunch and stiffen. Hello, DeBroer, she heard him say, rather formally. Where's Core?

Held up, Anton said. We don't need him, anyway.

She stepped from behind Alejandro. Anton was slouched in a morris chair, dressed in an ill-fitting suit, gazing with youthful disdain at Alejandro. It was the same young man who had questioned her at the cabin. Their eyes met, and Anton's widened slowly in surprise. He looked from her to Alejandro, who was still holding the child, and then back again.

Looks like I've been snookered, Anton said. Ellen, isn't it?

Alejandro demanded to see Robert Core.

Anton looked at Alejandro with stinging contempt. I told you, he said. We don't need him.

Then Anton looked at me, she remembered. And he smiled.

We're going home, Alejandro said curtly, and as he turned for the door, almost bumping into her, three other men who had been leaning watchfully on the wainscoting moved to block his exit.

As it happens, Anton said steadily, Core's got nothing to do with it. This is an agency matter. Too many, ah, violated directives. That kind of thing. Charges. And so on. You understand. My hands are tied.

His back to Anton, Alejandro handed her the sleeping child. They're going to arrest me, he told her quietly.

Just a minute, Anton said.

226

Go quickly, Alejandro told her.

The lady stays, said Anton, rising from his chair.

It was all happening much too quickly.

Alejandro turned to face the three men. For an instant she had the feeling he was going to do something ghastly and rash.

Anton raised his eyebrows and nodded toward the sleeping bundle in her arms. That your kid? he asked. Neither of them answered.

All the menace Alejandro had been holding so unsteadily in check seemed to leak away from him. He seemed to age twenty years in the space of five seconds.

Let them go, Alejandro said.

I'm afraid not, Anton said. You want me to break up a *family?*

She would never forget the derision on his face.

At that moment, Robert Core entered the room. He looked at Alejandro with surprise.

She was very close to fainting, and knew it, and tried to prevent it, but could not. The last thing she remembered that night was Alejandro scooping Rachel from her arms as she fell. . . .

And for what they did to the child, she was supposed to say thank you.

Ellen rechecked her watch by the diffused light of the nightscape. Months ago, she had quietly arranged for her impending departure — excellent quarters in Hawaii for a long-term stay. Ellen had informed no one of these arrangements. Frank Holsa was under the impression that he would be accompanying her to Switzerland in a few hours. It had been necessary for Ellen to create this impression, in order to forestall questions about the future. The captain's present usefulness was coming to an end. Frank Holsa was much too unpredictable for anything amounting to a long-term relationship.

As for Leonard — she would ask him to go into hiding, here in the States, to emerge again when, and if, it was indicated. Leonard would not be accompanying her, either. Leonard possessed that most valuable of assets, patience.

Leonard's shovel flew. When he had carved out a hole to his liking, Leonard put down his shovel, picked up the file box, and dropped it in. He stood back and studied his sandy pile of backfill for a moment.

With her mind cleared of all the incessant distractions, she would have been able to see him in a new light. All along, this had been Leonard's belief.

227

Mazatlán. He tried it out in his mind. Venice. He tried that one out, as well.

Leaning against one of the tower supports, less than two hundred yards from Ellen's car, Leonard wiped the dirt from his hands. There wasn't any reason to concern himself with Holsa or the coil any longer. He had already done what he could. Leonard had seen to it that the explosive charge placed inside the coil was at least twice as powerful as required. It would be a noteworthy send-off, when the time came.

In New York, Leonard remembered, they lost three chickens in a nearby coop.

Leonard kneeled down beside the hole, reached in, and pried open the lid of the file box. He emptied its contents into the dirt at the bottom of the hole, and his hands shook as he struck a match. This is the easy part, he was thinking.

Her lies had been consistent. Alejandro had pointed out most of them in the space of a ten-minute phone call. The pattern was there. The sickness was obvious.

Leonard straightened back up, watching to be sure that the notebooks caught fire. He had a final task to perform before he was through. It was the hardest task of all. No one should ever have to do it, he was thinking. Not even Alejandro should ask it.

Leonard took a moment to adjust his raincoat and arrange his hat. It was time for Ellen to retire.

*   *

Peter Cassidy realized that he was awake, and no longer dreaming of a hot air balloon high over the Pacific.

It took him longer to understand that this gradual dawning of consciousness stood for something. And then, finally, he got it.

Slowly, he raised his hands to his face and rubbed his eyes, concentrating on bringing his vision into focus. He was on his back, still on the motel bed, and something was wrong. He felt cold and wet. His joints wouldn't loosen. Everything felt out of whack, all his moving parts.

He rolled his head to the right, and looked over at the electric clock on the chipped table by the opposite bed. A few minutes past seven. Out since noon, about seven hours. Dark outside. A light burning in the bathroom. His pants, draped neatly over a chair.

His pants — Sig's pants — on the chair. Still life with pants.

Peter lay still for a while, trying to figure out what it meant.

An hour passed before he could sit up.

*   *

228

He became aware of an unpleasant odor. He looked down and discovered that his legs, and a portion of the bed, were soaked with urine. He looked at the clock again. It didn't make sense. He looked at his pants again. And then it did.

He still felt like hammered dog shit, but now he knew why.

He shook his head vigorously, trying to dislodge the last of the cobwebs — trying to retrieve the colonel's private number, which he had memorized from the card the colonel had given him. He attempted to stand up, and fell down, and made it to his knees, which was good enough for dialing.

As he leaned against the table for support, waiting for the colonel to come on the line, Peter tried to remember everything that had happened to him since that night, almost exactly one week ago, when he came home from the mountains in the dark, and lit a fire in his wood stove, and ignored his mail, and tried to get drunk. Doctor Cassidy. Mr. Cassidy. Peter, if I may. The good soldier's call. Snippets of mind-film, a kaleidoscope of impressions; half-glances, deceit and suspicion. . . .

"Cassidy," said Robert Core. "Where are you?"

The colonel's voice seemed to be coming from the bottom of a two-hundred-foot well. "I was drugged and put away in some motel," Peter said. "Leonard did it."

"We'll come get you," the colonel said.

"Uh, no, Colonel, it's not me, it's. . . . Colonel, what *day* is this?"

"It's Friday!" the colonel roared. "What the hell did you *think* it was? There's no time for — "

"Leonard put me out for a day and a half."

"Cassidy, if you *know* something — "

"Colonel," Peter interrupted, "have you ever heard of something called a resonating coil?"

The line hummed. "The question is," said the colonel, "how did *you* hear about it?"

"I've just seen one, Colonel. Yesterday, I mean. Alejandro Hunt designed it, and Frank Holsa just finished building it. What it is, is some kind of pulse-beam weapon that you can — "

"Peter, there's less than four hours to go — *where is it?*"

"The Pons Concert, in Marin, on Mount Tamalpais. And Colonel, you're right, there's no time. They're going to fire up this coil when The Who take the stage."

"When who — "

"Which could be any minute."

"You're absolutely sure the coil is there?"

"Mount Tamalpais, that was the plan. The place'll be a madhouse, I don't know how you're going to — "

"Stay on the line, Peter, and somebody will — "

"No, Colonel, listen. It's not Alejandro. Alejandro's not Klaatu." Peter paused for a deep breath. "If you want to know who it is, Colonel, then you have to guarantee me two things — "

"My God, Peter, there's no time for — "

"You have to clear David, and you have to guarantee the safety of Alison Atwood. DeBroer thinks — "

"Alison Atwood is in the hospital, completely safe," the colonel said rapidly. "As for Atwood — you have my word."

The funny thing was, Peter believed him. "It's Ada, Colonel. The coil is Ada's. I'm the only one who knows — "

The colonel signed off without another word. Peter didn't wait to see if anybody else was going to come on the line.

He allowed himself a few more minutes of recuperation, then willed himself to his feet. When the attacks of dizziness abated, he lurched across the room and fumbled his way into Sig's pants, breaking the zipper in the process. He drank several glasses of water from the bathroom tap, then headed for the motel room door, opened it, and stepped tentatively into the parking lot.

He fought his way slowly down the street, in the direction of the BART station he'd glimpsed on the way in. His vision was steady, but his balance was still precarious. He would hop a train for downtown, or call a cab, or steal a car. There was nothing to do but head for the mountain, however he could manage it.

If he was too late, then he was too late. He had decided to act as if it mattered.

Peter arrived at the BART platform, and found enough change in his pockets for a ticket. As he rode the escalator to the boarding platform, he saw lights down the track. The fates were handing him an inbound train.

This is my lucky day, he thought. Today I am reborn. I awoke from the dead, I caught my train, I did what I could. Except for Alison. Alison I did very badly.

He said a quick prayer for the Ace, figuring it was the thought that counted. He didn't know how to, but he did it, anyway.

For some reason, the train was packed. People gave Peter wide berth in the aisles, mistaking him for a wino — several days' worth of stubble and a wild-eyed look. He staggered into one of the soft blue seats, facing a twenty-minute ride to downtown San Francisco. His joints still felt weak and stiff, and he luxuriated in the delicious absence of muscular activity.

And then, strangely, Peter found himself thinking about fishing. About fishing and the fish. About how it had always been for him on the streams. He closed his eyes. He may have dozed.

He enjoyed fifteen minutes of rest. The train was in a tunnel beneath upper Market Street, the cars gently rocking as it began swinging through a curve at reduced speed. A toddler in tiny cowboy boots clamped onto Peter's leg for support. "Jerry, that's not nice," the boy's mother said.

There was a sound coming from the train.

The sound grew louder.

Peter could hear the other passengers begin to mumble in confusion. "What's going on, anyway?" Jerry's mother asked, directing it at anyone who might care to answer.

The sound seemed to come from everywhere at once. Peter was the only passenger on the train who knew what it meant.

I'm too late. Peter leaned toward the pint-sized parasite on his leg. *I'm stroked.*

It was the sound of a song, growing louder still.

And Peter recognized it.

TWENTY-SIX

THE MUSIC hit Pons like a hurricane. The same guitar he had strummed backstage was now being used as the instrument for solos so wild and modal that Pons got lost somewhere in the middle of them, every time. A portrait of Pons in heaven.

The captain showed up at 8:45, right in the middle of "Behind Blue Eyes." Neither of them felt inclined toward conversation.

Pons could see fights and assorted scufflings breaking out behind the stage. It didn't seem to be the fault of the fans. The on-site population of men in uniforms was multiplying rapidly, right before his eyes.

At 8:50, Pons looked at the captain, and wondered how he could keep the captain from blocking him away from the switch. Simple weight advantage — nature's law.

At 8:55, accompanied by the rising thunder of applause, four giant speakers, controlled by automatic lifts, tilted forty-five degrees skyward. The arena was alive with rippling bodies.

Onstage, the band kicked into the opening flourishes of "Won't Get Fooled Again." The arena roared.

At precisely nine, Pons licked his dry lips and turned to face the captain. "Augment," he shouted.

The captain reached down and switched on.

> Pick up my guitar and play
> Just like yesterday,
> And I get on my knees and pray
> We won't get fooled again. . . .

The sound intensified gradually at first. It grew louder, and louder still, but then the loudness seemed to peak out, and the sound seemed to grow, instead, in some other dimension of intensity. It became tactile; a snarl of electrical excitation. The sound of the sound became the feeling of the sound.

The ghost of electricity is howling in the bones of our faces, Pons silently intoned, paraphrasing his favorite New Testament prophet, Bob Dylan. Pons was standing, but could not feel his feet on the floor. He was breathing but he couldn't speak.

There was a moment, after four minutes of this blitzkrieg, during which the band produced a lone, pure, sustained tonic chord, and in that moment, Pons Grozniev succeeded, monumentally, in remembering his promise to himself. As a long series of guitar glissandos — great fiery towers of half notes, eighth notes, sixteenths — erupted from center stage, Pons threw off his glasses, turned, and leaped for the switch.

The captain was nowhere in sight.

Pons hit the switch. And nothing happened. The captain had anticipated this. Holsa had wired a one-way switch, and was now presumably on the way to the locked confines of his trailer, planning to turn off the coil whenever it pleased him.

Pons didn't have a chance.

The sound seemed to be coming from everywhere at once now, and again, onstage, the band brought forth a single, vibratory note, and sustained it.

Pons was the center and the center was everywhere.

Hoo-ooo. . . .

At seven minutes past nine o'clock, Pons slipped to his knees.

One minute later, the lights went out. The music stopped, and the darkness was upon them, all of them and everywhere. For one stretched instant, all was silence.

Then a series of unimaginable explosions erupted from the vicinity of the vans and semis behind the stage.

And oh, Pons thought, how it was when the lights went out! The things I saw in the dark! My Companion! And all the sweet children holding matches!

How it always was from then! From then on!

*　*

Alison Atwood, in her hospital nightgown, was sitting on the edge of the bed, impatiently watching TV. All the men with the questions were gone for the day. Asa was in his incubator, two halls down. It was a few minutes past nine P.M. The television, which someone had bracketed to the wall for life with four monstrous chunks of angle iron, glowed silently, neck-high, in the far corner of the room. *Entertainment Tonight.* It's time to get out of here, thought Alison. Asa, however, would be staying for a while. It seemed so ludicrous that David wasn't here. Initially, she worried that David would never get the chance to see Asa alive. Now she just worried, period.

She was about to press the nurse's buzzer, seeking to track down a pitcher of cold orange juice, when the television and all the lights in her room began to flicker, and then winked out.

That was the way it seemed. They winked out.

Alison remained seated on the edge of her bed, in total darkness, waiting for the power to come back on. She imagined that thousands of other people all over the hospital were doing the same, and then she thought, No, there are operations going on, and patients hooked to critical care equipment . . . like the Ace. . . .

Suddenly panicked, she stood and groped her way to the door of her room. She could hear movement in the hall; harried footsteps and muffled commands. Desperately, she tried to form a map in her mind. A left turn, and then another left . . . and then a right? She'd been to the preemie ward several times on her own, but without visual cues, in blackness, it was hard to be confident.

She entered the hallway. Flashlights threw bouncing stripes of light along the dark hall as doctors, nurses, and aides scrambled past her. "People!" said a nurse, meaning the patients, "you *must* stay in your rooms! Wait for the backup generator!" Alison ran across the hall and demanded directions, but the nurse doing the shouting simply ordered her back to bed. Alison looked at the flashlight, but the old nurse seemed to sense what Alison was thinking and she took a death grip on the flashlight with both of her mannish hands. Eerily, from behind a nearby door, there came the lost, keening wail of inchoate fear. The nurse turned abruptly, and Alison took off down the hall at a shuffling trot.

Alison made it as far as the second left turn, at which point the previously abundant supply of flashlight-bearing staffers gave out completely. Hugging the right wall, her arms out in front of her like a cartoon sleepwalker's, she hurried along the corridor anyway, taking chances in the dark. She upended a dinner cart, and a few steps later, something sharp brushed her cheek — the just-miss kiss of an open door. Alison kept moving, hoping deliriously that the next right turn would be, in fact, the next right turn.

Just to put my hands on him; to connect with the Ace across all this ink. . . .

Please make the power come back on, she prayed, with all the uneasy reverence she could muster. He *needs* those machines.

In midstride, Alison banged up against something solid, and crashed to the floor.

"God, who — are you all right?" Alison recognized the voice. It was Sandy. They were headed for the same place.

Arm in arm for safety, they headed for the nursery, with Sandy doing the navigating. Once inside, they were not alone. There were other nurses, and a few emergency beams for light, but not enough of either to go around. The Ace was in a private incubator and a private cubicle, but not a private room. There were others of his kind.

"Give us some light," Sandy begged, and mercifully, someone obliged. Sandy quickly checked Asa's computerized diagnostic and life-support equipment. None of it was working.

At that moment, the lights came back on. The machines did not. Like any good medical institution of its size, Alison's hospital was a client of the SEEK system.

Alison opened the lid of the steel-and-plexiglass incubator. There was no movement, not even a flutter, from the Ace. He was covered with bandages and strung with plastic tubes, a tiny purse-lipped wonder in repose. He could have been asleep. He had David's chin.

She felt dizzy. His head is so fine, she thought. So smooth and round. It fits in my palm.

"Hold the light steady, will you!"

Alison leaned over and picked him up. He felt so weightless in her hands. "He's not breathing. Oh please."

Sandy reached out and took him away, placing him gently back on the incubator table, all his lifeless tubes and pumps still intact. She bent at the waist and put her ear to his chest. "Go for a doctor," Sandy said, without looking up.

Alison tore herself away from the incubator and ran out of the nursery, looking for help; for another opinion; for a working piece of equipment; any mundane miracle at all, from a staff already stretched and overpowered. She spotted a doctor entering a patient's room, and barged in after the woman. A hulking black orderly was already there, standing beside the bed.

"Is he dead?" the woman doctor demanded.

"Lady, he's dead, and then some," said the orderly. He rapped his knuckles against the machine at the head of the bed, an intra-aortic balloon pump for cardiac patients. "Outa juice."

"My baby," Alison gasped. "He's not breathing." Alison grabbed the woman by the sleeves of her smock, intending to pull her back into the hall.

"She's did, friends. The time has came. It all Revelations now."

"*What?*" The doctor looked poleaxed.

"No, see, he's *dying!*" Alison screamed.

The doctor took root.

The orderly looked at the doctor with considerable scorn. "Lady," he said, "ain't you gonna go and save her baby?"

Alison felt the first twist of despair; the none-too-gradual loss of manufactured hope. Born too soon, sailed right through, checked right out.

Ace, don't go. . . .

*   *

In the city below Ellen, the lights were going out.

It was precisely as it had been in New York, except that the new coil was two hundred times more powerful than the old one. And this time, Ellen, at least, knew what to expect after eight minutes of operating time.

Back then, the song they had used for experimental purposes was "How Much Is That Doggie in the Window?" Music, even puerile music, was always the perfect test of successful communication. Music had a way of getting everybody's attention.

At exactly nine P.M., Ellen and Leonard had been among the first of the city's residents to hear the transmission of "Won't Get Fooled Again," as the Sutro tower resonated with sound. Within a radius of twenty miles, Ellen was certain, the sound was beginning to pour out of radios and televisions, bridges and flagpoles, stereos and power tools, computers and video games, pacemakers and paging devices, self-cleaning ovens and digital Mr. Coffees. . . .

The music was shimmering forth from all of these; from power transformers and utility stations; from the steel girders of big buildings and the copper plumbing of small ones. From metal, silicon, and niobium. Ellen had fulfilled her promise to the captain in that respect, even though the coil's frighteningly exponential accumulation of charge was not patently evident to him. Peter Cassidy had seen it only because he had been looking for it. In Ellen's view, Peter had turned out to be far more resourceful and committed and foolish than anyone, even Peter himself, might have expected.

The first four minutes of low-level transmission were the captain's. The last four minutes were hers.

From silver dog chains and lightning rods and stainless steel mixing bowls. . . .

From God's own hand. With help from Ellen.

It was now 9:03, and the concentric waves of electromagnetic energy from the coil were building, traveling far beyond the confines of the San Francisco Bay Area. The strength of the coil's output was increasing, and the digitized musical signal was beginning to decay as the frequencies shifted. In another minute, the song would be over. The coil would begin to resonate with the tuneless atomic hum of the SEEK system — and her work would be done.

Ellen backed away from the rocky edge of the viewpoint, where she had been watching the city darken, and started back for the car. Leonard was waiting for her there. Her boots made crunching sounds as she crossed the gravel parking area. She stumbled in the darkness as she tried to make out the car.

When she slipped the second time, she stopped walking, deciding, instead, to spend the final four minutes right here, in silent contemplation, motionless, concentrating on what she could sense about this extraordinary event.

She reached for a special moment of understanding, and came back, instead, with the memory of Rachel; the way Rachel looked as she sat on the hard wooden bench outside the courtroom, her eyes fixed on a gum wrapper which someone had left on the bench. When Rachel realized it was only the wrapping, and not the prize, a look of unalloyed disappointment crossed her face, and she shook her auburn hair. Ellen never forgot that look.

. . . And she remembered resolving not to cry in front of Rachel, as three men sat across the hall on another bench, watching. Her eyes were swollen from the effort of holding back. Rachel had never seen her crying. This was not the time to start. Rachel reached for Ellen's pocket, searching for a remnant of fabric, the last extant swatch of her favorite security blanket.

They can't do this. They can't take my child, someone will refuse to allow it. Alejandro will find a way to stop it. . . .

As Ellen recalled it, they wanted Alejandro to supply two crucial aspects of the SEEK system — the niobium circuitry it was based on, and a clever cryptographic code that Alejandro had devised for pro-

237

tecting the SEEK communication channels from outside interference.

The NSA had an idea, and they were calling it the SEEK system,
and they wanted Alejandro to make it real for them, precisely because Alejandro was the only one who could. Alejandro and niobium — the goose and the golden egg. A peerless technological lock.
In 1959, Alejandro *was* niobium technology.

They could have thrown the book at Alejandro over the unauthorized documents he'd used in his work with the coil, but neither the
NSA nor the Pentagon had wanted to do that. The last thing they
wanted was to see Alejandro in jail. They needed him. It was that
simple. He was the best of the lot.

The coil itself had nothing to do with it. The coil was not the
point. Presumably, Robert Core, who had so obviously played a role
in setting Alejandro up, had failed to grasp its true implications. Presumably, Robert Core could only see the coil as a failed experiment.
SEEK was all that anybody cared about, in the end.

Ada's child was not the point, either.

Of course, she was not Ada Stibbits back then. She was Ellen
Rosen. Her real name. God-given, as they say. She changed her
name to Ada Stibbits after she parted with Alejandro, during the years
she lived in Europe. She picked it out herself. Ada Stibbits, each
name a mirror, the same backward as forward. The elegant symmetry
of it.

They never gave her any more than the barest gist of what was
happening. Only enough to ensure her cooperation. If Alejandro refused to develop niobium technology for the SEEK system, the government was prepared to lay the case against Alejandro before the
public, letting politics take its course. The documents Alejandro
had misappropriated contained the names of wartime intelligence
agents, and the details of highly sensitive security matters. They gave
her to understand that she would be right there in the docket along
with him. The two of them could expect years of imprisonment if
they were lucky, and the fate of the Rosenbergs if they were not.

As for Ellen herself, they only wanted to scare her quite thoroughly. At twenty, she was scareable. . . .

It took less than one full day of unpublicized court time to end it
for everyone. If she had chosen to fight back, she would have lost
the child anyway. She knew that, but it did not help. She wanted to
plead with Alejandro, beg him to stop it — but Alejandro wasn't there.

In one stroke of the gavel, the mother of Rachel Hunt was declared unfit, and the child herself became a ward of the court, pending adoption proceedings. The adoption was to be a blind one, so that the unfit mother, so clearly unbalanced and distraught, could not "harass" the new parents.

Rachel was not the point of the proceedings. Rachel was only a by-product. The government simply argued that the "love child" had been living virtually wild in the woods, growing up untended and bereft of human contact, under highly questionable circumstances. Given the tenor of the times, and the importance of providing an object lesson, it was enough.

She had no job, no degree, no visible means of support without Alejandro. She wasn't married. The presiding judge in the case was seventy-six years old.

The pending charges against Alejandro were quietly dismissed.

A clean break, they told her. A chance for a new start.

They did it to get his attention. To cut down on his distractions. To show that they meant business. We were only by-products, Rachel and I. Civilian casualties. We were in the way.

They did it because they could. Because it lay within their power to do so. . . .

And never to know; never to see Rachel again, even after an army of private detectives. . . .

Spending thirteen years in Europe, eventually becoming a full professor of mathematics at the University of Geneva, and never knowing. . . .

Coming home in 1972, accepting the offer of a chair at Cal-Berkeley, and never finding out. . . .

Thirteen years . . . and a hundred new lifetimes. It was too far gone to be retrieved.

When Ada was first asked to do consulting work for the DID Corporation, she surprised herself by saying yes. It took great gall on their part even to ask, but of course it wasn't just her talent that interested them. In all the intervening years, nothing had changed for them. The colonel, and Anton, and all the others — they were still looking for the private line to Alejandro. They didn't know, or didn't want to believe, that she had stopped looking a long time ago. Other than Core, and Anton DeBroer, she met no one who had known her publicly as Ellen. There was the odd rumor about some sort of fling with Alejandro — but it was nothing. Folklore. The sciences were populated by the young, and if there was a single salient trait about them all, it was that they had no sense of history whatsoever. Nineteen fifty-nine. A.D. or B.C., it was all the same to them.

With the arrival of Klaatu, Robert Core had asked for her help. The colonel had been watching her ever since, but with the aid of Leonard, it had been possible to work around that. Ada went along with it. Ellen had her reasons.

Just before she closed her eyes, something caught Ellen's attention. A wink of stars above the hill; a dark shape moving across a darkened sky. She cocked her head and shielded her eyes with her hand, instinctively, as if the problem were too much light, rather than too little. As the object drifted past, going from north to south, she recognized it as a large airplane, a commercial jetliner of some kind, arcing silently toward the airport, following an angle of trajectory that did not admit of any debate. Without lights, its engines silent, the airplane was going to crash.

She watched this falling plane with sickened fascination, picturing the people inside: innocent bystanders in a less-than-perfect world. Perhaps someone she knew was on board. Perhaps some child.

She could not stop thinking about the passengers, and at the last minute, she distinctly heard them calling out to her. And she thought, *Egg in peril.* She felt herself falling with them.

She went down with them, as the plane became a fireball below Mount Sutro. And she thought: *Egg in flames.* Seconds later, the rolling impact reached her ears.

Ellen fell to her knees, exhausted. She was just so very tired.

For the first time in years, Ellen Rosen began to weep. And for just a few seconds, the sound of her weeping became the only sound she could hear.

Leonard came to her from across the parking lot. Awkwardly, he bent down and tried to comfort her. She pushed him away. She was moaning something about an airplane.

Leonard had been watching the same night sky as Ada, and there had been no air traffic of any kind for at least half an hour, maybe longer.

She mumbled something else, and Leonard leaned closer. But it didn't help. "Klaatu barada nikto," it sounded like.

It was too late.

Leonard pulled out a pocket flashlight and shone it on the back of her long, lovely neck. Like a swan, he thought. In his other hand, he held a disposable syringe. Tears were beginning to leak down his face, and he was afraid they would obscure his vision if he waited any longer.

If she thought about it logically, Leonard told himself, she would realize that this is what she needs.

It was 9:08, Pacific Standard Time.

*　*

When the lights went out, Peter saw it coming. BART was on the SEEK net.

The train lurched violently several times, then went into a skid. Peter pitched forward over the seat in front of him, and darkness gulped him down.

Hoarse shouts and screams rippled through the BART car. Peter was buried beneath a crush of bodies in the dark, and a squirming weight bore down sharply on his back. He felt two small hands still riveted like iron to his thigh. Peter bunched his legs underneath him, grabbed the child around the waist, and lurched upward, fighting to break free of the tangle of bodies in the aisle. Jerry was screaming, and above all the other screams, Peter could hear the dull thud of people kicking hopelessly at the windows. Peter fought for space at the back of the car. His eyes began to water and his breath came hot and harsh.

"Fire," someone shrieked.

No pleading voice of sanity rose above it all.

Peter placed his handkerchief over Jerry's mouth and tightened his grip against the child's struggling. There was no chance of finding Mom right now. Jerry bit through the handkerchief and into Peter's hand, as the unseen smoke thickened. Peter took shallow breaths and tried to hold them. A heightened wave of panic spread through the car.

Peter was never sure how much time actually passed before the lights began flickering and bouncing off the sides of the train. Flashlights dancing, playing off writhing figures and still forms prone in the smoke.

There was a splintering crash as the double doors split apart, and a rescue team with equipment packs and gas masks started pulling people free of the train. Peter and his unwilling orphan were the last to leave their car, or at least the last to do so unaided. Smoke blew out the door along with the passengers, and it was not much better in the tunnel between the inbound and outbound tracks. Peter carried Jerry, and when a woman in front of them stumbled, two rescuers scooped her up and dragged her along. Someone lost a shoe and it went skittering along the passageway, kicked and kicked again by the fleeing passengers.

Along with the rest of the pack, Peter trotted in the direction of a small square of light up ahead. When Jerry bit him again, Peter switched to an over-the-shoulder fireman's carry. The square of light became larger, and the pack began running.

When Peter burst into the station, he was one of the last to clear the tunnel. Emergency lights lit the smoke as it plumed and spun toward the high ceiling. There were policemen and stretchers; people sobbing and firemen coughing. A fat child fell hard and rolled helplessly, and lay still, one chubby cheek against the hard tile of the floor. Peter found a paramedic and handed over Jerry.

Then he sat down on the floor, the better to concentrate on his coughing.

How long would it take? he wondered. Peter very much wanted to know that. How would it go down, if Ada's broadcast reached all the way to the Peacemakers?

In silos across the West, in submarines off the Pacific. . . .

There wasn't any finger and there wasn't any button.

All of the missiles were linked to the SEEK central processing units at the NSA, Peter knew. Each missile was linked, in turn, to every other missile, so that whatever the SEEK system and its family of satellites raked in, the Peacemakers knew. Each missile rested in its sheath, inert but never dormant, processing data continuously, inputting the equivalent of the lost library of Alexandria every fifteen seconds or so. Each missile was packed with more than four hundred miles of connected niobium circuitry, radiation-hardened at great expense.

Peter had a picture of it in his mind. The effects of the coil would come to the memory banks of the missiles as a series of errors and glitches, caused by transient energy spikes all through the network. Miscues, soft errors. Gremlin electronics — individual electrons in the grip of the arcane phenomenon known as quantum tunneling, passing like magic bullets through energy barriers they could not ordinarily surmount. There would be much random brilliance in these errors, producing, in the end, a curious packet of data that might look, to the missiles, like a firing request.

And when the Peacemakers received a firing signal, they were programmed to interpret it as an attempt at group consensus. Even the president with his Hunt Code could not actually order an attack. He could only suggest it. The missiles decided the issue among themselves: In effect, they voted. It was supposed to be the ultimate in fail-safe redundancy — the tyranny of the majority was built right in.

At the end of this addled voyage of confusion, the missiles, sleek and soulless as sharks, would rise from their hiding places with a collective roar.

In Nevada, Utah, Alaska, the Peacemakers clearing their silos, thundering skyward. . . . And off the coast, the undersea Peacemakers breaching the surface of the ocean. . . . An accidental firing with only one possible outcome. . . .

When would you know? Peter kept asking himself. And he knew there was only one answer:

Any minute now.

TWENTY-SEVEN

O N MOUNT TAMALPAIS, the Pons Concert was over.
Rescue trucks and black-booted firemen dodged
each other in the backstage meadow, while the concertgoers filed
steadily out of the dark arena and milled along the path to the parking lot. There was no panic, only confusion. The harsh cough of
portable generators was the loudest sound on the mountain.

Pons Grozniev watched the odd procession of lights from his perch
behind the seats in the uppermost southern corner of the arena, as
far from the stage as possible. Below him, people were still lighting
their own way to the exits with an ingenious combination of materials — matches, Bic lighters, sparklers, glowing cigarettes, rolled
newspapers in flames, Tekna pocket emergency beams — anything
and everything that would actually work. Long before the auxiliary
power had arrived, a kid in a miner's hat had led several thousand
out the central exit, on the strength of his lone headlight. Glowing
hibachis, candles and hand mirrors; a kinetic sculpture of soft lights
and tiny torches.

The crowd was orderly. The strange new amplification of The Who's
finale, the blackout, the detonations and light from behind the stage —
none of these was clear evidence of something in the process of going
horribly wrong. As for the volley of explosions with which the show
ended: The explosions were the kind of thing The Who was famous
for. In the opinion of many, particularly those in the rearward reaches
of the arena, The Who had truly outdone themselves this time.

From up here, Pons could see the truth about the blackout. San
Francisco was down, and Oakland, too, by the look of it. The way it
turned out, thought Pons, maybe Peter and the captain were both
right. Dazed and glazed and temporarily hard of hearing, Pons didn't

know the details yet. He was more interested in staying out of jail for a few more minutes.

The Who was steamed, no doubt. Ditto for the other performers. Surprise amplification of that magnitude could get you electrocuted. Pons wished he had gotten up the nerve to let them all in on the secret in advance.

The coil, not to put too fine a point on it, was actually the lesser of the *two* momentous happenings Pons had taken part in that night. After the lights and sound had gone out; in that moment before the explosions when the air was charged with the pulse of the coil, and Pons's anxiety had reached its peak — Pons connected. That was the only way he could think of putting it. He opened a circuit he never knew he had. He emptied and refilled.

The exiting crowd of twenty thousand remained orderly and paced. Pons pulled his gaze away and turned to look down upon the nearly empty bleachers of the Pons Arena. Several rows below him, barely visible in the darkness, there were two people waiting for him.

One of them was his new Companion, the man with the crown of thorns who was there to save him. The other one was a policeman, who was there to arrest him.

Pons walked slowly down the hard wooden rows, and placed himself willingly in their hands.

*   *

Captain Crash lay in the bushes, groaning.

He was in no hurry to move. Patches of his clothing had been burned away by the force of the blast, and the skin was fiery red underneath. He was bleeding; he could taste it. His ribs, his left leg, his forehead — something felt not quite right about them all. He was badly hurt, that much for certain. Gingerly, he raised his head and twisted his neck, in order to take his bearings. He was flat on his back in a clot of leafy, aromatic bushes, almost twenty feet away from the rock at the edge of the backstage clearing where he'd been hiding when the explosions came. He must have crawled here.

The captain let his head drop back to the ground.

When he felt up to it, he pushed himself into a sitting position, his massive torso heaving with pain. So far so good. His forehead was cut and he kept getting blood in his eyes. He would have to move soon.

Didn't we do it, though, Frank Holsa told himself. *Didn't we just do it.*

The captain had been standing nearly two hundred feet away from the main trailer at the time of the explosions. This was no lucky accident. Frank had designed a remote-control switch, hand-held, for deactivating the coil, but he never got a chance to use it. The coil deactivated itself.

Overall, from his pixilated perspective of the moment, the captain felt safe in assuming that the experiment had been successful. He wondered, vaguely, whether Alejandro had appeared, as Ellen had promised, and whether he had missed that appearance.

At length, the captain swerved to his feet. The leg was okay, but the chest was almost unbearable. The captain touched his forehead with a tentative finger, and felt bone. He took several deep breaths as he stumbled hesitantly to the edge of the bushes. He took a quick survey of the clearing. Fire trucks and men with hats. Generators and emergency lights.

He looked at his watch, and discovered that it was almost midnight.

The captain was facing a diagonal sprint of a hundred yards or so, in order to reach a trail which led down the mountain to a string of deserted bungalows where he had stashed a car. He was to meet Ellen as soon as possible, in Mendocino.

That was the enterprise in a nutshell. He felt faint, and he wasn't sure he could pull it off. He gathered himself anyway, crouching low at the edge of the bushes, and began to make his move across the meadow. The tree-covered trail he was seeking was less than a football field away, but even a short run posed formidable barriers to a runner so low on blood and healthy tissue as Captain Crash.

He was intent on shuttling through the last nightmare yards of his sprint, his hand clenched against the pounding ache that had bloomed in his side the instant he broke into his downfield canter, when, inexplicably, he found himself bathed in celestial light. A great wind caught him up, and the ground began to vibrate.

He looked up. He saw a helicopter, flat black, with the DID Corporation logo emblazoned in scarlet on its side, blasting the clearing with the dust of its approach. As it landed, the captain became oblivious to his pain.

Alejandro, thought the captain, has come at last.

Dazed, the captain staggered off in the direction of the helicopter. He even ran.

Ellen would have to hack it on her own, the captain thought. He'd have to ask Alejandro about how she fit in, exactly.

As he approached the helicopter, choking in the dust, the captain caught sight of three cops as they broke away from the stage area and started running in his direction. Sorry, suckers, thought the captain, grimacing against the pain in his side. Gonna make like chariot of the gods here, get whisked away to who knows where —

The blades were whirling madly over the captain's head as he bent low and squinted inside. When he had succeeded in identifying the occupant, a great moan escaped him. The captain scuttled out from beneath the blades, howling, and broke into a jerky dash for cover.

When he fell the first time, the captain rose and resumed his escape.

When he fell the second time, three policemen were there to help him up. They let him bleed while they read him his rights.

A moment later, the door to the helicopter opened. Stepping quickly to the ground was its pilot and sole passenger, Colonel Robert Core.

PART

FIVE

TWENTY-EIGHT

THE DEBRIEFING, which lasted a full twelve hours, was conducted at the DID Corporation's divisional headquarters in Santa Clara, California. His padded leather chair was not comfortable, and the bristling bank of microphones on the narrow table in front of him was not designed to put him at his ease.

Videocams and shiny black shoes, the most memorable components of all Peter's worst-case nightmares, played a salient role in the proceedings.

The all-night session began shortly after Peter's arrival at the complex, less than three hours after the conclusion of the Pons Concert. Men he'd never seen before kept arriving and filing into the small, harshly lit room. They all wore suits, and none of them wore a name tag. Peter asked for the colonel, but the colonel, they told him, was in conference.

There were more eager spooks in the hallway. Peter could see them through the glass wall of the conference booth. They were milling around, trying to get inside. Their mouths were moving, but he couldn't hear what they were saying. There were at least fifteen people cramped into the booth with him already. Like they couldn't all catch it later, on the replay.

He answered all of their terse and telegraphic questions, answered them truthfully, to the best of his ability, even the dumb ones, even the sly. By the time it was over, absolutely everything Peter Cassidy knew for certain was on the record.

Alison and the Ace made it. That was the main thing Peter learned in the course of the interrogation session. The main damn thing. They were still in a Portland hospital, under guard.

A temporary Bay Area blackout; minor SEEK damage; spot outages from Vancouver to San Diego. Ada tried for an apocalypse, and did not get one.

The word for the day was *thankful*.

It was eight the next morning before they got around to asking him about the notebooks. Peter kept it vague. Hell, it *was* vague. Like he knew that much more, really, than anybody else. He had suspicions, that was all. He felt like telling all of them that he had finally managed to lose track of all the levels at once.

Peter was beginning to realize that none of the spooks in the room seemed to grasp the full significance of what had happened — or might have happened. It was understandable. Gone in a microsecond, over in a flash. After all, there wasn't much in the way of field data to work with. If you judged it strictly on the basis of the outside evidence — scattered blackouts, temporary upper-level disruptions, relatively minor lower-level damage, except for a few severe short-outs in SEEK-linked commercial equipment — well, it was a grisly mess, liability central, but you wouldn't necessarily comprehend the extent of the threat which the coil represented. Peter chose not to disturb that picture, pending a talk with Colonel Core.

When Peter inquired about any reported glitches in the Peacemaker system, they looked at him as if he were certifiable.

He couldn't have said exactly why, but he had a strong feeling that his earlier, muddled phone call to the colonel had paid off hugely.

By eleven, his listeners were apparently becoming disappointed with his answers. Peter, who had contracted a sore throat from all the talking, and a sour stomach from all the coffee he had pumped into himself in an effort to stay awake, took this as a heartening sign. He tried throwing out a few questions of his own.

He asked about the captain, and the captain was dead, of massive internal injuries. You try, he thought sadly. Maybe not hard enough, but, shit, you do try.

And Ada Stibbits was dead. Presumably a suicide, he was told. Peter wasn't so sure, but once again he decided to keep his feelings to himself. He didn't expect Leonard to turn up on anybody's doorstep soon with explanations.

Fish Dog was dead, too. But no one would say what the deal was with Anton. Or with David, for that matter. It was this omission which led Peter to demand to know Anton's whereabouts, at which point one of the men rose to ask Peter just exactly *why* he was so interested in DeBroer; just exactly *why* Peter so obviously had attempted to murder agent DeBroer in the street in front of the Atwood house. The man made it clear that this did not strike him as a rational response. In fact, it seemed to strike him forcefully as a prosecutable offense. *Murder* — that was the exact word used.

The guy had been saving up for this, Peter could tell.

Peter brought the proceedings to a full stop. "I refuse to answer any more questions," he said, "unless I am allowed to speak directly to Robert Core." It was time to find out exactly where he stood with the colonel.

Reluctantly, and after lengthy consultation, someone handed Peter a telephone. Peter dialed the number — he wasn't ever likely to forget it — and waited nervously through three rings.

"Yes," said the colonel. "What is it."

"This is Peter Cassidy, Colonel. They're giving me sort of a hard time here at DID Divisional." Peter looked out at his audience. They were all looking back at him.

"I know," said the colonel. "I've been watching."

After a moment's thought, Peter stared into the lens of the mounted videocam at the back of the room.

"Live on tape, as they say."

Peter gave the colonel a solemn wave.

"It's my way of being at least three places at once tonight," the colonel said. "I think they're about through with you down there."

"Colonel, they're insinuating that I ought to go to jail for threatening Anton with a gun. They think I was trying to kill him."

There was a pause on the colonel's end of the line. "Put somebody on."

"What about David Atwood, Colonel?"

"We'll discuss it. Put somebody on."

Peter handed back the phone. The man who had been badgering him picked it up and listened for a minute, and after that, there was no more talk about prosecutable offenses. All of the questions were unfailingly polite from that stage onward. Peter even began to wonder about his chances of seeing Alison or David sometime soon.

*   *

253

When they finally cut him loose, he was taken to the third floor, where he was fed and quartered in a spacious executive suite, courtesy of Colonel Core. Peter intended to shower and shave, but did not get very far in the direction of either chore before exhaustion claimed him. He walked across the carpet to the bed, turned back the red-and-black comforter, and fell gratefully onto the sheets.

⁜ ⁜

He was awakened five hours later by the insistent ringing of the bedside telephone. Peter eased himself upright and fumbled for the phone while he massaged his tangled hair.

It was the colonel, inviting him upstairs for dinner.

"Am I being charged with anything?" was Peter's first bleary thought.

"No, no," the colonel said. "Forget about that."

He showered and dressed quickly. Someone had washed and ironed Sig's shirt and pants for him in the interim. He could have slept another five hours, easily, but otherwise he felt okay. Through the floor-to-ceiling windows of the suite, he could see streams of cars jerking and flowing along the flux lines of the traffic grid below. To the south, he spotted a hump of smog hovering over San Jose, and beyond that, dimly seen, a line of hills. All things considered, he was happy enough to be right where he was. Happy to be anywhere at all.

Peter walked soundlessly along the carpeted fourth-floor hallway, scouting for the colonel's suite, and wondering what to expect. When he found the entrance, the colonel was there to meet him at the door, looking very casual, if preoccupied, in shirt sleeves, tan pants, and desert boots. As they shook hands, Peter tried to fathom the colonel's mood.

They had roast beef sandwiches and a bottle of wine at a small table overlooking the heart of Silicon Valley. The colonel's work suite was heavily populated with aides and secretaries. A steady stream of them filed past his chair, delivering documents, whispering messages, relaying phone calls. The colonel dealt with it smoothly and steadily as they ate. "We're dropping all Klaatu-related charges against David Atwood," he told Peter, when there was a momentary break in the parade.

"When can I see him?"

The colonel reached for his wineglass, and didn't answer right away.

Peter sighed, and put down his sandwich. "I thought we had a deal, sort of."

"Look," the colonel said. "David is going to do some time. Perhaps not as much as he deserves, probably more than he expects, but, in any event, he's doing time. There are other charges, the consequences of which he will have to face. Bear in mind that he was at least partially responsible for your own involvement in this affair."

"I haven't forgotten, Colonel." He tried hard to picture David, who was no longer exempt. He wondered, briefly, what David would be like at the other end of the stretch. I'll do what I can to help, he decided. I'm supposed to know that much.

"In the meantime, Alison Atwood and her baby will be taken care of financially. And protected, if necessary — but I see no reason to think that it will be."

"I presume Anton's dead," Peter said.

The colonel was about to speak, but changed his mind. Abruptly, he began dismissing employees.

"I presume that when you have a dead spook like Anton, nobody wants to talk about it," Peter said. "If he's merely absent without leave, then somebody really ought to tell me."

Evidently, the colonel did not intend to answer until the last aide had exited and closed the door behind him.

"He's dead," the colonel confirmed. "And nobody wants to talk about it, primarily because DeBroer was dealing with . . . outside parties. It's academic now. It's moot. But that's policy."

"It gives me the willies just thinking about it. Leonard gave me the same shot he gave Anton."

The colonel shook his head vigorously. "No, he didn't," the colonel said. "Ada didn't intend to kill you. Leonard was only trying to put you out of action for about three days, according to the lab report. The police found Leonard's medical bag."

Peter whistled. God bless Leonard, a man of his word. "I think Leonard may have killed Ada, Colonel. I begged him to call Alejandro, back at the motel."

A characteristic thought occurred to Peter just then. "Colonel," he asked, gesturing at the walls, "are we live on tape here?"

"No," said the colonel. "This is not a room in which that sort of thing takes place."

The colonel picked up an open pack of cigarettes from beside his wineglass, and tapped one free. His sandwich, with garnish, lay untouched on his plate. He looked sternly at Peter. "As soon as you found out where Holsa was hiding," he said, "you should have come to me."

255

After a moment of confusion, Peter said, "I didn't *know* enough. I felt like I was taking a chance on you, as it was."

"Nevertheless," said the colonel.

Peter waited for more.

The colonel took another sip of his wine. "I'm not sure you fully realize it, but you saved a significant number of lives by calling me when you did." The angry arch of his eyebrows softened slightly as he lit his cigarette. "You prevented a staggering amount of damage." He reached across the table and poured Peter another glass of wine. "Not that damage is in short supply."

Peter looked at the colonel. "You shut it down," he said. "It was your blackout."

"Selected portions of it," the colonel admitted. "And strictly on the West Coast. I wasn't able to shut down as much of it as I would have liked."

The colonel made it sound simple. But it would have cost him something, pulling the plug like that. It would have called for every ounce of grease, every chit he could pull in, to get the job done that fast.

All of it on my say-so, Peter was thinking. On my word alone. "The coil works, Colonel. That's what you're saying. You've known it all along."

"My personal acknowledgment will have to suffice. You won't be reading about it in the papers."

Peter had a picture of it in his mind: a device capable of firing off a burst of supercharged electrons, each of them behaving like a tiny radio transmitter gone berserk, disrupting an apparent span of frequencies from zero to well over 100 megahertz. . . .

"You should have seen the coil, Colonel. You could never have guessed, just by looking."

"To be honest," said the colonel, "I did see it, once. Another version, in nineteen fifty-nine."

"An early test. I wondered about that."

The colonel stared straight ahead. "Put it this way," he said. "There was no way of controlling the output. Whatever Alejandro had had in mind, the most obvious and immediate spin-off was as a weapon. When I convinced Alejandro to destroy the coil and all the documentation that went with it, I was first of all concerned with keeping everyone free of intelligence entanglements. The NSA was trying to build a corral around Alejandro at the time — "

"Wait a minute," Peter interrupted, "you're saying that *you* convinced Alejandro to deep-six this whole new, this entirely unprecedented avenue of — "

"Some of them are quite mad, you know," the colonel went on, in a low voice. "Almost all of them realize that the ability to disable your enemy's power grid and communications channels means that you have eliminated his chances of responding coherently to a nuclear attack. Given what you've seen and experienced as a result of Ada's exhibition," he said, "I want you to imagine precisely how tempting such a machine might be to people who think like that."

Peter didn't have to try very hard. The difficult part was accepting the fact that he'd been wrong about the colonel, too — in about a dozen different ways. The colonel would forever be the good soldier, Peter was thinking. But sometimes, good soldiers just naturally do the right thing.

"You might also be interested to know that I was unable to prevail upon the Pentagon to lock down the Peacemakers on such short notice." The colonel popped a crust of bread into his mouth before resuming. "Fortunately, your shielding held."

Peter sat there blinking.

"Your memos," said the colonel.

Peter's shielding held. Fuck the monkey if it wasn't true.

"Try to hold in mind, Peter, the possibility that other people, including myself, have been hard at work on this problem for quite a long time now. Your memos were our first real warning of how acutely vulnerable SEEK had become. We've quietly been attempting to design away that vulnerability ever since."

"Why," Peter asked slowly, "was I cut out of all this?"

"It was procedure. You were kept out of the loop. Sometimes procedure can be used to protect."

Peter looked at the ceiling, and closed his eyes. "Everybody shrugged it off," he mumbled. "Told me to go recalculate. For three years, I thought nobody was paying attention."

"You didn't have sufficient clearance. It's an entirely new ball game now, of course."

"Ada had clearance," Peter said, trying not to sound petulant en route to making his point. "She read the memos, too."

"She's been watched all her life," the colonel responded. "But we did not account sufficiently for Leonard."

The colonel regarded Peter calmly for a moment. "We'll have to scrap the Hunt Code," he said, "and we'll have to institute a major

SEEK redesign program, from the ground up. And of course, we'll be taking an entirely new look at the shielding question." Using a circular motion, the colonel neatly pared the ash of his cigarette against the glass bottom of his ashtray. When he finished, he looked squarely at Peter again. "Will you come back to work for us?"

The colonel was offering senior clearance in exchange for the further use of Peter's mind. Less than twenty-four hours after the fact, it was business as usual for the colonel. I got out of this alive, Peter was thinking. Let's leave it at that.

"My best friend's in jail," Peter said bitterly, "and his wife, who's *also* my best friend, almost got killed — as did their child. I lost the best goddamned dog I'll ever have, and a fishing pole, and a few other things — and you want me to just pitch in there and start building it up all over again. I mean, Colonel — I mean, I was never, I never liked the Boy Scouts, never joined. That was not my line."

"If you hadn't been here," the colonel said, "this all might have turned out quite differently."

"We got lucky, Colonel. I don't plan to stick around and see how it turns out the next time. I'm very intrigued about my — about the shielding, I'll admit it. And I'm as happy as you are about that phone call. But I've decided to cashier myself, Colonel. All I have to do is go fishing for a year or two and it comes true." Peter poured himself a final splash of wine.

The colonel raised his glass. "Here's to you," he said. "And to me."

Peter didn't know how to react. "All we do is speed things up. That's what I tried to tell Ada."

"Sometimes," said the colonel, "when you are in an unusual situation — "

"Nobody gets smarter," Peter said vehemently. "Nobody benefits."

The colonel turned in his chair, his gaze coming to rest on the DID parking lot four floors beneath the windows. There was only a smattering of parked cars, this being Saturday. " 'There is more to life than increasing its speed,' " the colonel said. "Do I have that right? If I'm not mistaken, Gandhi said it first." The colonel turned back and faced Peter. "It's never been any different. It didn't start with you."

Peter broke down and bummed a cigarette from the colonel's pack. He swore that he would quit again, as soon as he crossed the border.

TWENTY-NINE

O N THE MORNING OF Peter's final day at DID Divisional, he woke up early and discovered that some of his own clothing and personal effects, his actual jeans and his actual red L. L. Bean chamois shirt, along with a few odds and ends like his wallet and passport, had appeared overnight in the closet. It was a little eerie, but he remembered to thank the colonel for it, all the same.

Colonel Core had offered Peter a lift to the airport. In the company of the colonel, he proceeded downstairs and out the front door into the glare of the parking lot. The colonel was jingling the keys to a dark red company sedan. "You haven't told me where you're going, other than San Francisco International," the colonel said, as he unlocked the car. "It's not required, of course."

Peter told him anyway. He slid into the seat and settled back against the leather interior, content to let the colonel handle the driving.

When they reached the freeway, the colonel merged seamlessly into a tight line of northbound traffic, heading in the direction of Stanford and the airport. Peter didn't bother looking for old landmarks. They drove in silence for a while, neither of them feeling compelled to make small talk.

"Penny for your thoughts," the colonel said as the oversized hangar at Moffett Field came into view.

Peter straightened up in his seat, and adjusted the sun visor. "I was wondering if you could get the company to buy my neighbor a new car."

☆   ☆

259

Once inside the San Francisco airport, the colonel coaxed Peter into a nearly deserted lounge for a parting cup of coffee. "I couldn't help noticing that your passport is up to date," he said, as the waitress came and went. "I'm leaving for Guatemala now. I'm going to try to see Alejandro. Perhaps he will allow me to do that."

Peter had assumed all along that the colonel was headed for Washington, D.C.

The colonel cradled his coffee in both hands and watched the steam rising from the cup. "You're welcome to come along, if you want."

"I can't imagine why Alejandro would want to see me."

"I can't imagine it, either. But you're welcome to come, just the same."

Outside the window of the lounge, a bright orange 747 was taxiing down the nearest runway. There's a difference between what you want and what you need, Peter was thinking. "I don't think so," he told the colonel. "But thanks for asking."

The colonel lit a cigarette. "Will you come back to work for us?"

Peter watched the orange jet as it lifted off the runway and angled sharply skyward. "It's just a game, Colonel," he said. "Everybody loses, unless you count the money."

"Forgive me if I sound presumptuous to you," the colonel said, "but there was a time in my life, I think, when I felt very much like you do right now. It was nineteen forty-five, the year of the atomic bomb. Year Zero, Alejandro used to call it. I wanted nothing to do with it, and I remember thinking, 'Only a miracle can save us now.' "

The colonel paused. "But that's not the way it works."

"No miracles, Colonel?"

The colonel drained the remains of his coffee. "There's an old saying, which I first heard in the Middle East, years ago," the colonel said. He took some coins out of his pocket, and inspected them. "Trust in God," he said. "But tie the camel's leg."

Peter looked pretty severely confused, as he watched the colonel counting out his change.

"Do you know what it means?" the colonel inquired. "It means, for starters, that professionals don't go fishing for a year or two."

Peter wasn't thinking clearly. His mind was on other topics.

"There will always be people like Anton, and, once in a great while, someone like Ada. I very much hope that you come back."

Peter was still watching the jet. "All I ever wanted," he said quietly, "was a way out."

I will never understand these people, the colonel was thinking.

An hour later, Peter was on a flight to Portland.

THIRTY

I T WAS A BEAUTIFUL fish, iridescent silver with pale pink undertones, flashing and writhing in the clear water twenty feet below the canoe. Peter hooked it on the second Monday in June, on a red-and-white trolling spoon, using a light surf-casting rig that was perfect for big summer lake trout. Mainly he used the pole for oceangoing salmon aboard Buster's twenty-two-foot boat.

Peter kept a close watch on the horizon above the pines to the south, checking for the arrival of the float plane that brought supplies and mail on a weekly basis. He had three letters with him, and he wanted all of them to go out today.

A bald eagle soared lazily above him, as Peter brought the fish to the canoe. Alison had invited him down to Portland for the Fourth of July, and Peter was accepting. So the first letter was for her.

The second one was for David. *Don't cry for me, coastal British Columbia,* David recently had written. *I convinced the prison librarian to include Izaak Walton's* The Compleat Angler *in the house collection. Great stuff. I've petitioned the warden for a casting pool. . . .*

It wouldn't be that easy, Peter knew. It would be no easier for David than it would have been for him.

Which left the third letter, the one for Robert Core. It was a reply to the colonel's note of last month, in which the colonel inquired politely about Peter's vacation.

Peter heard the buzz of the low-flying seaplane. He watched as it appeared over the trees, bumped off the water twice, and then wallowed to a slow troll as the pilot brought it toward the dock on Buster's rocky peninsula. Buster came running out and started grabbing ropes, preparing to lash the plane to its moorings when it drifted in.

Peter's handwritten note to the colonel was a short one. *Nothing biting*, it read.

Gently, Peter released his catch, and rinsed his hands, and dried them on his jacket. For a few moments, he sat motionless in the stern. A sharp breeze moved across the water in his direction, breaking the lake into ripples. When the wind became too strong to ignore, he laid his fishing pole in the bottom of the canoe, and began to paddle.